THE FAT BULLDOG ROAMS AGAIN

By the same author

An Axe, a Spade and Ten Acres
Odd Noises from the Barn
The Travels of a Fat Bulldog

The Fat Bulldog Roams Again

George Courtauld

Constable · London

First published in Great Britain 1998
by Constable and Company Limited
3 The Lanchesters, 162 Fulham Palace Road
London W6 9ER
Copyright © George Courtauld 1998
ISBN 0 09 478990 8
The right of George Courtauld to be identified as the author
of this work has been asserted by him
in accordance with the Copyright, Designs and Patents Act 1988

Set in Monotype Garamond 12pt by
Servis Filmsetting Ltd, Manchester
Printed in Great Britain by
St Edmundsbury Press Ltd
Bury St Edmunds, Suffolk

A CIP catalogue record for this book
is available from the British Library

CONTENTS
Journeys and Diversions

CONTENTS

INTRODUCTION AND ACKNOWLEDGEMENTS

Like my last book, *The Travels of a Fat Bulldog* (Constable and Company Limited, 1996), this one is based on my journeys overseas as a Queen's Messenger: this time visits to thirty different countries, chosen from the quarter of a million miles I travelled between October 1996 and October 1997.

Being a Queen's Messenger, I am bound by the Official Secrets Act, so the following pages are not about my work as a Queen's Messenger, but where, what and whom I have been able to explore or see or do or meet during my spare times 'in transit'. Any opinions expressed are my own and in no way reflect the opinions of the Diplomatic Corps, the Foreign and Commonwealth Office or – particularly – of the British Governments during this period.

In my last book I gave a brief glimpse of family life between each journey, to emphasise the contrast between a hectic career dashing round the world and the placid life of a farmer whose year revolves with the slow-moving changes of the seasons. I give my family a bit of peace in this book; instead, as in my journeys, I occasionally stray up a sideroad or relax in a lay-by to remember previous journeys or to review the odd or the interesting.

I must thank Bernhard Garside, Superintendent, the Corps of Queen's Messengers, for 'vetting' the manuscript; all the Queen's Messengers with whom I have travelled, in particular Major Patrick Springfield,

Chairman of the Corps' Committee and Lt Colonel Anthony Bush; Jack and Betty Couldrey in Nairobi, Captain Richard Diamond in Mombasa, Dr Ricardo Badilla in Chile, Muqaddam Salim Kassim in Oman, Adrian White and András Török in Budapest, Nigel Hankin in Delhi, al-Mukhtar Hassan Ibrahim Jado in Jordan, Josh Green and Yun Qing in Peking, my cousins William and Caroline Courtauld in Hong Kong, my brother Sam and my brother-in-law Professor Jonathan Riley-Smith; and Ruth Thackeray for, once again, editing the whole conglomeration, tactfully pointing out PIs and OTTs (Politically Incorrects and Over The Tops), and picking through my ever-incompetent spelling. Any obsolete spelling peculiarities are mine, and did not escape her gimlet eyes – but if I prefer to spell Huang'pu as Wangpoo (as in my great-grandfather's atlas), that's how I'll spell it. I am grateful for permission to quote from 'Ah Vastness of Pines' from *Twenty Love Poems and a Song of Despair* by Pablo Neruda, translated by W.S. Merwin and published by Jonathan Cape; and *Collected Poems* by W.H. Auden, published by Faber & Faber.

New York, 2 October 1996. 'Enjoy!' she snaps.

Having slammed down my fried-eggs-sunny-side-up-with-two-rashers-of-bacon-and-no-hash, the waitress quits to intimidate the couple at the next table. I eat, staring out of the big plate-glass window at the early-morning walkers busy on the pavement. They include:

a stunningly elegant black woman, long, long legs in suede boots, her suit simply tailored in a camel-hair cloth of a twenty-ounce herringbone weave, her gold jewellery showing up exotically against her dark skin – she does not seem to walk, rather she moves with sinuous undulations like an eel swimming through the fronds of water-weeds;

three shifty, scurrying men in jeans and 'puffa' jackets talking agitatedly to each other with fierce, prodding gesticulations – two have shadows on the pavement, one seems to be without – he'll be a dead man by midnight;

another elegant woman, white, middle aged – she sees me looking and flashes a huge, toothy, gummy, extremely infectious smile and waves;

a jogger wearing shiny black tight shorts like corsets, seeing me still smiling (at the memory of the previous passer-by) – I receive an indignant scowl;

a man so nondescript, so featureless and dressed so conventionally that he is almost invisible, he could be a ghost of the pavements – but he is pulling a leash which tows a suitcase on little wheels, rather like Dr Who's nice little robot dog, K9;

two tiny schoolgirls wearing rucksacks;

a tall man who, although neatly suited and bespectacled in heavy horn-rims, sports a long queue of hair like a rocking-horse tail;

a tramp pushing a supermarket trolley. He has transformed it into the tiniest of mobile homes: downstairs, on the bottom shelf, is his bedroom, complete with sheets of cardboard, a roll of bedding, and a neat pair of tartan slippers; upstairs has two compartments, the dining-room/kitchen, with water bottles, grease-blotched bags of food, a mug and a billy can, the living-room is adjacent, complete with a folded newspaper, a roll of carpet and a clock.

I have decided to walk the thirty-two blocks to Barnes & Noble, the big bookshop on 18th Street. At present I am passing the United Nations, the great Hot-air Factory, and on an impulse I enter to walk around the lawns and hedges of the park that abuts it. There are many statues. The first that one sees is an impressive ball of burnished bronze, exploding to expose a crystalline interior of cubes and rectangles. The next is less subtle, infantile even: a six-shooter pistol with its barrel tied into a knot. I muse that it might be an idea to have the statue of a nude man, similarly knotted, outside the entrance of a monastery. There is a rather good Saint George and Dragon, the latter with its body made up from bits of military machinery. A man is beating a sword into a plough-share. A plaque says 'GIFT OF UNION OF SOVIET SOCIALIST REPUBLICS – 1959'; perhaps, after all, it is of a man beating a plough-share into a sword. I particularly like a spiky, multi-legged construction high up on the blank face of the east-facing wall, it resembles things I have noticed on my bedroom ceilings in hot and nasty countries.

Having stood in a queue sandwiched between a gaggle of Japanese tourists to the front and a giggle of Scandinavian girls behind, I enter a large pillared hall of marble cladding. There is not much to see: a stall giving out boring books and manuals, a small counter behind which a woman doles out passes. Above her is a banner announcing 'WOMAN AT PEACE'. Most of the women collecting the passes are squat and scowling. There is a trio of them wearing boiler suits; with bristle-cut hair-styles, they return my curious staring in a united glance of such burning disdain that I feel like a bit of bread on the end of a toasting-fork.

I carry on up First Avenue. I have forgotten if the bookshop is on Fifth or Sixth Avenue and stop to ask an amiable-looking, oldish woman if she knows. She makes absolutely no reply, but she pulls together the open flaps of my jacket and solemnly buttons them up. Then she walks away. A rum lot, the New Yorkers.

While I am still standing about, looking lost, and unbuttoning my jacket to let the fresh air in again, two tramps approach. One is immensely fat, and black. The other is thin, and had once been white. Now he is a mottled grey-brown. I have never seen such a filthy and scruffy creature. The only things visible amid the dishevelled and food-flecked tangle of beard and eyebrows is a round, red-veined nose and red-veined eyes; they look like a buzzard's eggs in a guano-encrusted nest. You could sow a good crop of turnips in his fingernails. Before now, the worst smell I ever smelt was the corpse of a sow in a cesspit; she was as exquisite as a primrose in comparison to this fellow.

They snuggle up to me. "Got any money man?' asks the black one.

He is very overwhelming: huge, with a neck so thick that it pushes up his earlobes and eyes that bulge out so much that they show white rings, as if someone had started to strangle him, and then had to give up. However, neither of them look as if they can run very fast, and their menacing obsequiousness is unpleasant, so I say: 'Yes, I've got masses, and I'm keeping the whole bloody lot.'

Immediately the black man's face splits in a huge watermelon of a grin.

'Hey, man, you sound like my favourite character on my TV.'

'Who?' I ask suspiciously.

'Now, let me see, he's English, like you. That's it! Dangermouse!'

We part, they a dollar or so better off, me musing a bit.

'Waddya think?' I have been in about five different queues to get here, to the top of the Empire State building. My neighbours all the way have been an abrupt little grannie and her husband, whose warty and brown face staring from below a huge six-gallon hat makes him look like a toad under a water-lily pad.

'Very tall,' I reply.

'Got nuttin' like it in Britt'n, I guess.'

'I reckon not.'

'Been there, to England. Me and Walt went, years ago. Didn't want to go again. Everything there so little, and so old.'

'Visibility twenty-five miles,' so a notice says. I look about. A pigeon lands on the wall and stares at me, eyeball to eyeball. It has had to fly up over one thousand feet to get up here. At least it did not have to queue, but like me it has flown over this city often and there is not much new to look at. I join another queue – for the exit lifts.

As I leave the building a man is exhorting people to 'come up and have a look-round. Ask me about it,' he says, 'it will be of no inconvenience to repeat myself. I do it all day. I do it at night too, in my dreams. I am approachable. Feel free to ask me questions: the view, the thrill, the speed of the elevators, the height – I'll let you into a secret folks, the height is 1250 feet or alternatively 381 metres.' He is thoroughly fed up, poor chap.

Near the synagogue on 51st Street I stop walking to write down the words above the door of the adjacent small plaza which was donated 'for providing some moments of serenity in this busy world'. I continue to the end of the street. Three police cars drive alongside. One then swerves out to block the whole road, one cuts across the pavement in front of me, the other stops next to me. I am suddenly surrounded by six policemen. 'Whatyougot in those bags,' shouts the fattest.

'Books.'

'Take them out and put them on the top of the car.'

I am not too fussed, some IRA alarm, I presume.

They stare at my heap of books, nonplussed.

'Where's your knife?'

'What knife?'

'The one you were pointing at the synagogue.'

'All I was pointing at the synagogue was this pen, which I am still holding.'

They stare at it, peeved.

'Even if it was a knife, do you think the synagogue would worry if I stabbed it?'

I suddenly remember that there are no IRA problems in New York. If anything, they are in favour of the murdering bastards. I notice that

the cars have a total of twenty-one lights, all busily flashing. There is an enormous line of traffic in 51st Street, being held up by the rear police car. Everyone is goggling at me.

'What the hell is all this about?'

'Now sir, no need to be disturbed, we are just doing our job. You come from England?'

'Yes, and I'm bloody well going back there at once if this is how you treat your guests.'

'Now sir, no problem. Just show us your passport.'

I produce my Queen's Messenger passport. Fatty looks at it, raises his eyebrows, hands it back, says 'thank you for your patience', nods to the others and without further ado they all get into their cars and buzz off.

I don't even have the consolation that they were rude so that I can complain.

The big Liverpudlian is driving me to the aerodrome. 'Had a good day?' he asks.

'Not bad, but I seemed to spend half the time queuing. And I was held up by the police.' I tell him what happened.

'That synagogue is used by the Jews of the United Nations. There have been so many threats against it that the police have a 'secret eye' looking at it. They must have seen you and thought you were some sort of bomber.'

'The police seemed quite efficient.'

'The average policeman in New York is as helpful as a chocolate teapot.'

We go under a flyover, the litter is dreadful, much of it seems to be hubcaps; the walling is covered in scrawls. The graffiti in America are abundant and ornate but unlike those in Britain not obscene, normally being initials or short names like Bob or Sam. 'It's because the graffiti scribblers are completely illiterate,' says my driver, 'they can't spell complicated words of four letters.'

Dusk is falling. Patches of jaundiced light gleam amid the drear and huddled shapes of a cemetery. 'Cold, it must be, for the people in those graves,' I say.

[13]

'Not a nice day to be dead in,' my driver agrees.

I wonder if that shadowless man I saw at breakfast is still alive.

 **Baku, 9 October 1996.** I am in the capital of Azerbaijan. I knew little of either the city or even the country until a month ago, when issued with my itinerary, and I was still not much the wiser until I landed here and was handed a useful pack of information including a map, and the following excellent summary:

Azerbaijan is about the size of Scotland, with a population of 7 million. It is a country of great variety: in the north and west the wooded mountains of the Caucasus rising to 16,000 feet, in the south-eastern areas arid, almost desert like steppe. At the Caspian Sea the mountains plunge downwards, to the Apsheron Peninsula where Baku lies. It borders with Russia (north), Georgia, Armenia and Turkey (west) and Iran (south). Baku is situated on a large bay in the Caspian Sea. It has a historic walled centre and many fine stone buildings, rather dilapidated, dating from the first oil boom in 1890–1905.

Also gleaned from the leaflets is the information that 'Health – medical facilities are extremely poor. There is a lack of basic medical supplies and modern equipment. Treatment is on a cash basis. . . . Inoculation against hepatitis A & B, rabies, diphtheria, TB and tetanus is recommended. . . . Boil water as well as filter it.' And from a list of *Strategic value/significance/important goods of Azerbaijan Republic*, 'Item 15. Snake poison, tarantula poison, scorpion poison.'

At present it is a clear, crisp autumn morning, but it can be very bleak here later in the year. The derivation of the name Baku is supposed to be from the Persian *bad kiu*, 'town of wind'. The wind is a violent north-north-westerner which persists throughout most of the winter. However there is rarely any frost. The average rainfall is little more than nine inches a year, which makes the local vegetation arid and thin.

What is special to the area is the presence of petroleum, both as crude oil and natural gas. The whole of the area is like a huge, oil-sodden sponge. The floor of the Caspian Sea heaves slowly up and down with the subterranean pressure, like the flanks of some colossal sleeping whale. Oil seeps from the ground (it was being collected and sold as early as the eighth century) and natural gas sometimes flares from the surface and ignites, a manifestation which caused great excitement in people who worshipped fire in one form or the other, such as Zoroastrians and some Hindus of pyrolatric sects. These came, often as merchants along the Silk Route, and built temples around some of the fires. One temple is on show where the fire has been artfully channelled so that flames spurt from all four corners of an altar, and glow within its cell-like centre. It is possible that the name Azerbaijan originates from 'The Land of Fires'.

The first oil-well ever sunk was the one drilled here in 1848. By 1900 rich oil-merchants had built grand houses in the city and by 1904–5 some of the less fortunate had shown the traditional human reaction to this in 'The Years of Anarchy', when many oil-wells and some houses were burned. The Communists kept this resentment fermenting so that the Red Army had a relatively easy invasion in 1920. However the Azerbaijani then regretted their acquiescence and 10,000 people were killed in 1930 by the Russian soldiery during anti-Communist riots. The Russians consolidated their hold in 1936 by the creation of the Transcaucasian Federal Republic, which included Azerbaijan, Georgia and Armenia: this was soon merged into the USSR. Azerbaijan declared itself an independent state in 1991 and fully confirmed its position as one of the world's nations by having aggressive – sometimes armed – arguments with its neighbours, particularly with Armenia.

Yesterday I went on a tour of the city, with a later visit to the botanic gardens.

The Old Town is built beside the sea and is delineated by walls whose age stretches from the twelfth to the fifteenth centuries. There are several good examples of medieval Arab architecture, of which a mosque built in 1078 is perhaps the earliest; there are a couple of domed buildings with central courtyards which look like caravanserai. I corkscrewed up the spiral staircases of the Maiden's Tower, a solidly

built defensive tower of several storeys, now used as a lighthouse. The oil-merchants' houses are charmingly ornate, with ornamental balconies and turrets and grand doorways, and scrolls and curlicues carved into the stonework. There is a park-like esplanade and some amusingly grandiose Russian public buildings, with towers and pinnacles in the Walt Disney kitsch style. Far out, the town degenerates into typical communist mass-produced shoeboxes.

There is a 'pantheon' of six large statues commemorating the type of men who are considered the real celebrities – almost heroes – of the local people: they are poets. I remember the Archdeacon Seraphim in Jerusalem telling me that he considered Turkish poetry the best in the world. Much of it is based on a tenth-century epic called the *Book of Dede Korkut*, which has been compared with the *Iliad*. The Azerbaijanis have been greatly influenced by Turkic literature. Poetry is the language and aspiration of them all, from the philosopher to the plough-boy. The Russians have waged a seventy-year resistance against the poetic protests of the Azerbaijani literati and many have died in prison or have been tortured into obedience.

The botanical gardens are on the outskirts of the city. A long time ago they were a horticultural oasis in a desert of indifference; now they are a derelict remnant of once burgeoning optimism. Much thought, love and money must have been spent on the place. But the flowerbeds have disappeared beneath a creeping barrage of weeds, trees have grown, and beneath them their seedlings have massed into copses; pools are dry and the long line of greenhouses have broken windows and palm trees bursting through their roofs. However, there are still some aged gardeners, a ghostly figure will rustle out from bushes and bow and smile and look wistful.

Today, as yesterday, my guide-cum-driver is Samir. He is typical in appearance to most of the locals. Genetically, they are a mixture of the invaders: the Mongolians under Tamerlane and Genghis Kahn, the Persians, Turks and Armenians; with a dash of the more peaceful visitors – Indian merchants, gypsies, Jews and Christian refugees from Islam. The result is small, stocky, dark and brown-eyed, with an impressive aquiline nose. Most of the men are moustached. They wear heavy knitted jerseys and shabby dark trousers and jackets, some of the older

men are topped by huge 'cor-blimey' caps, set four-square on the head, which makes them look like animated mushrooms. The older women wear frumpish dresses and the invariable Muslim scarf, most of the younger women do not.

Samir sports another local speciality, a chryselephantine smile of gold and ivory. His upper set of teeth consists of seven gold and one ivory one; below, he shows only one gold but five ivories. This lack of symmetry is disconcerting. I keep wanting to swap the gold and ivory singletons to make the whole display neater. He speaks a very basic English with a slight Texan accent and chain-smokes cigarettes of hand-rolled goat droppings.

His car is Russian: a Lada 1500. It is of a faded, pale blue outside; within, it smells frowsy, a combination of damp upholstery and cigarettes. We plan to drive about 100 miles up the coast of the Caspian, about an eighth of the total length of this, the world's largest inland sea.

The road out of Baku is badly pot-holed and furrowed. The suburbs degenerate into a shanty town of shacks; then an arid landscape of sand hillocks and industrial works. We pass a small oil-field. All is still, no people about, the chimneys and stacks smokeless, the pumps motionless.

'Run out of oil?' I ask.

'No', Samir replies, 'plenty of oil, no Russians. Many years they are here. They take oil. They take, they take. Then five, six years ago, no pay. "Where our money?" they ask. No one answers. They work, they work. Still no money. Russians sad. Still work. Still no money. Russians get angry. Go home. All stop. All finished.'

I have my side window wide open, the wind of our progress buffets my face. It smells of petroleum, my tongue tastes of oil as if it had been used as a dip-stick.

We pass a reservoir. 'Any fish in the water?' I ask.

'Many fish in water. Too many. They go to the latrine. Many birds on water. They go to the latrine too. The water, much shit. We drink it. We ablute in it. We cook in it. We wash our clothes in it.'

We have now driven through fifteen miles of industrial wreckage: an ironscape of ruin and rot and rust and dust, of abandoned wells and refineries and oil-cracking plants, all disintegrating amid a forest of

[17]

pylons, derricks, rigs, pumps, chimneys, flare-stacks and posts; a forest which seems to have suffered a great fire, for everything is coloured as if scorched and seared, the colour of corrosion. There is a skyscape of broken wires and cables which dangle and festoon from pylons and posts – also of piping which, having run alongside the road for a bit, will rear up and cross overhead, shedding lagging so that the pipes look like the stiffened corpses of leprous snakes.

It is hideous, but, oddly enough, not depressing. Perhaps it would be in the rain, but at present it is a balmy autumn morning. Also I met some British oil-men in the Embassy last night, and they told me of plans to clear up the area of all its pollutionary and obsolete equipment, to start again, clean and efficient.

Another pleasing event is that the countryside is moving in: a hawk perches on top of a fume-stack and looks calculatingly at a flock of pigeon which flutters amid the metallic fretwork of the distillery below; weeds are patches of green against the tin sheeting of a line of pre-fabricated living quarters; a butterfly flits over a clump of aster; brambles sprawl upon a concrete pad and the empty oil-drums which have been stacked on it; a squabble of hooded crows argue over the corpse of something large and ginger – a fox?

People are also moving in from the countryside, a roadside life is developing, an evolutionary civilisation. Shepherds tend little flocks of sheep which graze on the arid growth between the pipe-lines. Some of them are penned beside the road and studiously ignore their friends and relations who have been butchered and hang from the rusting cross-bars of pylons, being gutted and skinned. The dismembered joints hang from the poles and struts of makeshift stalls, or roast over fires whose smoke wafts appetisingly over the road. Two customers are inspecting a joint, they are both mounted on sturdy, Mongolian-type ponies. Other stalls sell fruit and vegetables. Crude housing appears as brief lines of ribbon development: hovels and shacks made from metal sheeting; converted caravans, de-wheeled and hoisted up on brick plinths. Heaps of log-wood are stacked beside each one. Sometimes there is a patch of cultivation where vegetables are grown. People bustle up and down the verge, buying, selling, gossiping – all utterly ignoring the traffic which moves along the boundary of their existence.

We have by-passed the seemingly hideous town of Sumguyeet and the industrial shambles is thinning out. The land is flat and featureless. The soil is sandy and has a thin fuzz of coarse grass with an occasional patch of broom and whin. The Caspian Sea is to our right, a pallid greeny-blue. Far to the front is a line of mountains, the foothills of the Caucasus. They are coloured a raw beige, more like the vast soil heaps of a series of quarries. The abandoned railway line is still alongside the road. I count a convoy of seventy-five oil waggons rusting in a queue to nowhere. Sometimes we pass a group of oil-pumps. They are called 'Nodding Donkeys', but they look more like birds: they stand on tall, spindly, stilt-like legs, their heads are beaked and their motion is similar to that of a bird drinking, as if bending down to sip and then raising the head to let the fluid run down the throat. Only a few peck and rear, most stand and brood, gazing into the far distance or staring down as if waiting for worms to appear.

After the settlement of Zarat, dominated by five-storey blocks of flats which loom above a clutter of shacks, we went through the town of Seeazan, of which we saw evidence several miles before our arrival: above it a large, flat, dark, beret-shaped cloud of pollution hung. We are now running alongside the mountain range. The land is more fertile, the slopes are covered with a blanket of green, small cultivated fields show recent ploughing, and many of the houses have hay or straw stacks beside them. Most of the houses look modern, and are unimaginatively rectangular with asbestos sheeting on their roofs, but at least they are built from the local limestone. The few older houses which exist are high and thin, with unfriendly tall, narrow windows, the upper lintel is usually pointed into something like a Gothic arch.

Samir and I have been trying to get on. 'What family do you have?' I ask.

'All ladies, no gents. Five ladies, zero gents. We try for gents: try, try, try, only ladies come out.'

'Still,' I say consolingly, 'it is a good bull that breeds heifers.'

'How mean? What is bull? What is heifer? What is breeds? Breeds is fuck, I think. I fuck heifers?'

He smiles eventually, but I think only to end the tedious chore of trying to understand my explanations.

[19]

The milometer says that we have done 110 kilometres from Baku. We have reached the town of Dava Chee. It is pleasant and airy; most of the houses have gardens and they contain many trees and bushes of walnuts, figs, Lombardy poplars, cypress and pomegranates; there is a bustlement of people walking along the sides of the streets.

I am fed up with the sea, and the mountains look inviting: I tell Samir to turn off and head inland.

Our road rapidly sloughs its thin skin of tarmac and becomes a meandering track of rubble and dust. Samir has to grapple with the wheel to avoid pot-holes and ruts but he does not mind, he is used to it. There are vineyards to either side, sometimes houses: low, white-washed, with very large lattice windows like the medieval weavers' cottages of Essex. Most of them have a haystack in the garden and an outside loo. The villages – hamlets really, because they seem to number a score or less of cottages – are cosy, often nestling in groves of Lombardy poplar. Flocks of geese waddle about on the banks of streams, horses graze further uphill, dogs scratch, men gossip, children stare and women toil.

The undulations of the hill-land are becoming steep as we climb into the Caucasus Mountains. We pass some men on horses, they wear picturesque round hats and capes or jackets slung over their shoulders. Fourteen kestrels rest on a telegraph wire; they must be about to migrate. The land alongside is becoming scrubby: brambles, elder, dogwood; the feathery plumes of dill or fennel grow by the ditch, also a yellow hollyhock. Is that the natural colour of the flower, before domestication?

We are perhaps about ten miles from our turn-off and are looking over a wide valley. On the top of a mountain opposite are the remains of a castle. Little is left of it: a tall, square-sectioned tower, a round tower, a down-sloping defence wall with a couple of turrets. It looks slightly like a crusader castle, so perhaps it was built in the period of the Kingdom of Lesser Armenia (1080–1375). Samir says it is called Gala-Aalti. He knows nothing else about it except 'it is old, very old. Not new, old. Old, it is, that big house, made many many many years ago. Made by old peoples.'

I want to climb up to it, so I tell Samir to get as near as possible.

It rears above us, still quite far away, I reckon I will have about a thousand feet to climb. It is now noon; I tell Samir not to expect me back for a couple of hours.

The mountain slopes leading up to the castle are very steep, and the mud beneath the autumn fall of leaves is very slippery. In many cases I have to haul myself up from trunk to trunk of the spindly trees, the oaks, hornbeam or maples which dominate the thick growth of vegetation. In fact it is so thick that I cannot see where I am going, all I know is that one direction is up, the other, down. I have become worried that I will get lost, so I have been tearing scraps of paper from my notebook and am skewering them to the end of branches to use as markers.

It has taken me almost one and a half hours to get up here. I am panting and sweaty. Around me are the low walls and scattered rubble of the ruins. The bleak tower looms above me. It is built of irregular limestone blocks with bands of pink brick on the upper heights. There are no windows or doors, just a huge gaping hole, too high up for me to enter. It discloses a tall, cheerless cell. The round tower is not far off, but on a separate pinnacle. I hunt about for artefacts: pottery shards, perhaps an arrowhead or musket ball. A glitter under a rock! I excitedly heave the rock up and look underneath . . . the crushed remains of a champagne bottle. Tuh! And I'd thought that I may have been the first person up here for decades. There is no more time to explore, Samir will already be flapping. Before I go I stand on the edge of the cliff upon which the castle is built and look over the great vale spread below, dotted with hamlets and cottages amid their copses and pastures. Ten miles away the land levels out into a flat plain; and then I see the pale misty blue of the sea which hazes away to the horizon, towards the great gulf called the Zaliv Kara Bogaz Gol, which I have always wanted to see ever since I read the name in my school atlas.

There is a shrubby honeysuckle growing in the rubble of the broken fortifications: it is about waist high and a dozen paces across. The berries are large, and of a beautiful translucent scarlet. I pick some to send to Kew Gardens. I put them in one of the collecting bags I usually carry (they are actually sanitary-towel disposal bags which hotels leave in their bathrooms – they are ideal for botanical samples).

A forty-minute scramble-slither downhill to the car, collecting the scraps of paper as I go, swinging and lurching down from tree to tree like some primeval man learning to walk upright. Samir greets me with open arms and cries of relief. I look at my map to see where we are, because Kew will want to know when I send them the seeds: I am not exactly sure but I reckon we are about latitude 41° 00′ N, longitude 48° 50′ E, and the castle is about 4500 feet above sea level.

Samir missed a turning and we are lost, but I tell him there is no reason to panic as if we drive with the sun behind us we are bound eventually to reach the coastal road. He did not understand me, so now I just point whenever we arrive at a junction.

We top a ridge of hills and see below a vale of desolation: an abandoned oil-field, a huge graveyard of lifeless bodies. We descend into a charnel of immobile pumps. Sometimes grouped into flocks, sometimes as isolated individuals, they are spread along the valley floor and are strewn along the arid slopes of hill and ridge. They are all still, all lifeless. Some bled to death and pools and clots of their life-blood congeal around each corpse. Here is a crane, like a dead dinosaur, its long neck stretched out along the ground, its sharp skull-like head lying on one cheek as if it was sleeping when it died. A conveyer belt has a long Cretaceous neck; its tiny head is poised over a heap of rubble, its last meal. A small pumping station is hunched over an intestinal jumble of pipes and tubes which spill from the gash of a missing panel in its side. A mechanical digger lies askew in a ditch, as if it had not quite finished excavating its own grave. Its fanged jaws are open to its last gasp. Another digger faces the rotting hulk of a bulldozer, both are mauled and scarred as if they had battered each other to death. A road roller overlooks the scene with blinded headlight eyes of broken glass. Metallic bones are everywhere: as skeletonic derricks, as the ribcage rafters of empty huts, as stacks of girders and cairns of waste scrap iron. There is the raw, meaty stink of crude oil. And everywhere the wind keens a dirge, whining and moaning through wires and cables.

We are back at the Embassy
'Chalksao – thank-you,' I say to Samir, as I pay and tip him. Perhaps

he will now be able to buy another gold tooth to complete his upper set.

The Corps of Queen's Messengers. The Corps of Queen's Messengers is to celebrate its 800th birthday party in 1999. This will be the anniversary of the appointment of the first King's Messenger known by name. He was John Hamelin, 'Messenger to the Lord King' (i.e. King John, who succeeded his brother Richard I on 27 May 1199).

But there have been Royal Messengers for much longer: from before the reign of Queen Boudicca to after that of Ethelred the Unready. All rulers have needed messengers, either because the task of taking messages was too unimportant for a busy ruler, or sometimes too dangerous: none likes the bearer of bad news or aggressive threats. The courier can vary from the humble runner with his message held in a cloven stick to the herald, smart in a playing-card uniform and accompanied by trumpeting fanfares to, finally, at the very top, someone like the Master of the Royal Horse whose job is formally to declare war on behalf of Her Majesty. (Nowadays that is normally done via a telephone call.)

Most of the messages taken by the Corps of Queen's Messengers are political, from the government via the Foreign and Commonwealth Office to British Embassies, High Commissions and Consulates throughout the world. The Corps is still officially an adjunct to the Royal Court, and when Her Majesty is at work abroad the Queen's Messenger brings both personal and official post.

In the days of King John the King's Messengers had to be freemen, but not necessarily socially smart. During the next 800 years our fortunes fluxed: sometimes we were personal friends of the monarch, sometimes we lived in the servants' hall with the chamber maids.

Our duties also varied, the conveyance of messages was not the only work, for example in 1397 the expenses for the High Sheriff of Norwich include: 'to one messenger of the Lord King for carrying a quarter of

Henry Ropere, traitor – payment 4s/6d.' On other occasions the King's Messenger was obliged to act as host to important hostages; for this he was usually paid nothing.

On one journey from a particularly nasty country I had sixteen seats in the front of the aeroplane, six of them taken by my escorts, the remainder taken up by the diplomatic bags. As he wished us farewell, the ambassador whispered to me: 'Don't forget to keep a low profile.'

We try to be unnoticed, but there are clues which can help the sharp-eyed to distinguish a Queen's Messenger. In the first place there are the diplomatic bags, sometimes up to half a ton of them. They are white and stamped in black:

H B M

DIPLOMATIC

SERVICE

(In this day and age, how many people need to be told that HBM stands for Her Britannic Majesty?) Other clues are the maroon passports bearing the words:

BRITISH PASSPORT

QUEEN'S

MESSENGER

COURRIER DIPLOMATIQUE

Inside is written: 'in the name of Her Majesty all those whom it may concern to allow [Colonel John Soap] CHARGED WITH DESPATCHES to pass freely without let or hindrance'. Lastly there is the badge. All diplomatic messengers need a pass, a sign of authority, whether it be the miniature assegai carried by the messengers of the Zulu kings, or the engraved brass plates of Imperial China. The Queen's/King's Messenger badges change in design with every new moanrch, the consistencies being that they include the insignia of the monarch, surrounded by the order of the garter from which the emblem hangs, the silver greyhound; the whole arrangement is suspended from a ribbon of garter blue. Nowadays these are worn only on ceremonial occasions;

[24]

for everyday use the Queen's Messenger bears his badge as a tie with a design of silver greyhounds carrying the royal crown. Because of this some Queen's Messengers are under the happy illusion that their nickname is 'The Silver Greyhound', but, as Lord Curzon said 100 years ago, when he came upon a Queen's Messenger packing his face with a large breakfast instead of delivering a vital message: 'Silver Greyhound indeed! A Fat Bulldog would be more apt.'

The history of the King's/Queen's Messengers is a long one of adventure and exploration, as colourful as ever since the end of the Second World War. Queen's Messengers were still travelling on horseback as late as 1949 (to Kathmandu). Within the last forty years there have been cases of our being attacked by pirates in the South China Seas, of train derailments in the Gobi Desert, of being hijacked (twice) and killed in aeroplane crashes (thrice). The site of one of the crashes was in the High Andes and the crashed aeroplane was not discovered for thirty-five years. All that was left of the Queen's Messenger and his load were his false teeth and the brass rings from the top of the bags. At the site of another crash it is reported that the Queen's Messenger was found as a skeleton propped against a tree: both his shin-bones were broken but his bags were arranged in a neat semicircle around him.

The latest bit of real adventure was during the Tien-an-men Square riots in 1995. Two Queen's Messengers arrived on the trans-Manchurian Express from Outer Mongolia. At Peking railway station they had to commandeer a couple of rickshaws. Upon these they piled the diplomatic bags, upon which they sat; they then ran the gauntlet of hostile crowds, a line of tanks and blocked roads. The rickshaw men earned well-earned tips.

At present the sixteen-strong Corps of Queen's Messengers travels to about sixty different destinations – although in some cases the Queen's Messenger merely lands there and quits in the same aeroplane. In addition there are 'Special' journeys which may take us anywhere. We each travel about a quarter of a million miles per year. Some people wonder why all this is necessary: there are fax machines; messages can even be bounced off the moon, having previously been coded by machines of the utmost ingenuity. But all messages can be intercepted; a code invented by one machine can be decoded by another. As events

over the last 800 years have proved, the most reliable messenger is still a middle-aged person with an ability to compromise and enjoy difficult situations and with a spare bottle of whisky to lubricate the wheels – or palms – of authority.

 **Valletta, 30 October 1996.** It was early morning today when I checked in at Rome aerodrome, ready to fly to Malta. 'Queen's Messenger,' I said, 'off to Valletta. I have two tickets, one for myself and one for the diplomatic bag, could I have bulkhead seats, together please. And two passes for your lounge, one for me and one for my escort here.' There was a little old biddy in the adjacent queue, checking in a large amount of expensive luggage and complaining about the surcharge. She had a dry little husband and wore the up-swept specs some Americans favour. She looked coldly at me then said: 'You're not my idea of James Bond.'

'Of course not,' I replied with calm dignity, 'I'm in disguise.'

When I go somewhere I often try to imagine myself in the place of the people who used to live there: hot, dry and dusty, on the banks of the Nile, watching Cleopatra sailing past in her barge with its purple sail bellying in the love-sick winds; in silks and peruke, as a courtier in Versailles, bowing to Louis XIV's chamber-pot as it is ceremoniously carried past; looking across the veld from the heights by Pretoria at the waggons of the Voortrekkers winding below. There is nowhere better for this vicariousness than a place of defence: a castle, a walled city, an old front line. I have always liked the idea of pouring boiling oil on uninvited guests, or waiting until they have climbed up to the top of a ladder and then tippling it over with a long pole, or hurling boulders down onto the heads of besiegers as they batter at my door. I spent much of my childhood doing this when staying in the Massif Central, in a castle with the lovely name of Château de Montrozier. In that part of France there seems to be a castle on top of every hill. They were all built as defence against the great enemy, the English. To my secret chagrin my cousins made me an honorary Frenchman and I had to play games

which involved repelling the sibilant-speeched pale-eyed invaders from the castle walls.

Castles are like cathedrals in that everyone has his favourite. Probably the crusader castle of the Krak de Chavaliers in Syria is considered the greatest of all, but I prefer Saint Hilarion in Cyprus, high on its mountains with its walls and arches and windows all higgledy-piggledy on the peaks and slopes. Poor frustrated Berengaria, the wife of Richard I, defenestrated herself there after she found out that her husband may have been Lion Hearted but was Lamb Libidoed. You can still look out of the actual window and see the rocks far below, where she landed. Even more evocative are the remote fortifications at the end of the Bay of Kotor in Montenegro; nearly forty years ago I wandered about the gateway which guards the seaward entrance and the castle high above it, and scrambled along the intercommunicated lines of battlemented walls and fortlets, and I was completely alone except two neat shadows in suits, Tito's police.

I am thinking about sieges because all afternoon I have been touring the ramparts of the capital of Malta, Valletta. The whole place seems to be one vast defensive unit. Everything is harmonised by the building materials: the pale, local sandstones and limestones. It is not only built from the rock, it is built into it: everywhere you look, even on a sheer cliff face, you will see loopholes, slits and gunports; walk round a cliff and perhaps there is a huge gully gouged out behind, full of rusting barbed wire and khaki-coloured scrap. Much of the fortification originated after 1565 when 30,000 of the Muslim troops of Suleiman II unsuccessfully besieged the island, defended by about 7000 knights of Saint John and their Maltese troops. The victorious commander, Grand Master de la Valette, made Valletta the most magnificent example of fortification of its type in the world. The British expanded and improved this, particularly round Grand Harbour. They then underwent their own siege, enduring, with the Maltese, the bombardment of 16,000 tons of bombs.

I have just left the Co-Cathedral of Saint John, one of the most astonishing buildings I have ever visited. It is rather plain and prim outside, almost Puritan; within, the floor is one mighty carpet of inlaid marble, an incredible complication of hundreds of coats of arms: the

marbles in blacks and whites, greys and blue-greys, honey, terracotta, red, tortoise-shell and many shades of brown and beige; the armorials are surmounted by crests of every chivalric headgear ranging from helmets and coronets to helms and mitres; they are swathed in mantling and held by supporters, many of these being skeletons. The whole floor is a graveyard, holding the élite of 'The Sovereign Military Hospitaller Order of the Hospital of Saint John of Jerusalem, called of Rhodes, called of Malta'. I found myself almost tip-toeing over it, trying not to draw attention from the hundreds of eye-sockets staring up at me. Around the walls are tombs, often surmounted by a statue of the occupant, periwigged and armoured and pointing meaningly at adjacent panels showing battles being fought or good deeds being done; and everywhere is the Maltese Cross.

I am now outside, basking on the ramparts. Near me, there is a little old man in shorts, with tattooed arms. He leads about a slow, fat and cross wife. He is muttering 'Can't recognise a thing now . . . all tidied up . . . it must be about here that Wilf copped it 'cos we found his foot in that doorway . . .'

Perhaps being in a siege isn't fun after all.

Lagos, 4 November 1996. It is a truth universally acknowledged, that if the world needed an enema, Lagos is where it should be applied. I first came to Nigeria as a businessman, shortly after 'Harold Wilson's War'. Peace had rapidly returned, money was flowing copiously (into the pockets of the corrupt and powerful) and 80 per cent of the population was aged less than eighteen. I had come here to try to get an order for the new unit I had founded in Courtaulds Ltd, the 'turn-key' furnishing organisation. 40,000 houses were to be built for FESTAC, the Festival of Black Arts; they were to be furnished and used as lodgings for visitors to the festival, then handed over to the populace. I came to offer complete furnishing, everything from design and specification to supply and installation. Our offer included 240,000 air-conditioning units, 80,000 corkscrews, 330 acres of carpeting, 120,000 ashtrays,

about 600 miles of curtaining, 3 tons of pictures and so forth. The package was worth £35 million. The two governmental ministers who fought to be my client finally came to at least one agreement: they wanted to be bribed equally – US$3,000,000 each. I refused, much to the despair of my agents and middlemen. So my competitors, the Yugoslav Government, got the order. Then there was a coup, the two ministers were among those executed and the Yugoslavs lost both the order and the bribe. The houses were never built, anyway.

Courtaulds Ltd was represented by a charming chieftain who had been the editor of the leading newspaper for many years, constantly in and out of prison for being critical of the rulers. I was grizzling to him one day about the inefficiency and dishonesty and he said: 'Stop complaining. Our country is the same as yours was in the days of King John or as Scotland still was 400 years later. We have a gang of barons fighting for position, exacerbated by a huge inrush of money from oil and the release of power through the withdrawal of British rule. In twenty years we'll have rectified things. Meanwhile, when a pot is stirred, the scum floats to the top.'

Well, twenty years have passed, but much of it is the same: the reception, for example. The less one wants to visit a country, the more ado the border bureaucrats seem to make of the administration of entry, causing it to be as difficult and tedious as possible: lengthy and complicated forms, suspicious interrogations, the pursing of lips as computer screens are scrutinised, the laborious leafing through passports in incompetent efforts to discover the visa. It would be much easier if we could all be completely frank and admit that the place is the pits and I am only coming because I must and I am quitting as soon as possible. As for wanting to live here, the idea is bloody ludicrous. At present there is a huge crowd of people jostling and pushing behind the immigration barrier; they exactly resemble my sheep at the gate of the shearing pen. And, like my sheep, they will get a nasty shock when they finally get through – they will be fleeced. As a businessman I was resigned to standing by apologetically, cringingly, impotently, while the customs officers plundered and looted my luggage. Oh, the ecstasy of having an escort who can growl 'Keep your filthy thieving fingers off the bags!'

That chaotic road from the aerodrome to the city is now completed,

but it still takes up to three hours to do the twenty miles during rush hour. What I remember as shanty villages of corrugated iron, or huge raw patches of building site, are now often new buildings or roads or flyovers, great tangles of them. There is still sad evidence of poverty and despair. Our car was stuck for some time next to an abject man in rags, sitting on the pavement, his head bowed as he watched his toenails grow. The prostitutes in the hotel are as numerous, but they are not as busy as before, no longer do they manoeuvre and patrol like army units, lines of them sit by the bar, sipping drinks, no longer is the conveyor belt of activity progressing up and down the lifts and along the corridors: AIDS.

5 November. It is gaspingly hot: not a breath of wind, the temperature is in the nineties and it is very humid; the window of my bedroom was completely steamed up when I awoke. I slide it open and step onto the balcony outside. The sea is about half a mile away, a long spit of sand separates its ruffled waters from the glassy flatness of a lagoon. Ramshackle huts and shacks have been built on the spit. They are on spindly legs, I can see them silhouetted against the sea. A kite is slowly flapping over the surface of the lagoon, just a few feet above its mirror image. Also mirrored are two canoes: long, graceful craft with up-rearing stem and stern. In one, a man sits immobile, brooding. In the other, a man is standing, adjusting something. Suddenly he throws it; it blossoms out like the skirt of a twirling girl, and the weighted net plops into the water. Directly below me are the palm fronds of the hotel garden, to one side the swimming-pool, eye-wrenchingly vivid with its mosaic blues and plastic furniture whites. Some people are already lounging on the extending seats and a man is painstakingly swimming up and down the pool.

We reckon that of all the places we visit, the three most dangerous for our 'time off' are, in order of danger: Rio de Janeiro, Kingston (Jamaica) and Lagos. I have therefore been strongly recommended not to wander around alone, mugging is almost a certainty. The High Commission kindly lent me a car and driver for a couple of hours. Having said I was interested in farming and gardening, I was taken to the allotment gardens of the prison of Kiri Kiri Apapa, past Tin Can

Island. I was not allowed out of the car, so did not see much, but the prisoners looked reasonably cheerful and from their indolence were evidently not being slave-driven. I was intrigued to see that the fencing between the men's and women's compounds was even stronger and thicker than the fencing between the prison and the outside world.

It is now mid-afternoon and I am being driven in the chaotic cataract of traffic to the aerodrome. I am well protected: there is an armed officer of the Diplomatic Police sitting beside my escort, and this is one of the few places where my car has a following car, with two more armed guards. We have a well-oiled system so that if we break down the Queen's Messenger, escort and bags can transfer immediately to the car behind, leaving our unfortunate driver to make his way back to base, preferably in his car if he can repair it without getting mugged and robbed. Both the Range Rover and the following Land-Rover are bullet-proofed. I always hate being in a bullet-proof car: there is very little room, my head is almost squashed against the roof, the claustrophobia is augmented by the fact that only the driver can open and shut the windows and doors and I keep on wondering what will happen if he gets killed, and the people outside start throwing petrol bombs. This driver is not skilled in driving our extra-heavy vehicle. The notice pasted on the dashboard says 'ABOVE 100 KM THIS VEHICLE IS UNSTABLE' but it seems pretty unstable at half that speed, whenever he swerves to avoid a pot-hole – and some of them look as deep as mine shafts – we sway and swoop and he grapples at the wheel like Captain Ahab after Moby Dick.

We have stopped. A decrepit yellow bus has broken down in front. It is being pushed to the verge by its passengers. Somewhat poignantly, inscribed on its rusted flank, is the proud boast: 'JESUS IS MY POWER'.

As we wait a policeman comes up. He taps on the driver's window. Being bullet-proof, it will not open. He taps again, angry. My driver is now in a state of frozen fear and just sits, staring ahead. The policeman gibbers at us through the glass. From here he seems all teeth and eyeballs. He unholsters his gun and points it at the driver, who has now turned an interesting pale khaki. My officer opens the back door and leaps out, his pistol pointing at the policeman. A guard gets out of the

other car and also points his weapon at the policeman. The policeman's eyes show white rings as they widen in shock.

The officer speaks to the policeman: 'May your testicles explode, you stupid man. What are you doing pointing your gun at this VIP vehicle?'

The policeman (who almost certainly was going to try to squeeze a bribe out of us on some trumped-up charge) says: 'All I wanted was to ask if you needed any help.'

The officer turns to me and emits a dramatic sigh of exasperation: 'Oh sir, what should we do with this foolish man?'

'How about thrashing the soles of his feet with the dried penis of a donkey?' I suggest. Everyone laughs heartily, even the policeman: his teeth sparkle in sunlit merriment, his shoulders heave, his cheeks are bunched up like apples, his eyes are sullen with hate. He resembles Ted Heath being reminded of Mrs Thatcher.

Now that we are on our way again the escort tells me that there was a police strike some time ago and during that period the crime rate dropped by 10 per cent. He says that his car was hijacked and driven away by three armed men recently. When the police came round a couple of weeks later to ask why he had not made an official complaint, he replied: 'What's the point, the hijackers all had polished shoes. The only people with polished shoes in Lagos are either the police or the politicians.'

There is a crashed van beside the verge, a mangled wreck. A pair of legs stick out from under the engine. 'That fellow is optimistic if he thinks he's going to get it going again,' I say.

'I doubt he thinks anything,' my escort replies. 'We passed here two days ago and I saw the head belonging to those legs a hundred yards further up the road. Ah, here it is again.'

Now I am flying to Senegal. There are three Nigerians in the other front seats: politicians or businessmen. They are rich and sleek and fat and wallow lethargically on the wide upholstery of the first-class seats like hogs in a mud patch. Yet as gross as they are, they have elegance, and the mass of gold they wear is very handsome on their dark skins: watches, bracelets, neckchains and amulets; one man even has golden spring-clips to keep his sleeves out of his food. All is atwinkle with

precious stones: the man next to me has a watch whose face has been surfaced with an icing of crushed diamonds. Clothes and accessories: a mohair suit, a shirt of the fairest white lawn, printed with a beautiful black design like a massive tattoo, a lizard-skin attaché case with matching lizard-skin shoes, a golden-buckled belt of ostrich skin, the lines of puckered warts showing from whence the feathers were plucked: all are immaculate, everything pressed and polished. My neighbour is huge: not only about six and a half feet high, but weighing about twenty-five stone. He could not put the table over his protuberant belly, so a tray was laid upon his lap and he had to hold the plates up to his face. Now that he has fed he sleeps, lounging on the seat like a sated seal; he still wears a small, white golfing cap, which he has never removed.

And as we hurtle through the air at 500 miles per hour, seated in our luxury armchairs, 30,000 feet below us the teeming hordes of the Black Continent toil, and starve, and breed, and toil and breed and starve again.

Cross-Channel, 18 November 1996. When Queen's Messengers deliver diplomatic mail to and from Paris, they go by van. The van is locked and sealed with a lead and wax seal and becomes, in effect, a large, reinforced, mobile diplomatic bag.

The outward journey yesterday was pleasant: an early-morning start from Whitehall, through the freshly rained-on Kent countryside, lit by the dawn; over on a cross-channel ferry; then on again along the attractive main roads of Normandy to the chaos of Paris.

James, the oldest driver, is chauffeuring me on this journey. Every time he turned the steering wheel there was a creaking noise.

'You need to oil your wrists,' I said.

'Very funny,' grumbled James, 'my last passenger suggested it was my spine.'

We discussed superstitions. James told me of two I haven't heard of. When he was a child, if you saw an ambulance, you would have to hold

on to your coat collar until you saw a dog. Some people would recite: 'Hold your collar, don't swaller, you'll never catch a fever.' A grey ambulance was the unluckiest, for that would be carrying contagious diseases such as measles or cholera. If you saw a man wearing a straw hat, like a boater, you'd say: 'First luck, straw yarn, second luck, straw yarn, third luck, straw yarn.' He didn't know why.

As usual, when in Paris, I stayed at my old friend Eléanore's penthouse flat in Avenue Gabriel. The stuffed pigs which were scattered about as pouffes have gone but the tiny little monkey who hates me is still around. Last time I was there it was wearing a crocheted skirt similar in size and shape to those covers some people put over their lavatory rolls. The monkey ripped it up and ate it, so Eléanore has made a dress for it out of a very expensive cashmere sock someone had left behind in a spare bedroom. Eléanore has snipped the end off the toe for the animal's head, two side cuts for its arms and a hole in the heel for its tail. As its walking posture is in a bent, Groucho Marx-style, the shape of the sock suits it – very chic and French in a horrible way.

After a very early start from the Embassy in Paris I am now on the ferry for the return crossing from Calais to Dover. On the ferry the Queen's Messenger becomes the guest of the driver, for it is the driver who has the privilege of using the Commercial Driver's Restaurant, so James is my host today.

The Public Café is already full. It is a cavernous canteen. The furnishing is spartan: linoleum, seats of metal tubing with plastic 'leather' and easy-wipe tables. There is a huge queue for food, it has to be collected on greasy trays and eaten with plastic cutlery; babies are being fed and changed, older children gobble and slurp, grannies mumble through their slipping teeth. The noise is deafening: shrieks from schoolchildren running in packs, the raucous laughter of lager louts, the blare of piped music. The smell is a combination of vinegar, fish and chips and the seasickness of previous journeys. In spite of all this, the prices scrawled over the food counter are very high.

In comparison all is quiet, elegant and efficient in the Driver's Saloon. The floor is carpeted. We sit in comfortable armchairs. There are tablecloths and napkins of white linen. The crockery and cutlery are plain but heavy and good. Uniformed staff are at the ready, one per four

tables. The only drinks are tea, coffee, fruit juice or 'nice cold, ice cold' milk; everyone is as sober as a judge. On each table there is a massive cruet which holds two sorts of mustard, mint sauce, mayonnaise, tomato sauce, 'chox' and the salt and pepper. The conversation is a murmur of foreign languages: French, Spanish, Italian, German, something Slavic.

You don't order what you want for breakfast, but what you do not want. I cancelled the fried potatoes and baked beans, so after the porridge (with cream and brown sugar) I only have the two fried eggs (sunny side up), fried bread, fried kidneys, fried bacon, sausages, mushrooms and grilled tomatoes – and, of course, the toast ('from brown bread, please') and marmalade ('thank you, the black, vintage, coarse cut') and coffee.

As we eat one of the drivers from another table comes up and taps James on the shoulder. 'It's Solly!' James exclaims, 'come and join us.'

'I'll sit with you for a while, but it'll do my reputation no good to be sitting at the same table as a driver of a titchy little truck.'

Solly sits. He is small and round and smiling with twinkling brown eyes. James points at him: 'Him and me used to drive the same bus route in Leytonstone High Road. Then we both got fed up with all that stopping and starting and argufying passengers and I joined the Foreign Office and Sol here took up the articulateds.'

After James and Solly have nattered for a bit I ask Solly why his reputation would be ruined by being with us.

'Talk about snobbery and class consciousness,' he says, 'the driving world beats the lot. Drivers of vans like Jim here normally won't speak to a driver of a lorry unless he's spoken to first, and a driver of a ten-tonner would give his seat up in a transport caff to an eighteen wheeler. With some drivers there's even a difference how they signal with their lights to other sized vehicles when on the move.'

'Sol here is putting on airs 'cos he's got one of the biggest vehicles of all and he reckons he's the King of the Road,' James says, not entirely amused.

I am down below and Solly has given me a brief tour of the driving cabin of his colossal Volvo. There are eighteen gears. The view is almost

as high as the view from the upper window of a double-decker bus. The whole of the cab is sprung as luxuriously as a good bed; in addition the driver's seat has independent springing. The seat seems to have more positioning levers and buttons than a dentist's chair. Behind the seat is a curtained-off living area, complete with bunk, wash-basin, 'fridge and basic cooking equipment. It is as neat as a pin, with no clutter or ornamentation except for a family photograph above the bunk and a Jewish star hanging from a switch on the dashboard.

We clamber up several strata of decks until we are able to emerge into the cold, gusty, salt-smelling outside world. We are near our destination. The white cliffs of Dover really are white. They really are cliffs. They look what they are: the edge of an island. On top of them the 'Key of England' broods: Dover Castle with its square tower and double ring of fortifications.

'How forbidding,' says a Frenchman to his companion, staring through the drizzle at the cliffs and castle.

'How welcoming,' I think.

There is a lout leaning over the rail. He is drunk – at ten in the morning. He starts to shout and swear and tries to pick a fight with a member of the crew who walks hurriedly away. A German glances at the yob, disgusted. He turns scornfully to Solly, James and me.

'So that is how you British behave if you drink too much.'

'Yes,' Solly says, 'we do drunk what your lot do sober.'

Someone is climbing up a gangway behind us. He has the most extraordinary booming voice, like a bullfrog. And it turns out that the voice emanates from a man who looks exactly like a bullfrog, very small and square. It is remarkable that such an impressive bass resonance can come from such a little body. He is followed by a taller, thinner man who at first sight looks like Salman Rushdie – bald on top, beard below, completely circular specs dead centre: somehow it seems as if his head has been put on upside down. He is wearing an 'ensemble' of bush-jacket and shorts, tailored in pale blue denim with brass press-studs. He and Bullfrog proceed down the deck, holding hands. James looks after them, and shakes his head. 'Dear me, deary me, what is the world coming to? Still, as they used to say, it doesn't matter what they do as long as it doesn't frighten the horses.'

[36]

'Extraordinarily thin legs the one in shorts has,' I say.

'I've seen better legs hanging over a bird's nest.'

An exotic couple are the next to come up the gangway. They lean against the gunwale between the German and us. They are both black, very tall and thin, with fine, aristocratic, Nilotic features. He is wearing an ordinary – but well-cut – suit, she is in an embroidered kaftan-type dress, with her hair of long thin plaits tied together with a golden ribbon. The squally rain clears and the sun comes out. As a non-artist I presume any outline must be in black, like a cartoon drawing, but I suddenly notice that the side of the woman nearest the sun is delineated in a fine line of burning gold. It matches the gold of her hair ribbon and jewellery. Her companion notices me admiring her.

'Er, rain,' I inform him, pointing at the departing squall.

He nods.

'Get any in your part of the world?' I ask.

'Rains the whole bloody time in Bingley,' he says.

'It always seemed to be snowing when I went there, as a yarn and fibre salesman,' I say. He is interested, it turns out that he is an importer of 'rare hairs and funny fibres'. We talk shop: I tell him how in Courtaulds our subsidiary William Hutchinson spun chenille yarns for weaving into the carpet-like tablecloths the Dutch use, and how Smith & Calverly tried to spin eiderdown, using continuous filament viscose as a binder yarn. He tells me of the difference between the hair of dromedary and bactrian camels and how he was once asked to collect slipe (hair from a dead animal) off grizzly bears.

The ferry has arrived and slotted itself into the disembarking ramp. I am back in the van with James and our little vehicle is in a line sandwiched between some mighty behemoths, grumbling and thundering and sending forth impatient exhaust fumes as they wait to be released out of the ship and into the soggy fields of Kent.

This has been a more comfortable sea journey than the one I planned as a fourteen-year-old schoolboy. I carefully wrote a list out, and although my spelling was nothing to be proud of I still treasure it: after all, it *may* become useful, sometime, perhaps when I retire.

A schoolboy's list.

Things needed for canoeing round the world.

Maps, tracing paper
Pens, pencils, ink, rubber, ruler, coloured pencils, geometry set
Paper, envelopes, glue, blank paper, file
Matches, wind-proof lighter, lanterns, candels
Wireless, spare parts
Primus, fuel
Tinned food & juices, salted & preserved food, condensed milk, meats, soup, fruit, fat, chockolate, biscuits, suger
Knives, forks, spoons, plates, mugs, tea set (for visiters)
Tin-opener (with bottle opener, puncher & corkscrew)
Pots, frying pan, kettles
Guns & ammo., (.303, .22, revolver)
Harpoons, shark hooks, hooks, rods & line, nets (hand, small, trawling & fine)
Knives (sheath, skinning, surgeons, pen, sharpener), kookery [kukri]
Tent, sleeping bags (waterproofed, 1 fur-lined), rucksack, mosquito net
Flannels, comb, toothbrush, soap, L-paper, mirror, sizzers
Boot & shoe cleaning stuff
Clothes (bathing, bed, arctic, tropical, waders, boots, pith-helmet, anerack)
Climbing boots, rubber boots, frog feet
Pins, needles, thread, buttons
1st. Aid (sunpeel, insect & snake bite, 1d-cilin [penicillin], quinine, casteroil, cottonwool, lint, stickyplaster, iodine, bandages, surgical spirit, stitches, water-purifying pellets, insect powder)
Thimometer
Watch, alarm-clock, compasses, sextant, sun & snow glasses, binoculars, micriscopes
Preserving spirit, tubes, tanks, alumn (for skin tanning)
Rope, spade, axes, ice-axe
About 5 canvas bags for souvenairs, etc., 2 sacks

Flags, fireworks (rockets), fog-horn
Tools, paint, paint brush, small pully system, splicing tools, twine, pre-
serving oil
String
Broom, bucket
Fire-extinguisher, extra planks, tar
Beads, cloths, small hooks, buttons, needles (for trading)
Books (Bible with funeral @ C), literature, novels, mags
Coach-horn, mouth-organ, drum
Seed, cage, grit, cuttle bone
Cards, travelling games
Champaine, brandy, tobacco
Dairys, log books
Camera, film, flash-bulbs
Life-jacket, rubber-dingy

George Courtauld.
Form 111A, Altyre House, Gordonstoun School, Forres, Morayshire,
Scotland, Great Britain, Europe, The Northern Hemi-sphere, The
British Empire, The World, The Solar System, The Milky Way, Space,
The Universe.   Summer term, 1952.

Rome, 13 December 1996. Rather an embarrassing breakfast in the small hotel. The dining-room was full of little old touristy couples. They all looked up at me as I clumped in noisily, then looked meaningly at each other, then down at their plates. The whole lot were as silent as mice. In comparison I thought I sounded like a farm: I crunch-crunch-crunched through my cereal like a rat gnawing through a barn door; the scrambled eggs were so runny I had to scoop and slop them up as if mucking out a cow-shed; I swallowed my coffee in gulps like the ladling out of a milk churn; my shy nibbles at the toast were magnified into the tramping of heavy boots over a gravelled yard; finally I developed a nervous cough which barked and wheezed like a tractor failing to start on a frosty dawn.

[39]

However, now that I am outside, the early-morning weather exactly suits my metabolism: a sunny sky with some shadowing clouds; a sharp, invigorating bite to the air with the temperature about 7°C. The Romans think otherwise and scurry off to their offices or shops wearing gloves and scarves.

I am walking up the Via Nomentana, a wide avenue of pollarded plane trees which leads north-east from the Porta Pia by the British Embassy into an expensive suburb area. It is mainly residential. The further I go, the more the blocks of flats are interspersed with large villas, mostly built early this century, their ornate style leads me to deduce.

Here is a middle-aged woman crying by a little parked car. Its side windows have been smashed in, by some lout stealing the contents I suppose. My heart turns over at the sight of her but there is nothing I can do, so I plod on.

I pass another woman who is solicitously wiping the running nose of her infant in a push-chair. Most men would rather eat ground glass or roll nude in nettles than do that. It is a woman's nature to want to wipe children's noses. Like squeezing spots. A long time ago, when I was fifteen, I rarely met a girl who did not have an irresistible impulse to squeeze spots. I never had many spots, but the few I had were absolute winners. My brother Sam never had spots. Instead he had an annoying (to him) little tuft of hair which stuck up from the crown of his head like a wren's tail. It would never stay down for long, no matter how much it was brushed and greased. It was called the 'Cocky-ollie Bird'.

'Your Cocky-ollie Bird is sticking up again,' I used to tell him, just as we were arriving at a party. It used to send him into a pleasing frenzy of fussing and pressing down and staring into the rear-view mirror and whimpering.

Thus reminiscing, I reach the park of the Villa Torlonia. I cannot make it out. One person in our Embassy said that it was abandoned, and so it seems to be, but another person said that it is still owned by the Torlonias, while someone else told me that it had been commandeered by Mussolini, who then lived in one of the park's villas. None of them had been there, the general opinion being that 'it is a gloomy, deserted garden of about thirty acres full of vandalised houses'.

The entrance is a gap in a long wall, marked by two classical kiosks, six-pillared and pedimented. To either side of them are four statues, beheaded by vandals. The entrance lamps are globes of glass surmounted by bronze eagles. The glass is smashed.

On entering I find myself in a grove of date palms. Beyond them a wide flight of curving steps leads up to a villa. It was built in the neo-classical style, by Giuseppe Valadier in 1806, I later discovered. There are lines of pillars below a portico which has been filled in with a bas-relief of a bacchanalian parade. There are half-drum porches to either side, also supported by pillars. The house had once been painted a yellow ochre, with the pillars in white, but now all the colours are faded and stained. The plaster of the walls is cracked; there are weeds in the roof and bushes sprout from the steps; lines of fern and moss grow down the walls beneath gutters which have spilled over; vandals have smashed windows and stolen shutters and the doors are chained shut. All of this is surrounded by fencing upon which notices hang saying PERICOLO. In spite of its sad decay, it is one of the prettiest and most charming of houses that I have ever seen.

Behind the villa the park is almost deserted – a few women with children, a courting couple sprawled on the grass, a tramp on a bench who looks at a jogger with contented scorn. It is calm and restful but slightly reminiscent of a cemetery: the cypresses and ivy and other sombre evergreens; the statues and obelisks, suggesting an Egyptian influence; the chained-up cast-iron gates which guard descending flights of steps that lead into crypts; the rusting urns and family memorials. I wander between shaggy lawns on paths of coarse white gravel. Much of the thirty acres is fenced off. I peer through the wire netting at paths, bosky and overgrown like abandoned canals, at tangles of bramble and clumps of glossy-leaved lords-and-ladies. I stand by a charming little villa built and ornamented in the Art Nouveau style. The Celtic convolutions of its cast-iron gates and balconies are in solid rust; its William Morrisy embellishments are mostly hidden by the green lushness of ascending ivy or descending fronds of ferns and scrub. The only sound I can hear is the warbling of a solitary bird. Here am I, a half-hour walk from the centre of Rome, and I could be in a secret garden in a fairy tale.

I come upon other abandoned buildings: some in Romanesque style, some in neo-Palladian – particularly impressive is one with its roof battlemented with twenty-four rusting urns; one villa has the brutish lumpiness of a sort of Fascist Sparta. Upon the older ones there is emblazoned an attractive escutcheon, presumably of the Torlonias: two shooting stars divided by a bend charged with five flowerheads. The Torlonias owned their prosperity to patriarch Giovanni Torlonia who was busy in the early 1800s, particularly during the Napoleonic wars which hit the old aristocracy of Europe particularly hard. Giovanni was a shopkeeper who built a fortune by lending money to the impoverished Roman nobility and then calling on their properties when they could not pay.

I pass a tall memorial to some of the Torlonias: a Corinthian pillar surmounted by an urn, dated MDCCCXXXXI and with family names inscribed in elegant letters. It took only twenty-five years for the usurer's kin to become 'respectable'.

Out of the park, and up to the Via Nomentana again.

The villas are getting even bigger and more ornate and their boundary walls longer with larger acres of garden to defend.

I arrive at the church of Sant'Agnese fuori le Mura. Saint Agnes was a thirteen-year-old who spurned the advances of a courtier in the court of the Emperor Diocletian. Indignant at the snub to one of his staff, the Emperor had her exposed naked, but her hair miraculously grew to cover her modesty. I cannot discover whether it grew from the top of her head, à la Lady Godiva, or whether she sprouted an over-all fuzz, like a guinea pig. Whatever her method, the Emperor, irked, had her decapitated, and she is now the patron saint of virgins.

Last month I was touring a church built by the Emperor Constantine; now I am in one built by his granddaughter, Constantia, around AD 340. (She was, no doubt, extremely worthy, but according to her compatriot, the historian Marcellinus, she was 'a fury incarnate', egging on her equally nasty husband Hannibalianus into violent revenges and vendettas.)

The exterior of the church is of brick, dominated by a good, square-sectioned tower. I enter. The most noticeable thing is the marvellous Byzantine mosaic in the half-dome of the apse ceiling. Amid the golden

glow of the background Saint Agnes stands as 'a bejewelled Byzantine empress in a stole of gold and a violet robe'. Stars are above her head and she has a pope as sentinel at either hand. My shoes clump noisily upon the marble flooring of the nave: to either side are Roman Corinthian columns, above is an ornate ceiling of carved and gilded panels, in front is a coffin, all around are glum people staring coldly at me. I've walked into a funeral. It's even more shy-making than breakfast. I tip-toed rapidly to the main entrance and stand meekly amid the undertakers.

To my right is an entrance to some catacombs. Something, a door perhaps, is moved within the depths below and reverberates in a muffled, subterranean groan.

A priest natters on from the pulpit.

I decide to leave and do so through a side door which opens to an ascending flight of marble steps. The walls have been covered with bits from the tomb inscriptions recovered from the catacombs. At regular intervals huge bunches of flowers have been hung. They are of plastic, and look as tawdry and out of place as does anything cheap and make-shift in elegant surroundings. The churchyards at home are becoming like this.

North-West Frontier, 30 January 1997. A sign tells us that we are leaving the Punjab and entering the North-West Frontier province of Pakistan.

My driver is named Raja Muhammad Younis. Like most Punjabis he is smallish and brownish and moustached and friendly; unlike most Punjabis he is neatly attired in a suit with polished black shoes. Another dissimilarity is that he is completely unflappable. The drivers of the Indian subcontinent are likely to be hysterical personifications of 'road rage': they proceed with the aid of screams, abuse and gesticulations, but Younis does not even use his horn. Every example of incompetence is greeted with a benign shaking of his head, every sign of aggression with a mild raising of the eyebrows. Other drivers find him infuriating. The car is a diesel Land-Rover Discovery, similar to the one I have at home, but he has a Union Jack on the windscreen.

My aim today is to visit some of the small hill stations where the British stayed during the hot summer months. These 'Little Englands' are based on Murree. I have visited there before so we have by-passed it and are toiling uphill towards a chain of smaller villages in the mountains ahead. The soil in the steep valleys below is of a strange puce colour, high mountain ranges undulate above, sometimes boulders have rolled off the slopes and lie on the road.

The uphill climb becomes steeper. Younis changes from third to second gear. Patches of snow appear on the verges. We skid slightly now and then. 'A bit dangerous, this road,' I say nervously. Younis agrees: 'This road is always turning, sir. But', he adds in a consoling voice, 'this road is not yet as bad as it soon will be. Past Sunny Banks it is always landsliding, very difficult to maintain. You will see, sir.'

A bus appears round a corner. It is packed with passengers, others hang onto the sides and are crammed within the spiked barricade of the roof-rack. It hurtles towards us, its chromium-plated eyeballs glaring, its fanged radiator snarling, its heavy valance of chained amulets swinging like a huge kilt, the swags of tinsel which festoon from its multitude of aerials all atwinkle: it resembles a manic amalgamation of a gypsy caravan with a Spanish galleon, driven by a kamikaze pilot and harried by a pack of banshees. In front, beside the driver, a small man sits, reading. I am impressed by his phlegm. 'Perhaps he is their resident Holy Man, and is saying prayers for their safety,' Younis suggests.

The ramshackle dwellings beside the road all have big stacks of logwood beside them; the chimneys wear flat hats, to keep out the snow; through my open window I can smell the sharp scent of resin. I feel young and aware and my senses are heightened: this is the sort of climatic condition which is exactly tuned to my metabolism. Most people I know seem to find the sun and a temperature of over 80°F ideally suited to their minds and bodies. I do not: in such circumstances I automatically walk in shadows or sit under parasols; the light dazzles my eyes and the dry air makes me sweat and I cannot think, for my mind is distracted by the discomfort of the heat. But the sight of snow, the slap of cold air on my cheeks, the smell of frosted leaves, the clatter of iced puddles crackling beneath my feet: once again I can outrun and

[44]

outjump anyone else and bestride mountains and ride in the night sky with the north wind through the aurora borealis.

Meanwhile, here, there are goats and chickens. A hen strolls across the road. Younis nods at it: 'You will observe, sir, that all of the poultry are white in this part of the world. I do not know why.'

We are now passing through Sawar Gali, one of the first of a chain of little villages called Gali. Gali means 'black', and refers to the soil, Younis tells me, but my ancient guide book says it means 'hilltop' or 'pass in a mountain range'. The dominant tree is now pine, but there are also oaks, walnuts, willow and a type of tall, thin, fastigiate poplar. Not many birds, a buzzard or kite now and then, wheeling over the canyons to the left of the road, some crows and myna: most birds have probably gone further down to the valley floor, where it is warmer.

We are now over 7500 feet. A ramshackle van dodders in front of us. 'MAKE WAY – VIP' is written on the back of it. Younis is quietly amused. There are a couple of donkeys, one loaded with turnips, the other with spinach. Younis and I agree that my children and his (like me, he has two boys and two girls) all hate turnips and spinach, also cabbage and most fish.

Khaira Gali: this is my first stop. At first sight all there seems to be of it are a few one-storey open-fronted shops in a corner of the road. There are no women around, only men, in large groups, all dun-coloured in their baggy *shalwar kameez* (knee-length shirt with loose trousers) and the *chador* (a blanket-like plaid round the shoulders). Many of them have impressive hawk noses jutting over bearded chins. They stand and stare. 'Poor people, it is quite sad,' says Younis, 'no work, they have nothing to do all winter but look at the traffic passing.' They seem friendly, however, and when Younis stops and asks the way to the church many crowd round the car, babbling. After some discussion a man climbs into the back of the car.

'Salaam alay kum.'

'Waalay kum as salaam.'

We shake hands, he holding mine in both of his and beaming closely into my face. He is tiny, with a grey beard and only a few teeth; he wears rubber boots and carries a small, elegant but rather useless-looking axe. He sees me inspecting it and shakes it. 'Wood, cut wood,' he explains.

[45]

He directs us up a steep track. We pass smart bungalows: shuttered, closed, blank-eyed – all empty. 'Rich people, summer only,' says Tiny Man. The roofs are piled with snow, about a foot deep, from them hang lovely fringes of icicles, glistening glassy rods up to a yard long, dripping diamonds in the sunlight.

We round a corner, the trail drops downwards. Below us is a small parade ground, built by the British a hundred years ago. Younis parks in it and we pile out. I wade through the snow to pace out the size of the drill square: fifty by eighty yards. Once it was a scene of miniature pageantry and busyness, now it lies silent and unused beneath its blanket of snow. Tiny Man opens his arms out to encompass the whole area. 'No soldiers now. Children now, play cricket here.'

I walk to the adjacent graveyard. It is in the garden of a large villa. Nothing can be identified, just a few long, narrow mounds humping up the snow. A long way from home. I quit the cold, lonely little place. 'We may as well carry on,' I tell Younis. He drives out of the parade ground and up the steep track and we get completely stuck in a drift. Younis is unperturbed. 'No worry,' he says, and sends Tiny Man off. Within a minute he reappears with half a dozen friends. They all push, shouting advice and encouragement. I slip and roll fatly into a deeper drift and they pick me up and dust me down with pats and cries of sympathy. Younis gets out and standing knee-deep in the snow surveys the situation. Unlike most people in such circumstances, he is not fussily anxious about his shoe polish or trouser creases. More debate. 'We will have to back down, our friend here says there is a path from the parade ground downhill.'

We descend a boulder-strewn mule track, squeezing between little stone-built dwellings. Women, at last: they are bending over baskets or bowls or are carrying pots or bundles; they freeze into position, surprised at our appearance. Finally we arrive at the 'main' road. We shake hands and wave goodbye to Tiny Man and now are on our way again. Somehow, throughout all the to-do, Younis has kept himself dry and immaculate.

The road narrows; the few open stalls are selling oranges, cauliflowers and turnips, a normally incompatible variety but all grown within ten miles of here; there are still not many birds, a crow now and

then, the occasional buzzard or kite circling over the great space of the deep canyon to our left; the car skids in the snow towards the edge of the road and my head prickles with alarm, Younis continues to look impassive. In the middle of the road some urchins are playing cricket; their wickets are built of snow. In the little hamlets the people loitering about are all men, the few women scuttle about in small groups and look uneasily around, as if of a persecuted minority; over the canyon, on the slopes of the opposing mountains, the flat tops of the terracing are emphasised by their tablecloths of snow. Younis says that wheat is grown on them: 'Very hard work, often just enough to feed a small family.'

We are near the next destination. A man tells us the way. He is huge, bearded, ragged and wearing dainty, gilded, female sandals: odd, even in normal circumstance, even odder in the snow.

Uphill again; the vehicles in front toil and grumble and pant out clouds of black smoke; Younis overtakes them at the most alarming places. 'That horseshoe on the back of the lorry is for luck,' he tells me.

'It's new, it should be old,' I reply know-ally, 'in England we have horseshoes above our doors to protect us from witches: they are very curious and when they see a horseshoe they like to count back on its prints to see where it has been, and how many steps it has taken. A very old shoe will keep them busy counting all night, and they can do no harm after sunrise.'

He looks doubtful: 'I do not think that will be very effective, I would prefer to take the risk and have a new, smart, tidy horseshoe.'

The only time I have seen Younis show any emotion is when he has just overtaken four vehicles and I ask him to stop, and they creep past, the drivers looking smug. I have seen an old-man's-beard, a wild clematis: festoons of grey pom-poms draped over the branches of a tall pine. I clamber up the steep slope to collect seeds, Younis looking disapprovingly up at me, then we drive on.

Nathia Gali is another Little England, 9000 feet above sea-level. We commission another volunteer to show the way and he navigates us up a series of lanes: more deserted houses, snow-filled gardens and cascades of icicles.

Saint Matthew's Church is cosily placed on a shelf in the hillside. It

[47]

nestles amid a grove of conifers. I get out of the car: there is a smell of pines, two crows call from some branches overhead, the crisp air invigorates but does not chill as the sun is warm. The church is wooden, the walls painted black, the Gothic-style windowframes white, the spire of planking grey with age. It is locked. Frustrated, I peer through a broken windowpane into the spartan interior: nothing much to see – a dozen pews, a simple altar, cold and bleak.

We quest around the humps of the graveyard. Nothing of interest but some prints in the snow; we all agree that they are of a fox.

Our next destination is the military town of Abbottabad. 'It is thirty-four kilometres – twenty-one miles – from here,' Younis tells me.

'Are you hungry?' I ask him.

'Yes, and thirsty too. But it is Ramadan and I can do nothing about it until nightfall.'

'When is that?'

'At five thirty-eight precisely.'

The road is being rebuilt, by the army. No one is at work today. Large pieces of wheeled machinery lie idle. The surface of the road is either slippery with thawing slush or skiddy with greasy mud. There is no retaining wall between us and outer space. 'What a drop!' I say meaningly as we skid towards the canyon. Every muscle of my body is working in defence: my stomach muscles banding like the hoops on a barrel, my toes curling up my shoes to my trouser bottoms, my buttocks gripping the upholstery.

'Very precipitous,' Younis agrees, leaning past me to look down.

Sometimes we meet a vehicle toiling uphill towards us. Even if it is bigger than us, a snow-plough perhaps, or if it seems more important, maybe a car bearing the emblems of a two-star general, Younis does not give way: he remains in the centre of the track and smiles pleasantly and quizzically at the driver of the opposing vehicle. To my surprise, after a minute or so staring back, they put on a sulky expression and reverse out of the way or squeeze past.

A bridge is broken-backed so we have to divert off onto a well-used track which leads down to the boulder-and-shingle bed of a river. Several lorry drivers have taken advantage of this and, having driven their vehicles axle-deep into the waters, are washing and soaping them

lovingly. Two men fill a large lorry with gravel. All that they have is a shovel. One holds the handle, the other helps him scoop by pulling at a rope tied on the handle, near the blade. Younis and I agree that it will take them a week to fill the lorry.

We see a sign: 'Abbottabad – 5 miles.' Younis changes up into fourth gear, the first time he has been able to do so for three hours.

Abbottabad was founded in the middle of the nineteenth century as a military and political headquarters. It still has a smart, soldierly air. There are attractive avenues of plane trees; trim pony-traps transport passengers along the shaded streets; tidy villas are set back in spruce gardens; there are parks with neat lawns; in a cantonment I see lines of cavalry horses feeding from white-painted mangers.

Saint Luke's Church was consecrated in 1865. It is now crumbling. The stonework is flaking; there is a hole in the wooden spire; the weathercock which surmounts it is standing askew – as if a living substitute, a pink-breasted brahminy myna is perched on the metal tail. A fat, clean-shaven man appears wearing a tweedy cow-pat on his head and bearing a large shiny key. He unlocks the door and I enter the silent stillness of the church. There are lines of pews, cane-backed for comfort when the weather is warmer. The altar is smartly clothed and cosy. On the hymn number-board a heading says 'The Third Sunday after Epiphany'. I check in my diary: yes, last Sunday, so this place is still in use. There are memorial plates on the walls, and they show many ways of dying: by influenza, for example, for four men of the 222nd Machine Gun Corps; by warfare for Captain John Paton Davidson, who 'fell at his post at the Crag Picket in the Umbeyla Pass (1864)'; by murder for Major Robert Adams, who was assassinated in Peshawa a hundred years ago.

Off again. Now we are travelling down the ancient Karakoram Road, the old Silk Route which extends from China into the Indian continent over the three massive mountain ranges of the Himalayas, the Karakorams and the Pamirs. The governments of China and Pakistan have co-operated recently in a massive engineering feat to widen the road so that it can take buses and lorries and fuel tankers – and tanks and soldiers and armoured cars. I have previously seen similar kindly offers to help build roads: in Bhutan from the Chinese and in Nepal

from the Indians. 'New arteries,' an international politician informed me. 'Tarmac Trojan horses,' I thought.

The valley is flattening and broadening out into a shallow river plain. Wheat-fields are to either side, sometimes orchards. The road life is busy: pony-traps, trains of mules and donkeys, a camel; there is a continuous fume from the traffic. There are many stalls selling oranges and Younis stops and buys a dozen which he haggles down from eighteen to fifteen rupees: about two-pence farthing each. 'They cost about twenty pence each in England,' I say. He is pleased.

It is only one hour and thirty-seven minutes before Younis can eat and drink, and dusk is not far off, but he insists we divert for a few moments to inspect some of the ruins of Taxila. Taxila was once one of the great cities of the Orient. From its foundation by the Persians of the Achaemenid Empire in 516 BC to its destruction by the White Huns in AD 455 it was a site of great activity: of political machinations and imperial rule, of trade, education and the arts. Its many invaders included Alexander the Great, the Scythians, Parthians and Kushans. One of its rulers was the great Ashoka (272–32 BC) of the Mauryan dynasty, who encouraged Buddhism and non-violence; the teachers of its university included the revered Sanskrit scholar Panini and the master of medicine Caraka. Its ruins cover twenty-five square miles. They have been classified into three separate sites, based on the cities which were founded during the millennium of development. The second city of Taxila is the one closest to our route, and Younis drives to a small car-park at its northern entrance. A plaque by the outer walling tells me that it was founded in 190 BC by Dementrius the Bactrian Greek.

I enter. The impression is of a tidy grid-work of foundations, low walls about three feet high, built neatly of boulders, each with a tidy infilling of pebbles, all this edged by close-cropped grassy paths. A guide appears. He is quasi-military, with a uniform and a beret. He leads me to an open cell with a dome in it. 'The Dome Stupa,' he says. A few paces off we see another cell with what appears to be an ornate altar in it. He points to a weathered lump carved into the side. 'A double-headed eagle,' he says, 'the Double-headed Eagle Stupa.' Another few paces. Another altar-like platform, it has pillars on it. 'The Pillar Stupa,' I am informed. His job done, the guide hovers around, looking needy.

I give him ten rupees. As if by magic, he vanishes to be replaced by a hawker. I am offered two ineptly carved forgeries. 'One thousand rupees . . . very well, eight hundred . . . for you, six hundred for both . . . a hundred each?' He patters alongside me, cajoling. He fiddles through his pockets and produces a coin. 'Gold,' he lies. 'Only seven thousand rupees.' He has said this so often and so unsuccessfully that the gilt has worn off the edges of the coin to reveal the leaden colour beneath.

A fascinating place, but a day's visit for the future; the last ten minutes have merely been the briefest of reconnaissances.

The villages alongside the road are lined with stalls selling a local speciality: urns and vases inlaid with mosaics of mirrored glass. With their impressive size, their undulating contours and the flash and glitter of the mosaics they are, in an interesting, exotic way, utterly hideous.

Through the Margalla Pass. The name 'Margalla' means 'a place to plunder caravans'. Once it was a dramatic and important portal to the subcontinent of India from the mainland of Asia. Now it has been demeaned by roadworks and buildings, and looks merely like a chip out of the ridge of hills.

Dusk: we are nearing Islamabad. Assemblies of lorries have been corralled together like herds of huge beasts and are being washed, watered and fed. Flocks of crows fly off to roost, a flight of parrots streaks overhead, their long tails and crescent wings cutting through the cold skies.

I say goodbye to Younis: a nice man, sympathetic to others, appreciative of his surroundings, well tempered; he has driven me with skill for nearly 150 miles.

'Khuda hafiz' – God be with you.

Names. Ragnar Hairy-breeks, Eric Bloodaxe, Harald Bluetooth, Olaf the Anthead, Ethelred the Unready; Charles the Bold, the Bald, the Fat, the Simple, the Wise, the Foolish, and the Mad; King Og, King Gub, King Fulk; Cartimandua, Queen of the Celts; the Seneschal of the Land of

Oc, the Count of the Saxon Shore, the High King of Tara, the Emperor of Trebizond, the Akhund of Swat; James Stewart, the Wolf of Badenoch; Lars Porsena of Clusium, Tamerlane of Transoxiana; Saint Ursula (and the 11,000 Virgins), the Venerable Bede; Snorri Sturluson; the Empress Presumptive, Mary Palaeogus (née Balls); Frederick Barbarossa, Ivan the Terrible; Hengist and Horsa; the Black Prince, the Fuggers of Antwerp; Chetewayo, Montezuma, Pokahontas . . .

Thus the names and titles roll on, some sonorous, some impressive, some ludicrous, all part of my schooling. It was often the names of people which made my history books interesting, not what those people did, or when, or why or with whom.

Similarly, one of the pleasures of travel is of meeting new names and titles: Mr and Mrs Quackenbush and Miss Margaret Bollwinkel (cocktail party, Washington); Ms Cherry Wun Mann Suk (China Air stewardess); His Royal Highness, King of the Five Million Elephants and the One White Parasol (Thailand); the Black Scorpion, His Royal Highness Eruohwo II (JP), the Ovie and Leader of Thought of Uvwie Kingdom, and Colonel David Dung (Nigeria); Her Highness Princess Ashi Dechen Wangmo Wanchuck, His Worship the Ramjam of the Bumthang Valley, and Dasho Pasang Wangi, the Dzongdag Tongsa of the Tongsa Dzong (Bhutan).

Bhutanese has some lovely words. I particularly like *dzong, dzongda, dzonpon; gonkhang, ramjam;* a *thondrol,* a *thrimpon* and the *Tashi tagye* − fortified monastery, district officer, fort commander; temple for guardian deities, junior official; a large religious scroll, a judge and the 'Eight Auspicious Signs').

Some of my local Essex villages have good names, ranging from Steeple Bumpstead and Dolt's End to Tolleshunt d'Arcy and Wendens Ambo. For a long time I insisted on calling Stanstead airport by its proper name of Stanstead Mountfitchet, but there can come a time when insisting on principles can appear mere affectation. My wife Dominie and I holidayed recently with some of my American cousins in the Carolinas, and I was delighted by the names of local villages: Possumtrot, Rabbit Shuffle, Lizard Lick, Turkey Den and Stiffknee Knob. Even the names of the apples in Cousin Sam's orchard were pleasing: crow's eggs, sheep's nose, bellflower, limbertwig, winesap, black hoover and Betsy Deacon.

One evening in North Carolina we went with some of my cousins to visit a friend who lived in a house built in the Southern Georgian style, with white-painted weather-boarded cladding and a large portico held up by huge white pillars. It was twilight. We sat under the overhanging pediment, the shade of the loblolly pines reinforcing the duskiness; lawns ran down in deep emerald-green sweeps to the still waters of a dark lake, where the occasional leaping bass or bream sent rings expanding toward the bank. As we sat, rain started to patter on the leaves overhead and scuffle the surface of the lake. Then lightning flashed on and off, but we were protected and snug in the cover of the portico. The rain intensified and a smell of wet leaves and damp ground percolated into the warm, humid air. Our hostess was a svelte blonde in a white trouser suit, elegantly draped in a wicker chair. While we sipped at tall, cold glasses of white wine and nibbled sugared pecan nuts, she talked of the names of American rivers, the old, primitive appellations which sometimes are the only memorial left of the Red Indians who had named them. She spoke in the local accent, a loooong, sloooow, sleeeeeepy Saaaaaaathern draaaawl, stretching out the ancient names into a sensual sequence of moans and purrs. She made the Ohio sound like a greeting called out from an angel many miles afar, the Shenandoah and Missouri lasted for eons of murmurous crooning, while the Mississippi became a series of long, slow kisses; she crooned a lullaby of the Noibrara and moaned of the Monongahela. Then it was my turn, and somehow I think I made rather less of an impression on her when I spoke proudly of some of my local waterways: the Ouse, the Foulness, the Crouch, the Blackwater and the little old Peb.

 **Bethlehem, 21 January 1997.** Perhaps because of my Sunday school teaching of fifty years ago, I find it strange to see road signs leading to Jericho, Jerusalem (City Centre), Bethany or Bethlehem. It is towards the last of these that I am being taken by Zosimus, my Christian/Arab driver. He is also acting as my guide; having taken many Embassy visitors round the sights he has become a knowledgeable companion.

In the centre of Jerusalem the traffic was all abustle, with all the different elements of it seemingly hating each other: tourist buses trying to dominate army lorries, tradesmen's vans jostling with taxis, private cars with the yellow number-plates of the Israelis cutting in on the blue of the Palestinians. Now that we have reached the suburbs, the traffic has thinned out and become better tempered. The roads are getting more and more cracked, the buildings more dilapidated, the people more scruffy but somehow more smiling.

The flags above my head are in green and black. There are posters of Arafat's semi-shaven features on the walls. The dominant car number plates are no longer yellow, but blue. We are in a Palestinian area.

We top a high road and in between some buildings I can see a skyline of sharply undulating mountain ridges. One hillock is particularly noticeable amid this irregularity because it is a perfect cone.

'What is that mountain that looks like Mount Fuji?'

'That is not a mountain, it is man-made, on the orders of King Herod. It is called the Herodium,' Zosimus replies.

I decide to explore it after I have visited the Church of the Nativity, which is the aim of this journey.

We must be entering a Christian area: we pass the Good Shepherd Store; a fruiterer's is called the Holy Manger, the hillside in front is clustered with belfries, only one minaret among them.

'When do we reach Bethlehem?' I ask.

'We have reached it.'

Bethlehem used to be separated from Jerusalem by five miles of semi-desert, now it has become a scruffy suburb of the capital.

We reach the centre: Manger Square. Small and cosy, full of parked vehicles, the pavements milling with slowly perambulating Christians, Muslims, tourists and pilgrims. A Christmas tree dominates the scene, together with an out-of-date plastic banner on a wall saying 'Merry Christmas'. One side of the square is made up of a line of arcaded shops; opposite are some public buildings, the largest being the police station. A mosque is at one end and the Church of the Nativity takes up the whole of the other side.

The church was built by Constantine around AD 325 over the cave in which Jesus is believed to have been born. The outer walls of the church

are of the local building material, an attractive, white-tinged-with-pinky-yellow limestone, and are a multi-faceted confusion of buttresses, lean-tos, ledges, pilasters, pediments and blocked-up doors and windows. The roof is an irregular line of different heights and angles. The entrance door is tiny, anyone entering has to bend almost double to get through it and the heavy stone lintels and jambs have been polished and stained with people's clothes like the edges of a mouse-hole rubbed by fur.

Having stepped through, I straighten up and walk through the gloom of a narrow narthex to enter the main body of the church. It is like entering another world: an astonishing difference from the sunlit shambles outside. The empty hall around me is a scene of lofty, spartan simplicity. High above, the beams and posts of the roof timbers are spread out like those of the great medieval tithe barns of Essex. The floor is flagged and clear of furniture. To either side are avenues of colossal Corinthian pillars, forty pillars in all, once painted scarlet, now faded and patchy. On each one, barely distinguishable, I can see the image of a crusader knight; they are standing in four ranks like the ghostly shadows of some long-gone army. There is no ornamentation in nave or aisles except for the remains of Byzantine mosaics, patches of them still existent on the plastered walls. In exotic comparison, at the far end, over the heads of a group of pilgrims, I can see a blaze of colour and decoration: the chancel with the apse, altar and side chapels.

I wonder among the forest of pillars. Zosimus tells me that the knight on the fourth pillar in the front row on the right is Knut, King of England and Denmark. (This is not the Canute of Turning-back-the-Tide fame, but his great-nephew, a genuine King of Denmark but an unsuccessful 'Pretender' to the English throne.) He is just discernible as a tall shadowy figure wearing a long mantle and bearing a shield of the round-topped-pointed-bottom Bayeux tapestry type.

Being Church of England rather than Roman Catholic, if I pray at all it is generally to God rather than the saints. However, in this case I touch the pillar and, looking up into the faint face, ask him to pass on up Higher at least two requests: please could Candy have an easy birth with her baby, and could the baby be OK; incidentally also, Candy and Alex are thinking of including Knut among his names, and if it is a girl perhaps they would call her 'Knutkin' or something.

'My son-in-law is half Norwegian,' I explain to Zosimus, a bit sheep-ishly.

'That King Knut killed many Norwegians,' Zosimus says, 'the cru-sader on the pillar next to him is the Norwegian King Olaf. King Knut killed him too. But they are friends now, probably.'

The only objects visible on the nave floor are wooden panels which have been removed to expose some mosaic, and a rather peculiar contraption: a metal can sprouting a ringlet of taps under which are plastic buckets. 'It is full of water,' Zosimus says, 'it stands here absorb-ing what I heard a young pilgrim call "the Holy vibes" and then people fill little bottles from it and take it home.'

The font is obscured in the gloom of the right-hand aisle. It is a massive, octagonal chunk of stone. 'This is the well in which the three Magi's star fell,' Zosimus says.

Before inspecting the complexity of the chancel area, I walk up a narrow corridor and find myself in some cloisters. They enclose a small garden of four grassy plots, each with an orange tree. In the cross-roads of the intersecting paths a statue of Saint Hieronymus stands. He is holding a notebook and plume and is looking heavenwards for inspira-tion. Behind him there is a door. I enter: the Franciscan church of Saint Catherine.

'All this looks very clean-cut and modern,' I say to Zosimus.

'That is not very surprising, this was built in 1881.'

It is nearly midday and monks are assembling for the noon mass. They are neat in their chocolate-brown habits girded with white cords but their footwear displays an astonishing variety, ranging from the reg-ulation-issue sandals to trendy moccasins, dapper brogues and a pair of shabby tartan carpet slippers worn by a minuscule monk with a vague smile.

Zosimus tells me that the Franciscans are one of the three Christian orders who have zones of influence in the church, the other two being the Armenians and the Greek Orthodox. Like the Church of the Holy Sepulchre in Jerusalem (which has six different sects within it), the different groups of Christians seem to be in a permanent state of loathing, jealousy and possessiveness. 'They even argue who sweeps where, and who keeps the dust. Over there, there is a column with three

nails: from one nail the Latins may hang a picture, from another the Greeks may hang a picture, and from the third nail nobody may hang anything. The star which marks the birth-place of Jesus was once moved by one of the sects and the row over this led to a quarrel between France and Russia and the argument turned into what you call "the Crimean War". Round the star there are fifteen lamps which are always burning, they are specially rationed, six of them are Greek lamps, five are Armenian and four are of the Latins.'

We return to the main church and walk up to the busy end, the chancel. Compared with the stark simplicity behind me, there is a profusion of ornamentation: hanging oil-lamps and cut-glass chandeliers, framed pictures and icons of beaten silver from which swarthy faces peer, crucifixes and candlesticks. The main altarpiece, with its cumbersome mass of figures and carved panelling and gilding, reminds me of the after-castle of the Swedish galleon, the *Veda*. She sank immediately after launching because of the weight of 70,000 carvings. Above all the tumult is a crucifix, but this is not the dominant item: strangely, the focal point, the centre for all this busyness, is a silver bird hanging from chains. I presume it to be a dove, the Holy Ghost, but a second look reveals an imperial double-headed eagle surmounted by a crown – God and Mammon and Politics are not unseparated. But why not?

I descend a flight of semicircular marble steps and am in the maze of caves and passages below the altar. The first cave is the Grotto of the Nativity. It is dark and warm and smells of incense. The walls are covered with heavy hangings of painted leather. Below a small altar I can see the silver star which marks Christ's birth-place. The little flickering lamps illuminate the words around it: *Hic de Virgine Maria, Jesus Christus natus est.*

A couple of paces away there is a small altar which marks the site of the manger. I brood a bit and then wander off into the other caves: tombs of saints, the Chapel of the Holy Innocents, the study and chamber where the brainy but tetchy Saint Jerome pondered and wrote and translated the Vulgate. Suddenly, far above my head, a great bell tolls, then the monks start chanting in plaintive solemnity as if from some unattainable far-off place in the clouds.

I return to the Grotto of the Nativity. It has become full of

anoracked pilgrims and their body heat has already affected the atmosphere. There is a nun acting as guide. Her eyes are of a gentle brown, her expression is serene, her voice is limpid, liquid, loving, soft, sibilant: – 'zis is ze plaice where de Bébé Shesus wass born, ziz is de ferry spot where de Bébé Shesus first saw de loffing faze of His dear mosser, Mary, der Maddonnah. And dis here iss ze Hollie Manger, where Mary, der Maddonnah, wrapped up de Bébé Shesus in Hizz swaddlin' cloze.'

Best that she stay a nun, as a married woman she could goad even the mildest of men into a frenzy of irritation.

A guitar twangs, the pilgrims' eyes go all glassy, they start to sing *Silent Night*. I am irked to hear that the ones singing it in German are louder than the ones singing it in English.

Zosimus and I leave. As we ascend the flight of steps a monk dashes past, his teeth gnashing in the recesses of his beard.

'He is going to discuss with the nun her unauthorised guiding,' Zosimus tells me.

We step out into the harsh sunlight of Manger Square and I tell Zosimus that I want a short stroll round the little town before we go to the Herodium. We enter a cobbled street beside the mosque. It is full of bustling shoppers and idle amblers. Every sort of shop is offering its wares: grocers and butchers and fruiterers; clothes and shoes and hats; a grimy forge complete with anvil is sandwiched between the golden glitter of two jewellers. There are delicious smells of things being baked, or toasted, then a marvellous waft of fresh strawberries. The tourists's shops are full of kitsch – plaques of the Last Supper in mother-of-pearl, olive-wood crucifixes with plastic Christs, glass bubbles with good shepherds kneeling at the manger (if you shake them snow-flakes swirl about), a stack of crowns-of-thorns. What on earth do you do with them? Wear them? Is there a little back room with a looking-glass where you can try them on?

Most of the people are small and brown-eyed but there is the occasional flash of blue: crusader's eyes, like those of Zosimus.

The road to the Herodium zigzags between steep hillocks and wadis, at last we are in proper countryside with bare rock and silt-filled vales where people have ploughed and tilled for the oncoming spring.

The artificial hill of the Herodium is about 300 feet high. It was built by Herod the Great around 20 BC as a combined summer palace, fortress, administrative capital and personal monument. After his death it was taken over by the Romans. The Zealots held it for four years, during which time they built a synagogue and ritual baths. Once again it was taken by the Romans. It fell into disuse until it was inhabited by a group of Byzantines, probably monks, between the fifth and seventh centuries. They built four churches on the site. Finally it was deserted to the desert and the bedouin. In 1962 archaeological excavations started in the 'upper' area, ten years later they started on the 'lower' part.

The 'upper' is the hill. It is unique in its size and shape for that period of history. It was the site of the fortress. I have now climbed up to the top. There is a wide walkway all around, which is about 200 yards in circumference. Below me, within the volcano-like crater, I can see a complex of cells, steps, doorways, ramps, walls and foundations, the remains of living quarters, dining-rooms, storerooms – even of a bath. The circular perimeter has an appendage in each point of the compass: three are defensive half-towers, the fourth is the solid foundation of the circular keep. Originally it was at least five storeys higher, so the whole edifice must have loomed about 400 feet above the surroundings. With its towers and battlements and pennants and perhaps gilded roofs it must have seemed, to the approaching visitors, like some legendary home of the gods.

Like the Masada pinnacle by the Dead Sea, also the site of one of Herod's remarkable palace-cum-fortresses, there are ingeniously constructed channels and tanks and underground cisterns designed to catch and store water in case of siege. Evidence of a siege which actually took place is a heap of crudely carved round boulders, each about the size of a football: they were made by the Zealots during their siege by the Romans. It must have been fun rolling them down the steep slopes and skittling away the assaulting soldiers.

I turn, to overlook the scenery below: nearby, agricultural land, rolling countryside of olive groves and areas of plough and pasture; further off, undulating aridity merging into hills, pale brown and sharply crinkled like crumpled-up wrapping paper.

Just below I can see the remains of the 'lower' complex. This

included the main palace and the areas used as guest's quarters and offices, also baths and a formal garden. The excavations are dominated by the walls of a rectangular pool, itself in a rectangular enclosure which was once pillared. The pool covers about an acre and served both as a swimming-pool and a miniature marina. A large stone stump in the centre marks the site of a pavilion. They must have had some terrific parties there. I bet they didn't ask any of those po-faced high priests.

Herod the Great was the Herod of the Slaughtering of the Innocents, not his grandson, the Herod who fancied Salome.

As a schoolboy I always had an unvoiced admiration for King Herod: anyone who could be so unpopular in both heaven and earth, and seemed to care neither jot nor tittle, had an impressive grandeur. And the more I know of him, the more I admire him. His long reign (thirty-six years) was one of relative peace and prosperity. Religious freedom was tolerated. The arts and sciences blossomed. Herod was nicknamed 'The Builder' with good reason: he managed to combine the talents of architects, engineers and artists to undertake an extraordinary series of buildings and rebuilding, of which the most famous is the reconstruction of the Temple in Jerusalem. He was a remarkable split personality of the good and the bad: he was cruel and loving and clever and unscrupulous and kind and brutal and brave and tyrannical and tolerant. He was partly a savage tribal chief, partly an efficient and sophisticated administrator. He had an excellent brain and outwiled the most subtle of priests and politicians, but he also had a superb physique, excelling in riding, archery and throwing the javelin; such was his enthusiasm for the sports that he is responsible for rescuing the Olympic Games from oblivion. He was attractive to women – managing even to father a child, Herod Philip, off Cleopatra. Magnificently, as a present, she gave him his personal body-guard of 400 Celts. He had nine Queens (including Queen Doris), but although he was passionately in love with his Queen Mariamne, in a fit of 'insane jealousy' he had her executed, and then was tormented with remorse for the rest of his life. He was immensely extravagant, and yet melted down his gold and silver to buy Egyptian corn for his people during the great famine of 25 BC.

John Romer sums him up very well in *Testament*:

In his palace at Caesarea he was a splendid Hellenistic king, a man decorated with silks and jewellery, a man with stables filled with fine desert horses, a man who built a dozen Corinthian palaces, the rococo dreams of a fierce and wily desert warrior. At holy Jerusalem, however, Herod was a pious Jew, relatively sober, god-fearing and mindful of Jehovah's Laws.

What a play Shakespeare would have written on Herod!

 **Brasilia, 13 February 1997.** 'The Backside of the Moon': this is the assessment by the Royal Institute of British Architects of the largest of the world's 'Planned Cities'. It is Brasilia, declared open in 1960 as the new capital of Brazil. It was created on the 'Purist' and 'Modular' theories of the town planner and architect Le Corbusier, via his disciples Oscar Niemeyer (Order of Lenin) and Lucio Costa. These theories postulate that a city should be set out on mathematical principles which could be co-ordinated with 'mechanised, bureaucratic control'. A vast socialist ideal where people, all conveniently equal and unvariable, are to live out ant-like existences of obedient conformity. Plonked in the dusty, scrubby centre of the country, this politician's dream was conceived and born in just over three years: the idea, the planning and design, the construction and the populating.

It is delineated in the shape of an aeroplane: the cockpit contains the parliament; the fuselage is a long, wide mall lined with governmental and municipal buildings; commerce is grouped in the area where the fuselage and wings connect; the wings are mainly living quarters. There are two focal points. They are less than two miles apart: the TV Tower – a tall pylon, about 715 feet high, which duplicates the mechanical efficiency of an oil-rig rather than the superfluous ornamentation of the Eiffel Tower, and the twin twenty-eight-storey columns of the Congress Building. These are impressive because of their height rather

than for any other reason, and they have been ingeniously placed so that the slit-like gap between them frames the sunrise on 21 April, Brazilian Republic Day: a cement Stonehenge.

I started this early-morning excursion from the TV Tower and am walking down the fuselage. This broad runway is of four main roads divided by bands of parkland. It is 405 paces wide (I have just measured this out), but many of the buildings are even further apart so that they loom as the lonely gravestones of a gigantic cemetery, a graveyard for Gullivers. Other skyscrapers are clumped together, like the stacks an infant makes with bricks.

The city has been sited on a plateau which slopes down in a series of terraces to a V-shaped artificial lake. Thus, as I descend, the views to either side and to the front are across obscured valleys whose further slopes climb out of far-off dead ground. On these facing slopes new buildings are sprouting: rich men's villas in lush suburbs, poor men's hovels in shanty towns euphemistically called 'Pioneer Settlements'. Bulldozers have scraped the green skin off the earth on the construction sites. The patches of raw soil have the livid redness of burned flesh, but as time passes this fades to a dusty pink.

The city lives around me like a huge, impersonal animal: the corpuscular traffic flows along the arteries of the roads, the air-conditioning units roar as the buildings inhale oxygen and regulate temperatures, heavy lorries bring in food and provisions and the sewerage system excretes waste products: only of fragile flesh and blood are the few indigent human beings, insignificant parasites and pests which salvage for scraps in unclean crevices and sip water from the public fountains and sleep beneath the ornamental trees and shrubs.

This place is designed for vehicles, not people. The basic walk areas are the parking spaces around each building. There are pavements, but they are narrow strips of cracked tarmac alongside some of the roads and they are liable to peter out suddenly, leaving me stranded under a flyover or hovering indecisively at a cross-roads. However it is pleasant when I am able to walk upon the lawns of tough, springy, broad-leafed grass. There is a profusion of municipal planting: good trees and shrubs, including fish-tail, imperial and coconut palms, bougainvillaea and hibiscus; the most beautiful is a medium-sized tree with a mass of

vivid purple flowers, yesterday my escort told me it is called an 'ipiroxa'. In some flowerbeds each bloom is set exactly the same distance apart. I suspect the gardeners use their feet to measure them out. It looks odd and unnatural but not unpleasant. Hiding amid the blades of grass I find a weed, a tiny blue iris.

Although architecture is meant to be the prime attraction of the city, I am unimpressed. The basic shape is the shoebox, like the Russian-built apartment blocks of Ulaan Baatar, the only difference is that most of them have been up-ended as skyscrapers. There is a limit to what you can do with a shoebox: you can decide on basic type – burly and squarish for boots, tall and thin for winkle-pickers, flat and narrow for sandals, broad for slippers, the child's size 4s and the hobbledehoy's size 12s; for ornamentation you might have broken lines of balconies or staggered lines of windows, pilaster strips in different-coloured cement, a grandiose portico or tinted glass in panels. (The tinted glass that covers our Embassy creates a permanent twilight so that electric light has to be on all day.) It is apt that the lines of twenty governmental buildings near the 'cockpit' look like two ranks of huge filing cabinets, that the Banco do Brasil is like a massive black safe, that most of the hotels resemble air-conditioning units and that the living quarters, the 'superquadra' (superblocks) are similar in design to the cabinet-covered walls of a mortuary.

Such buildings might be pleasing if arranged aesthetically in tableaux of rectangles and squares, but most are not. An additional detraction is the obvious shoddiness of the building materials: everything is flaking, cracking, missing bits and splotched and streaked with stains.

The artificiality of the city has repelled Nature. There are hardly any birds. I see more birds on my lawn at sunrise than I can see now on the huge expanses of grass and parkland around me. There is a small flock of pigeons, a grackle, a couple of sparrows – that's it. There are not many insects either, apart from a plenitude of dragonflies; in half an hour I have seen one swarm of gnat-like things, less than a dozen butterflies, and no bees, wasps or beetles. There are a few large anthills. I prod one with my shoe, nothing emerges: an idle species of ant perhaps, maybe *mañana* is infectious.

Neither do I have many fellow pedestrians. Those I see are of the

lowest rung of the pecking order: small, dark and shy; they do not have the intrusive curiosity, enmity or friendliness you encounter in most of South America. I pass a dumpy frumpy woman with a lumpy grumpy boy. He stares at me then speaks to the woman. I cannot understand Portuguese. I guess he said either 'They are green, his eyes' or 'That gringo has a round head.'

On the back of my map there is a list 'interesting places to visit'. First in the list is: 'THE BUS TERMINAL – This H-shaped, four-level structure located at the intersection of the city's two main Axes contains an information booth, post office and waiting rooms.' Thrills.

Actually it is not as dull as it sounds because there is a tented market nearby. I am in a crowd at last, within the market, shaded by awnings and trees. There is a pleasant busyness: housewives bustle about with shopping bags, stall-holders are arranging their wares, a man pushes a trolley laden with sticks of sugar-cane. There is a variety of smells as I stroll through the canvas alleyways: of the leather of shoes, the cotton of jeans and rucksacks, a spicy-sugary smell from a confectioner; a delicious tangy almost irresistible scent from a barrow laden with split-open melons and peeled pineapples. As I snuffle at this aroma in appreciation I get a nasal-wrenching, eye-watering whiff from a baby being carried past.

The cathedral is a round building, basically a tapering and waisted tube of glass reinforced by upsweeping ribs: it is a cross between a crown of lamb and 'Paddy's Wigwam', the Roman Catholic cathedral of Liverpool. Much of it is below ground and the interior is pleasant, the airy space illuminated by the cool blues and greens of the stained glass; there are clean-cut lines and curves in the marble cladding and in the simple, elegant altar. Three silvered angels hang on strings from the roof, swinging slightly like pantomime fairies.

Outside the cathedral is the campanile. Like the cathedral, it is not inelegant. The stand is of four tapering buttresses meeting at right angles. On the top of the taper is perched the belfry: a five-pronged fork. Between the tines of this fork are the bells, four of them. They have never been rung as a carillon as after it was built it was estimated that all bells pealing at once would cause this incompetent erection to snap apart.

A fifteen-minute stroll past the cathedral and the twin towers of the Congress Building loom above me. To either side, on the platform-like building which is the main body of this complex, there are two huge, simple, white adornments. The one to the right is beautifully shaped like a saucer. The one to the left is a dome. It is slightly the wrong size in relation to its companion, and it worries my sense of symmetry and balance. When we drove past it yesterday my escort said: 'The saucer represents a receptacle for ideas, the upside-down bowl represents what happens to them.'

At last: an attractive governmental building. It is the Palacio do Itamaraty (the Foreign Ministry). Its tall columns and high arches reflect the flickering surfaces of the water gardens set around it. These are islanded with formal beds of tall pampas grass and papyrus, the lush leaves of elephant-ears and arum; the formality is relaxed by irregular clumpings of water-lilies. But behind the building is one of the grossest eyesores of all: an office block whose eight shelf-like storeys, all covered with a huge grid of iron bars, resemble a massive broiler unit, a factory where gigantic hens are imprisoned to lay ton after ton of useless eggs.

I have reached the far side of the main square behind the Congress Building. Surprisingly it is unlike many similarly grandiose spaces, not being dominated by the mausoleum of some dead and stuffed politician. It will be, I daresay.

At the very far end is the Pantheon (the Temple of Liberty and Democracy). It is a white building which, according to the back of my map, 'is a creation of the architect Oscar Niemeyer. Its structure resembles a dove.' It looks more like a tortoise to me.

I enter. There is a circular reception desk. Within the circle sit three attractive girls who scream with merriment when they hear that I am English and come from England.

'Your Princess Di is beautiful, are your princes handsome?' one asks.

I think she learned that from a phrase book.

They hand me a leaflet which tells me of the works of art upstairs. There are only two of them. One is a gross stained-glass window of a few coloured blobs which, apparently, 'reminds us of the form of a stylized map of Brazil and, in a few parts, the structure of a tree. The work is done on a 180m² surface and, among its components, 16 tons of iron.

The glass, in purple, red and white colors symbolise introspection, passion, and peace.' Like much of municipal art, bulk is considered an acceptable alternative to beauty.

My leaflet offers more statistics on the other 'work of art', the intriguingly entitled *Mural of the Inconfidence*, 'painted on a canvas stretched by an aluminium frame and covers a total area of 84m². It is divided into 7 parts . . . The first part represents the burning of the looms.' My heart hardens: anyone who burns looms is not on my wavelength.

Another panel represents the *Death of Claudio Manoel da Costa*: 'The poet's body is buried close to where he was hung. Despite much research, it is not known to this day if he was killed, hung, or committed suicide.' Talk about inconfident.

I am walking back to the hotel. Near the TV Tower I see an eyesore that, although in antithesis to the general theme of the area, is somehow grotesquely compatible. It is a McDonald's. It is a little square building standing on its own. In the 'garden' in front there is a child's play-frame: a large construction of plastic piping, writhing and pink, like intestines; the pipes snake from plastic compartments with huge cyclops bubble eyes; neatly aligned beside this blot are tables and chairs, glaringly white in the sunlight, each table with a white plastic parasol hovering hopefully over it, like a tart lifting her skirts. It is a disgusting little factory for the modern human being, a machine designed to convert agricultural products into sewerage.

My escort is waiting for me when I arrive at the hotel, aptly designed like a chest of drawers. He has just arrived from his flat. He gives me an identification card. It has his address on it:

SQN 908
Bloco W – 786
5/7a
70000 Brasilia DF

'What is it like living here?' I ask.

'I don't live here. I work here. At weekends most of us leave this dull and sinister place and fly the thousand kilometres to Rio.'

I have been to The Future. God help my great-grandchildren. Let them be rebels.

Birds – – – I am sitting up in bed with jetlag, the lag being the four hours' difference between Essex and my last journey, so I am bushy-tailed and bright-eyed while Dominie is wrapped in the deepest slumber next to me, as are the cat and two pekineses on the eiderdown, the miniature mottled dachshund under it, and my mongrel labrador/spaniel gundog snoring in the hall below. A misty dawn is light-ening the bedroom windows. It is going to be a sunny spring day. Cocks crow and dogs bark to one another across the river valley from farm to farm: Parley Beams, Ravenshall, Munns, the Martins, Westwoods. The garden is waking up, the first sleepy twitters are over and it is becoming alive with song, many blackbirds, but also the thrush. The blackbird is just the better musician of the two: it sings, while the thrush whistles, and the blackbird does not keep on repeating himself. Woodpigeons have begun to woo in the evergreen oak whose shadow has overcast the Lower Lawn for over two hundred years. I hear the staccato rattle of a yaffle in Botany Bay Wood, a quarter of a mile off. A moorhen suddenly chirrups amid the sallows of the Wild Pond. Sparrows argue in the farm-yard and house martins twitter under the eaves. At intervals a chain of noise intrudes: the twit-twit-twitter and sliding-down scale of the willow warbler. Further off, a mile across the Colne Valley, rooks are cawing a parliament in the colony near Greenstead Green.

Being unmusical I had to learn my birdsong phonetically: the
'little bit of bread and no cheeeeeese'
of the yellowhammer, the thrush's interrogative

'Did you do it?
Did you do it?
You did! – You did! – You did!
I saw you! I saw you!'

[67]

the

'I do love you, I do love you'
'I love you, too – I love you, too'

of the pigeons. Later, I learned others: one day, by Lake Nakuru, Kenya, the unhappy emerald-spotted wood dove was mourning

'my father is dead
my mother is dead
all my relations are dead
and my heart goes boom – boom – boom.'

Some calls need no words: I still remember my scalp crawling as I heard the baying of the Hounds of Hell as they harried the souls of the damned above my nursery ceiling (brent geese); the crowing of a jungle cock in the foothills of the Himalayas, waking me up with its annoyingly incomplete 'cock-a-doodle d – cock-a-doodle d – cook-a-d'; the frenzied, mounting anxiety of the brain-fever bird as it yelled hysterically at me as I climbed the hills near Islamabad.

A collared dove has just landed on a windowsill. Odd how birds have that pecking movement with their heads when they walk. Dinosaurs are meant to be closely related to birds, did they walk like that? It must have made the approach of Tyrannosaurus Rex even more frightening: deliberate, mincing, macabre. Could some of the dinosaurs whistle, like birds? The dawn chorus of the Jurassic age could have been ear-splitting: the song of Iguanodon, as loud as an air-raid siren, echoing from crag to crag; the tremendous warbling of Stegosaurus; the bittern-like booming of the Brontosaurus in his bog, the trilling of the Triceratops, the thunderous quacking of the duck-billed Saurolophus, and far above one's stooped, shaggy back, the lark-like twitters of the Pterodactyl. Or did they crow?

Egg collecting was an approved hobby when I was a small child: the sudden flash of a chaffinch from a hedge or of a lark from an expanse of pasture, and then the long, long wait for the birds' return so that one could pinpoint the exact location of the nest; the wonderful beauty of

[68]

the turquoise beads in the hair-lined cup of a hedge betty's nest and the complexity of the feather-packed mossy bag that the bottle-tit had built; the sickening experience when climbing down a tall elm with a rook's egg in my mouth, slipping and involuntarily clenching my teeth – then something squirming alive on my tongue. My egg collection lay in its multi-drawered cabinet, like rows of jewels and semiprecious stones: the jade of the nightingale, the turquoise of the starling, the jasper of the tree pipit, the lapis lazuli of the pied flycatcher, the rubies of the pipits, the malachite of the corvids, the pearls of martins and the scribbled onyx of guillemots.

From eggs I became interested in the birds themselves. My first bird book – and still my favourite – is *British Birds* by F.B. Kirkman and F.C.R. Jourdain (Thomas Nelson & Sons, 1930). It weighs nearly four pounds and is best for browsing through by the hearth in the evening. It has 200 superb colour plates with captions such as 'Long-tailed tits building their nest', 'Red-backed-shrikes in their larder', 'Roseate-tern bringing a fish to its young'. It is always with a flash of pleasure I see these old English friends of my childhood in some far-away setting: a pintail duck on a river in Bhutan, an arctic tern on the River Tuul in Outer Mongolia, a flock of fieldfare in Lapland and a swallow flitting above some turbid pool in Botswana.

Because I travel to so many far-off places, it is the exotic and unusual I like to recall. High above the mountains of the Eastern Himalayas a flock of yellow-billed chough rotate as if in a great bowl. They fold their wings and pitch earthwards with such childish glee you can almost hear them saying 'zzzzoooomm!', then they hurtle through the pass below me and swoop up to wheel once more round the mountain top. High above the Pacific Ocean, off the coast of Costa Rica, two large birds are flying, languorously, idly, with alternate flaps and long glides; the setting sun shines pink through their wings; they are roseate spoonbills. In the leafy upper reaches of a jungle giant, a macaw fossicks, scarlet and gold, like the phoenix on fire. The flocks of millions of flamingo round Lake Nukuru (strange to think that that beautiful sight is producing fifty tons of guano per day). The crane families, standing in the sun-dial shadows of the telegraph poles in the Gobi Desert. A Mauritius kestrel, streaking overhead, once only four left in the world. The high, wheeling cross of

a lammergeyer above a peak in the Karakorams. On the tundra, a flock of funny little birds with huge eyebrows, horned larks. The lovely blue flash of the azure-winged magpie in a temple complex in North China. Sun-birds and humming-birds, iridescent jewels hovering and darting amid the scarlet trumpets of hibiscus and the waxy flowers of the frangipani. The charmingly hideous green barbet of North India, slinking rat-like along the branch of a jungle tree, its back is a sort of sickly green, in front it is an unhealthy, almost nude pink, it has red-rimmed eyes and bristles round its beak; alternatively the peacock, a sacred idol, picking its hundred-eyed way through the sewage ditches of black Bengal. The Hindus say the peacock has angel's feathers, the devil's voice, the walk of a thief and cries at night in fear of losing its beauty.

One of my pleasures about birds is their names. The local Essex names are not normally descriptive, except perhaps the cold-arse bird (missel-thrush) and the bottle-tit (long-tailed tit); more terse is jib (sparrow), yaffle (green woodpecker) and hawchat (whitethroat). None of these is as vivid as some I have met abroad, such as the Caribbean arrow-up-the-arse (long-tailed tropicbird), crack-pot soldier (stilt) and income-tax inspector (frigate bird, a parasitical sponger on other birds). In the United States there are excellent bird names: the red-faced warbler, the sage thrasher, the western wood peewee, black Phoebe, the yellow-bellied sapsucker, the golden-crowned kinglet, the boat-tailed grackle, kiskadee, the blue-faced booby and the common loon – what a play could be written with a cast like that!

Some of my favourites throughout the world can be grouped in categories:

The most long-winded
Slender-billed chestnut-winged starling
Large necklaced laughing thrush
Brown-headed stork-billed kingfisher

The most alliterative
Paddyfield pippit
Tufted tit-tyrant (my favourite)
Mugimaki flycatcher

[70]

The quaintest
Fire-fronted bishop
White-bellied go-away-bird

Back to the bird's ancestors. What colours were they? Stephen Cave in Barbados told me that that island does not have its own parrot, as do several of the other islands, because Barbados, being coral rather than volcanic, does not have a rich, fruit-producing soil. He also says that eating fruit causes birds to develop bright colours. I wonder why most sea-birds are white. Why are penguins black? Perhaps they could not find each other in the snow if white. Why are the patterns on birds symmetrical, and not irregularly blotched as on cows? Come to think of it, it is only domesticated animals which have irregular patterns, why? . . .

My musings are interrupted by a thump. Millicent the cat has leapt off the bed. In three more bounds she is on the windowsill: but the collared dove has gone.

 **Budapest, 26 February 1997.** Wilf Cracoe was the alarming and dictatorial foreman of a weaving shed when I was learning the trade thirty-five years ago. He is now over seventy, but still at work, as an independent consultant. He is here in Hungary advising some of the newly de-nationalised textile mills on their modernisation. I meet him by chance when I step out of the Embassy and as we have nothing to do for the next six hours we decided to explore Budapest together.

We began our walk along the Váci Utca, a pedestrians-only road lined with good shops.

'Ek, that's a comedown,' says Cracoe, 'here we are, miles away from home, in one of the romantic cities of the world, and the first shop we come to is a bloody Marks and Sparks.'

We see an art gallery. Cracoe insinuates that if I want to go round it I must be some sort of latent homosexual. Grumbling, and embarrassed lest someone from Rochdale be there to see him, he follows me

in. Once in, he cheers up, for he sees a painting of God the Father and his Son and both are balding. 'You can't win, whoever you are,' he says, pleased. I quite like the modern swirly etchings of pretty girls lurking in flowery bowers, but a lot of the other work suggests that the Hungarian art pupils have just discovered Salvador Dali and Aubrey Beardsley. The modern art of Hungary seems exuberant and happy. In comparison, the earlier art seems incredibly gloomy: sad families having cheerless picnics in damp meadows; wretched peasants in hovels receiving bad news; a desolate landscape with three dead trees, a stagnant pond and a cow which needs worming.

We carry on down the street. It is a pleasing bustle of local shoppers and tourists, but there are several beggars. One old beggar sits cross-legged in the middle of the walkway. He is dressed in a shabby suit. His hair makes a shaggy halo round the dirtily blotched dome of his balding head. Cracoe tosses him a coin, one of extreme monetary insignificance. The old man inspects it, raises both hands to heaven, wails out in a show of passionate gratitude, and bending down bangs his head against the pavement beside Cracoe's feet.

Cracoe moves away, discomforted. 'Sarcastic old bugger,' he complains.

Further on a hippie-type is squatting on the flagging and puffing through a long wooden tube. It produces a reasonably melodious panting sound, interspersed with the occasional hoot or hum or buzzing; in accompaniment he raps the side of the instrument with a little stick, making tappings.

Cracoe stops and stares at him. 'What a way of earning a living!' he exclaims.

The hippie looks up, scowling. 'Up your's too, matey,' he says.

Near the end of the Váci Utca there is a large building whose ornate brick façade and pediments are reminiscent of a Victorian railway station. We enter it and find outrselves in a large, airy market. The first floor is divided up into sections, of which the largest are those for fruit, vegetables and the butcher's. Cracoe laughs to see a row of little piggies' heads on a shelf. There are many sausages, of every shape and size, festooning from beams, dangling in bunches from hooks, in multi-yard-long coils, neatly sliced, on platters. 'Not very pretty', Cracoe says

fastidiously. In the fish section, in the basement, there are glass tanks, all ajostle with large carp, goggling and gobbling in despair; there are some sturgeon, with their armoured sides and long spatulate snouts they look like strange, alien spaceships.

Just over the Danube from the market is Gellert Hall, a Baroquish building constructed around some of the natural thermal baths which abound in this area. We enter and read a signboard which points to places such as the 'Massage Room', the 'Women's Only Baths' and, intriguingly, the 'Inhalatorium'. Do you go there to sniff in fumes and steam?

A frightfully ugly woman approaches. She is built like a beer-barrel. Her beefy, knotted arms show beneath the short sleeves of her pink satin blouse. She is bow-legged and has huge feet and teeters in an ungainly manner and in high-heeled shoes, pink, to match her blouse, I suppose. Her make-up has been lavishly applied with a palette knife, somewhat smudgily. She has lost several teeth. She asks us the time. Unable to speak Hungarian, Cracoe shows her his wristwatch. She smiles a gap-toothed grin and asks again. Impatiently Cracoe taps his watch, obliging her to concentrate.

'American?' she asks.

'English,' we say.

'Not so rich, huh?' she says, disparagingly.

'Goddamit, she's a prostitute.' Cracoe is indignant that she thinks him desperate enough to need someone as ugly as she.

'Go away,' he says.

'Huh?' she growls, her eyebrows beetling.

'Bloody 'ell, she's not a tart at all,' Cracoe says, 'she's a bloke. Bugger off.'

Off she/he/it goes, laughing.

We cross the river again to find somewhere to eat. We enter a pleasant little restaurant of the chintz-tablecloth-and-candle-in-a-bottle ilk and discover too late that the proprietress is one of those who consider an arch motherliness as part of the ambience. The heavy-browed, baggy-bosomed woman hangs about us clucking and commenting on every

mouthful: 'You like-a?' she keeps asking. Unfortunately me no like-a: what's this, this reminder of Micky and Minnie, my pets of fifty years ago? – and of those little bundles of chewed sacking I used to find in the corners of the granary? – and of the squeaking and scuttling and panic when we took the stacks of sheaves apart for thrashing? What it is, is that soup, salad, goulash, the vegetable bowls and the sauceboats are all beset with horrible sweet peppers: some red, and disguised as tomatoes, or chillies, or bits of meat; some green, and pretending to be sliced beans or cucumbers; some ground up into pastes – a variety of camouflages but all with that unmistakable musty, fusty, yukky taste reminiscent of the smell of a mouse's nest. Normally I am not fussy about food as long as there is plenty of it, but I cannot abide those disgusting sweet peppers.

I have some beer but Cracoe says he will have a bottle of local wine. The proprietress pours a bit out and Cracow makes a great palaver of sniffing it, staring through it and finally taking a gulp.

'You like-a?'

'Pardon me while me eyes water,' he replies. 'I've drunk smoother battery acid, but I'll have it, it'll help take the plaque off me teeth.'

Later, in the Embassy, having said that I do not particularly like Hungarian food, I am told that it is a combination of French cooking, via Vienna, together with the cooking of the peasantry of Central Europe: much of it is based on *rántás*, a roux of flour and pork lard whose taste is disguised with the heavy application of spices, particularly chilli and paprika.

Over the Danube again, crossing from Pest to Buda on the Bridge of Chains, designed and constructed by the British in the style of the suspension bridge of the Thames at Marlow, Buckinghamshire.

Rather like the Mongolians (from whom they have a dash of blood), the Hungarians often have very exaggerated features. In the Hungarian case it includes thick eyebrows, large, heavy-lidded eyes, deeply carved lips and chunky, angular faces: the result can be either exotically attractive or remarkably ugly. You are less likely to see a mousily plain girl in Budapest than anywhere else in Europe. However, the woman who has just come to lean over the bridge next to us is thin and pinch-lipped, she

is wearing a large hat with feathers and from it a sharp face looks out as lethal as the barb on a fishing hook. Cracoe fancies her.

'Hello,' he says, 'got a sister for my friend here?'

'You've got to chat them up, they like a bit of sexual innuendo, repartee, like,' he says cheerfully, not a bit abashed that she had given him a look that could have flayed the hide off a hippo and stamped off.

We climb the path which zigzags up the steep face of the citadel and at the top we lean over a fortified wall to look at the view, over the river at the city of Pest, spread out on the plain which extends towards Transdanubia.

My father spent much of his youth between the wars visiting the exotic and fashionable places of Europe and he said that Budapest was the most romantic and delightful of all the capital cities, even better than Paris or Vienna, but he had a penchant for Hungarian girlfriends and that may have made him biased. The setting is certainly attractive: the great river winding between the low-lying city of Pest on one side and the towering plateau of the citadel of Buda on the other, but Budapest is remarkably devoid of buildings of architectural interest. When the invading Turks were ousted in 1686 they left a city in ruins and so everything is comparatively new: the 860-room palace behind Cracoe and me was completed in 1905, the nearby Coronation Church had the last of its many restorations completed in 1896; but from afar the setting helps to create the right illusion. Over the water I can see the Houses of Parliament (finished 1902) and from here the 'Gothic' edifice looks mighty fine with its forest of spires and flying buttresses, directly in front of us the basilica of the Leopoldstadt is almost as impressive as London's Saint Paul's. However the dominant architecture is of the bulbously grandiose style which might be called 'Bourgeois Baroque', somewhat similar in concept to our 'Victorian Gothic'.

Having brooded over the view, Cracoe and I walk to the military museum. The exhibits drive the point home that if you must enter the messy and frightening business of killing and being killed, then at least you can make it better by making it handsome. There are pictures and examples of exotic uniforms, gay Hussars, fierce Lancers, daring Dragoons, debonair Carabineers; banners and colours; armour and weapons; chains, plumes, cockades, medals and decorations. All the

officers look brave and dashing and display every variety of facial hair, as Cracoe says: 'from the teeny 'tache to the stoat looking out of a bear's arse.'

Cracoe is fascinated by a suit of jousting armour: there seems to be no place in the helmet for the armour's occupant to look out. I suggest that perhaps he had his page running alongside his horse, shouting instructions such as 'Put your lance up a little – higher – to the left – now down a bit – easy now – DUCK!'

There is not much of British history here: a Mills hand grenade, a Lee Enfield .303 (heavens, I am part of history), a photograph of the Yalta Conference with Stalin and Roosevelt exchanging sly glances across Churchill's portly tummy; in the Toy-soldier and Model Room there is an effete-looking Scots Guards officer in porcelain. I remember when I first met Cracoe, reporting for duty in the weaving shed.

'Public school and Guards, eh,' he said, looking me up and down and handing me a broom to sweep the flooring between the looms, 'how come that I've never met an intelligent Guards officer?'

'Presumably because the intelligent ones avoid you,' I replied. I thought it quite a deft and witty answer, but we never became bosom chums.

On the staircase there is a magnificent painting of a cavalry charge, some of the horses bolting like rabbits, ears flat back, eyes popping, one cavalryman has just been shot in the chest and has the horror of the knowledge of death on his face, another urges his steed on with both hands at the rein, he holds his sabre between his teeth and his eyes are ablaze with excitement.

We walk back over the bridge. There is a man fishing at the centre. His bait undulates in a jamjar: leeches. 'Does he lower a leech on the end of his line so that it can suck onto a fish?' I wonder.

'Unlikely,' replies Cracoe.

Over the bridge we part, I to turn right to the Embassy, he to carry straight on to his quarters. We shake hands: although we were never friends, it is still pleasant to meet someone from the time when one was young and eager and learning new things – even if it was just how to sweep the 'fly' off a weaving shed floor.

Cairo, 6 March 1997. So, this has not been a wasted morning after all: I have seen four things I have never seen before – never even imagined . . . but to go to the beginning . . . Having arrived in Cairo last night I have a late breakfast overlooking the Nile while brooding that this morning will be a waste of time: I will be in one of my favourite countries yet will have no time to do anything much; only three hours free in Cairo before I set off for Jordan. I have a guide book on Egypt from the Halstead library and am looking in it to see if there is anywhere near my hotel on Roda Island which I have not visited before.

Here's something: within a ten-minute walk along the banks of the island I will come to the Manyal Palace, the old palatial residence of Prince Mohammed Ali, brother of the Khedive Abbas II and cousin to King Farouk. It was built in 1903 and is full of 'bizarre kitsch', the book says. The oddities include 'a stuffed, hermaphrodite goat'. I will go there: it will be nice to tell Dominie when I get home that I have seen a stuffed, hermaphrodite goat.

The walk up the east bank of the Nile is as relaxing as ever: although it is already a hot day, the pavement is soothingly shaded by trees; a few people sit on the riverside benches – they are mostly rather prim and solemn courting couples, with an occasional fisherman or a vendor of tea. The traffic moves hectically alongside, hooting and jostling. I like the insubordinate way the drivers toot at the traffic policemen when they get fed up waiting for their signal to move on.

I enter the palace grounds, under a fortified gateway. It seems a pleasant place, although slightly run down and dusty, as is all of Cairo. I am the only foreigner here and it is an oasis of peace as I stroll through the garden, along paths edged by low hedging, past flowerbeds and under the shade of palms, banyans and other trees. There are some small fountains, but none playing. A hoopioe lands on a lawn beside me and raises and lowers its black and white crest angrily; perhaps it has a nest nearby. An old gardener is on the top of a very tall date palm sawing off the dead leaves. His bare feet on the jagged stumps of previous leaves must hurt.

The main building in the centre of the garden is the Resident Palace.

[77]

It is tall and rather sinister, built of something concrete-coloured, embellished with Nouveau Islamic designs; the roofing is overlooked by a square, box-like room on a stalk. Its large windows on every side help make it look exactly like the control tower of an aerodrome. A dome on top gives it an oriental look. A sign outside says that the palace comprises a Fountain Hall, Dining-room, Mother-of-pearl Room, Mirror Hall, Blue Saloon, office, library and 'shammas' for smoking and drinking tea.

I enter. A haze, a multitude, a plethora, a swirling squirming of ornamentation hits the eye. The décor is what interior designers call 'busy'. There is not a square inch without a bit of decoration: the ceilings are of ornately carved and painted woodwork, the windows are screened with 'bobbin-work' turned wooden screens, the floor is of fussily patterned wooden veneers, which creak like a wicker basket as I walk on them. Everywhere there are rugs and carpets: strewn on floors, draped on furniture, hung on walls. Dominant throughout are the tiles, not only on every particle of walling; there are patterned mosaics in the most unexpected places. I am reminded of the clerihew by J. and E. Carter on the architect of St Pancras railway station and the Albert Memorial:

> Gilbert Scott
> might have been a lovesome thing, God wot,
> if he had resisted the wiles
> of the manufacturers of encaustic tiles.

After going through the Fountain Hall I enter the Mother-of-pearl Room. Like the now-vanished Amber Room in St Petersburg's Hermitage, there is just too much of it, one's senses are sated: mother-of-pearl is imbedded in the walling and the window screens, it is in gleaming chips on the legs of the furniture and as inset mosaics on the table tops, it gleams hither, it glows yon. In heavy contrast is the battery of ottoman couches all around the walls, upholstered in oriental jacquard designs. The floor is covered with superb rugs whose multitude eliminate each other's subtlety of design into a mere jumble of scribbles, splotches and meandering fussiness. The whole scene is illuminated by hanging globes of glass, painted in a style compromising between Early Pharaonic and Art Nouveau.

[78]

The Dining-room seems sad: here people had fun and laughed and talked and been convivial; now it is silent and dusty and the silver needs polishing and the tassels hanging from each chair – seventeen tassels per chair – look frayed and ridiculous.

The room next door is like a man's club with heavy armchairs and chesterfields in buttoned leather. There is a fine set of about thirty portraits of men in huge, ballooning turbans, some of them with fountains of feathers spraying out from the top; the men sport beards varying from the sinister spike to the fluffy Father Christmas; poses range from the welcoming, open-handed gesture to the threateningly half-drawn sword.

By the end of my tour round this house my eyes are so dazzled by the display of opulence and bad taste that they are fuzzy and blinking as if I have been looking at the flickering stripe-and-zigzag effect of a haywire TV screen.

Next building – the Throne Palace. It is basically one room: long and low, dominated by a huge gilded sunburst on the ceiling and the alternate armchairs and sofas, all upholstered in red velvet, which line the two longways walls. At the far end squats the throne (a red sofa) and the thronelets (armchairs); these are flanked by a pair of massive and ornate candelabra. Some portraits hang along the walls. The men portrayed all have three things in common: fat faces, beards and magnificent uniforms. The one I am standing opposite at present has a uniform of yellow silk: a short jacket of the 'bum-freezer' type, a spotted cummerbund, and a magnificent pair of plus-one ballooning trousers, all this surmounted by a scarlet fez; the man holds a sheathed scimitar in one hand, and props himself up by holding onto a ship's cannon with the other.

A tiny, besandled guide has been accompanying me around this room, indicating obvious things such as 'throne', 'picture of Nile and camels', 'big carpet – Turkish', but now he shows me something rather odd: he points at the foot in one of the portraits, of a man in multi-medalled uniform. The toe of one of his boots is pointing towards me. Little Guide takes me by the arm and places me to one side of the picture. The toe is still pointing at me. Then we go to the other side. Toe still towards me. 'Like eyes of Mona Lisa,' says Little Guide proudly.

Out into the garden once more. At the back of the Throne Palace there is an open room meshed from the outside with wire netting. I peer through it and see two dry, dejected, hang-head skeletons, one of a camel, the other a pony: someone's favourites, once? No stuffed, her-maphrodite goat, though.

The Private Museum: a notice outside says it is of fourteen halls. Big enough to include a stuffed, hermaphrodite goat. I am getting quite excited.

I now have another guide: youngish, moustached; useless, as he does not speak English. He tries to hurry me round, which is irritating – and unnecessary as there is not a single other tourist in the whole complex. Many things are delightfully labelled, including a shell-shaped silver gravy boat with a merman handle:

A SILVER DISH LIKE A BOAT
WITH THE STATUE OF SOME PERSON
FROM A BOVE HOLDING AN OAR.

The museum is mainly equipped with furnishings and house fittings: pictures, lighting, crockery and cutlery, furniture, carpets and, particu-larly, a mass of embroidered wall hangings. The whole lot is in the style of utmost ornate opulence. There are hubble-bubbles in blown and cut glass; egg-cups ('porcelain envelopes') in profusion; a one-thousand-piece set of silver dining cutlery, including fish knives (I can almost hear 'Phone for the fish knives, pharaoh'); one of King Farouk's thrones, Art Deco in style, in slabs of pink and grey marble, and upholstered in green leather; flywhisks, inkpots, silver stirrups in the form of clogs – but no stuffed, hermaphrodite goat. I am very disappointed. It must be somewhere here. But Useless Guide does not understand English: how do I mime 'stuffed, hermaphrodite goat' to make him understand? I can think of several ways, but in each case he may get my message severely wrong, and they are quite touchy, some of these fellows.

Sadly, I leave the museum and make for the entrance, having pressed an undeserved 50-piastre note into Useless Guide's hand.

As I make my way down a hedgy path, an arrow points to Hunting Museum, 'Properties of the former King Farouk'. I enter a long, low

room. Glass-panelled cabinets are to one side, all full of stuffed, moulting birds. Opposite is a multitude of animal's heads. Just insde the door is a pair of magnificent tusks. Next to them is an oddly shaped table, roughly the shape of the African continent and about five foot long. It is made out of an elephant's ear! What peculiar mind thought of making a table out of so inappropriate an object? Peculiar Mind obviously had a full-time job with King Farouk: the cabinets are full of unexpectedly used materials such as a coffee set made out of rhinoceros horns, a pipe whose stem is made from the hairy shin of a gazelle and the bowl from its antler, necklaces of teeth and claws, a pendant made from the jaws of a stag beetle, candlesticks from the legs and talons of a vulture and . . . what on earth is this? It is 'A whip made from Fish's Whiskers'. It is about a foot and a half long, with a silver handle. Whatever gave Peculiar Mind the idea of chastising anyone with fish's whiskers? And what fish has whiskers that long? Perhaps the barbels from some huge Nile perch, but maybe this lash looks a bit like the sting from a string-ray. And what's this, this necklace made from a row of fusty little objects set in gold? They are humming-birds' heads! 'Necklace of bird's heads made for Queen Farida'. Peculiar Mind's masterpiece! It's one of the oddest things I've ever seen. It looks absolutely ghastly now, the row of poor little moulting skulls, but I have a guilty feeling that I may have thought it magnificent when the birds were young and like iridescent jewels, and the Queen, too, was young and beautiful.

I carry on down the exhibits. There is a case displaying a pleasingly macabre arrangement of glass eyes. There is an array of traps, ranging from a gin-trap for an elephant to (ludicrously different) the ordinary mouse-trap. There is a case full of ostrich eggs together with a stuffed fledgeling; there is a huge lobster and a tiny tortoise ('aged 36 days'), there are many cabinets full of beautiful butterflies and moths, and remarkable beetles. On the walls there are skins – I pace out a snake's skin, seven paces – and the animal heads.

In the same way that the mummy of the Pharaoh Sekenenre shows his final horrified expression when he was clubbed and axed to death, so these animals seem to have their last expressions preserved. But most of them are not disagreeable except, perhaps, a lion, whose expres-

sion is one of intense chagrin, or of a water buffalo, who looks as surprised as any cow would be when suddenly shot while contentedly grazing in its pastures. The line of a hundred or more gazelle heads all display a friendly curiosity, as if thinking 'Who is this nice fat man approaching me, waving some deliciously tempting tufts of grass in my direction?'

BANG!

I have been accompanied by another annoying guide. At least he speaks English. He points to a stuffed owl: 'Owl,' he says. He points to some dead snakes in a cabinet: 'Snakes'; he continues to practise his English on me for the scorpion, turtle, crocodile, even the horn of a narwhale, but abandons it when we reach a show of stuffed chickens and he 'cluck-clucks' and 'cock-a-doodle-doos' instead. We reach the end of the room. He points to the head of a goat: 'Goat. Mother and father together.' It's the hermaphrodite goat! I stare at it, baffled. How do I know it is a hermaphrodite? It could be any old goat. Surely, they should have stuffed and mounted the other, more interesting end? The guide points to a photograph above the head. It is of the goat, when alive. He points at its udders: 'Mother goat.' He points to its balls: 'Father goat.' He is wreathed in smiles, as proud as if he was related to it.

On my way out I pass the private mosque. I kick off my shoes and enter it. Another frantic shambles of ornamentation in tiling and carpeting and woodwork, but the large panels of mosaic with Allah's different names in black calligraphy on white backgrounds are attractive.

As I walk under the entrance gate a toothless little guide darts out of a side door.

'American?'

'English.'

His eyes light up: 'Winston Churchill. Come, he visits here.' He leads me up an ornate flight of stairs into a *majlis* (assembly room), which again has an over-carpeted floor and ottoman couches set all along the walls. Toothless One leads me to the central ottoman. There is a noticeable dent in the seating. 'Churchill, he sit here. You sit.'

So I sit where Churchill sat and Toothless One bobs up and down in front of me, smiling and rubbing his hands together in anticipation of a 50-piastre note.

I walk back to the hotel. So, this has not been a wasted morning after all: I have seen four things I have never seen before – never even imagined: a table made out of an ear, a whip made out of a fish's whiskers, a necklace in gold and humming-birds, and a stuffed, hermaphrodite goat.

 **Unwanted neighbours – – –** Sometimes I am the first person to board an aeroplane, often the last. The big concern when embarking is who is to be my neighbour, perhaps for a whole day and night. In the rare cases when it is someone attractive I dump my bag down in front of her so that she can read the label which helps us in our quest for discreet anonymity. Bright yellow, it reads:

ON HER BRITANNIC MAJESTY'S SERVICE

PERSONAL LUGGAGE
OF THE
QUEEN'S MESSENGER

I then look about piercingly.

Usually it is some businessman or politician and as soon as I have sat down I put on the earphones and pretend to listen to the piped music. This is to avoid having long conversations. Sometimes the neighbour can get a sentence or two in and I have made a brief list of the opening remarks which I thought particularly depressing:

Addressed to me
  'Where's yer gun?'
  'I say, do you mind awfully, but my wife and I are on our honeymoon and she's been put right at the back and anyway she's terrified of flying

and I'm sure you'd be terrifically kind and make our honeymoon a success and exchange seats.'

'I seem to be some sort of Jonah. Something always goes wrong in any plane I'm in. Last time it was the man sitting next to me. He sort of shuddered. Then he died.'

'I do not care if this is your seat. I am a Member of Parliament and I will not be moved.'

'Hellooo, I'm Cyril.'

'No offence chum, but if there's one thing I can't stand it's a toffee-nosed pom with a plummy voice.'

'It cost me a bloody fortune to pay for a Club Class seat. Am I right in presuming that as a tax-payer I'm also paying a bloody fortune for *you* to fly Club Class?'

'Excuse me, pliz, I have this foot itching. Do you mind if my shoes and socks I am taking off?'

Addressed to the stewardess

'Ta, darling, I'll have a large one, and you can leave the bottle.'

'I see I have only *one* sick bag.'

'My husband will bring the baby in a minute.'

'Do you have any flea powder? I've just come back from Calcutta.'

'Might as well have the champers, though it does something cruel to me flatulence.'

Holiday, Sri Lanka, 11–23 March 1997. Our driver-cum-guide is called Mr Kariyawasam but he has suggested that we call him Kari. He is slightly taller and paler than the average Sinhalese and has a fine aquiline nose rather than the standard small spud. His father's forename was Carlos. I suspect that there is a dash of Portuguese blood in him somewhere. He is a Buddhist and his normal expression is a serene half-smile which resembles Buddha in one of his contemplative moments. He is married with three sons, the oldest of whom is at a technical university. The lovingly polished mini-bus is his. It is a twelve-seater,

although there are only four of us holiday-makers: Dominie and me and our friends Julian and Diana. Kari is a polite and deferential driver; he even gives way to bicycles. Perhaps he has the inherent gentleness of a Buddhist. I, being an impatient and ruder Christian, find myself continuously pressing an imaginary accelerator.

'No hand signals,' I say disapprovingly of a little three-wheeler taxi which overtakes us on the inside and then suddenly turns right across our front.

'They will be losing their arms if they do hand signals, sir. Their limbs will be completely broken off.'

He has been driving us through the outskirts of Colombo, the capital of Sri Lanka, threading through the traffic, largely three-wheeler taxis – trishaws, honorary insects zigzagging about like whirly-gig beetles or bobbling past us in Indian file like busy little expeditions of woodlice. The city has now degenerated into a scruffy shambles of ribbon development, ranks of small, open-fronted shacks from which things are sold, everything you will need and other things you never will: from gym shoes to gemstones, tractor parts to turtle-shells, writing paper to rice flails. After hunting and harvesting, selling things seems to be the basic instinct of the domesticating human being. Even when we leave the last suburbs of Colombo the roadside is lined with stalls. They come in coteries: there may be half a mile of people selling cane furniture; then there will be the section of cashew-nut sellers with smiling women enticing customers with come-hither wavings; then there may be a line of stalls selling only brightly patterned pillows and cushions (stuffed with kapok whose fluffy, burst-open pods hang from branches overhead); then perhaps the fruiterers, with displays of jak fruit, pineapples, bananas and coconuts.

The coconut is the oriental equivalent of our pig, 'of which you can use everything, except the squeal'. It seems that they can use all of the coconut palm but for the rustle of its leaves: the timber for building, the fronds for thatching or basketwork, the underbark as a textile, the flowers as a source of drink (toddy, or if made alcoholic, arrack), the husk of the nut (coir) for matting, the shell as fuel or as vessels, the 'meat' as food or oil and the juice not only as a drink but, with one type of coconut whose juice is sympathetic to the human body, as a cheap substitute for plasma in hospitals.

Kari says that there are three different sorts of coconut but twenty-three different types of banana. We stop at a stall and buy a bunch: small, fat, soft, warm and pink, like a financier's fingers.They are delicious, creamy and scented: 'the only bananas I have ever liked,' I tell Kari. 'They are normally only liked by Muslims,' he says with esoteric disparagement.

The country is small, smaller than Scotland, but the scenery varies immensely: from mountain ranges to dales and plains; from savannas, swamps and sea-shores to semi-arid scrublands and rain-forests. At present we are passing through a lushly verdant area of agriculture, a park-like effect of expanses of paddy fields edged with clumps of coconut groves or orchards of bananas. Water buffalo graze in the harvested rice stubble, each beast with his white, graceful attendant, a cattle egret waiting for the browsing animal to stir up an insect.

There are extraordinarily magnificent trees which have been planted as shade-bearers on the side of the road, sometimes in cavernous avenues. They have relatively short trunks, from which massive branches tower, bearing domes of small leaves, among which a fuzzy pink flower can be seen.

'Impressive, those huge trees,' I say.

'Very, very lovely', agrees Kari. 'We call them rain trees because they have leaves which close at night, like pairs of little green hands. And they trap the dew and the night dampness and in the morning the leaves open and there is a nice rain of little droppings.' Another noticeably beautiful and tall tree (*Tabebuia rosea*) is rather like our Essex 'gean', the wild cherry, except that the ascending cloud of flowers are pale pink rather than white. Each flower is trumpet-shaped and about a hand's width across. They come in ball-like clumps, like rhododendrons. In some of the more formal areas I see the tree which has been urbanised throughout the tropics, possibly because it can look completely artificial. The mast tree (*Polyalthia longifolia*) is a tallish, elegant evergreen with a smooth, greyish-brown trunk. Its leaves are extraordinary: of a bright and glossy green, they are about nine inches long and elegantly lanceolate; their wavy margins and brilliant sheen resemble plastic sheeting. They are often used in wreaths.

The average dwelling we pass is a two-roomed shack built entirely of

local materials, either brick or wattle and daub, with a roof of plaited coconut palm leaves. This roof has a large overhang; sometimes there is an awning also of leaves, or of corrugated iron. The front of the house has one door and one window. There is a little detached hut at the back. The gardens are busy: bananas, manioc, pineapples; perhaps shaded by a jak tree bearing fruit the size and shape of a marrow, but covered with densely packed green warts. 'One jak fruit will feed a large family for a whole day – and usually does,' Kari tells us.

The hamlets often have a pump as a central point for social life. Women fill large water jars from them, children wash under them or just spray each other. The larger villages always seem crowded and abustle. Many have a clock (occasionally even an accurate one) at the main cross-roads. The inhabitants are small and dark, some almost black. They are not a good-looking people on average but have pleasant, friendly faces. Many of the woman are elegant in saris; most of them have long ebony pigtails. About half the men wear sarongs rather than trousers. There are neat groups of schoolchildren, the girls in crisp white dresses, the boys nondescript. Sometimes one will see a Buddhist monk in saffron robe and with the yellow parasol which is a sign of office. Most people are on foot or bicycling.

Local elections are to take place on Saturday. The political parties have hung their colours everywhere, sometimes as banners, usually as lines of thin plastic ribbons festooned over roads or along telegraph poles. The dominant colours are blue, red or green. Each party has an emblem: everywhere, on hillside rocks, on milestones, the walls of bridges, in the centre of the road, people have painted a chair, an elephant, a bell or a chicken. There are many posters showing the candidates: some smiling ingratiatingly, some scowling like 'Wanted' posters, some looking worried, or important, or caring.

It is becoming less inhabited, there are patches of wilderness, a burgeoning of bushes and a flourishing of undergrowth. We stop at another stall and buy a pineapple. Kari slices it up into longitudinal segments and we nibble as he drives on. The soil has changed from a reddish pink to a gingery orange.

The road surface becomes terrible. 'Tighten your bra straps,' I tell

Dominie. 'Everything that can wobble is wobbling, talk about "jogger's nipples",' she replies worriedly.

We stop to stare over the limpid waters of a shallow lake. It is one of the most beautiful places I have ever seen, and with the most intense colours. The vivid blue of the tropical sky is reflected in the waters. The undulations of the shoreline are marked out by clumps of coconut groves with shaggy green fronds and golden nuts. Of a paler green are the banner-like leaves of the bananas. Lilies grow in large patches. Some are flowering: the blue of the lotus, the creamy white of the common water-lily, the leaves in lovely shades of hazy green or pale powder-blue. Sometimes we see the turquoise, azure and red of a kingfisher flashing across the scene like a firework; in contrast, the blue herons and white egrets remain frozen in fishermen's expectation. In England we have the drab black moorhen; here we see the purple moorhen, vivid with scarlet beak and legs, violet body and green wings. Less gaudy, but just as striking, is the elegant pheasant-tailed jacana whose white, black-framed wings flitter restlessly amid the lily-pads.

'Do you like it here?' I ask Kari.

'I like it extremely. I have a very peaceful mind in this place.'

As we stand and stare, some rice harvesters on the other side of the road pause to look at us. One women scratches herself with the point of her sickle; quite elegantly, I think.

We drive on. Occasionally we meet large tumbrils piled high with woven palm fronds and pulled by pairs of oxen. Nets of fodder are hung on the end of the central waggon shaft, so that the beasts can browse as they go. Kari says that they travel up to two days to deliver their load. A palm-frond roof lasts only about three monsoons. Other animals seen include a small brown, fuzzy mongoose who suddenly dashes across the road; a speckled lizard four foot long and a snake even longer; water buffalo who work or wallow in the paddy fields; utterly indolent dogs who snooze on the road, sometimes in the exact dead centre. We come upon an elephant lurching down the verge, its trunk fastidiously sniffing and sweeping the way before it. There are many desiccated corpses hanging on the electric wires: flying foxes.

'They are landing on the upper wire, sir. Then they swing upside

down so that their head touches the wire beneath. Flash! Puff! Dead bat,' says Kari.

Our arrival at the Country Club near Dambulla is pleasant: a white-bearded old man who is the 'chamcha' – professional sycophant – greets us with pressed-together hands, bowings, deferential smiles and oriental fawnings. Minions in attractive uniforms of golden shirts and maroon sarongs bustle out and deal with our twelve pieces of luggage (who would have thought that normally I can travel the whole world with little more than a sponge bag). The entrance building is light and airy with a huge open roof and large swimming-pool below it. There is a park-like garden of lawns and trees. Just visible through the trees is a large reservoir. The sinister, gaunt shapes of long-dead trees stand ghostly in the waters; cormorants perch in their branches; dug-out canoes drift over the mirrored surface; fishermen doze in the humid heat. Our rooms are individual chalets, a bit dark but cool.

We have had three fascinating days touring the ruined cities of the lost civilisations of Ceylon. I had always assumed that the island was a bit of a backwater, dominated by its larger neighbour: India's equivalent of the Isle of Wight. Not at all: encompassing civilisations which inspired other, more famous, civilisations, it developed a strongly individual artistry, achieving amazing technical achievements in hydraulics.

Unlike many countries, Ceylon has a recorded history of great antiquity. This is called *The Mahavansa* (The Genealogy of the Great). It was written by Buddhist monks as an epic poem with intersecting notes and short accounts. It includes a thousand-year history of Ceylon from the landing of the Aryan Vijaya, the first Sinhalese king, in 504 BC; some of Buddha's history and genealogy; a summary of Indian history; and a hagiography of the Buddhist king Devanam-piya Tissa, who introduced Buddhism into Ceylon. The history of the island reveals a complicated sequence of attempts for ascendancy to the throne, including invasive attempts by the Princes of India.

One after the other three great cities were built by the Sinhalese kings: firstly Anuradhapura, which was founded in the fourth century BC and finally destroyed – by Tamils from South India – in 992 AD; secondly Polonnaruwa, in use between the eleventh and thirteenth cen-

turies; finally Kandy, which successfully resisted the colonising efforts of the Portuguese and Dutch but finally succumbed to the British in 1815.

Kandy is still a living city; the two others are now many square miles of abandoned and evocative ruins. *Dagobas* dominate their shambles of crumbling walls, leaning pillars and the occasional still-in-use temple or altar. A *dagoba* is a shrine which contains a relic of Buddha or one of his disciples. All *dagobas* are built to a similar format: a central dome, which has to be in the shape of a bell, a pot, a bubble or a heap of rice; a tiny, hidden cell within it where the relic is deposited, like the sarcophagus within an Egyptian pyramid; a central spire or tower, at the very summit of which there is a crystal or jewel which reflects the sun's rays; an encircling area of sand or paving; and a boundary wall pierced by four ornamental entrances. They can be huge. The largest we walked round – clockwise, as it is still a place sacred to Buddhists – is called the Jetavanarama Dagoba and is constructed with enough brick to build a wall between London and Edinburgh one foot thick and ten foot high; the crystal on top of Ruvanweli Dagoba (built 161 BC) is a foot-long pyramid of quartz which sparkles 150 feet above the ground.

There is also a statue that sparkles. The best-preserved building in Polonnaruwa is the church of the Thuparama Buddha: it still has most of its roof; its walls, seven feet thick, are covered with good stone carvings. There is a statue of Buddha within, carved from dolomite. Quartz crystals are embedded in the rock. It is dark and gloomy beside it until a man with a candle appears. He flits the flame up and down the statue's face and it seems that the Buddha's cheeks are glistening with tears. Perhaps they are, for at the altar end of the temple there used to be the figure of a larger Buddha. A specially sited window high up in the facing wall would direct a ray of sunlight right into the face, lighting up the lapis lazuli eyes so that they shone in the gloom. Gone, but for a shattered bulk, vandalised.

There are other memories of these three days, a mixed confusion. Prime among them is the sacred Bo tree. It was planted 2000 years ago which, Kari said, makes it the oldest tree in the world. I didn't argue, but he was wrong: there are many yews and sequoias twice that age, and a bristle-cone pine over 8000 years old. Kari also said it is a type of

banyan, and he was probably right there, but I reckon that with its smooth bark and pointed leaves it is more like a poplar. It even sounds like a poplar when the warm breeze makes a papery rustling through its foliage.

As we crossed the flagged forecourt of a *dagoba* it was so hot that my bare feet began to get scalded and I had to throw my notebook on the ground and hop onto it. Then the sweaty foot print wouldn't take the ink of my pen.

Then there is the memory of the Temple of the Tooth in Kandy. We joined a queue and eventually were able to look through the doorways of three rooms (one door in ivory, the next in silver and the last in gold) to the complicated ornamentation and vivid gleam of a large golden shrine. Within it are six other shrines-within-shrines, like Russian dolls. The innermost one contains a tooth of Buddha. I glanced at it and immediately a monk by the viewing niche pointed urgently at something of even greater importance beside him: the offertory plate. Having contributed a greasy 20-rupee note I was then hustled out.

Equally vivid is Sigiriya, a fortress built 1500 years ago on a vast block of rock which rears 400 feet out of the surrounding plain. At its feet water gardens and boulder gardens are laid out. Kari said that they were inspirations for the gardens of Persia and even Japan. I think he was probably exaggerating, as the Persians must have learned much of their garden design from earlier Mesopotamian origins, from Babylon to Luxor, but the amazing techniques and artistry of the Sinhalese may have had some influence. The hydroponics of their kingdoms were so ingenious that they developed basin-to-basin levelling techniques, similar to those of modern canals, bathing pools and water gardens made crystal-clear by ingenious settling pans and filters. They even managed to raise water by up to six inches per mile with the clever use of centrifugal force round corners, in the same way that a space rocket is naturally accelerated by swinging it round a moon or planet.

By the time the three days were over we were sated with ruins, even with Buddha. 'I'm not sure if I ever want to see a ruin again, and I think I've seen Buddha in every possible position,' Dominie said.

After all that Kari drove us to a luxurious hotel in the mountains, by the Huias Falls, 160 feet high. The mini-bus toiled up the mountainsides

and through acres of tea plantation where the women picking tea leaves were dressed in colourful saris and shawls so that they looked like butterflies against the dark green of the tea bushes. However, when we met a gang of them toiling uphill to their village we saw that most of them are small and wizened with dreadful teeth. They are all Tamils, imported by the British from South India, the Sinhalese reckoning tea-picking a contemptible occupation, Kari told us, rather snootily. He said that their maximum pay is eighty rupees per day. 'No matter, eighty rupees are enough for food and clothes. There are no shops for them to buy other things.'

Later I walked alone through the village near the hotel. Unpleasantly persistent and clinging children pleaded 'Money? Money? Money? Bon-bon? Bon-bon?' Not surprising, I suppose, considering that the equivalent of one pound sterling is more than a day's pay for their mothers.

Even later, in the still calm of the late afternoon, Julian, Kari and I wandered downhill. The air was warm and heavy and spicy. We walked through an enchanted forest of scents: from the clove trees which were clumped about in glossy green hillocks, the cinnamon trees, the tea bushes, there were wild vines climbing up nutmeg trees which Kari identified as peppers. Amid this scented paradise the birds were mobile jewels, as their names suggested. Julian spoke them out as he scanned through his binoculars: 'There's a yellow-browed bulbul – an orange-breasted blue flycatcher – a pair of crimson-throated barbets – some green pigeons.' A minute bird flitted from a bush: 'The smallest bird in Sri Lanka, a pale-billed flower-pecker,' Julian said. Kari pointed to a couple of charming little birds, fan-tailed flycatchers, who flirted and fidgeted amid the branches of a flame tree. 'We call them "drunken pipers," they are always moving, and their song is a pretty whistling,' he said.

The river ran below us, amid its great boulders, sometimes collecting into still pools; through the gaps in the treetops we could see mountains towering, topped with pines. Big brown bags hung from the massive branches of a forest giant: they were the honey-filled nests of a forest wasp. 'The honey is very strong and only used for medicine,' Kali told us. He picked up the strange flower of a cannon-ball tree. 'This represents the time when Buddha was preaching and it rained. This little

knob in the middle of the lower petal is Buddha, the little spikes all around him are the people listening, and the pink and gold upper petal which leans over them represents the giant cobra who leant over and sheltered them all with his outspread hood.'

We returned to find our wives lounging by the swimming-pool, wearing large straw hats, sunglasses and sipping iced soda water. Julian and I gulped down daiquiris. Each one cost two days' pay for a tea-picker. I should have felt guilty. I didn't, particularly.

We have reached the turn-off to the tented camp near Tanamalwila where we are to spend the next three days. The approach is down a rutted, dusty track. To indicate the way, cattle skulls have been nailed to trees, some are painted silver.

We have arrived at the car-park. It is an expanse of threadbare soil delineated by white-painted stones and dominated by an arrangement of dead elephant: its skull and crossed thigh bones. Our morale is a bit low: we are tired from the three-hour journey, zigzagging down mountain roads, bobbling and bucking over appalling surfaces; made lethargic and breathless by the immense mugginess of the heat; dispirited by the arid unfriendliness of the scene. A man appears. His clothes are dirty, his expression testy, his face unshaven, his teeth horrific, like long brown interlocked fingers. He is accompanied by four urchins. Reluctantly, they haul our luggage onto their shoulders and totter off down a thorn-edged footpath. We follow. 'This looks interesting,' I say brightly. This place had been my idea. Dominie and Diana remain mute.

The layout of the tented camp is pleasant, amid the boles of large-branched trees. Each tent is shaded by a thatched roof and fronted by a small fenced-in veranda containing two 'rustic' armchairs. A larger arrangement of canvas, wood and palm roofing is obviously the bar; behind the counter lounges and scratches a bored man in a greasy T-shirt. Another large expanse of roof must be the dining area; it contains two large tables, and on the pews alongside them are rows of sunburned faces that simultaneously and silently turn round to stare at us with that hostile curiosity with which new boys at school are greeted.

We inspect our tents. They each contain two iron beds. Upon them

are two greyish sheets and one small pillow. The beds are six feet long, exactly my length, but Julian is five inches longer. The other furnishing is a small table, upon which is the lighting: a torch – mine with an almost-flat battery. There is just room to squeeze between the table and the beds, but not enough to accommodate all our luggage. The lavatory is a tented compartment adjacent, the ablutions a hosepipe screened – partly – by sacking. Dominie and Diana still have not uttered a word, but their lips have tightened into buttonholes.

I flop onto one of the twig-built chairs in my veranda. With a cacophony of creaks and crackles it swirls askew and, having transformed into a heap of kindling wood, subsides beneath me. For the first time since our arrival, Dominie laughs. Julian, who has assumed an air of stoic cheerfulness, hurries towards the bar. He confers with the churl behind the counter. There is a terrible cry of astonishment and despair: 'No ice?' 'No ice!'

Dinner was good. It included buffalo curd with coconut syrup: delicious, the former tasting slightly nutty, the latter darkish, with a tang of toffee. The two nationalities present assumed their characteristic personalities, the French remaining peevish and secretive, the Dutch open and friendly. The Hollanders are a happy lot and I can hear them still singing and laughing as I lie on my bed, writing this by the light of my torch. A drop of sweat has just run off the end of my nose onto the page.

Next day: up at six o'clock; shave under the cold tap, razor in one hand and torch in the other; the breakfast we had ordered is non-existent, the cook having overslept, but we are finally issued some tepid tea and coffee; the light of dawn outshines the flickering of the hurricane lamps; we embus and start off on an hour's drive to Bundall, an area of bird-filled lagoons and saltpans. Women are sweeping leaves off the beaten earth in front of their dwellings, others are arranging the produce for sale in the little stalls of pole and thatch. It is election day and politicians and their cronies hang up posters and streamers and harangue people from vans which sprout bouquets of loudspeakers. People look peaceful, but Kari has just told us that the next two days are to be under curfew, and we will not be able to leave the tented camp.

A heat haze shimmers over the lagoons. They are full of waterfowl: ibis, stilts, whistling duck, plovers, sandpipers, pelicans, storks, flamingo. A bit further inland the muddy verges of the freshwater ponds are pock-marked with the prints of elephants. There are about 2500 still roaming wild on the island. We finally see one. He is scratching a shoulder against the trunk of a large acacia tree. I take a photograph of him. In this one photograph I manage to include a crested hawk eagle perched in the upper branches of the tree, three peacocks crossing the grass in front, two egrets, and in the large pond between us some spoonbills and a painted stork. All is idyllic, except for the human beings. Nellie stares disparagingly at us and then ambles off, gliding through the scrub like a grey barge.

Kari sighs: 'The elephant, they have become very rude and cross, too many people.'

We had a good lunch at the Peacock Beach Hotel near the seaside town of Hambantota. Afterward we sat in its veranda overlooking the sea. The waves broke rhythmically on the golden sands. Butterflies flitted among the exotic flowers of the hotel garden. Overhead fans kept the afternoon heat at bay. Ice tinkled in our tumblers of freshly pressed lime juice and soda. Dominie and Diana looked at each other. They raised their eyebrows. They nodded. Within a moment we had driven back to the tented camp, packed, paid and quit and have now checked into the hotel.

It is late afternoon. Dominie is in the warm waters of the swimming-pool, floating amid the scented, waxy petals which have fallen off the frangipanis which are clumped around and overhead. Diana is lounging on a deckchair, reading; there is a large palu tree (*Palu mimusops hexandra*) above her, amid its glossy dark green foliage crows pick and argue over its yellow berries. Hibiscus is flowering behind Julian as he sits in a bathing-suit and straw hat, examining a golden oriole through his binoculars. Three long-tailed monkeys silently appear, glance at us and then bend over to drink from the far edge of the pool. A huge black and white butterfly flits amid the flowers of that most lovely of all bushes, the peacock flower (*Ponticiana regina*) whose flowers resemble dancing girls in frilly dresses, holding golden sprays of stamens. Julian gets up and strolls towards the bar where a little brown man in uniform

dozes amid the scarlet swathes of a bougainvillaea. Dominie catches my eye. '*This* is what I call a holiday,' she says.

Young influence – – –. The first Sinhalese I knew was a great influence in my life, making me out-of-date before my time. Before I went to school, I had a governess. Miss Pearson was small and brown and sometimes rather fierce, but I loved her. Her father had been a Scotchman, her mother Sinhalese. She would often talk of the times when she was young, and when she spoke, every sentence was a poem: concise and vivid as a haiku. She told of her life as governess to the family of an officer of the army, one of the guardians of the British Empire, in the olden, golden days before the Great War. Soldiers in scarlet, brass and burnished steel drilled to the calls of bugles, stately women in long white dresses glided across vice-regal lawns, Indians salaamed and pulled the punka ropes to fan verandaed rooms where supremely confident people lived amidst the panoply of an everlasting Empire.

Rajputana, Burma, the Transvaal – all places were the same to her, for although her naïve wonder took in new sights (camels plodding across drifting sands, forests of rhododendrons, the wailing babble of spiced bazaars, the songs of troop-ships gliding through burning sunsets, durbars, mob riots, cholera, Zulu drums), everywhere for her was characterised by the same people whom she loved. All parade grounds held for her the crash and thump of British soldiers: Pompadour and Fusilier, Hussar and Highlander, Ghurkha and Artillery, Cavalry and corps. She makes me think of silver teapots reflecting cooling afternoons.

The Empire is dead. In a Fulham Road bedsitter, Miss Pearson faded out with leukaemia. But each day was just as wonderful to her untired mind, each tiny act of kindness vivid evidence of God's domain, each leaf of potted hyacinth as much a natural marvel as they were when she was a girl. She dreamed without heartache of the past, where although Death and Arrogance were gods, there was no dingy meanness or drab-

ness of intent. When she died, old Colonel Napier met her at the barrack gates and took her by the hand to a place where the angels are in gold and scarlet, and the sun never sets.

All that remains of her is a cheap notebook filled with her neat copperplate writing, the walnut tree in my garden which she had planted from a nut fifty years ago, and some of my own opinions: out-of-date perhaps, but I hope also embodying principles of honour and responsibility and a sense of romance and wonder that she instilled in me. I hope I have succeeded in passing on at least some of this to my own children and grandchildren.

Pretoria, Easter Day, 30 March 1997. As it is Easter I must go to church: Easter, Christmas, Harvest Festival and Armistice Day are my four 'musts'. Before I go I put, easily accessible in the right-hand pocket of my jacket, the D clip I use to hold the diplomatic bags together. It is a sad reflection on the state of the world, especially of the 'new' South Africa, when a man walking to church has to take such precautions.

It has been raining. There are almost no cars or people and it seems a deserted city as I walk down Pretorius Street and then Schoeman Street.

Here is Saint Alban's Cathedral. I have arrived much too early. A nice woman who looks exactly like one of the hierarchy of Colne Engaine's Women's Institute comes up, introduces herself – Deaconess Gladys Dawson. She asks about my tie. 'A silver greyhound carrying the royal crown – a Queen's Messenger,' I say. 'I go round the world delivering confidential messages for the Government of her Britannic Majesty.'

She takes me on a tour of the cathedral. It is built out of a craggy pinky-yellow rock in two styles: Gothic at the east end, modern in the main body. There are four impressive but garish stained-glass windows on the south wall, a font gracefully shaped like a goblet, a couple of cosy but rather stark side chapels, a weird bishop's throne which looks like the dentist's chair for a Martian, a simple but dignified apse with altar and three elevated alcoves to each side, and a large seat-with-canopy which came from our Ely Cathedral.

'Who was Saint Alban?' I ask.

'A Roman-British citizen. He dressed himself in priest's garb and was executed on Holmhurst Hill in England. He is usually depicted with a tall cross and sword, with his head in an adjacent holy bush and the eyes of his executioner falling out.'

'Tuh,' I say sympathetically.

As I sit in the pew waiting for the service to start Mrs Dawson comes up to me. 'We have decided that after the sermon is over you will finish off by telling us, from your experiences in going round the world, how all the world will be rejoicing on this Easter Day.' She is so friendly – and determined – and I am so aghast, that I do not have time to refuse, so I am spending most of the service worrying and scribbling down notes.

The bishop is away and the service is being taken by Dean Jo Seoka. The acoustics are bad, the tall roof echoes rather than amplifies, so that the singing of the choir is distorted and muffled. But the singing of the individual people is superb, even the ugliest and craggiest of the women warble like the 'drunken pipers' I was listening to in Sri Lanka just over a week ago, a whole ocean away, with my Dominie.

In the recesses to either side of the altar six girls are standing. They are all black, dressed simply but impressively in white albs overlaid with red chasubles. They look mighty fine, statuesque, two of them are rather pretty . . . Sorry, God, I'll concentrate on my sermon.

My turn. I walk up the tile-paved nave. I had forgotten that the rubber heel has fallen off one of my shoes. The improvised knuckle-duster in my jacket pocket is clanking, in my trouser pockets the loose change of three different countries tinkles together.

'Click – squidge – click – squidge – click – squidge – jingle – jingle – tinkle – tinkle – tinkle – clank', I sound like a troop of cavalry – *after* the Charge of the Light Brigade.

When I reach the lectern and look up I see a mass of friendly black faces looking back. There are a few whites and some Ghanaians, looking impressive in their robes and head dresses. I swallow. 'Homilophobia – fear of sermons,' I think irrationally. I wonder what fear of giving them is?

'Good morning. It is a pleasure – though a bit of a shock – to meet you like this. I am a Queen's Messenger, someone who travels on behalf

of her Britannic Majesty or her government throughout the world, a quarter of a million miles a year from China to Chile, Kathmandu to Kuwait, Norway to Neasden (*sorry, God, a bit over the top, but I cannot resist a good alliteration*). If ever I have any spare time there are two places I try to go to, the cathedral and the botanical gardens – combining things spiritual and temporal. Today is especially important that I go to church, for it is even more important than Christmas Day. If I wasn't here I would be 7000 miles north, in my village church. It is a typical English parish church, built about 700 years ago, using bits and pieces from earlier times, prehistoric sarsens, Roman tiles, Anglo-Saxon bricks, and with some extra additions put in during the reign of Henry VIII. (*The congregation is beginning to look glassy-eyed.*) After church my wife and family, our children, their wives and husbands, the grandchildren, and some special friends, twenty-three people in all (*the twenty-fourth is here, all alone, being stared at*) will be sitting down to lunch. They will be eating lamb in – a perhaps macabre – memory of the Paschal Lamb. It will be home-grown, from my farm.

'Sometime ago I was in Jerusalem and went to the Monastery of the Holy Cross where grows, they think, a tree which is the great-great-grandchild of the original tree from which the Cross was made. There I met the monk in charge, the Archdeacon Seraphim. I said that I sometimes felt a bit guilty that I was fattening the sweet and woolly lambs so that they may be butchered. And he said: "Don't worry, the sheep probably domesticated the shepherd, to make him feed them and pay the vet's bills." I suppose, today, that the Archdeacon Seraphim is busy in Jerusalem celebrating Easter, as they are in all the many other churches I have visited throughout the world. I may not speak for them, just share, like you, in this celebration, but I will be presumptuous enough to send greeting from Saint Andrew's Church, Colne Engaine, Essex, England, to Saint Alban's Cathedral, Pretoria, in the continent of Africa.'

At least, that's what I meant to say, but once I have stood up to speak I seem to forget everything until I find myself sitting down again.

After the service was over I was invited to the adjacent hall where I had a cup of tea and a hot cross bun and shook hands with a lot of friendly smiling people.

Then I went on my errand.

The first thing to do was to steal a flower.

The flower I stole was from a red hibiscus I had noticed just outside the south door of the cathedral. I tweaked it guiltily off the bush when no one was looking – except God, and if He was around He would not mind. (Well, He might. I sometimes think that He is rather disagreeable, but Jesus wouldn't mind, He is the One on our side.)

Now the familiar walk down Church Street. A few more people are about. Most of the white men are in shorts. The people of Sri Lanka would laugh to see it: to the Sinhalese, the only people to wear shorts are schoolboys. I reach the grim barracks of Church Square, where a couple of slobs lean against the statue of Paul Kruger: huge pink faces, wobbly great bodies, close-cropped hair, scowls. I look at them, thinking what revolting lumps of superfluous meat they are.

I meet a peeved and piggy eye. 'What are you staring at, man?'

'Fuck alone knows,' I reply (not a nice reaction from someone who has just given a sermon). But the answer must have satisfied them, as they make no other remark.

At last, the cemetery. Go to the military area. Quest about. Here it is, the memorial to the fallen from the Brigade of Guards. Pay my respects. Walk past other soldiers' graves. Nod a greeting to those of the Essex Regiment. Back to the civilian area. Quest about again. Can't find the grave that touched me during my first visit here. Ah: 'THELMA MINNIE (Tookles) . . . died . . . aged 3 years 10 months.' I lay the flower on the little girl's grave. Perhaps I am the first person to do so for eighty-nine years. As I look at the tiny, abandoned little rectangle over the long-dead Tookles a surge of loneliness takes me by the throat.

So I will go back to the 'ethnic' restaurant and eat an ostrich for lunch. For dinner there yesterday I had smoked impala followed by kudu steak. It was rather nasty, with a nose-catching tang which suggested it was over-hung, and with flaccid flesh which implied that, like most game, it was very tough and had had to be pounded to a jelly.

I ask the waitress if I am eating breast or thigh of the roast ostrich and she merely smiles, looking embarrassed. The bird is rather a disappointment, dark and tough, with the consistency of aged veal. It would probably be nicer if carved into thin slices rather than chopped up into steaks. It tastes fair, more like chicken than game bird; Dominie

would do better with it, boiled, with rice and white sauce.

But she is basting the lamb at present, at home so far away.

I have been asked to an Easter evening party by a member of the High Commission, who kindly arranged for me to be driven there by car. I am sitting in front; behind is another guest, an instructor from some British Governmental agency, sent here to teach the locals some trade or language. He just nodded when I got into the car, didn't even have the manners to reply to my 'Good-evening'. Pompous prick.

The driver and I chat, mainly about other people's bad driving and our own families.

'What is your tribe?' I ask.

'Xhosa,' he says.

The little pillock behind me leans over and says right into my ear, in a clipped, mouthing voice which is heavy with disapproval and dislike: 'And your tribe, may I ask?'

'The Huguenots.'

He havers for a bit, then says, 'Never heard of them.'

'From Stellenbosch, mostly, the Huguenots are,' says the driver.

'Yes,' I tell him, 'a lot of us went there 300 years ago when we were driven out of France; they are still quite a big element in the wine-growing trade. But my own family went straight to England.'

We carry on nattering, the driver and I. There is no more conversation from behind, just a simmering silence. Where once the British spread learning and tolerance throughout the world, now many of our bureaucrats contaminate it with petty-mindedness and built-in resentment, founded on their own bad education and inherited chippyness.

 **Mauritius, 2 April 1997.** The Island of the Dodo – I arrived here yesterday evening. Having hung around in the deserted Arrivals Hall for forty minutes I telephoned the High Commission to find out why I had not been met. The duty officer, sounding aggrieved, said they were not expecting me. I said I was extremely annoyed and would wait no longer,

they could book me into the normal beach hotel and come and collect the diplomatic bag from there. I then changed some dollars into Mauritian rupees and took a taxi to the hotel – which, I must admit, is very comfortable and luxurious. I have a two-roomed suite with a balcony overlooking the sea.

I ate in solitary state, sulking, the little white diplomatic bag sitting in the chair opposite, creating puzzled stares from the holiday makers feasting all around me. Eventually someone from the High Commission came to collect the bag. She was a jolly girl with her Mauritian fiancé, so instead of being the fierce and angry officer I had intended to be I melted and they sat and had drinks while I finished my meal.

It is the crack of dawn. God knows what time my mental clock should say it is: in the last month I have been to three continents, one sub-continent and have changed my watch five times. In the last four days I have taken four aeroplanes (one of them was so old and quaint it had a Bible in an easy-to-open box next to the entrance, instead of the normal fire extinguisher) – and I will have three more to take in the next two days. However, I am up early as I only have till noon before the car comes to collect me from the High Commission. At present I am sitting in my balcony, scribbling this, sipping a cup of coffee and looking at the sun rising over the sea, just visible between the plumes of coconut palms. After this I will start off with a swim among the coral, then I will have breakfast, then I will have a bicycle ride to the nearest village, then I will explore it, then I will bicycle back a different way, then I will have another swim. Then I will pack and go.

The water is quite warm. I am being cautious. The first time I swam here I was nearly drowned and spent several hours trying to get back from the rollers and undertow on the reef. The sea-bed near the hotel is an aquatic litter dump: bottles, boots, plastic bags, tins, stuff dumped from yachts and rubbish from the hotel; the coral is dead or dying. What a filthy animal the human being is. It is better here, further out. Some big silver fish shaped like missiles have just shot past. There is one specially odd fish which looks like a rectangular black box with white spots. A

tiny species of fish lurking in the crevices of coral looks like chips of blue stained glass. I am amid a shoal of a beautiful black and yellow striped angel-fish: flat, with a long streamer flowing from the tip of the upper fin.

A twerp in a motor-boat putters up to me, frightening them off. 'Taxi?' he asks.

Breakfast, often the best meal of the day: 'fruit' juice made from hibiscus flowers, bacon, eggs, sausage, tomato, good coffee, toast and proper marmalade; I sit under the great spread of the open-air thatched roof and look out over my book at the gardens and the snow-white beach and the turquoise sea beyond.

It is a happy, attractive place. Everyone is here to enjoy themselves. There are a lot of children running about. A young mother is holding her baby and smiling down at it: there is something very appealing at such a sight, as the medieval painters of the Madonna and Child knew. A painting of a man in the same circumstances would be accurate if it showed an expression of mild disgust on his face.

There are a lot of honeymooners about. Odd, most of them do not talk: some smile secretly at each other, others look askance. Just shyness, one hopes. Lots of oldies too. There are a couple of them at the next table. She has been rocking with laughter after he had read out from a newspaper that a new pop song is called *Fly High, Lesbian Seagull*. Many of these old people have saved a lifetime for this holiday. They are the sort of people who would scrimp and save and then take a first-class ticket on the *Queen Mary*. Prescott, as a good old-fashioned social-ist, boasted that when he was a steward on a Cunard liner he would deliberately tip soup over the laps of the first-class passengers. And it is likely that he and others of his ilk are going to be our rulers in a month's time.

Perhaps, then, someone will pour things over *his* trousers.

To hell with this bicycle ride. I have been going a couple of miles and all I have seen are the green walls of sugarcane plantations. I feel like an ant in a golf course. The road surface is terrible – a real ball-breaker – and it is becoming very hot. I'm going back to swim, there's an hour before I pack and go.

 **Nairobi to Mombasa train, 21–2 April 1997.** Landed here this morning and checked in at the Mutheiga Club, which is the traditional place for Queen's Messengers to stay while in Kenya: mahogany and chintz and stuffed animals and bosky gardens. Had lunch there with Henrietta's in-laws, Jack and Betty Couldrey, and discussed what I should do for the next three days – this journey involving a longish wait while they assemble return bags for me from Dar es Salaam, Addis Ababa, Kampala and the Seychelles. I do not report for duty until 20.15 the day after tomorrow.

The Couldreys told me that it has been raining, and that it is going to carry on raining so that all the 'mini-safaris' are off. To think I have been praying for the stuff in England for the last three months. I told them that my daughter-in-law Lucy had said that she had been on the Nairobi-to-Mombasa night train and it had been quite fun. I could catch the train tonight, explore Mombasa tomorrow and return tomorrow night on the same train. Betty said that she thought it a pretty ghastly idea, but they would drive me to the station so I could buy a ticket and reserve a cabin.

18.00 hours. The first-class cabin, plus two meal chits (dinner and break-fast) and a chit for bedding amounts to 3000 Kenyan shillings, about £34. I stroll down the platform, along the whole length of the train. At the rear there is a very old-fashioned guard's van and another waggon with three doors, one each for DRIVERS, FIREMEN and GUARDS. Then there are thirteen carriages, which include a restaurant car, the first- and second-class sleepers and the already-crammed-with-people third-class sardine tins. Finally there is a goods waggon and the engine: a large diesel with a snub snout like a King Charles spaniel and a long dachshund body, once painted blue. The driver is a tall black man with a big white smile and a small grey oil-cloth. I return to the sleepers and look for my name on the rows of cards on the outside of the sleeper carriages. I find it on coach 9, cabin E, which I am to share with a W. Anagawi. The passengers next door are called Mrs Croc and Mrs Pronk. I'm longing to see what they look like, but they seem to have barricaded themselves in. It is a bit of a shock to find I am sharing a cabin. I had thought that it would

be like our Peking-to-Ulaan Baatar journey and I would have a cabin to myself. I have reserved the lower bunk by strewing it with the only things I've packed – in a Muthaiga Club laundry bag: a thriller, a notebook, a toothbrush and razor, and a Queen's Messenger tie in readiness for an unexpected formal occasion. As well as the two bunks there is a wash-basin with a mirrored cabinet over it, a cupboard, and a ladder to get up to the top bunk. The whole thing is panelled in imitation wood and formica. The bunks are longer than those of the Trans-Manchurian Express; as a result the corridor is much narrower and it is only just pos-sible for two people to pass. As most of the passengers in the sleeper classes seem to be adolescents with huge rucksacks, there is much nipping in and out of doors. I did a quick reconnaissance into the lava-tory at the end of the carriage and almost fell down it; it is merely a metal-reinforced hole in the floor. Fortunately I prepared for this journey by taking the indigestion pill which gives me instant constipation.

I wander up and down the platform again: it is quite a pleasant station, reasonably clean, busy but not hysterical, well signed. All the signs are in both English and Swahili – the Swahili for 'station master' is 'steshen masta'; you can't help sounding like a politically incorrect comedian if you say it aloud. The Swahili for 'lavatory' is 'choo'.

Back in my cabin. W. Anagawi looms in the doorway. He is huge and dark and menacing: he looks like the heavy-weight boxing champion of hell.

'Ah am William,' he says, enveloping my hand in his vast one. He dumps a rucksack on the upper bunk, sits down, dons a dainty little pair of gold-rimmed spectacles, opens a well-thumbed Bible and proceeds to read it.

A steward enters. He takes our chits for the bedding and tells us he will make up our bed while we eat. He says 'many thieves about at night' and shows us how to lock the door and fix the mosquito screen over the upper windows. I am extra glad I chose the bottom bunk, the upper window is rather obscured by the mesh.

19.00 hours. We move off. There is a tinkling noise coming down the cor-ridor. It is the steward with a metal xylophone calling for the first sitting for dinner.

The tables in the restaurant car are laid with heavy canteen-style crockery and cutlery. William and I sit at one of the tables together. We are joined by a taciturn Asian with a crutch and an ex-colonial called Tom M***. He is in his mid-sixties, wirily fit, with an aquiline nose and hawk-like eyes beneath lowering eyebrows. He knows a couple of Queen's Messengers (R.J.A. and J.O.H.) as he was in the Kenya Police with them many years ago. He has had an interesting life: having left the Kenya Police he went to various parts of the Middle and Far East and Africa, specialising in flying aeroplanes for the surveyors in National Parks, doing things like counting the flamingos in the chain of lakes down the Great Rift Valley and assaying herds of elephant. One of his more peculiar jobs was counting turtles' eggs off the coast of Africa. He flew a Club Piper from which turtle nests could be seen from the air; the aeroplane could then land on the beach and the eggs counted. A couple of years ago he was called out of his retirement cottage somewhere near Guildford to help manage a newly developed Nature Reserve/Game Park near the Tanzanian border.

He has not been to Nairobi for twenty years and he is doing a nostalgic final tour before he returns to Surrey. He says he is astonished and appalled at the change in the places he has just visited. He says the chief cause of unpleasantness is not corruption or incompetence, which admittedly exist in abundance, but the sheer numbers of people: the vast crowds and the traffic which cannot be accommodated by pavements and roads which were designed decades ago; the collapse of public services, especially those affecting hygiene, such as rubbish collection and public lavatories; the building on a vast scale but still not able to keep up with the shanty town growth – all this resulting in squalor and ugliness, poverty and aggression.

Now that he mentions it, I realise this is equally true of many other places that I have been to, most recently Colombo and Kandy in Sri Lanka where the vestiges of previous civilisations, from Sinhalese to Victorian British, are being swamped by overpopulation.

Dinner is drab: tepid and watery vegetable soup; I then have a 'beef' curry, the meat apparently butchered off the rubber soles of brothel creepers. The others have chicken with snow-white goose-pimply flesh;

a school pudding like the sponges you clean cars with, blobbed all over with lumpy custard.

Our beds are made up by our return. William shyly undresses and puts his pyjamas on when lying on the top bunk, wriggling like a maggot in a chrysalis. When he drops his shoes onto the floor they make a noise like a couple of ten-pound haddock hitting the deck. I am now lying looking out of the window. Sheet lightning is flashing, silhouetting the shapes of trees against the sky: shock-headed palms, flat-topped fever trees and the extraordinary upside-down outline of the baobabs.

06.00 hours. Breakfast has just started. I am sharing a table with an affable, burly South African with a daughter (pink adolescent spots) and son (bony adolescent knees). Breakfast is toast plus a horrible jam, adequate fried egg and sausage, bearable coffee.

We have remained stationary throughout breakfast. I ask a passing waiter what is happening.

'No problem, the goods train in front is derailed.'

09.00 hours. We are outside a small railway station called 'Wangala'. A sign says 117 kilometres from somewhere, presumably Mombasa. Tom M*** has joined me looking out of the window and tells me that we are on the edge of Tsavo National Park where he once used to work. On the other side, about 400 yards away, there is a large road.

Me: 'I think I may have to hitchhike.'

He: 'If you do, don't stick your thumb up. It's an insulting gesture. If they stop at all it will be to beat you up.'

There are a lot of people walking up and down the railway line, looking important but being futile. There is a terrific variety of hats: tweed flowerpots, Muslim pillboxes, a baseball peaked cap worn back to front, the official dark cap, something small and greasy like a fish and chip bag, a hideous creation in pink imitation leather with a light blue peak, the trilby, the hubcap, the little-knitted-number-with-a-bobble-on-top.

We have moved on a few miles to a station called Bachuma. Like all the other stations it is immaculate: lines of painted white stones, flowerbeds, well-planted trees and shrubs, areas of ginger-coloured

beaten earth without a single weed, attractive buildings painted cream with chocolate-coloured doorframes and windows. I go with Tom to the station master's control room and he shows us round: glistening brass, polished steel, great heavy cast-iron handles for moving the signals and points, many neatly aligned brass plaques saying 'Bachuma – Best Kept Station – 1914' etc.

11.30 hours. We have been waiting about six hours. The Nairobi-bound train from Mombasa is passing us. It stops. Directly opposite me are a crowd of jolly young Americans. They tell me that they have been stuck in the train since nine o'clock last night and will arrive in Nairobi just in time to miss their aeroplane. The train moves on. All the passengers in both trains wave and smile and shout 'Good luck!' and we are on the move at last.

The scenery is almost entirely of thorny scrub, and the countryside pretty flat, no animals, the occasional interest being the odd tree cactus, railway station or hamlet of thatched shacks. As we pass the hamlets children run up and wave and scream.

The carriage is beginning to smell from the lavatories at each end. Thank God for that constipation pill! Talking of God, it turns out that William is a Jehovah's Witness. He broached the subject and I said how very interesting but I am Church of England and he did not persist.

13.30 hours. It is becoming more cultivated. There are large areas of tilled soil amid coconut palms; cattle, goats, more and more waving children.

The shanty towns are getting closer together. There are deep valleys, the track meanders along the top of ridges – I can sometimes see our engine and the first few carriages curving along in front.

We are now entering the outskirts of Mombasa. The first sight of it is of two huge flame-stacks of a refinery, one of which is emitting balls and billows of scarlet fire amid a great plume of carboniferous smoke.

The train goes past a big bay; the beach is black and smelling of oil.

The oily smell is now being replaced with the rancid stink of a vast rubbish tip. Gangs of people pick through the trash.

The rubbish tip goes on and on.

Houses – shops – the station at last: pleasant, open and airy.

I wave goodbye to Tom, who has donned a tiny rucksack and whose aquiline face is surmounted by a ridiculously inappropriate teeny prep-school type sunhat in white linen.

William and I share a taxi and he drops me at the Mission to Seamen, in Mogadishu Road. I had decided to make the Mission my base, if possible, as the man who runs it is our Honorary Consular Representative, the Reverend Captain Richard Diamond.

The first sight of the Mission is pleasant: grounds including ornamental trees and shrubs, a tidy car-park with clean and respectable cars, flags on masts, striped awnings, an airy building of which the most noticeable area is the bar with a long counter supported by wooden barrels and with walls decorated with ships' insignia. To one side there are offices, a games room and an outside swimming-pool. The little chapel is attractive. The font is a large ship's bell, turned upside down.

There is only one person in the bar, a large friendly Tasmanian with a beard. He buys me a pint of Ice-cap lager. Jim has bummed around the world sailing yachts, to Zanzibar, Indonesia, Fiji: all over the Indian and Pacific Oceans; now he is thinking of settling down and starting up a prawn farm on the coast of Kenya.

I ask him what Captain Diamond is like. 'Good bloke. Efficient, too. But a strange man really – he used to make pies in Cape Town. And talking of pies, he has got a finger in every pie you can think of. At present he is trying to make money by selling microlights to the local people, but they keep killing themselves before they can pay him. And talking of the devil – here he comes.'

I had presumed that his Reverence would be like the old priest of the South China Seas I sometimes met in the Seamen's Mission in Hong Kong: white-haired, battered and toothless after bar-room brawls, scarred by attacks from pirates and prostitutes. Not a bit: he is a dapper, stocky man with a neat crop of grey hair and dressed in crisp cottons.

More Ice-cap all round, my order this time. A sailor comes in and tries to borrow some money from the Captain and is offered goodwill and sympathy but no money. 'He comes off a Croatian ship whose owner is owed $480,000, so hasn't been able to pay his crew for seven months.' Lack of money is a great problem around here, AIDS is another. I ask him if the people locally are like the Caribbeans in which

marriage generally takes place when people are in their fifties, and meanwhile the men are roving 'studs'. This way of life is starting to happen in urban Britain.

'Not a bit,' he says, 'there is very much a tradition of working away from home – at sea, in the mines, on the railways – the wife stays at home and tends the farmstead of three to five acres. The women are generally fairly well behaved, or discreet at least, as they live in a village community: presumably the men are as promiscuous as men often are when they are away from home a long time.'

Mugging is becoming an increasingly unpleasant problem. The police are useless. People take the law into their own hands. For example, he had to interrupt a sermon recently because of the sounds of shouting and arguing outside. He ran out and saw the bloodied wreck of a mugger who had been caught and beaten up by a crowd. A collection was being made among them to buy petrol. The cause of the noise was an argument between those in favour of buying a fourteen-inch tyre against those who preferred a sixteen-inch tyre. There were a couple of policemen standing by looking on.

'Why don't you stop them, they are going to necklace him?' the padre asked.

'But they haven't started yet,' objected a policeman.

The bar is filling up. A group of people are talking about Zaire: the advance upon Mobutu's beleaguered Kinshasa by the 'rebels' under Kabila. The general opinion is 'same trough, different pig'. A tall man tells me that he tried to do some trading with the Zairean government and the politicians he met 'were almost brain-dead, having passed through corruption and debauchery to satiation and indifference'. A small man buys a round. He is in shorts, has grey hair in an urchin cut and knows the Essex coast; he kept his first boat in West Mersea. It was a lifeboat of the type which used to be carried under the wings of Lancaster bombers. He bought it for £500. He primped it up and sold it in Holland and with the profit bought a tug with which he used to tow barges up and down the Dutch canals. Later, he chartered crews in the Mediterranean, finally buying a schooner and inventing a patent Bermuda rig on the two top-masts so that he could sail it with only one extra hand. These old sailors never seem to stay still for a minute, so

different from the sedentary life when I started in Courtaulds Ltd, when one's promotion was almost planned from the very first day and one's pay was accepted as one's age plus two noughts.

18.00 hours. Richard Diamond's driver has taken me back to the railway station. I am pacing up and down the platform. I see I am to share my cabin with a Dr Fuad. A sleek man in a well-cut but loudly striped suit bustles up: 'Ah, my friend, we were together last night and here you are back again!' I do not know him from Adam, he's not my nice old William, unless he's shrunk, slimmed and bought a vile gold watch with diamonds all round the dial.

'If you want, I will get you a nice cabin, all to yourself.'

'Thanks, so long as I don't have to pay extra.'

He loses all interest in my well-being and vanishes towards the restaurant car. It is twilight. Crows are noisily cawing as they settle for the night in the trees next to the platform, and flights of flying foxes flitter-flutter overhead, to the nearest orchards I suppose. A lovely anvil-shaped cloud towers in the sky, lit up by the setting sun. That means more rain and maybe thunder. As I return to my cabin I hear a sequence of staccato noises emitting from it like someone unsuccessfully trying to start up a chainsaw. It is Dr Fuad: the bloody man was farting. He has the grace to look thoroughly abashed when I enter and stare at him in amazement. He is a wispy little person dressed in black, with a pillbox hat and a long thin goatlike beard. I hastily depart, leaving him to sit amidst his own miasma.

20.00 hours. Dinner was not good: tinned asparagus soup, tough mutton chops, the same pud as last night. The head waiter turns out to be the smooth man who offered to find me an empty cabin. We should have left an hour ago. I wander off and see the station master standing outside his office, surrounded by worried-looking people in uniform.

'Why have we not left yet?' I ask.

'No problem. There has been a derailment.'

'But that was yesterday.'

'This is another derailment. Different place. Different goods train.'

'When will be cleared so we can move off?'

'We may know in an hour. I will come and tell you at 21.00 hours.'

'Bollocks,' I think, and return to my cabin and the flatulent Dr Fuad.

The electricity is turned off: the fan in the cabin stops, the lights go out, I cannot even read: I lie and sweat.

21.00 hours. A knock on my door. I see by the light of a lantern that it is the station master. 'I tell you what is happening. What is happening is that we do not know. It is derailed in a very isolated spot. More news in one hour precisely.' He leaves. I continue to lie on my bunk and fret: the Americans on yesterday's up-train said that they were going to miss their flight. What flights are there from Mombasa aerodrome? Are there buses? How long will they take? Can I hire a car?

I can't just lie here doing nothing. I go to the station master's office. There is a small crowd of worried people outside it. The station master is a large man, dignified in spite of an Arafat-style five-day stubble. He has an assistant, also in late middle age, but very neat.

'I'm sorry,' I say, 'but I must be in Nairobi by tomorrow evening. If things get worse, will you be able to organise alternative transport – flights?'

He says that a Norwegian woman has already asked that question and is in his office with one of his assistants, telephoning the aerodrome. I enter to hear Miss Norway saying down the telephone: 'No, absolutely not. It has taken twenty minutes to get through to you, I will hang on here and *you* ask the man on extension 2016. I am sorry, but I am not interested if you are just a trainee, hurry up.'

The Norwegian girl is about twenty, her blonde hair in a pony-tail, a pretty plumpish face but too young to show much character in it: a bit like the young Queen Victoria.

We wait. She speaks down the telephone again: 'No more flights tonight! What times are tomorrow morning's flights? Seven o'clock is the first. Will there be room in any of the flights? You cannot be sure?'

We look gloomily at each other. We hang about. Our little crowd becomes a bit bigger. The station master speaks down another telephone. He turns to us: 'News, at last. You will not be moving off for at least ten hours.' There is a howl of rage from the assembly.

I eventually force my way through the snarling mob and find the

station master and his assistant cowering behind a desk. Miss Norway is leaning over them.

'You'll have to organise buses, or something,' I say.

'This lady from Norway has already told us to do that. It is done. There will be buses for the first- and second-class passengers. Coming in one hour precisely.'

The crowd hangs about. 'I suppose the other passengers do not know about it yet, perhaps they should be told,' I suggest to the station master's assistant.

'Certainly not,' says Miss Norway, 'there are only three buses.'

This girl is continuously five paces ahead of me, as I am five paces in front of the other passengers. Her resemblance to Queen Victoria is becoming striking.

The crowd is becoming more angry, egged on by The Screamer. The Screamer is a tiny, middle-aged Austrian female who wants her money back. She has a large husband with a pot-belly and a sad, apologetic smile. The Screamer's voice is as shrill and as persistent and as loud as a band-saw going through a baulk of teak: 'You should have told us – you should have told us – you should have told us when we were boarding – we could then have gone to the airport – you are a stupid, *stupid*, STUPID man – we want our money back – I am not going in a bus it will be a death trap – on that road – a death trap – a complete death trap, particularly at night – we want our money back – we will go to a hotel – WE WANT OUR MONEY BACK – GIVE US OUR MONEY BACK – I SAID GIVE US OUR MONEY BACK – WE WANT OUR 6000 SHILLINGS – even if we go by bus, a bus is only 500 shillings, so two of us cost 1000 – and we paid 3000 twice – so – WE WANT 5000 SHILLINGS BACK IF WE GO ON THE BUS – but we don't want to go on the bus – we want to go to a hotel and we want you to pay for the taxi – what do you mean there are no taxis at this time of night – NO TAXIS NO GOTTDAMIT TAXIS SAUEREI GOTTMITSCHWEIN . . .'

There is a small knot of angry Asians, including Fuad the Farter:

'YES!
WE WANT OUR MONEY BACK!!
NOW!!!'

they shout.

The station master stands, looking sad and impassive, and rather noble.

Over the heads of the rapidly increasing and vociferous crowd, and through the metal grill of the station gates, I see the buses arrive. I streak through the mob, assess which is the bus in best condition, board it and see Miss Norway is already seated at the back by the exit door.

'It will be pretty crowded there, right at the back,' I call out to her.

'Maybe, but it is the safest seat. You heard what that loud woman-person said about the dangers.'

Forty years ago I would have hurried over and sat next to her – the 'Charmingly Shy Englishman' ploy, probably – but now I get into the seat I was aiming at: the only one alone, and with the best view, right in front beside the driver (although he and I are separated by the covering of the mighty diesel engine).

The bus fills up. The seats behind me are at a slightly higher level and are now crammed with passengers. The stowage lockers below them have been filled, and the extra baggage clutters up the central passage: cases, parcels, bales, tourists' tom-toms, rucksacks, some cooking kit.

23.45 hours. We move off on our 310-mile journey. The bus, although battered, is relatively modern, and the driver and I have a panoramic view of the darkened streets of Mombasa through a huge expanse of windscreen. The driver is burly and impassive, an introductionary nod has been our only communication, the thunderous roar of the engine and the yowls of changing gear cogs forbid other intercourse. Besides, he must concentrate. The road (the A 109) is not quite wide enough for two large vehicles to pass, both of them have to put their outer wheels off the tarmac, down the two- to four-inch drop onto the churned-up mud of the verge. This is done at high speed. An additional excitement is the erratic influence of the multitude of pot-holes, deep and jagged, real tyre-rippers. These cause the vehicles to swerve involuntarily. Sometimes a driver will suddenly make an evasive zigzag to avoid a cluster of pot-holes; this is worrying if we are in the process of over-taking him. Even without the holes the road surface would be appalling; it is like driving over sheets of corrugated iron, the continuous bobbing

up and down is beginning to abrade my back on the hard rear of the seat. The male passengers sitting over the wheels must be in a permanent state of 'convoy cock', but all I can see of them is the whites of their eyes reflected in the front screen. We play a sort of game of 'chicken' with the approaching traffic: we charge each other at top speed with headlights blazing, then at the last moment we dodge a few inches out of the way, blaring our horn at the same time. I am kept continuously alert by the sight of accidents, I reckon about one every twenty miles: the very first one we saw was just outside Mombasa, a lorry lying on its back, some people on their hands and knees peering into the flattened remains of the driving cabin.

I am now writing this in the harsh light of a petrol station. We are here thanks to Miss Norway. After a couple of hours our driver stopped; he and a lot of other passengers debussed, lined up like a firing squad and peed into the ditch. Miss Norway ploughed her way through the baggage in the nave and when the driver returned she said: 'The women cannot do this. Stop somewhere where there is a proper lavatory.' The driver did not understand her, or pretended not to, he just shrugged and lit another cigarette: the African male is often reluctant to take orders from women. Miss Norway turned to me: 'You tell him,' she commanded.

I called the driver to attention and pointed to Miss Norway: 'choo', I said. 'Choo-choo, next petrol station.' He nodded dourly.

06.00 hours. A grey, rainy morning: I have passed the last few hours in a semi-conscious daze, lolling half-asleep in my seat, kept awake by the bum-numbing battering below and having to keep leaning forward to relieve the painful abrasion on my spine from the back of my seat, continuously startled into frightened surprise as headlights sear through my half-closed eyelids and sirens bellow in my ear. The streets of Nairobi are drear and wet and dirty and relatively empty.

06.15 hours. The bus rumbles into the station yard. We stopped during the journey a few times, perhaps a total of half an hour, so we have travelled at an average speed of over fifty miles per hour, but we were travelling well over eighty on many occasions. There are only three taxis

parked in the puddled and pot-holed expanse of yard. Hastily thanking and congratulating my neighbour, the driver, I leap out and hurry over to the nearest taxi.

'Muthaiga Club, how much?'

'800 shillings.'

'Nonsense, it is not more than 400 shillings.'

'800 shillings or nothing, it is far, it is raining, there are plenty other passengers.'

Without further ado I hurry off to the next taxi and agree on 500 shillings, being too tired and sleepy to argue. As I am driven away I get a last sight of Miss Norway, bargaining with the first taxi driver: she'll have his guts for garters if he tries anything funny.

Bliss. I am in the Muthaiga Club. I have had a hot bath and am now sitting down to a huge, old-fashioned British Empire breakfast. A flock of ibis caw in the flame trees outside, an orange-flowered hibiscus nearby nods in the warm wind, a smiling waiter has poured me another cup of coffee. The discomfort and worry of last night were worth it, if only to heighten my appreciation of the present. That could be the point of all this travelling.

A callow youth and his car. *Spring 1960.* When my father's father died he left almost all his assets and possessions to the oldest and most perseverant of his five mistresses. Later, when I was a youth, this woman died and one of the assets escaped the leeches who claimed to be her inheritors so I became the owner of an orange grove in South Africa. It was small; the income was just large enough to pay my mess bills as a National Service officer and later my expenses as an undergraduate at Cambridge.

One sad day I received a letter from a Swiss consortium saying that they had bought all the orange groves around mine, and intended to buy that as well. I wrote politely back, saying I did not want to sell. They wrote rudely back saying that if I did not, they would cut off my irriga-

tion supply. I replied that then I would set up a mildew and greenfly rearing station.

I lost the financial quibble, but I did get a lump sum in compensation. Hastily, before my father could give me sensible advice, I spent much of the money in buying a large and impracticable car from another undergraduate who had been unwise enough to marry and then, too late, had discovered that women, once married, hate draughty cars.

Some people find the details of cars excessively tedious, if not incomprehensible, others are rivetted. I show below the specifications of mine in a way that will enable the uninterested to skip over them in one glance:

LAGONDA – 4.5 litre. Type M 45

CONSTRUCTION: 1933

ORIGIN: Great Britain

ENGINE: 6-cylinder Meadows (Henry Meadows Ltd). 4.5 litre, 88.4 mm × 120.6 mm bore and stroke

CAPACITY: 4,429 cc. O.H.V. push-rod operated, 2 per cyclinder. B.H.P. 115 at 3,200 r.p.m. with standard compression ratio of 6:1. Head and block in cast iron, both detachable. Crank-case in light alloys with 4-bearing crankshaft. White metal bearings in bronze shells

IGNITION: dual – by B.T.H. magneto and independent coil and distributor firing two sets of six plugs

CARBURATION: dual, by two horizontal S.U. carburettors

CLUTCH: single plate

GEARBOX: 4-speed close ratio independently mounted, 11.56, 7.36, 4.76, 3.66 to 1

BRAKE: 4-wheel mechanical

CHASIS: Wheelbase 10'-9"

SPRINGS: semi-elliptic

MAXIMUM SPEED: 100.56 m.p.h.

ACCELERATION: 0–60 m.p.h. in 14.6 seconds

CONSUMPTION: 17 m.p.g. (city conditions), 20-gallon rear tank

WEIGHT: 3880 lbs

COACHWORK: open 2/4 seater designed for Sir H. Newbold; racing wings, down-swept boot

COLOUR: British Racing Green

*

The car looked magnificent and although not fast by today's standards it felt like riding a warhorse of the gods when she went thundering and booming down the streets of Paris or Barcelona, her long green snout quivering in front, her iron-studded tyres sending out sheets of fire when I accelerated round sharp corners or raced off at traffic lights. It was extra exciting at speed as she was inclined to 'float' all over the road, and she took about a hundred yards to stop. She had raced in Le Mans in 1934 and come honourably somewhere in the middle. In the days when she was built the Lagondas had their own special place in the lore and legend of cars, particularly in the noise. To connoisseurs all the best cars had their distinctive sound: Hispano Suizas screamed, Bugattis roared, Lagondas boomed and Rolls Royces just sighed. My car was extra fortunate, for it was close enough to the horse and carriage world to inherit some carriage fads, and the U on a number plate was meant to represent the lucky horseshoe. My car's number was AUU 295 – two horseshoes.

It was the long vacation. Three months with nothing to do, with a car of my own, and all the roads of the world spread out before me. (Actually, I had a lot to do, according to my tutors of Political Thought and of Anthropology, but as far as I was concerned Plato, Aristotle, Machiavelli, Malthus, Moore, Hobbes, Marsilio of Padua, William of Occam and any other pontificating pedant could get lost, together with the tribes of the Nuer, the Xhosa, the Ngwato, the Ankole, the Tallensi and even the little old Pygmies.) I packed my bathing-suit, dinner jacket, toothbrush and razor, two each of ties, pants, socks and shirts, my passport and my address book. Then I leapt into the Lagonda and hurried to the continent of Europe.

Having wandered round France for a bit, staying with a variety of friends and relations, I decided to go to Spain. I went via Andorra, entering at the Envalira Pass, 9000 feet up in the Pyrenees. Andorra is well known as one of the smallest countries in the world, with an area of about 180 square miles and a population, when I visited it, of 20,000 people – probably three times that amount now, if Maltheus was correct. It is a co-principality, being ruled partly by Spain (represented by the Bishop of Urgel) and partly by France (once represented by the Conte de Foix, but now by the President of France). The country was

founded in 784 by Charlemagne to act as a buffer to protect France from the Moors. However it was captured by the Muslims and only became a country when peace was declared at the end of the thirteenth century. My AA book said, rather rudely, that its chief source of income was from tourists, smuggling, and the sale of postage stamps. In those days the AA books had interesting and quirky information for the traveller, and their patrolmen wore riding breeches and saluted any car bearing AA badges.

The scenery was magnificent: massive, snow-capped mountains, gorges, cliffs, wooded valleys, waterfalls and tarns, the whole partly obscured by mists and clouds and, unfortunately, by rather too many electric cables and pylons. My Lagonda's radiator was inclined to boil at high altitude, and I had to top it up several times with snow-melt. I finally reached Andorra-la-Vieja, the capital: about the size of Steeple Bumpstead; rather Swiss in appearance, with chalets and timbered houses and people looking as if they had been scrubbed clean in the snow. I stayed the night in a tiny hotel built mainly of logs and with huge projecting eaves.

Early in the lark-filled morning I took the long downhill road into Spain. It may be different now, then it was a zigzag route of different widths: narrow, or very narrow. Sometimes cliffs reared above me, sometimes precipices plunged below. The early-morning sun warmed my forehead, cascades cooled it again as they spattered their spray on my face as I drove past. The wind lightly buffeted my cheeks and tousled my hair. Little green pastures lay tucked into tiny valleys and folds between the mountains; lower down there were cool woods of scented pine or single stands of magnificent sweet-chestnuts.

It was among some chestnuts that I saw the house with the girl. The road had flattened out for a bit, the mountains climbed up on my right, but more gently so that the stream rushing downhill was a torrent rather than a fall. A small valley was to my left, with little pastures and groves of fruit trees. Along the road, half hidden by the tall chestnuts, was a long stone house. It was old, but elegant. The stone was grey, the iron-work above the doors and windows was black. The entrance was large, with double doors big enough to take a carriage. There was a coat of arms carved on the lichen-blotched keystone. The balconies on the first

floor were also carved in stone, with elegant balustrading and sills. From one of the balconies a girl leaned. She was about my age, perhaps a bit younger, about seventeen. She had an immensely long plait of thick black hair, which hung down as if she were the Princess in the Tower. Her eyebrows and eyelashes were also jet black, particularly noticeable on her pale face: the 'sooty fingermarks' which some of the Spanish and Irish have. I slowed down and stopped below her. I looked up at her. The first impression was correct: she was beautiful. I waved. She paused, waved and laughed. Then, wet and timid youth that I was, not having enough daring or resolution to do anything else, I drove on. I got a puncture ten miles on, then an oil leak. I suspected that my Lagonda thought that I had let it down.

Vienna, 29 April 1997. As I set off on the drive from home, I can just see in the dawn light that my stable clock is saying 4.35. This is a typical Queen's Messenger journey: three days, based in Vienna, taking a total of six aeroplanes. All Queen's Messengers like going to Vienna because we go in pairs, using our Embassy there as our base and staying at the same old hotel, so we can have dinner and breakfast together. On this journey Patrick S*** is my fellow Queen's Messenger.

Two milk-floats are the only traffic on the lanes and streets through Colne Engaine, Earls' Colne, Coggeshall, Feering and Kelvedon but the A12 is already quite busy when I get on it near Witham. I pass Hatfield Peveral and hear the five o'clock news on Radio Melody, mostly about the General Election the day after tomorrow. At the Chelmsford by-pass I hear a funny tune on the wireless, the percussion doesn't seem to be keeping in time with the music. Now there is a series of alarming bangs. Oh my God, it's my big end going . . . I am losing power . . . sputter, sputter. There's a sign saying 'SOS Telephone 2 Miles'. Made it. Telephone in the little box. Give efficient policewoman at other end my AA Relay number and ask her to tell the AA to hurry as I must catch an aeroplane from Heathrow at 9.55. I say that I am a Queen's Messenger and she must telephone the Resident Clerk in the Foreign Office to

sitrep Queen's Messenger Patrick S*** and ask him to bring my bags and paperwork to Heathrow as well as his own; also, if I miss the aeroplane, could he take my bags on to Vienna and give them to Rüdi, the meeting driver, to take on to the Vienna Embassy (luckily I do not have to deliver any of them until tomorrow) and leave my passport, tickets etc. with Heathrow Security; I will make my own way to Vienna by a later flight.

The policewoman seems brisk and efficient: I stand miserably by the telephone box, watching the increasing spate of commuter traffic until she rings me back and says 'all tickety-boo at the office' but the AA won't be here for an hour.

I finally move off in a hired car (which will be paid for by the AA) at 6.40: the driver says if all goes well it will take no longer than an hour and a half to Heathrow – plenty of time still for me to check in and meet Patrick.

The M25 – we have been going quite well. The driver is taciturn and a bit dozy; this morning he has already driven from Chelmsford to Gatwick and back.

A hold-up in front: 'Must be an accident, we don't normally get hold-ups here at this time in the morning.'

We creep. I keep looking at my watch. All the traffic is diverted off the road. We follow a huge convoy which seems to be heading the wrong way: north. More diversions, more standstills. The driver turns the wireless on for the news – the IRA. The bastards have put out bomb warnings on the roads to Gatwick and Watford.

Telephone Dominie from the hired car at 7.40 to tell her what has happened and not to worry if she sees my car being towed back. She says it arrived five minutes ago.

This driver is utterly futile. He is obviously lost but won't admit it. We arrived at a T-junction, a road sign said 'WATLING STREET'. 'Oh good, this is the old Roman road to London,' I said. Then the great dunderhead turned *right*. 'Now we're going north, we want to go south!' I wittered. 'What makes you think we're going north?' he asked. 'Look where the sun is, for a start, and if we've hit a north–south road from the east, we must obviously turn left to go south.' When I get annoyed, the top

[121]

of my head itches and prickles, perhaps a remnant of the primitive hair-on-end sign of aggression. (Do the more primitive primates have the ability to stand their hair on end?)

He has been wandering around in a desultory manner for the last half hour; we have already gone through a place called Bushey twice, so I have got a road map from the boot of his car and we are now heading in the right direction on the A312.

I arrived at Heathrow at about 10.45, so checked in on the next British Airways flight to Vienna, the 15.00. Sat in the lounge for over three hours, nibbling Twiglets and reading.

I arrive at Vienna airport and see the tall figure of our driver Rüdi towering above the other people in the arrivals area. As usual, he has a broad smile under his long, wispy walrus moustache. Patrick arrives ten minutes later, from his day flight to and from Sofia. Off we go in the Embassy car.

'What in your notebook are you writing?' asks Rüdi.

'Dandelions.'

'For why are you dandelions writing?'

'There is a terrific lot of them about, on the side of this road, I thought it might be interesting.'

'I do not think so,' says Rüdi crushingly.

Pause.

'Now what is it that you are writing about?'

'I am writing that Rüdi is driving at about a million miles an hour and I am sweating with fright.' Rüdi laughs merrily and accelerates: 'I may be famous, if you put me in your book,' he says.

The ambassador Sir Antony Figgis and I were at Cambridge together. He and his wife Mayella asked me to dinner. The outside of the Residence is handsome but a bit sombre, the inside is attractive and elegant and was full of servants hovering about with trays of drinks. There were about forty guests, and the ambassador introduced me to a variety, all interesting and pleasant enough, ranging from a banker who wants to work with Courtaulds Ltd to the ginger-haired and amusing Irish ambassadress. I sat at the end of the table, amid the rather jolly

wives of bankers and traders. No one seemed to be sulking at being at the bottom of the table, but how many wars or resentments have been caused by people being placed 'below the salt'. After dinner I walked back through the park, and along several side streets, using the great illuminated spire of Saint Stephen's as my beacon. I am now writing this in bed before midnight.

May Day. The Conservatives under the Tin Man want to abolish it, to annoy the socialists. The Conservatives I have always voted for would not have shown such petty spite or historical ignorance. Nor would they have wanted to scrap *Britannia* or talk of substituting Queen's Messengers for an impersonal industrial unit like Group 4. As far as I am concerned, Conservatives conserve what is good and what makes us uniquely British; the changes or innovations they make are primarily to meet new conditions and to protect the helpless. It is Election Day back home, presumably the next government will be another socialist one, but will actually admit its leanings.

The requisites for being a communist seem that one should be small, ugly, dark and annoyed. Patrick and I are spending the early morning wandering round the streets of Vienna, looking at the May Day parades: red banners; marching, rather sullen crowds; people shouting through loudspeakers; uninspiring bands, but all well behaved. They are so well behaved that I am getting disappointed. Some children march past, holding red balloons. 'How about lighting up a large, ostentatious cigar, and using it for popping one of those children's balloons, to get the crowd a bit more animated?' I suggest to Patrick.

'For God's sake,' he mutters, 'it's bad enough that you stand here in a businessman's suit. The very sight of those pinstripes is enough to annoy them.'

We ramble through the streets towards the Dorotheum, the auction house. To either side the shops are all aglitter: jewellery, porcelain and glass, bags and gloves, parades of toy soldiers in the exotic uniforms of the Austro-Hungarian Empire, confectionery shops arrayed with coloured, edible jewels and heaps of chocolates – especially the ubiquitous 'Mozart's Balls'. The squares of Vienna have a charming assortment of street 'furniture': fountains, well heads, statues and of

course the groupings of café tables and parasols. But the streets are often so narrow that one may walk past what seems to be a mere row of shops and will miss the skyscape of domes and urns and wrought ironwork, and lower down the ornamental windows and sashes, the balconies, coats of arms, wreaths in plaster and foliage in marble; the pillars, pilasters, pinnacles, pediments and plaques; the wrought-iron brackets holding lanterns and inn signs; the gold of brand-new gilding and the green of old verdigris: the eccentric juxtapositioning so that Art Deco may be next to Imperial Baroque next to Gothic next to Ultra-modern.

As usual there is a mass of interesting stuff in the Dorotheum, but there is also a lot of rubbish: great clouty bits of furniture with crude and heavy carvings, much of it similar in style to the Spanish – huge wardrobes, box-like cupboards, chunky tables and chests; of Germanic influence are cuckoo clocks with fir-cone weights, chandeliers made from antlers; there are horrible Art Deco and Art Nouveau ornaments – dancing twelve-year-old nymphs, dogs with their heads cocked engagingly, Egyptian goddesses in bronze and ivory, droopy lampshades which look as if they had melted in the heat. Some of the military paintings and prints are interesting: cavalry charges, gallant officers in exotic uniforms, a city besieged. There are many icons, presumably imported from the newly liberated East, I quite like the one of Saint Nicholas of Myra – the original Father Christmas – with fluffy beard and red dressing-gown and, at his feet, the three children pickling in a tub whose corpses he is reputed to have revived. In the silver rooms the few bits of English silver stand out clearly amid the continental stuff. Our shapes are more elegant – stately, almost – the ornamentation less fussy and intrusive. Even the colour is different: English silver has a deep glow; Continental silver has a bright sheen which at its worst looks tinny, or chromium-plated.

Patrick has now flown off to Kiev and I am writing this while sitting under a parasol by a pavement café and having a cup of coffee. There is a fountain nearby. Some undergraduates are sprawled on the steps and talking earnest twaddle about their motivations. A man with a mongrel in a tartan overcoat is playing a flute; the music wafts over the heads of the pedestrians.

[124]

Just my luck, a loonie comes along and sits at the next table and starts shouting. 'Juliano! Juliano!' he yells. He is oldish, with a round, red face, neatly but oddly dressed in a home-made suit of a harlequin mixture of green, blue and purple patches. The manager of the café comes out like an angry hornet and buzzes agitatedly round him. He takes no notice: 'Juliano! Juuuuuuliano! Juliano-Juliano-Juliano Juliaaaaaaano!' he continues to bellow. I sit, writing all this down and concentrating on not catching his eye.

He suddenly leaps up and hurries off.

Rüdi had taken me to the aerodrome so that I can catch the Air Austria flight to Zagreb. Having checked in, I hurry up to the British Airways first-class lounge to nick the newspapers, but some antisocial swine has already done it.

In the waiting area there is a nun: tall, crisply smart in black and brown, with an aesthetic, bony white face. Poor thing. She is wearing wire-rimmed spectacles and a stark black watch with a black dial. I imagine that most women with her elegance would like at least one tiny touch of vanity.

My flight is to be on a Tyrolean Dash 8/300. It has two propellers and fifty seats. I follow the nun up the steps of the aeroplane. Well, well – vanity after all, her shoes are immaculate and expensive and have three-inch high heels. Her leather belt is polished and hand-stitched.

My seat is next to the nun. She is holding a Croatian passport in one hand and a rosary of large, polished black beads in the other. She must think that I am some sort of weirdo but I cannot stop peering closely at her habit: I can hardly believe it, but I think it is tailored from the finest bombasine, a fabric hardly seen since I tramped the streets around Commercial Road as a young yarn and fibre salesman: a silk warp with a two-fold worsted-spun weft. Her wimple is woven from a very fine long-stapled cotton yarn, completely free of slub or nep, and between veil and habit she has an ornate shawl of crocheted lace. I take another close peek and look up – oops – I received a cold, ice-blue glare right between the eyes.

The engines rev up and we begin to take off. The nun grits her teeth, leans back with her eyes tight shut and thumbs rapidly through her

rosary. You'd have thought someone like her would welcome a fatal accident.

Lunch on the aeroplane: two slices of shiny pink plastic folded neatly and placed on a small slice of white polystyrene, a thicker pink slice, mottled, half sunk in some greenish slime which the nun might describe as a 'mess of potage', and two tiny gherkins – a vegetable as nasty as the name suggests. For pud, something yellow and absorbent, which has already sopped up much of the thin red juice it is soaking in. Neither the nun nor I eat any of it. The nun settles down to sleep, but every now and then her eyes snap open and she glares suspiciously at me.

Busy six hours: arrive at Zagreb mid-afternoon to exchange bags. Take off about a quarter of an hour later; met by Rüdi at Vienna aerodrome; liaise with Patrick and the Embassy escort who helps me onto the next flight back to London; the office, then HOME!

My birthday tomorrow – fifty-nine! God, how old. And I have to go back to London to talk on the Debbie Thrower Show on Radio 2 about my last book being reissued as a paperback. And the election results – presumably Labour will get in. I hope Candy's boss, of whom she is very fond, isn't one of the ones to get the chop. (Next day: Labour land-slide, but Nicholas Soames was returned. Also next day: a message from the Embassy. After returning the car there last night, Rüdi went off on his motor-bicycle and was killed in an accident. What a waste of such a gentle, likeable man. We all will miss him very much.)

 **Ankara, 8 May 1997.** I have a chameleon mind which subconsciously adapts itself to its surround-ings: so if I am in a dank, gloomy place I feel dank and gloomy; if all around me are full of *joie-de-vivre* and excitement, so am I. As I step out into the heights of Ankara at seven o'clock on a warm, sunny morning just after breakfast, I get a sudden illogical wave of pleasure: a foreign place to explore, new people and places and things to see. I have planned to spend all morning walking around

Ankara, and I have two aims which make this walk purposeful: to see a tree, and to buy an axe head.

The tree is *Corylus colurna* – the Turkish hazel or Constantinople nut tree. I bought four of these recently on an impulse, mainly because I dote on hazel nuts but also because of the description in Hilliers' catalogue: 'a remarkable, large tree of very symmetrical, pyramidal form. The striking, corky corrugations of the bark are an attractive feature.' It grows up to eighty feet high and is apparently a magnificent sight when covered with its 'lambs' tails'. The nut harvest from a big tree must be immense. My little saplings are only waist high: it would be interesting to see a large tree growing in its place of origin. I presume that there will be at least one growing in the parks near the Embassy.

This city is basically unattractive, constructed *en bloc* seventy years ago and now beginning to fall apart. Its great virtue is similar to that of Amman: it is built amid a series of hills and gorges which give scenic interest; one always seems to be looking down steep streets or up at hillsides cluttered with buildings. These, although ugly, are often roofed with terracotta pantiles which makes the city appear, from afar, much more venerable and cosy than it is. Clumps of tall fastigiate poplar add a touch of nature and hide, with their fountaining leafy branches, some of the starker concrete wallings. A few of the gorges are too steep for construction, and many of them have been turned into parks: plantings of semi-wild trees and shrubs between which thread precipitous paths and steps. The two parks near the hotel are typical of this. One is called the Segmenler Park, the other is the botanical gardens.

The former has a stream running down the centre, at the bottom of the valley. It is collected in shallow pools which spill over stone-built waterfalls. Pools and the stream are paved with squared cobbling. It is not as attractive as it should be because there seems to be no wild life in the water of any sort, neither flora nor fauna. I discover the reason why when I reach the source, a large pool in an amphitheatre: the waters smell strongly of chlorine. During my perambulation along the stream I kept an eye out for the nut tree. The season here is about the same as in England: the same weeds are flowering in abundance, mainly dandelions and daisies; also flowering are the apples, plums, cherries, snowy mesphilus, Judas trees, mahonia and forsythia; the trees beside the water

bear pussy-willows and lambs' tails. Magpies look down at me from the holes in the sides of their large round nests. But no sign of a nut tree. I stroll on, past couples who sit primly on the park benches. Generally the good-looking girls are in jeans and T-shirts; the plainer ones in the normal Muslim kit of headscarf, cardigan and frowsty frock. I suppose if you can't be pretty you may as well be good. A bearded man tries to sell me a sheep skin. If I wanted a sheep skin I'd skin one of my own. Another man is selling rugs, good ones presumably, but I do not need one, so thank him politely and sidle off.

I have left the first park and am still walking uphill, now in the botanical gardens. The plantings here are more formal and more varied than in the Segmenler Park, but there still is no sign of the nut tree.

I have reached the foot of the Atakule Tower, which sprouts like a great mushroom 400 feet above me. You can get a view of most of Ankara from the revolving restaurant-cum-lookout at the top. No need to go up it: from here I can see my next destination, the Citadel of Ankara, and the scale on my map tells me that it is almost five miles away as the crow flies. I have already been walking for about an hour, so I'd better stop brooding at the view and start off at once.

Having turned about at the tower, I have been walking downhill for the last half hour, but I could not relax because the pavements were interrupted by many little and unexpected steps. I walked through three basic areas: first the diplomatic and governmental – quite good modern buildings with excellent gardens; then the residential quarters – relatively quiet with blocks of flats and offices; now the ground is levelling out into the valley bottom and I am in the shopping area. The window-dressing is still in the 1950s. In the cobbler's the shoes are neatly displayed in their open boxes, in rows according to size; a food shop exhibits tiered stacks of tins and biscuit boxes; in the clothes shops the models, hairstyles and all, are of brown plastic, chipped and cracked, with jerseys folded and heaped into piles, hangers of trousers aligned on racks, skirts pinned to the walls, gloves and socks, all knitted from scratchy-looking wool, splayed out fanwise on the flooring. There are many street vendors selling rings of something brown and baked and covered with seeds: simitos. I buy one – 15,000 lire, which sounds a fortune but is only about seven pence. A bit dull, just bread; not unlike those bagels and pretzels

which Americans make such a fuss about, making them a sort of folk-food, but which taste like ordinary buns or biscuits.

There are two policemen at the cross-roads nearby: one is leisurely and graceful, his arms sinuously undulate like a Siamese dancer's; the other is impatient and abrupt, he jabs fiercely in various directions and peep-peep-peeps at his whistle. Both men are equally ineffective, neither technique works, no one takes any notice of them. The traffic is appalling, and adds to its offensiveness by emitting huge quantities of pollution. The distant hilltops are hazed over with a brownish mist, my mouth is dry and has an iron taste in it.

This steep uphill lane which leads towards the Citadel is full of jew-ellers' shops: lots of gold bangles and necklaces on display, all defended by heavy iron gratings. I come to an antique shop. Some of the items are labelled in English; one label says 'Circumcision Box'. The box is mainly brass with painted plaques on the top and sides. It has a lock and key. Who on earth would want to steal the contents? And it is about nine by five by four inches. Surely, that is huge for what will be put inside? It reminds me of an unkind remark made about one of my father's Jewish friends, rather small and wrinkled: 'When they circumcised Lord ***, they threw away the wrong bit.'

I am looking up from the foundations of the Citadel. Between its fifteen defensive towers the walls resemble huge slices of pinky-puce fruitcake. Among its irregular chunks of stone are embedded the marble butts of pillars, neat blocks of ashlar, tablets inscribed in Roman, a crudely hewn Christian cross, carved lions – all this in a jumble of Galatian lintels, Roman arches, Crusader battlements, Ottoman windows. Sometimes a pigeon will flap from its nest in a lancet window. Swifts scream and wheel above my head. Why are there no raptors? This should be an ideal place for something like the hobby, fast and agile enough to catch those swifts.

I tramp the cobbled streets and courtyards inside the Citadel. Little houses lean and lurch and are flaking, built for tiny people, some of the door lintels are lower than my shoulder. The gaps between the upright beams are filled with a herringbone arrangement of bricks or tiles. One building is so old and rickety that the arrangement looks like rows of starving old men, the beams their arms, the tiles their ribs.

I try to enter the battlemented fortlet at the top. From it flies the Turkish flag. Its main entrance is locked and there are military-type notices; there is a side door but it is obscured by a line of washing and a bundle of barbed wire.

I see plenty of women and children. The only men are a grizzled old man selling plastic buckets and basins, and a man with tractor and trailer selling potatoes and onions. The people living in the Old Town are officially classified as 'needy', but I reckon that they are happier and more content than the frantic milling mob below them, and they seem prosperous enough to produce a great many fat, well-dressed children.

I am now at the highest point of the Citadel. To get here one has to pass a defensive barricade of women knitting with fine steel needles and selling the resulting lace mats and embroidery. The main construction is a semicircular wall, perhaps the remains of a huge round tower. It is pierced by lancet windows. They seem a bit pointless to me: I look through a couple and all one would see of the enemy is their heads three or four furlongs away, out of shot, or eyeball-to-eyeball once they have scaled the walls and peer back at you through your window. I am standing on the wall, about five feet thick. The swifts and swallows are now flying below me. The view is magnificent: a panorama of red-tiled roofs, minarets, poplar trees, skyscrapers; at eye-level to my right, at the other end of the Citadel, the flag is flying from the military post; directly opposite, over five miles away, the mushroom shape of the Atakule Tower where I was two hours ago. There is no one here but for three small children standing near me, flying a kite. Odd, below is a city of millions of people, yet not one of them wants to come up here to have a look, or even to sit and think; not even any tourists.

I leave from a great arched gateway to the nearby food market. Most of the stalls are selling sacks of pulses, nuts, corn, cereals and dried fruit. Behind them I find the hardware shop where I once bought some sheep bells. I remember there were some large axe heads, of the size I want. I have lost my seven-pound axe head and nowadays English ironmongers only stock weedy five-pounders or less. There are metal containers of every size and shape, mattocks, adzes and pickaxes, scythes, sickles and bill-hooks, scales and knives and everything you need in metal except for axe heads.

Back in my hotel room. I have been walking for about five hours, much of it uphill. Neither of the intentions of my walk has been fulfilled: no nut tree, no axe head. But I feel content enough. I have broken one of my rules and have taken a drink out of my room's mini-bar, a bottle of local beer. I have taken off my shoes and socks. The socks lie on the floor, steaming and twitching. I pick them up and put them in one of the sanitary towel disposal bags I always carry for botanical samples. Time to pack and go.

 **The strange French – – –** Most Englishmen of my age have mixed emotions about the French. It is annoying that we were successfully invaded by a small band of Frogs in 1066. It is strange that they play rugger, and can even beat us at it. There was Brigitte Bardot, but there were also those hairy little crones who sat in doorways and stared and knitted.

The food: for an Englishman, there was something almost pervertedly debauched in eating frogs and snails, and garlic, and runny cheeses with pungent smells. Those tiny peas – a sort of greedy infanticide – salads with all manner of peculiar leaves in them: burnet, rocket, dandelion, watercress, sorrel – how recklessly carefree to browse on weeds. Veal – typical of the French cavalierly to interrupt the natural process of development into beef, and to smother the result in sauces made from wine, and cream, and toadstools. Those matchstick chips: golden and brittle, how pertly unlike the pallid English chip with its bad attack of brewer's droop. And of course to eat all this while sitting, unconcerned in the middle of a pavement, staring at the fascinating people chattering past: and it is not even raining.

My feelings about the French are even more complicated than those of the average Briton. Just off the city-port of La Rochelle, in the stormy waters of the Bay of Biscay, there are several islands. The largest of these, the Ile d'Oléron, is where my family lived until 1685 when Louis XIV revoked the Edict of Nantes, thus causing thousands of Protestants, the Huguenots, to flee to the more tolerant states of

North-West Europe, British South Africa and British North America. My family went to London, and set up as silversmiths; a hundred years later we turned to textiles and moved to North Essex.

I still have some French relations. When I first visited them I discovered that although the British are adept at producing eccentric men, the French can hold their own with dotty females, with two of them in particular.

Bordeaux, in parts, is one of the most elegant and sedate cities I have visited. Forty years ago, when my Lagonda boomed over the bridge which spanned the river Garonne, I could see, along a five-mile long curve of the river, a crescent of wide quays bordering its waters, with a background of tall mansions and warehouses; on the other side were rows of merchants' houses, solidly built in the traditional French materials of stone, slate, iron and lead. Between them, silent and stately, squares opened up, seemingly each with a statue of a mounted general. The whole city was planned in the eighteenth-century fashion, with wide streets, and radial points or open spaces which added emphasis to important items such as the cathedral of Saint André, the Grand Théâtre and the two rostral columns which serve as lighthouses.

I had come to stay with Madame Croixrouge. She was the matriarch of one of the old merchant families of the city. She lived in one of the larger mansions in one of the smaller squares: it seemed to take up most of the side of the sleepy, tree-filled enclosure. The house was extremely dirty. The shutters sagged at their hinges. The metalwork on the balconies was rusting. However the doorway was filled with a pair of well-kept double doors. There was a smaller, human-sized door let into one of them. The ornate handle of a bellpull dangled beside it. I hauled at it and something tolled within. Silence fell. Nothing happened. After a few minutes I pulled the bell again, but more urgently. My carillon was ignored. A seemly wait of a few minutes, and then a pumping action on the bellpull. Silence once more. Then scuffling noises, the squeak and scrape of bolts being drawn and clank of locks undone. The door creaked open and revealed a small woman standing in a courtyard. She was dressed in the traditional garb of the concierge, a rusty black dress, wrinkled stockings and huge, dirty shoes distorted by bunions: they

looked like boulders barnacled with limpets. A greying moustache added another touch of authenticity. Five strings of massive pearls subtracted from it.

'You must be George,' she said in a throaty murmur like Eartha Kitt at her most velvety. 'MacKenzie is out, shopping, so you must open these doors to drive your car in.'

After my car had been comfortably ensconced in the cobbled yard, my hostess led me indoors.

The entrance hall was colossal. Tier after tier of stone balconies rose towards the indistinct gloom of the ceiling; a howling draught caused the tapestries to billow and the chandeliers, draped with cobwebs, to sway. A beautiful marble staircase reared up from the marble hall and separated into two sweeping wings which reached the first floor. An empty fireplace gaped blackly opposite the stairway, the stuffed head of a rhinoceros glowered above it, a tiny but utterly hideous tartan rug stretched out before. Madame Croixrouge saw me looking at it. 'Hélas, MacKenzie presents me that, to my infinite regret,' she said. There was little other furniture or ornamentation: a battered sedan chair mouldered in a corner, a heap of old swords, pikes and carbines was stacked in another; a large Gothic chest was against one wall. That was all.

My bedroom was hardly more cheerful. The huge posted bed was slightly aslant, and rocked horribly when I put my luggage on it. The overhead tester was solid oak, with dusty ostrich feathers at each corner. It must have weighed nearly twelve stone and did not look at all safe. I resolved to sleep away from the bed, rather than in it. There were five pictures in the room, two Fragonards, a Watteau, a Picasso and an incompetent daub by a child. My hostess pointed proudly at it. 'My eldest son, mon choufleur Guillème, he paints that when he is a sweet little child. Now, hélas, he is fat and bald and boring, but he is still quite nice. You will meet him and the rest of my family at dinner, before the dance.'

I have rarely heard anything more seductive than her voice when she said 'mon choufleur Guillème', just like the purring of a contented panther. It was a pity, I thought, that she looked more like a very old and battered pekinese.

Dinner was pleasant enough: the dining-room was warm, the food

good, the company amusing. Madame Croixrouge had invited her five sons and their wives, also a married British couple who were local wine shippers, the British consul and his wife, and her eldest granddaughter with whom I instantly fell in love. She was not outstandingly pretty but she had her grandmother's seductive cooing voice and a fascinating way of laughing, throwing her head back so I could peer past the glittering rows of pearly teeth into the moistly pink cavities beyond.

Madame Croixrouge's entrance before dinner was dramatic. The rest of the party had assembled in the hall. A small fire had been lit on the heap of ashes, corks and cigarette ends which covered the hearth. MacKenzie, a freckled and wiry little man in his early seventies, was dealing out the drink.

'It is either whisky or beer,' he said. 'Madame wishes this to be a British night.'

'Neither thanks, I'm not thirsty,' I said.

He looked at me with amazement. 'Jinks, at last I know what a "callow youth" is,' he said.

'Don't mind old MacKenzie, a bit eccentric,' whispered one of Madame Croixrouge's sons, 'war wounds. He has told me that he was wounded fighting with the Highland Light Infantry during the First World War.'

'Surely not, mon frère,' said another, 'he has intimated to me that it was the King's Own Scottish Borderers.'

'Non,' interrupted one of the wives, 'it was the Seaforth Highlanders.'

'Actually,' said the consul, 'he was invalided out of the Catering Corps after having an eardrum perforated by the explosion of a ten-pound tin of fermented peas.'

'Whatever, he has his uses,' said another brother, 'for example, he sleeps with our mother and that makes her more content.'

Our hostess descended the stairs. The flight of steps had been designed for dramatic entries, and Madame Croixrouge made the most of it. At first I could not see much, just a twinkle or two in the dusty gloom at the top of the staircase, but as she descended the twinkles became more numerous and I was able to discern their origins. The lowest came from some shoe-buckles, then from the jewels which

studded the *skian dhus* which she wore tucked in the garters of both stockings. Her sporran looked home-made from the corpse of a small, tawny creature (later, I learned that it had been a dearly loved cat called Alphonse), star sapphires glittered where its eyes once were. Her right hand, encrusted with diamonds, played idly with the basketed hilt of a claymore. Her plaid, whose tasselled fringe disclosed its origins as a travelling rug, was held in place by a Cairn Gorm brooch the size of a golf ball. The tartan of her stockings was MacDonald, of her kilt, Royal Stewart and her plaid was of the MacLeods. The whole ensemble was crowned by a French sailor beret, blue with a red bobble. Eight terriers followed her downstairs. They were of that nervy, testy species which yaps whenever you catch its eyes. The dogs had no individual names, collectively they were called 'Le Clan MacCroixrouges'.

Her family let out a variety of resigned sighs. MacKenzie ground his teeth so that his cheek muscles palpitated in and out.

We danced to the music of a very ancient gramophone. It was all Scottish dancing, of course. MacKenzie was kept busy: he had to wind up the gramophone, hand out the drinks and partner his mistress. The last thing I remember of that evening was standing to attention while Madame Croixrouge played *God Save the Queen* on the bagpipes. Every clansman of the MacCroixrouges was howling in concert to the piping, MacKenzie was mopping his eyes within the secret confines of the sedan chair: I could not tell if his tears and the howling of the clan were through nostalgia for their banks and braes, or anguish at the excruciating piping of their mistress.

After my stay with the Croixrouges I drove my car to Biarritz to stay with Cousin Eugenie. In the same way as Madame Croixrouge was keen on Scotland, so Eugenie was fond of royalty.

She lived in a flat in one of the few old buildings left which overlooked the Atlantic. Her rooms were swathed in heavy velvet and encrusted with gilded carvings: large pelmets over the windows, swarming with flocks of cherubs and cherubim; massive picture frames, emblazoned with the coats of arms of those portrayed; plaques, either of shields from which sprouted pikes, swords and other weapons, or wheat-sheaves holding together sprays of flowers, streamers of fruit and swags of vegetables. The chimneypiece of the drawing-room was

similarly burdened with gilding and carving, but, more to my taste, nude nymphs held up the mantle shelf and writhed around the frame of the looking-glass above it. Compared with these massy fixtures, the furniture looked spindle-shanked and unbalanced, mostly Louis XV and XVI: Rococo commodes, tables and chairs, all curves and undulations, their lumpy bodies on skimpy little bow legs like dachshunds; secretaires with marble tops, boule friezes and fluted legs; Baroque sofas smothered in brocades and brocatelle. Cousin Eugenie slept in a state bed and she still insisted that the covering should be of the traditional thirty-three parts.

A grand piano took up much of the drawing-room. It was burdened with framed photographs. All the men in the photographs wore ornate uniforms heavily embellished with medals, ribbons and badges, the features of most of them hidden under hair: beards, moustaches, Dundreary whiskers, mutton-chops, bugger's grips – the lot. The women were generally tall and elegant, wore tiaras and evening dresses with their trains curled around their feet, their elegantly long necks festooned in rank upon rank of pearls.

'Do you play that piano?' I asked Cousin Eugenie.

She allowed an inscrutable smile to flit over her well-chiselled features, as white as snow with powder and with a scarlet slash for a mouth: 'Poor Rudolph,' she replied obscurely, 'for him, the only music was the singing of the wolves.'

Conversing with her left me completely at a loss, she was incapable of answering anything directly and replied with hints and innuendoes of such complexity and obscurity that I was left weltering in doubt and confusion. Questions like 'What time is lunch?' were answered with 'I never liked the peacocks, myself, but the old marquese used to laugh and say that we should only have the quails' eggs before the guns fired the evening salvo.' 'Where is the nearest shop which sells postcards?' was met with 'We always went in the landau to the chocolate house. Just a small troop of hussars behind, we liked to go incognito, of course.' Her most abstruse reply was 'Better an adjutant who has an unnatural passion for the regimental mascot than a padre who smokes a pipe.' The chain of thought which prompted that remark was my observation that my brother Sam still bit his fingernails.

Strange people kept coming and going. Most of them were old, handsome and melancholy, some were more unusual: a small man wearing an embroidered dressing-gown, the deposed sultan of an Indonesian island; a shifty type with a Lancashire accent (learned from his nanny, apparently) and a suitcase full of scents and soaps, whose mother had been princess in some Ruritanian kingdom and his father a communist commissar; two gloomy Jews dressed in the deepest black, who told me that they were always in mourning at this time of year, it was the festival of the ascension into heaven of their ancestor the Virgin Mary. Cousin Eugenie's particular friend was a small and wispy female, dressed in expensive but nondescript grey silks and voiles. 'Poor Catherina,' said Cousin Eugenie one evening, as the wispy friend left, whittering goodbyes, 'she has remained unmarried, for although she inherited her father's immense estates, she also inherited his large cavalry moustache.'

On my second day there Cousin Eugenie pointed to the telephone: 'Pick up that machin-chose there,' she said, 'and dial 6. It will be answered by the hall porter. Tell him we are going for an outing and desire my conveyance to be waiting outside.' I did so, rather dubiously, but the porter answered civilly enough and with no apparent surprise.

Cousin Eugenie appeared from her boudoir. She had donned her clothing for the journey, an immensely long coat, gloves, a muff and a huge hat with a veil, and she carried a rug embroidered with Napoleonic bees. 'A souvenir, one is not related to those Corsican paysans.' We rattled down to ground level in the palsied birdcage which served as a lift.

Her transport was parked alongside the kerb, just outside the door. It was a bath chair, of wickerwork, with a handle at the back and a tiller at the front which was attached to the fore wheel.

She settled herself in, adjusted her coat and the rug about her person, and then stared at me. I looked vacantly back.

'You have both the privilege of passenger and the pleasure of postilion,' she remarked, somewhat tartly. I had grown used enough of her to realise that she meant 'Push'. Off we set. She was a rotten driver, quietly dithering. We zigzagged along pavements, we rammed lamp-posts, we wandered into doorways. Every time we did so, she blamed

me. I could now recognise the reproof 'the Kara-Georgeviches liked the excitement of the boar hunt, but they were rather nouveau riche, I regret.' 'It was unfortunate that the Admiral could not swim, and of course his epaulettes were absolument énorme.'

At least she was no speed maniac. 'Slower,' she kept saying, 'we are not escaping the assassins.' However, if I dawdled too much, I would hear some remark such as 'The dear Maharaja used to tell me that even the sacred beast of Shiva should sometimes be woken from its dreams of the Upper Plains.' Occasionally her gloved hand would appear from the depth of her muff as she graciously replied to a greeting; sometimes I would have to stop when she decided to chat.

It was all very peaceful somehow. From afar I could hear the subdued mumble of the Atlantic rollers as they broke on the beach; gulls squawked above our heads; Cousin Eugenie's veil fluttered in the sea-breeze; courtly old men and elegant old women bowed and smiled and nodded. Occasionally I would meet a pusher such as I, usually a nanny with a pram, but sometimes another bath chair propellant, and then we would bow and nod and smile in comradeship. And as we progressed Cousin Eugenie reminisced about royalty and relations, friends and servants; deposed, or dead and gone, or retired or mad or ill.

 **Jerusalem, 14 May 1997.** I have delivered the diplomatic bags to the Jerusalem Consulate and have been told that I can have four hours free. I thought I'd go and see the tombs on the Mount of Olives. This is one of the most important places for Jew, Christian and Muslim to be buried for it is where the Last Trump is to be blown, and those buried there will be the first in the queue outside the pearly gates. (Personally, I think hell will have begun when one finds oneself standing in a queue with one hundred thousand billion other people, and some shortsighted old dotard with reference books and a team of winged bureaucrats fussing about him. It will be worse than the immigration department at Lagos airport.) As I arrived at the parking space above the Jewish section, the guides – aware of my nationality because of the Union Jack pasted on

my windscreen – swarmed towards me yelling: 'The Crook!' 'The Crook!' 'I show you the Tomb of the Crook!' Sad irony that the modern pilgrim to the Holy City is presumed to want a visit to Maxwell's grave as his priority. Actually I did want to see Maxwell's tomb, to see if there are any suitably insulting graffiti upon it, but I was too ashamed to admit it. Having pottered around a few graves, I returned to my car and asked my driver Zosimus where he could take me that I had not been before.

'Have you been to Yad Vashem, the Martyrs' and Heroes' Remembrance Monument?'

I told him that I have never wanted to go, thinking that it was perhaps an intrusion into somewhere private and special for Jews; and even if not, I would be sickened by what I saw. Zosimus told me that I must go: even he, a Christian Arab, with no particular affection for his Jewish neighbours, understood more about them after he had been round.

Yad Vashem is a ten-acre complex of buildings and gardens in memory of the people who suffered in the Holocaust. It is about twenty minutes' drive from the Old City of Jerusalem.

Zosimus squeezes our car between long files of parked tourist buses and I disembark. Having bought a disgracefully expensive tourist guide, I walk up the Avenue of the Righteous Among the Nations to the Ohel Yizkor, the Hall of Remembrance. This is a square block of a building, a mixture of huge boulders cobbled together with plain concrete walls. Inside, it is dark and impressive. An eternal flame flickers in a hearth of spiky, blackened stalagmites which look like a random huddle of folded bats' wings. In front of it is a simple slab. This covers a vault filled with human ashes collected from most of the death camps. I am joined by a gawping gang of tourists, all from the same bus, mainly American and late middle-aged. The men are mainly pot-bellied, the woman with fleshy, sunburned arms; both sexes wear shorts and gym-shoes and floppy sunhats and dark glasses and they tout cameras. Their holiday appearance seems very inappropriate in these stark surroundings. Equally inappropriate are my fatuously unsuccessful attempts to keep on the cardboard skullcap known as a *kipa*, with which I was issued at my entry.

[139]

Next I got to the Holocaust and Heroism Museum. The permanent exhibition here is mainly pictorial, some posters and press cuttings, but usually photographs which illustrate the growth of anti-Semiticism in the Nazi world. It tells of a not-unusual tale of human stupidity and ignorance creating bigotry, and the resulting progress from rudeness to unkindness to cruelty to unspeakable horror. The first scenes are of bullying and harassment, the next of persecution and control, followed by destruction and death: a sequence of events which starts from the loutish behaviour of individuals to its co-ordination into the more thorough systems of state control. I am reminded that in Montenegro a Serb professor told me that he hated Italians and Croatians more than Germans, for the former took more pleasure in their cruelty; with the Germans it was nothing personal, they were just taking pride in their efficiency.

The scenes of mass misery are terrible, but not as moving as of individual suffering: a small boy, his peaked cap at a Just William angle, holding his arms up in surrender while soldiers aim their guns at him; an old, frightened man with a white beard surrounded by a mocking crowd of beefy Teutons; a woman, clutching a child to her body, her back to the man who is about to fire a rifle bullet into her head. It shows lines of people queuing for the gas chambers, of emaciated bodies lying helpless in rows on concrete floors, of corpses being shovelled into the incinerators, of rotting flesh and skeletons. It is all a dreadful reminder that the human body which can be so beautiful can also look so horrible, that the human spirit which can be so inspired and proud can be so afraid and abject and ashamed. Shame is a surprisingly dominant element, not just the shame of deliberate humiliation, of a gang of mocking louts overseeing some upper-class Jewish women scrubbing a pavement, but the sort of senseless shame which makes some poor naked girls who, although in an ecstasy of terror, yet try to hide their nudity from the firing squad.

And it all ends with victory: with pictures of the vanquished murderers: great big butch brutish surly scowling women; insignificant men looking scared and mean and wearing overcoats which are suddenly too big for them.

I step outside into the clean, pine-scented sunshine. A steady trickle

of people are exiting beside me. I try to analyse their reactions by their faces, but most people are expressionless, even the groups of adolescents and army recruits who, in the early stages of the exhibition, were looking bored or even giggling one to another. What can a Jew feel? 'Indignation' may sound trite but there must be much of it. Someone in the Embassy told me that she had been 'emotionally drained'. I am the opposite, my mind is bursting with emotion: rage and pity, and I feel ashamed that my hatred for the perpetrators is almost as intense as my pity for the victims. After all, it was rage and hate which started it all.

A furlong off is the Children's Memorial. I descend down an open, narrow passage, past some enlarged photographs of children's faces and into what seems to be a vast darkness lit with thousands of tiny flickering lights. It is as if I am stepping into outer space. Apparently there are only five little candles, but a complexity of mirrors turns this into an infinity. I tip-toe a maze-like course in the heavy gloom, following arrows only just visible upon the floor. The silence of my progress and the stillness of the darkness all about make me feel as if I am floating through the hollows of space between the stars. I do not know if anyone else is here, but I feel utterly alone, with just the faint, far-off trumpeting of a shofar and a slow, sonorous voice tolling out the names and ages of murdered children, one and a half million of them.

I stand outside, calculating: if they are reading out names at about eight to the minute, it will take 130 days to read them all. The group of tourists emerges. All are silent, a few are wiping their eyes. Their holiday clothes seem no longer tactless, just rather pathetic and joyless.

I wander around the gardens. Every tree and bush bears a commemorative plaque. There are many sculptures. Some are obscure: the amoeboid blob or the jumble of scrap-iron which may have meant a lot to the sculptors but which means damn-all to me, but most are of a high standard. I particularly admire – it is impossible to like, it is too horrific – the tangle of charred, skeletonic limbs and bodies called the Monument to the Victims of Death Camps, but although it is dramatic it seems to have no heartening message. Just 'For us the past was frightful – and we have no future.' Many of the other sculptures, like the

photographs, demonstrate the trite fact that the Way to Death involves an awful lot of queuing.

Zosimus has managed to park right by the entrance. As I get in the group of tourists trudges past, towards their bus. Faces are grim, some of the women have red noses.

'This is not an easy place for a Jew to visit,' I say.

'Or a German,' replies Zosimus.

Or any human being, capable of shame or pity.

I am on the way back to Tel Aviv and I thought I'd go via the Arab village of Abu Ghosh and see the Crusader church. The diplomatic bag I have got is large, nevertheless I am taking it with me rather than leaving it in the car.

I ring a bell by the locked door. A monk comes out, looks at me, looks at the bag, and having pointed curtly at the tradesmen's entrance disappears, the door self-locking behind him with a click. Peeved, I ring again. Pause. I ring once more. A man pops out, a different monk but the same sort of farce: he espies the bag, says 'Rien aujourdui, merci' and vanishes before I have time to expostulate.

Ring again.

'Tu es encore là! Tire toi!'

'I want to get in to see the church,' I shout.

He looks dubious: 'What is in that bag?'

'That is my concern, if I want to carry it about it should be no worry for you.'

Looking uneasy, he lets me in.

The great hulk of the church has an impressive, spartan simplicity. There is a large and airy but dank and gloomy crypt. Voices echo up from it, monks are sweeping the stone floor, making exactly the same scraping-swishing noise that I hear when my stables at home are being swept clean. The main body of the church above it is lofty and dark. I can just see a few frescoes, tatty and scabby but interesting as they are rare examples of the period when the artistry of Byzantium and Francia overlapped. It all would be serene and peaceful but for the presence of a couple of little monks who keep twittering about and looking at me out of the corner of their eyes and counting the candlesticks as I pass.

Havana, 28 May 1997. I haven't been to Cuba for some time. It is interesting to see the difference that three more years of Communism have made. For a start, it is quieter. There is even less traffic – Havana's traffic this Wednesday is similar to that of London on a sleepy Sunday morning. Although the great old dinosaurs of the Chevrolets, Buicks and Cadillacs still lurch and rattle down the streets, there are fewer of them, many have died of old age (even the youngest is nearly forty years old – since Castro took power) and they are terribly expensive on the scarce petrol. There are more people on bicycles, more motor-bikes with sidecars, very large crowds of people waiting at bus stops. Communism always seems to equate with queuing. The bus stop has taken the place of the parish pump as the communal meeting place. Secondly, everyone seems more subdued. My escort told me that is because the police and military have been harassing the populace recently. Although the people in Havana look reasonably fit and fat, the hunger and poverty in the countryside is dreadful. I saw some evidence of this as I flew over yesterday: much of the agricultural land looked threadbare, there was almost no vehicular traffic on the country lanes. Therefore many people have been illegally sneaking into Havana. As a result the Ministry of the Interior organised a sweep of the streets of the capital. Suddenly the city was filled with even more uniforms: police, military and the Avispas Negras, the 'Black Wasps', the élite units of pro-Castro men. They stopped people in the streets – even woke them up in their houses – and if they did not have the appropriate passes they were trucked back to the rural areas, about 110,000 people in all.

My hotel, not the dingy little pit I had stayed at previously, is a new skyscraper: clean, smart, efficient, slick. There are in-house shops and they sell expensive things: jewellery, leather, pictures, and no longer do you have to fill in a form in quadruplicate just to buy a postcard. However, at the entrance of each lift and at the bottom of each stairway there is a black-suited civilian with sharp eyes and a walkie-talkie.

I am having an opulent breakfast. Unlike the previous hotel the clientèle is not longer bullet-headed East German and Slav trades-union leaders with their frowsty wives, instead it is full of sleek men in well-

tailored short-sleeved shirts and with snake-skin belts holding up neatly pressed trousers. Many are French businessmen, following their nation's skills as the industrial vultures of the world. But what is left to pick in this desiccated corpse of a country? Even fifteen years ago I found it impossible to do business with the Cubans: on one contract we agreed that as they had no money they could pay us in four and a half million oranges; by the time their bureaucrats had finished with the paperwork all the oranges had gone mouldy.

I set off at half past eight for a morning's walk around the city. The sky is clear, there is a slight wind, but it is already hot and muggy. There are many low walls, often enclosing semi-abandoned building sites. Every wall has its perchment of men roosting on it: one man is working a power drill on a bit of pavement, seven men sit on a wall beside him and watch. The idle always seem to like to watch the busy: is it nostalgia, or gloating? The long seaside wall along the Malecón is no longer aligned with the pairs of lovers it had last night; they have been replaced by single men, and the occasional fisherman.

I pass a sign of emerging capitalism: a disused building plot with people standing in the shade of large parasols selling hand-made toys, dolls and horrid little ornaments made from coral and shells; there are even vendors of sandwiches and orange juice. This private enterprise is not likely to last long. Some time ago the government allowed the creation of 'palladars'. These are small café-cum-restaurants in people's houses. They are usually sited in the front rooms, with the whole household being involved, the wife doing the cooking, the husband the waiting and the children the washing-up. A maximum of only twelve customers is allowed. A proportion of the turn-over, of course, is paid in taxes. They have been so successful that they have been taking business from the state-owned restaurants so, in retaliation, the government in April increased the taxes to Cs22,000 per month – the equivalent of £2200 per year. This, as planned, has all but wiped them out. Another disincentive has been the banning of the sea-food fishermen. These used to go out to sea, floating with an inner tube around them and their frog-flippered feet working frantically below. The government took a dislike of this difficult-to-control activity and has banned it.

The city is getting more dirty, and uglier. I am enraged to see even

more of the charming coral-built houses have been bulldozed down and replaced with the ugliest utilitarian buildings in the world. Their paint is already flaking, their plaster is scabious. The public statues are rusting, the ornamental pools are empty – but for litter – their concrete linings cracking in the sun.

I walk past El Floridita, the bar popular with Ernest Hemingway. He is a local cult hero. Although he would have hated the spartan regime he did not have to endure it, being a favoured friend of Castro. (He also admired Hitler: there is little difference between the International Socialism of Communism and the National Socialism of Fascism.) When he is mentioned I always remember what Clive James said, on being shown round the Hemingway villa by a reverentially deferential guide. 'All around you,' whispered the guide to the awed trippers grouped about him, 'you can see, on the walls, the head of every animal that Ernesto Hemingway had shot.'

'Except,' murmured James dryly, 'his own.'

A honey of an answer: quick, witty, apt, and immensely annoying to all around.

I pass a room full of relaxing people in uniform. Through the open window I see that there is a television in a corner depicting Castro pontificating. Cuban television seems to be entirely football games or Castro talking. I cannot understand how the population can bear it: although Communism is bad enough, it has been borne by stoic millions; but Castro's speeches are interminable. He must have a massive conceit: the world's biggest windbag and bore.

There is the most astonishing dog in a side street: one of the oddest looking animals I have ever seen. It is the size of a bull-terrier. It has a tuft of bristle at the end of its tail, and from the root of the tail to the top of its head runs a punk-style ridge of hair; elsewhere it is as bald as a stone. Its nude body is bi-coloured a vivid pink and an inky blue-black, blotched haphazardly except for its balls: neatly, one is blue, the other pink. Neither it or the woman who is leading it seem the remotest bit embarrassed by its macabre appearance.

I am now sitting in the veranda of the Hotel Inglaterra, a 120-year remnant of elegant times: all brass and polished mahogany. I am drink-

ing a Ron Collins – Tom Collins's rather common Caribbean cousin, made of rum. I have just noticed how extremely fat are many of the Cubans – the politicians and bureaucrats, not the ones starving in the villages. They must be the fattest people in the world, except the Boers and Polynesians. Perhaps it is because their diet is based on sugar and pasta.

Off again, walking through the back streets. Sometimes a cock will crow from above, then abruptly cease as if muffled. Otherwise the streets are so quiet I can hear the echo of my footsteps off the peeling-plastered walls. I have seen so many women with bad squints that I am wearing out my fingers crossing them against the evil eye. The whole place has become so sinister it reminds me of a walk I had forty years ago.

Montenegro: An eerie amble. *Summer 1956.* A couple of years ago there was a sale of farmhouse chattels near Steeple Bumpstead. On an impulse I bought an ancient stamp album, a ragged old book dated 1910 with smudgy prints of the relevant stamps on each page. The little boy who grew up to be the old farmer had not collected much, and I made no great bargain, but I treasure the book for its evocative names of countries and states long dead and forgotten: Inhambane, Jubaland, Kouang Tcheou, Zambezia, Corisco, Cundinamarca and Fernando Poo. Also included was Montenegro – the Kingdom of the Black Mountain.

Montenegro became part of Yugoslavia under Tito. Now, although not a kingdom, it is once again a state, part of the squabbling mini-countries that make up the Balkans. It is situated in the mountainous country between Albania to the south, Serbia to the east and Bosnia and Hercegovina to the north. It is peculiar in that the inhabitants are totally dissimilar in racial type from its neighbours: the Serbs, Croats and Albanians are short and dark, the Montenegrans are fair and, together with the Highland Scottish, are the tallest people in Europe.

In the gap between leaving school and starting my national service I went to Venice, and from there I wandered down the Adriatic coast of Yugoslavia, finally ending up in the Bay of Kotor. The flowery guide book of Montenegro waxed lyrical about the little town:

In the last bay of Boka Kotorska, at its very end, retired among cliffs and encircled by walls, stands Kotor.

Looking at it from the approaching ship, it seems as if one were coming to the end of the world. The rocks pressing it between their sides, the tops of which touch the clouds, do not permit one to imagine another world beyond that wall. The border is delineated much too roughly to allow somebody to gather enough courage and throw his fancy across the pathless Kotor hinterland.

The old Kotor, within the town walls, is full of calm, dozing, and as if sleepy. Narrow, high houses, from the windows of which neighbours may shake hands across the street, are hindering the access to light and sunshine. A kind of permanent twilight reigns there, and the steps of the passers by resound dully in the stone paved streets, leaving to the visitor the impression of being in a shrine which has Mount Lovcen as ceiling.

When the Republic of Venice was at her most powerful she needed more people to man her huge fleet than she could supply from her own populace, so sailors were recruited from all the towns and villages down the Adriatic Sea, among the coves and islands of the Dalmatian coast. The Bay of Kotor supplied many of these men, and in part of the bay some of them built a village in imitation of the city they had served, a kind of mini-Venice.

I came upon it by chance, when I decided to go for an early morning walk along the road which followed the shoreline. I had spent the night in Kotor police station, due to a misunderstanding between me and the local police: I had taken a photograph of a Montenegran peasant, picturesque in his embroidered waistcoat, blue breeches and white silk stockings and had been unaware of three of Tito's submarines in the waters behind him; the police arrested me as a spy. When they discovered I was not a German (they loathed Germans almost as much

as they loathed Italians), but an Englishman (they doted on the English, perhaps because they had not yet met our football fans), they were full of apologies and tried to usher me out of the comfortable cell into which they had previously thrust me. I declined: I had been sharing the meagre amenities of my hotel room with a delegation of six Bulgarian trades-union leaders who liked sleeping with their windows shut and their orifices open. I spent most of the night playing backgammon with the policemen, and when I finally went to bed they tactfully left the door of the cell half open so I would not feel ill at ease.

I plodded from the police station comfortably full of the Montenegran equivalent of porridge. Although the scenery was beauti-ful in a placid and isolated way, I began to feel uneasy. There was utter silence, as if the whole countryside was holding its breath. The high mountains round the fjord-like bay shadowed waters that were still and dark and deep. A lovely three-masted sailing ship, her full suit of sails spread, glided across the surface as if on a ghost wind like the Flying Dutchman. Two shadows slipped and slithered amid the rocks above and behind me: Tito's secret police. This predatory stalking, incompe-tent as it was, still made the hackles on the back of my neck prickle. Apart from them, it was only after ambling along the dry and stony road for over an hour that I saw any sign of human life: the campaniles and roofs of a grand city. I thought, at first, that it was far away. To my sur-prise, within a very short while I was at the outskirts – the distance had been an illusion. Everything was about a fifth of the size that I had pre-sumed: the campaniles were hardly taller than telegraph poles, the palaces were hardly bigger than seaside chalets. The weirdness of the place was accentuated by the solitude: there was no one in sight, and my footsteps echoed hollowly as I walked on the flagstones which paved the broad high street. The width of the street yet again gave the optical illusion of size to the buildings, and made the street seem even wider and more impressive. It also gave a shocking gigantism to the first person I saw, looming hugely and silently in a doorway: he had no nose or fingers and was dressed in rags. I strode on, stiff-legged with unease. A thin, ashen-faced wraith on crutches, also festooned in rags, fluttered and tottered round a corner and at the sight of me froze into immobil-

ity, staring. I noticed three more people, sitting on a doorstep: their faces were greeny-white, their eyes haggard, they were missing parts of themselves. As I continued to walk down the centre of the street my clomping footsteps began to sound like someone rapping on a huge door, a summons which was bringing out more ill-made scarecrows, coldly curious, hostile, but furtive. I began to feel like the knight in Bergman's *The Seventh Seal*, returning from the Crusades to find his home town dead of the plague and the flitting shadow of death at his heels.

I suddenly realised that I was in the middle of a leper colony.

I stopped in my tracks, spun round and hurried back.

Perhaps worse than the silence which accompanied me in was the thin, derisive tittering which followed me out.

Muscat to Nizwa, 14 June 1997. Queen's Messenger Patrick S*** served in Oman as a regimental artillery officer in the army of His Majesty Sultan Qaboos bin Said al Said. Patrick has sent a message to one of his former brother officers, Muqaddam [Lt. Col.] Salim K***, that as Queen's Messenger Courtauld has a free day here, could he take him to somewhere interesting. So, having landed at half past seven this morning, been driven to the Embassy where I deliver the bags, then to the Muscat Intercontinental Hotel where I shower and have breakfast, I meet Salim in the hotel lobby at ten o'clock.

Salim has retired as a full-time soldier and is now in 'security'. He is forty-two, burly, with a smiling round face and a black beard. He wears the local dress of a long white *dishdasha*, under this he has a sort of petticoat serendipitously called a *woozah* and the whole outfit is surmounted by a *kumma*, an embroidered pillbox cap. I know it is ill-mannered to ask about his womenfolk but as he tells me that he has nine children I reckon that he has more than one wife, although Iqbal, one of my Abu Dhabian friends, always said that one mother-in-law was more than enough for anyone.

Salim drives me down the pleasant streets of Muscat. The locals have

employed good architects who have combined the basis of Arab design (the tent and pavilion, together with influences from the Moguls, the Mamelukes and the Ottomans) with the particular characteristic of Omani domestic architecture (influenced by the defensive buildings of the Persian and Portuguese invaders). The result is an attractive and competent modern compromise. Most of the houses look both sturdy and elegant: they are low and white and have arches and vaulted doorways and are closely girt about with boundary walls. We drive through long avenues of date palms, most of them bearing heavy crops of fruit: golden, red or brown. 'Anyone can pick them and take them home, but if he sells them he gets punished.' Salim says. We do not pass many shops, and none of much interest except a surprisingly versatile one that advertises: 'Dentist, Dermatologist, Gynaecologist'.

We are travelling south-west towards Nizwa, a fortified town about one hundred miles from Muscat.

It is flat at first but as we head inland we climb a thousand feet to Fanja. The scenery to the right is dominated by a stark range of hills called the Jebel Nakhl, to the left the view is mainly of hillocks which look more artificial than natural: like heaps of rubble left carelessly by excavators, and spoil tips and slag heaps. The main colour is sandy pinky-gold but the colours are getting more varied as the hills turn into mountains.

After Fanja we drive along the Wadi Samail which runs below the twenty-five-mile-long base of a range of mountains called the Jebel Akhdar. The rock is extraordinary, of every shape and texture and colour: poisonous-looking greens, beiges, greys, pinks and puce; the only colour one does not see is that of vegetation, the rocky aridity resembling the surface of the moon. There are both sedentary and volcanic rocks, such as sandstones and granites, but the main conformation is of layers of water-laid strata. In many places this has been completely tipped on its sides so that the layers are standing on edge, creating huge cliffs which barricade one side of the flat-bottomed wadi down which we are driving. On the other side the terrain is more hillocky. Stone or mud-brick towers are positioned on the top of some of the knolls. They are mainly sentry posts and are only big enough to hold a section-sized squad of men.

'Your neighbour comes and visits you at night, uninvited, and the sentry in the watchtower will ring a bell.'

Salim tells me that there used to be many tribal conflicts. There are about 250 different tribes. Most of the contention was over three things: access to water, ownership of palm trees or goat grazings. Most marriages were inter-tribal, but now many more marry from outside, they meet the 'outsiders' at school or university.

Salim, like most of my Arab friends, cannot resist the telephone. He spends much time steering with one hand and talking down the telephone which he holds in the other. He is quite good at overtaking but is not so good at getting back to our side of the road having done so, which makes it quite exciting when a bus or army lorry – the two main vehicles – are approaching us. There is not much traffic, even from the few villages that we pass. The villages are snugly tucked into oases, shielded by groves of date; mangoes and limes trees are planted amid the palms.

We stop at Izki and buy petrol: it costs 120 baisa a litre. A bottle of water is 200 baisa a litre.

'But I prefer milk to water,' Salim says, 'the milk of the camel is the best milk of all. It is nicest when drunk straight from the camel, warm, and full of little bubbles.'

I get out of the car to inspect a small shrub – a type of myrtle, I suspect. The sun is overhead, it is nearly noon. It is searingly, stiflingly hot, around 45°C, Salim reckons. In 1442 Abd-er-Razzak, a traveller in Oman, wrote:

The heat was so intense that it burned the marrow in the bones, the sword in its scabbard melted like wax and the gems which adorned the handles of the khanjar was charred to coal. In the plains the chase became a matter of simplicity, for the desert was filled with roasted gazelle.

Having filled the car with petrol, we turn due west for the twenty-mile drive to Nizwa.

Nizwa. The present city-fort was built in the seventeenth century by Sultan bin Saif, first Imam of the al-Ya'ribi dynasty. For nearly 300 years it was the centre of government, serving as palace, house of parliament and chief dungeon. As we approach it we have to drive over the wadi bed which is covered with a shallow spread of water from a flash flood. It is lovely to see such abundance of water, particularly in contrast to the shimmering heat and the arid dryness of the mountain range behind. The town is reflected on the waters: it is long and low and battlemented. Flags fly from the walls and from the top of a large, drum-shaped keep which dominates the roofscape. Most of the colouring is of a pinky-beige plaster but a beautiful dome and minaret hang over the mosque and they are of a vivid blue overlaid with a tracery of gold.

We enter through the *bab* (main gate), a wide portal of thick wooden panels, joined with massive nails. Within, the living, trading and defence areas merge into a busily built interior which is attractively warren-like: tall, mud-brick houses lining narrow streets; shops and souks; a muddle of little alleyways and squares; of steps and narrow pavements; of arches and pillars and buttresses; here and there a wall has a mosaic; there are cool areas of shadows. People drift from one patch of shade to another, shuffling in their sandals. The keep which dominates the town is 280 feet in circumference and 100 feet high. The lower two thirds of it was filled with earth and acts as a gun platform; the cannons have a full 360° field of fire. The battlemented upper walk was for the defending musketeers. We enter a door which leads into the flight of steps built inside the walls of the keep. The stairs zigzag up, at each corner there is a door which can be shut against any invader. There are also 'murder holes' from where projectiles can be thrown. Another method of defence is the machicolation from which boiling honey can be poured on those below (what a waste of honey, why don't they use ordinary oil?). After climbing the 100 feet we are on top of the circular walkway. The town snoozes below us in the midday sun. It all looks very peaceful. But it was only about forty years ago when those cannon were last fired in anger.

We descend to explore the souks. Each souk has a different smell: the appalling smell of fish from one, the raw iron smell of meat from another, the sticky smell of the date souk, the female scent of jasmine and sandalwood from the jewellers and goldsmiths – perhaps this smell is from the customers, unlike Saudi or much of the Gulf many of the shoppers here are women. This souk is of two long corridors, very high with finely wrought rafters overhead and floored with irregular slabs of rock. There are cubicles to either side. Each cubicle, when not in use, is shuttered with tall, elegant panelled doors with large brass nails. The whole effect when closed (which it is, as it is now after noon) is more like a formal university library.

The women here do not wear the mask with such strict rigour as in much of Arabia. However masks are for sale, and Salim and I try one on with sycophantic laughter from the shopkeeper. The view through the eyeholes cut in the stiff black cloth is adequate, but it is terribly stuffy inside; it must be appallingly claustrophobic for women to have to wear this as well as their black bell-tents.

We enter a shop-cum-restaurant. On the walls and from the ceiling hang every sort of armament: the sharply curved Omani dagger (*khanjar*), shotguns, rifles (especially the Lee Enfield .303), bandoleers in festoons, stuffed with cartridges of every calibre up to the .577. There are also gin-traps and bird-traps; shelves of crockery and cutlery in brass, porcelain and terracotta, of goat skins (for holding water), camel saddles, rugs, carpets and big balls of yarn, chunky silver jewellery, money boxes and wedding chests. Salim takes down a long sword. I think it looks fairly useless as the scabbard is of a rather tawdry embossed silvery metal and the grip is too small for my hand and has no hilt. But when Salim draws it I feel both edges of the blade which are as sharp as razors and you could slice a man's head or arm off with one swipe. I rummage puzzledly through the contents of a bowl: it contains semi-transparent pieces of material in chips and blobs, mostly yellowish or amber-coloured. The shopkeeper is a studious, neat man in an ash-grey *dishdasha* and with gold-rimmed spectacles. 'Frankincense,' he says. 'Before we made our money from oil, this was our main source of riches. Every temple in the world, from the Hindu temples of India to Egypt and Persia and Greece, even the Jews

and later the Christians, they all needed the incense from burning frankincense for their rituals, and we were the only people who could grow the tree from which the frankincense resin is harvested. [I think he may be wrong, and that the tree also grows in Africa.] Our production reached 3000 tons per year.' He rummages in another bowl, full of coins. 'Here is another interesting thing,' he says, picking out what I recognise as a Maria Theresa thaler, 'even though all these were made in 1780 [or were minted more recently with that date on] they were the most important coin here until 1968. To you, only riyals five.' As I have already bought a couple of these in Dubai for a fifth of that price I politely decline, but Salim buys an attractive rug of black and red stripes with large tassels.

The restaurant part of the complex consists mainly of little rooms where a whole family or group of friends may dine in privacy. The basic furnishing is of a carpeted floor, cushions all round the walls and attractive circular mats of straw or raffia about four and a half feet across. On these are placed shallow platters of almost the same diameter. A different food is put in them: one may contain layers and layers of a very thin pancake-like bread; another may have rice, usually mixed with spices and maybe vegetables; another may have bits of meat. A similar dish is inverted over it to keep the food warm and on top of it all another round mat is put, in the manner of a tea-cosy. This covering is slightly conical like a coolie's hat.

Like many Arabs, Salim is fascinated by water. We leave the fort and go to a picnic area upriver. It is a bit municipal with its seating areas and parasols of thatched palm fronds, but reasonably pleasant, with lawns of irrigated grass, flowerbeds, bushes which shimmer with the singing of the cicadas. The river is mountain fed. Some of the flow has been diverted into an attractive artificial pool built of the local rock. The crystalline waters are of a strange, silvery blue-green, similar in colour to the leaves of my cricket-bat willows. An old man with a shy smile is lolling in the pool; he is holding a small and even more embarrassed infant who is presumably his granddaughter – or an offspring from one of his younger wives. Salim kicks off his sandals, lifts the hems of his *woozah* and *dishdasha* and blissfully paddles in the shallow waters of the

upper steps. I reluctantly decline, knowing my cheap shoes (bought from the scrap merchant in Coggeshall) have leached their colours onto my equally cheap socks.

Off to see some more water, about half an hour's drive away. This is in a *falat*, an irrigation channel which runs from the mountains, through the castle-fort of Birkat al Mauz and out into the adjacent village. The channel is lined with a lush, light green weed. There are red dragonflies like airborne embers. A castle-fort in comparison to a military fort is basically for domestic use. Birkat al Mauz was the governmental seat and main residence of the Lords of the Green Mountain (green rocks, not grass), and Salim says it is very luxurious inside with 230 rooms, some with beautiful ceilings and polylobate lintels over doors and windows. We knock on the door. It is locked, and no one answers, so all we see is the rather forbidding exterior: a square main keep with circular corner towers, and an outer wall battlemented with the traditional pointed crenellations. Salim tells me that it has fallen only twice to an enemy. The first time was in 973, to the Persians. The second time was during the Jebel War of the 1950s, after withstanding a siege of three months. The defence was under the command of the then Lord of the Green Mountain, Suleiman bin Himyar, Sheikh of the powerful Bani Riyam people. He finally had to admit defeat against the combined forces of the Sultan of Oman and his British assistants.

We have arrived at Salim's army headquarters. The barracks is mainly for the artillery. The gates are newly painted, the entrance road is lined with flagpoles from which flutter pennants, stones are painted white, tanks and gun pieces are stationed on plinths – all very British. We enter the officers' mess. Also very British: a long entrance corridor, lined with photographs of uniformed fellows sitting on tanks or beside artillery pieces. The occasional camel adds a local touch. I enter the main room and see to my astonishment that it is dominated by a large bar and behind the bar is arrayed a vast profusion of alcohol in tier after tier of bottles, stack upon stack of cans. A cheerful gang of officers are leaning against it: some are wearing *dishdashas*, they are either reservists such as Salim or men who are 'off' today; others are in camouflaged battle dress, they have been busying around the desert and mountains this morning;

the remainder are in service dress, they have been pen-pushing. Everybody is extremely welcoming and cheerful. The conversation is very similar to that of any group of men: slightly disparaging jokes on each others' abilities and activities, a friendly rivalry. The attitude of the officers is very similar to those of British officers compared with foreign officers' messes I have visited: these men are casually relaxed and unaffected and talk of many things – unlike, for example, in the American bases in Germany and Belgium where the men seem to be obsessed with sporting statistics and gossip, or in South Africa where the general intellectual level seems to be at the spot-picking age of a prep school, or the French who are much more formal and stilted. However, like the French, they have the very good manners of speaking English, even to each other, so as to include the stranger in their conversation. The main differences from British officers is the lack of talk about women, the occasional impulse of the officers to hold hands and the busy rubbing of noses when Salim greets his best friend, Raaid (Major) Umor Kahlifa.

The men, on average, are slightly shorter and more burly and round-faced in comparison to my friends from the Emirates, but there is one particularly impressive man with a long, coffin-shaped face, a huge hooked nose, aquiline eyebrows and a beard like a black dagger.

After a glass of lager and four large vodkas and water – presumably they are not selling camel's milk at the bar – Salim takes me off for lunch in the mess-room. Umor and a couple of others have come too. We eat with our hands, though I have to use a spoon for the rice as I cannot perfect the technique of rolling and squeezing and squashing and kneading it with my fingers until it forms a ball of the right size and consistency to pop into my mouth. The mess stewards have served a platter of biryani and a big fish with a mawful of nasty teeth. My hosts very kindly keep handing me large chunks of this fish, with their right hands of course. I have an unease that I will also be handed their well-manipulated little balls of rice.

After the meal I view the most remarkable thing I have seen in the whole encampment: the lavatories in the latrine of these desert warriors are *pink*.

*

We are returning to Muscat on a different road, heading due east at present. The mountain ranges are behind us, the scenery is of undulating wadis dotted with the slag-heap type of knoll and hillock.

We stop at the market of a small town and Salim buys two crates of dates which resemble small golden eggs: one seven-kilo crate for his mother, the other for his wife. (It turns out that he has only one: he must keep her busy.) There are little terracotta vases which hold about a pint of water. This is cool because of the transference of latent heat by the evaporation of the liquor percolating through the earthenware. You can buy a vase of water for ten baisa, about six pence. A stall-holder is selling dried fish. Some are split open rather like kippers and dried in the sun. There are sacks of small silvery fish which look like minnows. Salim takes one, breaks the head off and offers me the little body. It was probably a freshwater fish as it tastes almost of nothing, not even salt, just slightly musty. Salim says that the nomadic Arabs like dried fish as it can be carried around for months without deteriorating.

We stop again at Bidbid where Salim buys two tubs of halwa. At the back of the sweetshop the halwa is being made in a large copper cauldron, the honey and nuts being stirred until the whole thing thickens into a very rubbery jelly. It is slightly like Turkish Delight rather than the Turkish halva where the nuts have been ground up and the consistency is firmer.

We are entering Muscat. Salim takes me to his house. It is typical, with the enclosure wall so closely round the building that there is only a narrow corridor each side and a little more room in front where he can park his four cars. It is shaded with maybe a dozen trees: mangoes, pawpaws, limes.

I enter. 'Keep your shoes on,' he says; perhaps he has noticed my socks. The interior is busy, with much ornamentation on walling and furnishing, many photographs of desert warriors, and swords and medals hung up. A string of children comes up and kisses his hand and solemnly shakes mine, the younger ones then run off skipping and giggling and the elder ones fetch coffee and biscuits. A couple of friends drop in and they talk about the price of dates. Salim mourns that he paid too much today for his fourteen kilos.

[157]

Back to the hotel. More cups of coffee with my turn to be host to Salim and his friends.

Time to part. Salim hands me the tasselled rug and the two tubs of halva: 'For your family,' he says, 'goodbye, we will meet again.'

Inshallah.

 **Budapest, 9 July 1997.** When I took off this morning from Vienna I saw, from the aeroplane windows, the watery skirts of the Danube spilling over her banks into the fields and woodlands to either side. Here, further downstream, in Budapest, every one is excited: 'Have you seen the Danube!' 'Have you seen the Danube?' they all ask. As my car travels along the riverside road, the people sitting on the pavement are dangling their feet in the floodwaters hurrying past; normally there is a ten- to fifteen-foot drop here. The water is rising at such a rate that they are expected to pour over the embankment roads early this evening – after my departure; I am here for only six hours.

Having completed my business in the Embassy I decide to do my normal wander up the Váci Utca, the shopping street. I enter the art shop which is always full of interesting things: an extraordinary mixture of antique furniture and knickknacks; old and modern art; paintings, prints and statuary.

A few times in my life I have been so entranced by something for sale that even though I could not afford it I have had an irresistible impulse to buy. The first time was as an Officer Cadet near Chester when I spent a whole week's pay – three guineas – on a terracotta flagon, thrown with such exactitude that it looked as if it had been blown, like glass, rather than turned from crude clay. Then there was the set of blue Bristol glass beakers I bought when an undergraduate at Cambridge; the Queen Anne period ship's desk with forty-eight drawers, eight of them secret, which I bought in Bonham's for the same price as a Mini car (£420); the huge, almost black amethyst pendant I bought for Dominie in Bond Street; the Mongolian hunting scene sold to me behind the monastery in Ulaan Baatar.

Today is such a day. In a glass-fronted cabinet there are two prints. They depict two scenes from Bartók's opera, *Duke Bluebeard's Castle*. They are of complete simplicity: on heavy white paper; the only colours are blue and black on one, with an additional rectangle in red on the other. The first picture is basically of a female figure, tall, elongated, dressed in solid black: a few strokes of a pen to make a face – serene, wondering, alone, curious, apprehensive – Juliet, the wife of Bluebeard, looking through the first door. The other picture is almost a solid block of blue, but with that face again, beside a white glimmer which represents another secretly opened door; the scarlet rectangle denotes the approaching Bluebeard. The artist is János Kass (pronounced Yanosh Kosh).

'How much?' I ask.

Too expensive, I think, but I hurry back to the Embassy to collect my wallet.

Longlegs is in her office beside the reception area, her booted feet on her desk, her large sleepy eyes scanning an article on procreation in *The Observer* supplement.

'Chimpanzees do not need to put on kinky rubber clothing to have sex,' she says.

This is a subject to discuss later. Meanwhile: 'Please write on a bit of paper, "What discount will you give me if I buy both?"'

Back to the art gallery.

'Ha mind a két képet megreszem, tudnak némi a'rengedmény adni?'

My tongue is now in a complete knot. Everyone looks worried and uncomprehending. Someone takes my bit of paper and reads it to the others. There is a little huddle of negotiators: a man with a pony-tail too young for him, a sophisticated woman in a blue suit, and a lumpy hausfrau type. They natter together; computers are produced; I flitter dollar notes temptingly under noses, murmuring 'Cash, cash'; a figure is written on a piece of paper; I write another; they follow on after more natter with another; we all smile and shake hands and I pay and quit exultantly carrying a tube containing two rolled-up pages.

That's a fortnight's pay gone for a Burton.

'So, you bought them, let me see,' says Longlegs.

'Nice, you have good judgement, I thought they would be of fat naked ladies.'

'You're been reading too much of *The Observer*.'

I collect my guide book and sally out to explore. The guide book, *Budapest: a Critical Guide*, is my favourite of all the ones I have read, mainly because of the quirky character of the author, András Török. I particularly like his lists: lists not only of useful things such as 'The Most Important Accessory to tour Budapest with (a pair of binoculars . . . to help examine the façades and spires)' and 'The Best Antique Shop for Art Nouveau', but of his own particular fads. These include:

The Most Mysterious, Oversize Stone Lady,
The Waitress with the Nicest, but not Sexy Smile,
The Best Place to Feel that You are Just a Piece of Dust, Doomed
    to Failure,
The Naffest Lampshade Specialist,
The Ghastliest Public Building.

I read it over a bowl of goulash. Török says that one of the 'musts' is the Historical Portrait section of the National Museum: it is a 'must' I have not 'done' so will 'do' in the three hours I have spare before I fly back to Vienna.

The museum is a neo-classical building fronted by a large flight of steps upon which has amassed a group of people characteristic of those always sitting on museum steps: young, earnest and meek. Before going upstairs to the Historical Portraits section I divert into a room of almost reverential silence and gloom. It contains only seven objects, discreetly lit: they are the Hungarian royal regalia. It is with a shock of recognition that I see that famous crown with its askew terminal cross, the crown that was depicted on the Hungarians' postage in my stamp collection of fifty years ago: the medieval crown of Saint Stephen. It looks slightly like the head of a hippie girl, wearing a circlet of enamelled plaques, the golden pendant chains hanging like plaited Rastafarian locks threaded with beads at the tips. There is also a sword, an impressively simple orb, a short sceptre with a carved terminal in rock crystal, an ornately embroidered twelfth-

century cope and two fine chests, one in wood and iron, the other a silver casket.

Apart from various characters of the Austro-Hungarian Empire, mostly Habsburg, I do not know many famous Hungarians. They have been famous discreetly away from English history books: Admiral Miklós Horthy, remarkable because he had no fleet, no coast, even; a couple of musicians, Liszt and Bartók; Ladislao Biro who invented the Biro pen and . . . er . . .

The tour of the Historical Portraits section leaves me none the wiser except for the sad discovery that the Esterházys, who had always seemed a most romantic family, had hideous women and effetely ridiculous men, with a penchant for embroidered tights. Most of the uniforms are very exotic, with the accessory of a rug or pelt flung over one shoulder. Some of the jewellery is fantastic, one woman has twenty-eight ropes of pearls round her waist. There are attractive jewelled feathers: I remember that no one in Hungary could wear a feather unless he had slain a Turk. It could be interesting to write a book on feathers.

Back in the Embassy. A conversation with Longlegs: 'Before my father married, he had a Hungarian girlfriend.'

'Very sensible. She was pretty, this girlfriend?'

'So he said, he said she was lovely, she had auburn hair like you, and would suddenly dance and twirl down the banks of Danube, for no reason.'

'And, so?'

'And so he went home, and became a businessman, and married a French girl.'

'That was happy?'

'She was my mother. But he remembered Budapest, and when I was small he used to recite a Hungarian rhyme his girlfriend had taught him, it started with something like 'Oz zip-a'foyee popnok' and ended with a lot of 'pippi poppi fappi paps'; it means something like 'The archbishop of Popnok has a wooden pipe, therefore the pipe of the Archbishop is made of wood.' Do you know it?'

'I know it. My father taught it to me also. I will write it down for you.'

And she writes:

> Az Ipafai papnak
> fából van a fapipája,
> mert az Ipafai
> Papi pipa csak is fapipa.

'Hmmm, it doesn't look like it sounded.'
'I will say it to you.'
And she did.
'Yes! That's it! That's the first time I've heard it in forty years.'
'So, today, you will be taking home two pictures and a memory. And you will be leaving poor me to drown in the Danube, not to dance down the banks, or do the twirlings.'

 **Rome, 14 July 1997.** A disappointing start to the morning. I had a letter written by a Knight of Malta. It was addressed to:

Dei gratia Sacrae Domus Hospitalis Sancti Johannis
Hierosolymitani et militaris Ordinis Sancti Sepulcri
Dominici magister humilis pauperumque Jesu Christi custos

and it went as follows:

Eminent Highness,
My brother-in-law George Courtauld, who is a Queen's Messenger, is often in Rome in the course of his duties, but has never seen the Priory of Malta on the Aventine. I would be most grateful if he were given permission to visit it. He will be in Rome on Monday 14th July and I am taking the liberty of writing this introductory note for him to take with him.
Sincerely your confrère,
Jonathan

I rang the bell at the portal of the Palazzo Malta, in the Via Condotti. A dry little wisp of a man admitted me and ushered me into the porter's lodge. He took my letter. He telephoned. There was a longish wait

during which Dry Wisp and I smiled shyly at each other now and then. A burly man appeared. He did not speak English. My Italian is a picked-up babble of words in Latin, Spanish, Italian and Portuguese which is just enough to puzzle anyone to whom it is addressed. Burly Man took Jonathan's letter, and my letter from our Embassy for the Holy See, and my visiting card. He smiled, shook my hand; there was a squeaking as Dry Wisp opened the gate and the next thing I knew was that I was back in the street.

I walked the hundred yards up the pavement to our Embassy for the Holy See to whinge. The ambassadress was away on holiday. 'So is the Grand Master of the Order of Malta,' says the charmingly named Mr Dewberry, the First Secretary, 'the Pope is away, fishing, and when the Pope goes on holiday so also does all of religious Rome.' He kindly said that if he is contacted by one of the Grand Master's minions he will tell them that I will be back in Rome on 23 September.

I am now in Saint Peter's basilica, having walked here along the Via Condotti with its smart shops and elegant women, then the Via Tomacelli and over the Tiber on the Ponte Cavour. The Piazza Cavour is dominated by the huge façade of the Palazzo di Giustizia (begun in 1889 but not completed until 1911 because of interference from sub-terranean springs), which looks like an over-decorated wedding cake in the heat slowly collapsing under the weight of its grandiose ornamenta-tion. I continue round the fortifications and drum tower of the Castel Sant'Angelo and finally enter the great colonnaded circle of Bernini's Piazza San Pietro in front of the church.

Here it is all amill with priests and nuns and monks and troops of well-behaved schoolchildren. It irks me to have to compare all this Papist energy and bustle with the inefficiency and lassitude of the Church of England. In all my travels I have seen no sign of any of our missionaries sallying out to fill the gaps left by retreating com-munism with a spiritual alternative, no sign of any resistance to the advancing hordes of Islam; instead, the hierarchy publicises excuses for ignoring beliefs and commandments which although defined in the Bible are unappealing to the perverted, the idle, the doubting or the dishonest.

[163]

I have been sitting on a step, scribbling out this peevish tirade: time to enter the cathedral.

I have mixed feelings about Saint Peter's. Individually, there is so much beauty and excellence of artistry – the architecture, the sculpture, the metalwork, the paintings. But in totality it is such a conglomeration, such an *embarras de richesses*, that it seems to have neither the cosy, crammed-with-history business of Westminster Abbey or Canterbury, nor the stark elegance of Durham or Ely or Rheims, nor the religious ambience of Tournos or Torcello. Entering Saint Peter's is rather like stepping into a colossal box of sweets. However, today, whether by design or luck, the whole interior is dominated by the dramatic simplicity of the golden crucifix high on top of the altar canopy: a ray of sun through a window in the dome is lighting it up like a beacon.

I inspect some of my favourites: firstly the simple little monument to

+++
IACOBI+II+MAGNAE+BRIT+REGIS+FILIO
KAROLO+EDWARDO
+++
IACOB+III

Above this, their epitaph, are the busts of Bonny Prince Charlie and the Old Pretender; between them is the sternly dressed Cardinal of York. The princes are pudgy, balding, glum, like a couple of unsuccessful pork-butchers from Perth in discussion with their accountant.

Next, for contrast, I visit Bernini's monument to Pope Alexander VII. At the apex, towering above the onlooker, is the marble effigy of the kneeling pope. He is a dapper figure with a Van Dyck beard and opulent robes. Below him are three females: a peaceful one looking down at the globe, upon which she rests a foot; a worried one holding a grossly fat and charmless baby; and one lurking behind, almost indistinguishable. They are all in white marble. Around them is a massive blanketing of red and brown marble. From this shawl a gilded skeleton struggles to get free: he has managed to extricate one arm and it sticks out towards the viewer, brandishing an hourglass.

I finally pause to look over the teeming black heads of half of Japan at that amazing figure of sorrow and life and death and flowing drapery,

all fossilised into marble: Michelangelo's *Pietà*, the grieving Madonna holding the corpse of Christ.

Now out in the open again, in the harsh glare of sunlight. Two of the Swiss Guard are near me. One holds a halberd, the other wears a sword; they are smart in their striped uniforms but instead of the armoured helmet with red plumes they are wearing berets. I have never liked the beret, a most unsoldierly garb. Why does anyone want to put his (or indeed her) head into a lopsided bag? (Still, there are a lot of folk, braver and better than I am, who think otherwise.)

I have two hours left before I am on duty, just about time to walk back to the Embassy. But I have already got slightly lost, although I know approximately which way to walk, because of the sun. The bridge I have just crossed is not on my map. I stop at a police car which typically has been parked so that it is completely blocking the pavement. I show them my map. It is old and linen-backed; I found it in one of the less-used bits of furniture at home. The police puzzle over it, then one of them notices the date on the bottom, 1876. They break into impertinent demonstrations of merriment and gesticulation. Then they point out my position and I carry on up the Corso Vittorio Emanuele II, non-existent on my map; it may have been bulldozed along the route of the former Via dei Bianchi Vecchi.

I am now sitting on the steps of the grandiose monument to Victor Emmanuel. Because of its shape, and the rows of upper pillars, the Romans have nicknamed it The Typewriter. I rather admire it for its peculiarity. The king sits astride a colossal horse. His magnificent mustachios stick out each side of his face like the wings of an albatross. I hear an American reading from a guide book: 'The equestrian statue of Victor Emmanuel is forty feet long.' I calculate that that must make the distance from tip to tip of his whiskers nearly five feet. Such magnificent appendages deserve such an unabashedly opulent and conceited memorial. There is a group of Italians sitting near me. Odd thing, the Italian language: it seems so sonorous and poetic when in print, or when sung, yet even the prettiest of Italian girls seems to speak it with a metallic screech. Does language affect people's mentality? Does the unsubtle aggression in Arabic make the Arab inherently aggressive? Do

the complications of Kikuyu make the Kikuyu a philosopher? Do Germans shout belligerently because German is an angry-sounding language? I can always annoy my French cousins by suggesting that the paucity of their language (they use circumlocutions like 'peu profond' because they do not even have an exact word for 'shallow') is the reason for the meagre amount of Nobel Prizes awarded to the French compared with the English. Alternatively, I think it may be because of the French obsession with 'logic': you cannot be inspired if you don't have moments of irrationality, in the same way a species cannot adapt without the occasional mutation. I remember hearing somewhere that your name can affect your personality: the round letters of the murmurous tones of Oona Curlicue will create a more contented personality than spiky, hissing Letitia Skittle-Wickett.

It is one o'clock and I am back at the Embassy. I check to see if there is any answer to my enraged telephone call yesterday evening, asking who was responsible for forgetting to book me into the hotel, so that I had to wander around looking for a spare room elsewhere. As usual The System had sprung into action: the buck has been passed as quickly as a game of pass-the-parcel in Belfast, and has finally come to rest on the desk of a junior underling who is away on holiday.

Now lunch: all that I want – a pleasant little restaurant, a smiling waitress and large quantities of food sodden with olive oil. I was interviewed for a Dutch newspaper recently and the interviewer started off: 'I have read your book and it seems to me that your great interests are lots of food and pretty ladies.' I must admit I relish my victuals. I even remember a meal I had on my first holiday ever, over fifty years ago.

Cyprus: the House of Sin. *Summer 1947.* It was soon after the war. My parents decided to take themselves and their two small children to a country where, for the first time in eight years, they could eat beef steaks and oranges and chocolate and bananas and lobsters and sticky puddings

smothered in cream-and-treacle and steak tartare and avocado pears and things-with-garlic-in-them and anything that was not corned beef or spam or rabbit or whale meat or cabbage or boiled potato or turnips or swedes. They wanted to laze in the sun, swim in a warm sea, meet amusing people and be fawned on by waiters bearing tray loads of dry martinis.

They chose Cyprus.

It was over fifty years ago, but I still remember it well. There were palm trees, their leafy fronds looking exactly as depicted in the *Illustrated New Testament for Primary Readers*. The beaches had sand, not Essex mud: it was yellow and at noon was too hot to walk on. Fishermen caught octopi. They turned them inside-out to kill them. There were real castles: I found a cannon ball embedded in the turf of the Castle of Kyrenia; I looked through the window of the Castle of Aeos Hilarion out of which Berengaria, the wife of Richard I of England, had committed suicide. There were real beggars in real rags: two of them, fat and friendly; they sat at each side of the exit of the Dome Hotel and sold the flowers they stole every morning from the public park. The policemen had huge moustaches dyed red with henna. Some people who lived in a ruined monastery let me blow through a conch, just like a mer-boy. There were the little Turkish boys who took me fishing and there were the little Greek boys who turned tortoises or crabs upside down so they baked alive in the sun – I have always preferred the Turks to the Greeks ever since. There was THE HOUSE OF SIN. It had been named thus by some of the staider members of the British Colony.

'You should avoid that rather unsavoury crowd,' said Mrs Wollerwacker, buttonholing my father as we sat by the swimming-pool of the British Country Club in Kyrenia, 'I saw you talking to the one they call "Filthy Francis". Sir Francis S***, actually, but I regret that he does not live up to his title. Need I say more,' and she arched her eyebrows significantly.

'He's a friend of mine,' my father said, 'he was in SOE with me. One of the bravest men I have ever met.'

Mrs Wollerwacker looked nonplussed: 'An exception I suppose. Perhaps he suffered in the war and it's affected his personality. But as for

the others – dissolute, I'm afraid: drunks, the lot of them; pederasts, some of them; and one or two of them even originate from very obscure parts of Central Europe.'

'Do you know any of them?' my father asked.

'Certainly not! But we know of them. There's Joyce M***, always inebriated, the co-habitué of a strange dark little man with a broken accent, Pedro, they call him. He seems to have no other name. Then Osbert R***. He was a doctor but now writes poetry – that's what he says, but we happen to know that he writes the most incredibly filthy books for the Obelisk Press. Then there's Niké, a Greek film star – need I say more – and of course she has an admirer who – to put it nicely – is a frightfully common and ill-bred person from Wales. Then Izzy Something or other: "Izzy", there, need I say more [and she pointed in an equally common and ill-bred, if meaningful way at her nose], then there's the one they just call "Faber", she never wears any shoes, and a painter with a beard called Grimshaw.'

I thought of asking why he called his beard Grimshaw, but remembered that children should be seen and not heard.

We could not take Mrs Wollerwacker's advice, for Filthy Francis had already invited us to lunch the next day.

The house was small, plastered with yellowish stucco and with a vine-covered veranda along the front. There were two small balconies outside the first-floor windows. A merry but blowsy blonde sat and swayed on the top of one of them. Like the house, she too was plastered. (That was my father's joke.)

'Welcome to civilisation,' she shouted excitedly at us as we dismounted from our ancient taxi; then she raised a glass to her lips, leaned backwards to take a swig and somersaulted over the edge of the balcony through the vine and onto the hard earthen floor of the patio. I was so horrified that the screams of concern and anguish are still as clear as yesterday:

'My God, Joyce has *killed* herself.'

'No she's still breathing.'

'But blood is coming out of her *ears*' ... 'that means a fractured skull' ... 'it's not blood, it's wine' ... 'how very significant, somehow' ... 'take her to her bed' ... 'who was she sleeping with last night?' ... 'for GOD'S

SAKE, any bed will do' . . . 'what about a hospital?' . . . 'you were a doctor before they struck you off' . . . 'well, how is she?' . . . 'seems alright, lucky she was so boozed, it made her relaxed, put her in my bed' . . . 'but it's not your turn' . . . 'Oh for God's sake, have you no decency' . . . 'Huh! I know you, huh! I saw . . . Ah, here's George and Claudine' . . . 'My God, they've got a couple of little brats with them' (that made me feel really welcome) . . . 'Who's turn to scratch up the lunch?' . . . 'mine but it was yours to go shopping, and if you remember you refused to . . .'

Lunch was eaten on the patio. The vine above our heads was sparse and wiry, no one had watered it so that many of its leaves had withered and the small bunches of grapes hung in mildewed clumps. The packed earth of the floor was stained with the unhousetrained efforts of Winston, Ike, Monty and Margaret-Rose, a quartet of unkempt terriers. We ate off a trestle table made from a couple of old doors and some orange boxes. Instead of a tablecloth the surface was covered with a glutinous and multi-coloured paste blended from marmalades and jams, soups and sauces, treacle and liqueurs; all this reinforced by the bonding agencies of cigarette ash and bread crumbs.

There was nothing to eat except fruit, cheese and bread. The cheese smelt musty and was, I now realise, from goat's milk; the bread was stale, but at least it was soft, being sodden and soppy with the wine which had been spilt over it. The fruit was blotched with moulds and bruises, and was attractive only to a variety of wasps and bluebottles. A bunch of bananas took pride of place: not the handsome, all-yellow fruit I had seen in pictures, but a clutch of festering black and jaundiced fingers which had split and oozed pus-like juices over the other contents of the chipped enamelled wash-basin.

'Have you ever eaten a banana?' asked Filthy Francis.

Few people are better judges of character than small boys. I immediately recognised the fact that Filthy Francis not only couldn't care less if I had eaten a banana, but thought children alarming and repellant.

'No,' I admitted.

He tossed one over. I ate it. One of life's great disappointments: I had been told about bananas for eight years; one of the treats in store

when the war ended would be to eat one – and it tasted like insipid soap.

A man was seen reeling towards us from the road. He was wearing a dinner jacket, but no shoes and socks. He was six foot five, immensely fat, had a thick coating of stubble on his chin and was holding a hatchet.

'Damn it, here's Carl, hide me,' said a stunningly beautiful woman with pitch-black hair and violet eyes. She was hustled indoors and under a bed.

The man with the hatchet arrived.

'Where's my wife?' he shrilled in a surprisingly alto voice. He had a Polish accent.

He was placated with alcoholic offerings. Finally he burst into maudlin tears about no one loving him. Everyone assured him with there, there, of course everyone loves you, but he came back with no, nobody did, in fact, everyone hated him, particularly Zoë, his dear beautiful wife, she hated him terribly and it made him so hurt and unhappy. He then got up and was sick in a corner. Then he sat down on the ground, immediately fell asleep and began to snore. The conversation revolved acrimoniously over the subject of who should clear up the mess. Agreement was reached that it was the job of whoever was Carl's friend; further discussion concluded that Carl had no friends, didn't deserve any and would never have any.

'May I get down?' I asked.

A man with an alarming black beard scowled across the table at me.

'You haven't finished your bread and cheese,' he said.

I looked towards my parents for protection, but they were out of earshot at the other end of the table.

'It's stale,' I objected.

'Stale!' exclaimed the man, his teeth glinting alarmingly amid the wild dishevelment of his beard. 'Do you know how many people would give their life's blood for just a scrap of that feast spread before you?'

'No, sir,' I piped uneasily.

'Millions. Bloody millions.' He stabbed a long, gnarled finger towards my plate: 'Eat it,' he snarled.

So I ate it.

Jerash, 21 July 1997. The livery of the Air Jordan aeroplane is in black, grey and gold, one of the smartest of all airlines. I think it a great pity that British Airways are changing theirs into trendy daubs and sploshes – for a cost of $60,000,000 apparently. I would much rather fly with the plain but reassuring uniform of a staid old English butler than with the tarty make-up of some skittish floozy. Cairo was almost invisible in smog and sand when we took off, but the air cleared when we flew over the desert of Sinai and I could see the ghost rivers in the sands below, evidence of the lushness of times past, long before even the Old Testament was written and Moses and his people wandered lost amid the dunes and gravel plains.

We land at Amman at 17.20 hours. I am met by the Embassy driver, my friend the Mukhtar, Hassan Ibrahim Jado. A Mukhtar is a sort of hereditary councillor, and we discuss sheep: his community having several flocks, while I have one (whose numbers are limited, by the urban, alien, interfering, pedantic, nasty, domineering, bureaucratic tyrants in Brussels, to 105.7 head of ewes). Hassan complains that home-grown mutton costs six dinars in the butcher's (a price similar to English lamb), while the inferior ('tastes worse, difficult to bite') mutton from Russia and Romania is only four dinars. I tell him of my problem with Ramses and Rambo, two of my new tups. I had kitted them up in kinky leather harness, with colour pads on them to see which ram was tupping which ewe, but for a week nothing happened, no sign of a red or blue patch on a ewe's rump. At last, a patch of colour – on Rambo's nose: I'd purchased a pair of homosexual sheep.

Hassan tells me that after I have delivered the bags to the Embassy and checked into my hotel, he will drive me to Jerash so that I can have a look around.

We are on our way to Jerash, a town whose name is derived from the Greco-Roman city of Gerasa. The verge of the road is busy: there are many sellers of figs or delicious-looking melons, dark green with paler green longitudinal stripes, other people are selling pots of coffee from tall kettles which steam over fires; a gang of road workers sit outside

their tent, one of them ladles water from an amphora-in-tripod whose design goes back to the Bronze Age. I tell Hussan that I first visited Jerash about twenty years ago, as a businessman, driving down from Damascus, sinister with its 'toenail factory', the HQ of the police, staring slitty-eyed at the populace; the whole city infested with pictures of the senior socialist, President Assad. Hassan says that he was in Iraq recently and it was the same there: 'It is very strange, everywhere I look, there is Saddam Hussein looking back at me, from pictures on every piece of wall.' Hassan and our ambassador went to visit the Anglican church. Everything had been vandalised or stolen, even the doors and windows had been taken away, confirming Saddam Hussein's regime to be the sneak thieves among the nations. Hassan was amused to see that the face of President Bush had been painted on the floor of the entrance of his hotel, so anyone entering it had to trample over it.

Hassan keeps sucking sweets. He offers one to me. They are made from caffeine and are delicious: 'To help me stop smoking,' he says.

'When did you give up?'

'Two years, five months ago.'

The ancient site of Gerasa is in a valley amid the highlands of Gilead, about thirty miles north of Amman, on the Damascas–Amman–Petra road. Nothing seems to be mentioned of it in the Old Testament, unless it represents Ramoth Gilead. It was reputed to be colonised by Alexander the Great – but few cities in the Classical East seem to escape that distinction. Josephus wrote that in 83 BC it was captured by Alexander Jannaeus, a Jewish king-priest, and subsequently rebuilt and burned down several times until it became safely protected under the aegis of the Roman Empire: in 63 BC Pompey, having completed his conquest of most of that area, included Gerasa into his newly created Province of Syria. Although the neighbouring Nabataeans had some influence in the style, it was the Romans who were the basic architects and builders, much of the work visible at present being undertaken between AD 130 and 180, during the reign of the Antonines. It gradually lost power for four main reasons: the shrinking of the valley stream and other water sources due to climatic changes; the loss of political and trading influence, especially through the shifting away of the trade

routes after the destruction of Palmyra (AD 273) and the growth of the Sassanian Kingdom; the withering of the Roman Empire; and, perhaps above all, earthquakes. However, in AD 350 Christianity gained entry and Gerasa became a bishopric: there are the ruins of at least thirteen churches within the walls. The Muslim conquest of AD 635 mortally wounded the city which was finally destroyed by earthquakes in AD 747.

It is thought to be the most complete of all Roman provincial cities. It is an early example of town planning: there is the main street, crossed at right angles by lesser streets, all are colonnaded. The main public buildings are to the west of the main street, on the higher ground. They include temples, shrines, theatres and of course the ubiquitous baths. The whole area of 1300 acres was surrounded by 3000 yards of walling, eight feet thick. This was pierced by six gates. The population of the city was 18,000 at the most.

When I was here first it was late spring, and the desert round about was beautiful with wild poppies, anemones and hollyhocks. Now all is sere and dry in the heat of summer, and it is beginning to gloom over with the approaching twilight.

We enter the city through the Triumphal Arch, a triple gateway raised to celebrate Trajan's visit in AD 129. A minute's walk and we are in the Forum. This is an extraordinary one, being oval rather than circular or straight-sided. Its circumference is marked by about sixty Ionic pillars (the number changes each time I count); most are restored with their lintels in place. In the middle there is a crowd of a couple of dozen Iranians. We stare at each other with mild dislike: they perhaps critical at my large pinkness enveloped in boating jacket with brass buttons, and grey flannels; I not liking their dour, bearded faces and grim black robes. We carry on, between the Corinthian pillars which avenue the main street, the Street of Columns – 260 of them to either side of 650-yard length. It is evocative to see ruts in the hard limestone flagging, eroded by the wheels of chariots and carts of people long dead. There are pavements along the street: once they were shaded by awnings so that the citizens could window-shop in all weathers.

We have reached the Nymphaeum, to the west side of the street. This is a two-storey building acting as a shrine to Nymphs. The stonework is ornately carved and is reminiscent of Petra. Once, there were statues of

maidens holding jugs and ewers from which poured streams of water into marble-lined tanks. Sadly, the fountains have gone and the tanks, in which visiting nymphs may have disported, have been dry for centuries. I peer over the lip of the huge saucer of pinkish stone which has been placed in front of the building, but it is bone dry.

There has been much restoration since I was first here twenty years ago. Obviously I have no objection to the excavations, the unveiling of the buildings and streets from their mantling of desert sand; and I cannot grumble much on restoration, certainly not when they have re-erected pillars and replaced tumbled stones, but the work on the North Theatre seems to have been a bit heavy handed: in certain areas none of the original building is visible behind the newly installed masonry. The Temple of Artemis has been officially vandalised: as we stroll uphill I see, vividly noticeable amid the ancient stones of the platforms and columns of the temple, two flights of newly laid steps, as pinkly raw as a baby's bottom. But still, Artemis' temple remains the most impressive of all the ruins, as befits the patron goddess to the city. The most remarkable of its remnants are the colossal pillars over fifty feet high. Artemis' statue was once on a raised platform at the west end – no sign of her now; destroyed by invading Muslim or Crusader. Hassan and I stand on the platform and look at the city spread below us. A human skeleton is horrific, but the bared skeleton of a building or city can be beautiful. Only the bones of Gerasa remain: once all the buildings, even the pillars, were painted in vivid reds, blues, greens and yellows, now all colour has been bleached away by the sun and rains of a millennium; the roofs were once tiled with red pantiles, the shops and lanes shaded with awnings, all gone; but it is perhaps even more beautiful in its stark simplicity. Hassan and I stare through the twilight at the forest of pillars, the hunched backs of some of the buildings; the warm evening breeze whispers through the dry grasses and flowers stems; as we look the muezzin begin to call out from the minarets of the adjacent village and spotlights are turned on and the whole city glows into a ghostly existence.

Much of the masonry from the wallings, monumental gates and stairs of the temple were used later for building the ensuing Christian churches. There are several of these within a hundred yards of the

Temple of Artemis, but we avoid their jumble of walls and cells which are becoming dangerously obscured in the gloom and walk round their mazy muddle until we are below the South Theatre (capable of holding 5000 spectators) and the adjacent Temple of Zeus. A left turn downhill, through the now deserted Forum and soon back in the Land-Rover heading towards Amman and dinner and bed. I will be flying back to Egypt tomorrow; home the next day, to see Dominie and tell her about the ancient city whispering its memories in the mountains of Gilead.

 **Macao, 5 August 1997.** Mike C*** is the 'incoming' Queen's Messenger, on his way back from Outer Mongolia. We both have a full day here 'in transit', with nothing to do, so we have decided to go forty miles up the western coast of China, to Macao, 'The Wickedest city in the East', full of gamblers, drug addicts and naughty women.

> A weed from Catholic Europe, it took root
> Between some yellow mountains and a sea,
> Its gay stone houses an exotic fruit
> A Portugal-cum-China oddity
>
> Rococo images of saint and Saviour
> Promises its gamblers fortunes when they die,
> Churches alongside brothels testify
> That faith can pardon natural behaviour . . .
>
> And nothing serious can happen here.
> W.H. Auden, 'Macao', from *Journey to a War*

Macao can be defined as a city-state, perhaps comparable with present-day Monaco or medieval Venice or even the Athens of the Classical age. It is officially termed a 'Chinese territory under Portuguese administration'. It will be handed back to China on 20 December 1999. It was founded by Portuguese traders and missionaries in the middle of the sixteenth century and the ensuing 400 years have resulted in a unique

blend of two cultures, occidental and oriental. The total area is about seven square miles and consists of a peninsula and two islands, all linked by bridges or causeways. It has many old, interesting and picturesque areas, mostly on the peninsula, but its attraction to the majority of its visitors is its enormous choice of casinos. Within these day-made-nights the gamut of gambling games is played, not only the conventional Western ones such as roulette, black jack, baccarat and boule but also the Eastern such as *fan-tan* and *dai-siu*. There are also hundreds of slot machines known locally as 'hungry tigers'.

It is not entirely committed to idleness or frivolity: Macao is still an outlet for rice, fish and goods, also a big producer of textiles and clothing.

To get to the ferry Mike and I have to walk through the peculiar temperature differences of Hong Kong, either of Nature or of Mankind: the muggy heat of the open air; the blissful coolness of the air-conditioned shopping malls. We pass through an alleyway where a shop is selling extremely explicit little figurines of couples copulating in a variety of usual and unusual positions. Mike stops to inspect them: 'These are ivory and expensive,' he says, 'but there are plastic copies which are quite cheap and I often buy a pocketful. They are very useful when at cocktail parties as guest of some of my primmer and more respectable friends. I put one or two on their mantlepieces when no one is looking – conversation pieces: for the guests during the party, for the hosts when it is all over and they are clearing up.'

We arrive at the ferry terminal and our passports are stamped; there is some extra, puzzled scrutiny as they are Queen's Messenger ones, burgundy, with the personal Royal coat-of-arms. The immigration/emigration staff have not seen their like before. By 10.30 we are leaving port in a large catamaran, the twin-hulled *Turbo Cat*.

It is a smooth crossing: we skitter over the calm waters between the islands of the archipelago. After an hour we arrive at Macao.

At first sight, from the sea, Macao looks very like Hong Kong: much of the former coastal shallows are now reclaimed land covered with skyscrapers – offices, flats, hotels and the convolutions of aerial roadways. Amid all this one sees the Macaoan speciality: the huge casinos

with lumpish embellishments – golden domes, fatly limbed balconies, huge nameboards in neon lighting.

Having landed, we decide that although there is a lot to see, because of the short time we have (seven hours) and the appallingly muggy heat, we will concentrate our sightseeing on the famous ruined church of Saint Paul's and the conveniently adjacent Citadel. This will entail rambles through the little side streets and markets and squares during which we should get an overall feel of the place.

As we walk up the waterfront we decide that, in comparison to Hong Kong, Macao is much quieter, there is not nearly as much traffic and there are far fewer people on the pavements. The people seem less animated: in Hong Kong they stand back and shout at each other, here they lean forward and whisper.

We reach the largest and best known of the casinos, the Lisboa. It is a massive and weirdly ornamented building with domes and balconies. We enter and go first to one of the slot-machine halls. There are several people working on them. Each person has a plastic bowl full of coins, from them he is shovelling money into the machines like a stoker at a furnace. I put a two-dollar coin in a slot, pull a handle; there is a trundling noise, a lot of flashing lights, three spinning pictures stop to rest to reveal a row of assorted fruits, and nothing comes out. So, that's my gamble for the day done.

We enter a large circular room with an ornate plaster ceiling above many baize-topped tables upon which a variety of games are being played. Although it is only about ten o'clock in the morning the place looks packed. The seated players are silent and grim. There is a triple bank of viewers looking over their shoulders. The dealers are young and sleek; they are the only people who smile, secret and despising, arrogant with their power of distributing despair or exaltation. There is little glamour, even the chips are ugly and practical, disks of mottled plastic, not like the lovely slivers of carved mother-of-pearl we have at home. The players are drab: here is a burly man in scruffy denims, he has just changed HK$10,000 into chips and sits with his face impassive, but he has trembling hands and his feet are wrapped tightly round his chair legs; there is a smaller man who ceaselessly fidgets with his jacket cuffs and pulls at his lapels but his face too is impassive; an adolescent puts

his last chip on a number, watches as it fails to come up and then suddenly springs to his feet and forces his way out. Poor fellow, he looks too young and too poor to have lost so much.

We leave to enter a meanderation of narrow cobbled streets and small squares: a blend of the *hutongs* of Peking and the back streets of small towns in the Algarve. This Portuguese/Chinese mixture is emphasised by the names above the shop windows: Edificio Fai Sang, Mobilia de Long Ngai, Agencia Comercial Man Meng, Firma Cheong U, Chong Siu-Importa Cao. In the pleasantly cosy main square is the Leal Senado (Muncipal Council), an elegant example of Portuguese architecture: inside it is full of the traditionally Portuguese blue and white tiling.

During our ramble we sometimes enter the churches we are passing. Macao was once the centre of oriental Christianity, generating an immense bustle of activity, sending forth streams of missionaries, churning out theological and philosophical treatises, teaching and tending. Like all such organisations it was occasionally assailed by either Nature or politics, perhaps the biggest wound being self-inflicted: when the Vatican ruled that the governing Jesuits and Augustinians were forbidden to admit 'ancestor worship' as part of the Christian routine. In its prime, Macao was reputed to have more churches than the Vatican, and certainly the 24,000 Christians here are well served. The churches are beautiful, particularly inside. With their ornate plasterwork, painted white like the finest icing sugar, and their ornamentation of fretted woodwork, often also painted in creams and turquoise and gold, they resemble gigantic wedding cakes, enfiladed by a multitude of saints. These saints do not look Chinese, most of them do not even look Portuguese, but Anglo-Saxon: the female saints have pink and white English-rose complexions; the male saints, particularly the beefy ones stripped for some painful martyrdom, look as if they are about to trot onto the rugger pitch. Some of the church contents are pleasingly quaint: Saint Augustine's contains the grave of Maria de Moura and the arm of her husband, Captain António Albuquerque Coelho, which was cut off in a fight with one of her suitors; Saint Antony was a 'military' saint and on his feast day the President of the Senate pays his image his wages and the statue is taken on a tour of inspection of the city battle-

ments. Saint James is another 'soldier', the official military defender of Macao. At night, sometimes, his image tip-toes off on secret patrol round the city: proof of this are his boots, which are occasionally found to be muddy. He was once allocated a soldier-servant to clean them. One day the idle man skipped his duties and next day was punished with a wallop on his head from the saint's sword.

We have now arrived at the most impressive church of all – although there is nothing much left of it. The church of Saint Paul's was originally called the Church of the Mother of God: I don't know why they changed its name. It was built soon after the settlement of the Portuguese: the cornerstone is dated 1602. A college for the teaching of Christianity was also built nearby. In its heyday it was described as 'the greatest Monument to Christianity in all the Eastern lands', so famous that it was showered with presents from all of Christendom. In 1835 God's attention was distracted and the building caught fire and now all that is left above ground is the huge façade and the flights of steps leading up to it.

It was probably designed by Italian Jesuits and was constructed with the assistance of Christian Japanese artists and craftsmen. Built from granite, the surface is durable enough to keep the carving sharp and new. Apart from the stonework, the ornamentation consists of bronze statues. They were cast in a nearby cannon and bell foundry.

The silhouette of the front façade looming in the sky looks like a great altarpiece. It is divided up vertically by pillars which continue above the roof-line and into the sky as a series of pinnacles. The horizontal divisions are of four tiers. The top one is a triangular pediment, the lower ones enlarge as they descend, and have arches and niches. The pediment is surmounted by a cross of Jerusalem; within the triangle of of the pediment is a bronze dove. By the shape of it, one is reminded that the dodo was also of the pigeon family. Also of bronze is the statue of the Virgin Mary below, and the lower rank of the four Jesuit Saints – Ignatius, Francisco de Borja, Francisco Xavier and Luis Gonzaga. The carving of the façade is like nothing I have ever seen before. It is a strange amalgamation of the Portuguese, Italian and Japanese: insular and unique, a one-off like the Easter Island statues or the Minoan bull frescoes or the Pictish stelae. Good examples of this here are the

[179]

bronze statue of Our Lady of Assumption with its framing of stone flowers, the peony of China and the chrysanthemum of Japan; the seven-headed hydra which has the comfortable appearance of another dodo; and the winged skeleton, half-dragon, half-demon. The head Jesuits of the church and the adjacent college were awarded the rank of Mandarin and one can see the socket mark for their Mandarin banners which flew in front of the church.

Behind and under the old floor of the church there is a crypt. It holds a stark and simple lectern; the altar is amid an artful jumble of huge old blocks of building stone. To either side there are narrow granite shelves, protected by strips of thick glass. We peer into the darkness of the niches and see human bones, neatly arrayed like ornaments on chimneypieces. There is a small museum adjacent. Most of the exhibits are little pottery figurines; there are a few interesting pictures, one of which is of a horrific scene of a mass crucifixion. Those being crucified (twenty-three of them) have expressions of stoic smugness, as if they know that they are BEING GOOD.

Out into the heat once more. Up a steep, cobbled walkway, through an arch and we are in the fort, the Citadel of Sao Paulo do Monte. It is like a cosy little park walled in by battlements. The many cannon, positioned to face out to sea, look more like toys than anything dangerous, although in 1622 a lucky shot from one (fired by a priest) landed in the ammunition store of a besieging Dutch ship, causing the potential invaders to retreat hurriedly. We squeeze alongside a great old cannon and peer between the teeth of the battlements at the town below. Intriguingly the most notable sound is not the roar of traffic but of air-conditioning units.

We have now walked on to the Protestant cemetery. It is walled, with a nice little chapel by the entrance gate. The building is a bit stark, especially in relation to all the Roman Catholic ornamentation we have seen elsewhere, but it is cosy with the seats and backs of the pews of woven cane, to let out the heat generated by long sermons. At present, I am sitting on a tomb in the graveyard. The 150 or so graves are aligned on two terraces: lawned, flowerbedded and shaded by large trees and shrubs – frangipanis, bauhinias and banyans. Pigeons coo and potter about. All is very peaceful in comparison to the causes of death which

were often sudden and unpleasant. There are many graves to seamen, as one can see from the nautical ways of dying: drowning, falling, disease, in battle. The spelling of the Chinese masons was sometimes a bit shaky: I have read 'REST IN PIECE', 'Commander of the Bark Calcutta', 'Our Saviour Christ to Meat' and 'SECRET to the memory' (of the Peninsular's Apprentice boy who was killed by a 'Fall into the hold'). The burials include Winston Churchill's great-uncle, Captain Lord Henry Spencer-Churchill, a Joseph Adams who was the grandson of John Adams, the second American President, Thomas Beale the opium king and Robert Morrison who translated the Bible into Chinese.

Back in Hong Kong. 'We've been to Macao,' we tell Keith, the security officer.

'Not many people about, were there? Almost deserted of tourists now, it is, and the hotel rates are as low as 20 per cent. It's the inter-triad warfare, you see.'

'Warfare!'

'For the last ten months Macao has been terrorised by fighting between the gambling Triads. At least sixteen people have been killed – one suspects that such low numbers are due to bloody bad marksmanship and incompetence as there have been several machine-gun attacks, bombings and incendiary raids.'

And Mike and I did not even see any naughty women.

 **Shanghai, 6 August 1997.** This morning I undertook the two-hour, 900-mile flight from Hong Kong to Shanghai and later this afternoon I shall be returning to Hong Kong on the same aeroplane.

Shanghai is a trading and industrial city sited on an estuary of the Yangtze, in a tidal tributary called the Whangpoo. My meeting escort, who had a mind for figures, told me that it is the largest city in China with over 7,000,000 bicycles and is China's most important port with the world's biggest accumulation of dockside cranes. Education and the arts are also here in abundance, with many theatres and museums and about 200 uni-

versities, polytechnics and 'learned societies'. Its period of greatest development started with the Treaty of Nanking in 1842 which allowed Shanghai to become a Western-dominated 'open' trading area. The contrasting but compatible abilities of Western entrepreneurs and Chinese merchants combined, like a warp and a weft, into a fabric of such strength that in spite of the complications of Chinese history Shanghai remained a great international trading centre and money market until the Communists took over in 1949. They thought it decadent, but they also wanted its money, so they plundered the liquid assets, but they did nothing in return. The lack of reinvestment together with the persecution of the money-making classes finally killed the goose which had laid the golden eggs.

Is this what will happen to Hong Kong?

Perhaps not. The Chinese government seems to have been taught a lesson, and a stock market was opened recently in Shanghai, and the 'market economy' is being lauded.

So there is little to see which is of historical interest. What is interesting is the commercial life of the recent past and the potential future. As I have only a couple of spare hours here I will go to the Bund, which is the best examples of both of these.

At present I am in the British Consulate-General. On the outside it is an ultra-modern building; inside, it is a bit like an English pub, with wallpaper which changes colour at a dado strip halfway up the walls, and 'ye olde oake' panelling: even the doors to the lavatories are oak panelled. When I got into the lift with fifteen men of Chinese/Japanese features I was interested to hear that their common language was English.

11.55 hours. Off we go, my driver has been asked to take me to the Bund via a few of the lesser streets so that I can get a good impression of life off the main roads.

The narrow streets are congested with traffic; there are many more motor-cars than bicycles compared with Peking. The wider streets are avenued with plane trees, with trolley-bus lines overhead. Tall, new office blocks tower above the single- and two-storey shops and living quarters. There are many shops and restaurants; one would not have

seen any of these in China twelve years ago, except a few of the state-run ones. Another sign of the fading of Communism is the plethora of taxis, I can count ten within thirty yards of me at present. There are many little tri-cars boxed in with canvas, looking like small mobile loos. Sometimes a washing line droops over the pavement: the one nearest me dangles four pink towels, a pair of socks, a bra, two T-shirts and some vests and pants. Stacked on the pavements outside the smaller dwellings are bicycles, pails and cooking equipment. People are all in summer clothes; some carry parasols. There are also parasols over the stalls of food and iced drinks sellers. Some of the young girls have their hair dyed brown and even a few of the young men have had their hair waved (all this is very much disapproved of by the older generation). An old man carries some ewers on a bamboo yoke. A mournful man stands sadly by his vehicle; few things are more abject than a broken-down tricycle.

Now the street is full of banners and advertisements printed on fabric.

My driver has become bored creeping about and is overtaking a stationary queue of traffic-jam, waving imperiously at the oncoming vehicles to get out of the way. He has now put on a roof-flasher and we go charging the wrong way up a side street. Now he is hooting aggressively. It is a bit unfair that everyone is scowling at *me*.

We have reached our destination: I leave the air-conditioned luxury of my car and enter the stifling heat and hurly-burly of the outside world. The car is parked beside the Peace Hotel. I have told the driver I will be back in two hours.

The Peace Hotel, formerly the Cathay Hotel, was built in 1926. A plaque outside says: 'Selected as Most Famous Hotel in the world 1991 by the Most Famous Hotel in the World Organisation'; sounds like a mutual back-scratching set-up. I enter through the revolving door into the marble, mahogany and brass lobby. It is just like any other good 1920s hotel, but all the famous old ambience is gone; it is no longer a centre of gossip and political intrigue and financial wheeler-dealing, just some raw-looking Australian tourists in shorts and a few suited businessmen in sibilant conversation by the reception counter. I leave.

It is now right in the middle of lunch hour and many people are

sitting on steps eating with one hand and fanning themselves cool with the other. Although the women of Hong Kong are often pretty, and can be rather sweet in a giggly way, they are inclined to be small and squeaky. The people of Shanghai are taller; some of the women have a svelte elegance – in contrast to the hectic scurry of Hong Kong, they seem more inclined to glide and amble – but perhaps that is because it is the lunch hour.

The Bund is the most famous thoroughfare in all of Cathay. 'Bund' is the old Anglo-Indian word for this waterfront broadway, the official name is the Zhongshan Dong Yi Lu. To landward it is dominated by a great swathe of colonial buildings of the 1920s and 1930s – trading houses, banks, hotels, shipping offices. The Westerners in this area were mostly British, American and French, and this is reflected in the architecture: at first sight it resembles Liverpool, with a touch of New York's Art Deco, and a splash (particularly in the florid interiors) of bourgeois French. Some of the buildings are faced with ashlar blocks. There are pediments, arches, pillars, clock towers and other outward evidence of commercial success. Alongside this crescent of buildings runs the main road, then further to seaward are wide, ambulatory pavements, strips of formal garden bedding and then the river. Here, the waters are about 400 yards wide and thirty feet deep, capable of taking vessels of up to 10,000 tons. There is a big ship moored in midstream, several others are moored alongside the banks, but most of the river craft seem to be on the move. Many of them are small barges with low silhouettes, they look like semi-submerged otters; there are scores of them and they all sound like little lawnmowers as they chunter upstream and down.

There is a notice board with a list of rules. Some are severe authoritarian ones such as the banning of 'any social activities'. However I rather like:

'Rule 5. Any action repugnant to the eye is prohibited in the area.'

The heat and humidity has become quite frightful, black thunderclouds are gathering; yet still the women sit in gossiping groups, dressed in summer colours so that their fluttering fans resemble the wings of butterlifes amid clumps of flowers.

A pleasantly smiling man with a fat, bland face approaches me. He is fanning himself vigorously with a paper and bamboo fan. 'Hallo,' he

says, suddenly shaking me by the hand. 'I am here on holiday, are you American?'

'No, English.'

'That is so charming and of great historical interest. I am a long-serving student of olden periods. I also am an artist. I can do something for you.'

He takes out a small piece of paper and some scissors: he gazes at me piercingly and starts to snip – he is an artist of silhouettes.

'No!' I cry, sidling away, 'no thank you. I'm sorry, but I have no money on me.'

'Oh!' he cries back, sadly, 'but you are so handsome.'

This at least is a relief: I was beginning to worry that my face empurpling with the heat and the hair on the back of my head rat-tailing with sweat were perhaps illegal actions 'repugnant to the eye'.

I pass a big statue of Mao Tse Tung – a thorough waste of five tons of decent bronze in my opinion. Next to him, smaller, but much more noticeable, is a plastic statue of a cow. It is wearing a striped T-shirt, yellow shorts, gym shoes and is poised on one leg in a coy dance. It is advertising Fujifilm. Mao is leaning back slightly and looking at it in disgust: Communism, sour and puritan and regulated, inspecting Capitalism, vulgar and exuberant and unruly.

And, as if in mighty disapproval, thunder growls and mutters, the sky is almost black, people start to scurry, a few big drops splash down – by the time I have reached my car I am soaked. Back to the Consulate-General – back to the aeroplane – back to Hong Kong.

Hong Kong, 7 August 1997. So, what's the difference? What has changed during the five weeks that this remnant of the British Empire was handed over to the Chinese?

Apparently, almost nothing, just the flags: the Red Banner of China rather than the Union Jack flies from public buildings; I felt a bit of a frisson when I saw the red flag over HMS *Tamar*, it was sad seeing the cenotaph bare, stripped of the colours of our army, navy and air force, it seemed as if

all that the Dead had fought for was finished, no longer relevant. And it is quieter: surprisingly, there are even fewer soldiers and police on the streets; everyone who can has gone away on holiday; there are not even many tourists.

Our new headquarters is an office block, no longer the cosy confines of Osborne Barracks. Keith D*** is the Chief Security Officer in charge. After I had delivered the bags he took me on a tour round it. The only ornamentation in the stark entrance lobby is a flight of three plaster cranes flying down the course of the escalators. Keith nodded at them: 'They have bad vibes, those birds, you see,' he said, 'they are not only flying out of the building, but they are flying westwards towards the sunset: a doubly unfortunate occurrence.'

'Why not paint them black, or some unlucky colour, then they could represent departing misfortune?' I suggested.

Keith shook his head sadly: 'No good, they are white, look, and that is an unlucky colour already, you see, so misfortune is totally upon us.'

This morning I have been invited to visit the Kadoorie Farm and Botanic Garden.

The Star Ferry (the *Twinkling Star* today) is full of commuters but the five-minute crossing from the island to the mainland is as enjoyable as always: the great cliffs of glass and concrete which edge the sea-strait, the water abustle with every type of craft from barges and junks to patrol boats and cockle-shell sampans. I disembark from the ferry and board the MTR (Mass Transit [underground] Railway) from Tsim Sha Tsui to Kowloon Tong via Mong Kok – I feel an Old China Hand now that these names roll familiarly off my tongue. The carriages also are packed with commuters. It is so crowded that belt buckles are rubbing together and people are reading their neighbours' newspapers and breathing the fumes of each other's breakfasts. As I look over the squash around me I think how thoughtful it was of God to have made us bipeds, ideally shaped for cramming into a train; how inconvenient if we were on all fours, and perhaps embarrassing – it is bad enough having to stare into someone's earhole or nuzzle into someone's armpit. At Kowloon Tong I change onto the KCR (Kowloon–Canton Railway) to Tai Wo. Huge residential skyscrapers sprout out of the ground like the

strange constructions of a massive termite. Mankind is evolving from a rural, individual mammal to an urbanised, social insect. As we go further north, the views become less domesticated and more attractive with craggy gorges, covered with luxuriant growth; much of it is blanketed by a morning glory with large, mauve, trumpet-shaped flowers.

At Tai Wo I leave the train and take a taxi for the last couple of miles.

My two guides are awaiting for me in the entrance of the farm and garden. They are two young Hong Kong Chinese: the senior is Mr Kong, who smiles a lot; the junior is Simon, who speaks English well. They take me into the entrance lodge and Simon explains the purpose and layout of the complex.

It was all founded in 1951 by Sir Horace Kadoorie and, to a lesser extent, his brother Lawrence. Part of it was developed into a wonderfully landscaped botanical garden, taking advantage of the mountain streams and the lush natural vegetation; another part was developed as a place for educating people into the methods of self-sufficient smallholding and market gardening. About 350,000 refugees and poverty-stricken peasants were thus educated – and often financed with plots of land and equipment. Later, an agricultural course for retiring Gurkhas was started up. The aim of the course was: 'to provide retiring Gurkha soldiers with basic agricultural skills . . . various aspects of animal husbandry, chicken and pig farming, fruit and vegetable growing, bee keeping and milk and curd making, . . . and how to culture pond fish.' Over 7000 Ghurkhas went through the course between its inception in 1968 and the last course in September 1996. After that, the *soi-disant* 'Conservative' British Government destroyed the Brigade of Ghurkhas so it was no longer relevant; also the agricultural land in Hong Kong has been so diminished by buildings and road-making that there is little room for market gardeners or smallholders. So the organisation changed itself into one specialising in conservation, particularly of Hong Kong flora and fauna, also retaining the focus on education, particularly appreciation of the natural world.

The site is on the side of a mountain range. Because of the valley ridges and angled sides it faces differing directions and it ranges in height from about 500 to 2000 feet, thus there are a variety of microclimates, both vertical and horizontal.

We embus into a jeep and Simon starts to drive up on one of the fifteen miles of roads that zigzag over the estate. Our intention is to make for the highest point (1975 feet) and sightsee as we descend. We drive through a pleasant mixture of landscaped farm-plots and garden beddings, alternated with wild scrub and forest. The labourers at work all seem to be women. They are of the local Hakka tribe and are wearing their traditional attractive hats like large straw discs with hanging pelmets of black gauze. We pass gangs of schoolchildren toiling uphill. They hold out weary arms in despairing attempts to hitch a lift.

We have reached the top peak, called after Kwun Yum Shan – a goddess of Love and Compassion. The view is magnificent, overlooking long valleys towards the waters sprinkled with the islands of the Tolo archipelago. There is a little copse of low trees and bushes at the very top. Amid them are the remains of ancient altars where farmers used to come and pray for good harvests: apt for a site which is concerned with farming. A fascinating aspect of this site is the 'Dragon's Breath'. This is the warm air exhaled from some holes in the ground. The holes are the mouths of long, subterranean volcanic pipes which lead down to the foot of the mountain. The warm air of the lowlands enters these tunnels and is wafted up by its lighter weight. The statue of the goddess Kwun Yum Shan stands in the shrubbery near one of the warm-air vents. She has a serene, brooding expression. She was sent to hell for refusing to marry and provide her father with an heir. Her compassionate nature was such that she turned hell into a paradise and was expelled for being a nuisance. She is now in heaven, having attained her status as a goddess. The scripture was crafted by Nicholas Dimbleby, who also made Sofka, the mermaid in my garden pond. I nod to the goddess and pass on Sofka's regards: sometimes I am so twee I get quite worried.

We start our descent. There are traces of old terracing on the hilltops all around us which are the remains of ancient tea plantations. We pass a scattering of pavilions pleasantly set in groves and on knoll tops. There is an aviary. Simon is particularly proud of the success they have had in breeding three threatened species: the blue crowned pigeon – enormous and gawky; the black-necked swan – bad-tempered; and the blue-gold Macaw – beautifully coloured and hideously screeching.

There is also an orchid 'haven'. There are 120 species of orchid in Hong Kong, thirteen of which are endemic. Many of them are disappearing because of picking and urbanisation. The orchid haven is attempting to rear and reintroduce the endangered species. I inspect displays of organic farming. There is a poultry section: Simon tells me that I am the first person ever to ask to see their broiler unit. The chickens in this unit are mainly given away to the employees, as bonuses. I go round the hatcheries and the meat and egg units. All the chickens seem happy and, although lit only by daylight, do not seem to go in for the feather pecking and anti-social behaviour one would expect. After a pretty lotus pond there is a raptor sanctuary. The aim of this place is to rehabilitate or alternatively to breed from injured raptors, preferably releasing those that recover back to the wild. I look at a collection of kites, hawks, falcons and owls, who seem to be in various stages of injury – mainly broken wings from vehicles. There is a mad eagle who tries to look at us by turning his head upside down. Most people would prefer and approve of this bird collection rather than the farmed chickens, but somehow I do not: I know that the idea of the bird-hospital-cum-lunatic-asylum is worthy, but the effect is utterly dankly despairingly awfully depressing.

We stop at the offices and I am introduced to a shy, serious, prim Chinese girl who is on loan from Cambridge University. She disapproves of pollution. She is keen on composting. She is worried about acid rain. She speaks warmly of the recycling of human excretory products. She dislikes the Lychee stink bug but admires the Chinese peacock butterfly. She offers me some of the orchard produce to sample: the macademia nut – in an almost globular, iron-hard shell, in taste slightly like a hazel, but more crunchy; the Chinese wampee – clusters of about thirty small fruits, teardrop shaped, coloured attractively with an 'old gold' skin and jade-green seeds around a jelly-like flesh, sweet and slightly astringent; the lychee – the white fruit of fleshy flaps wrapped round the glossy brown seed; a smaller lychee type which is called 'lychee's servant' or 'dragon's eye' – pleasant, although unattractive after being removed from its round brittle skin, being rather slimy with a translucent milkiness.

Mr Kang shows me an obituary on the founder.

Sir Elly Kadoorie, a Sephardic Jew who emigrated from Baghdad to Hong Kong, was the originator of the family fortunes. These were firstly built up through the monopolistic supply of electricity and a string of grand hotels, of which the flagship was the Majestic Peninsula on the Kowloon waterfront. All this was eliminated by the Japanese invasion and Elly was paraded gloatingly through the streets of Hong Kong and died in a Japanese camp. He had two sons. Lord Lawrence, who was the last of the colony's traditional Taipans and the first man from Hong Kong to be created a life peer, and Sir Horace, his younger brother. After the war the brothers picked up the traces and eventually assembled a fortune worth at least HK$2,000,000. They both felt that they owed the community for their good fortune and were generous with their patronage, particularly Sir Horace.

'Sir Horace was a retiring figure, kindly but shrewd. He was revered throughout the New Territories, where local bus drivers would flash their headlights and salute when he passed, and in Nepal which he continued to visit annually. His visits to there, particularly in his final years, became legendary. When he could no longer walk his chair was carried on the shoulders of devoted ex-Gurkhas. . . . In remote regions where hundreds had gathered, some having walked for days from their homes, it became clear that this was less an exercise in relief aid than a mystical celebration of life brought about by the visits of a great soul. He died at the age of 92, in April 1995.'

He never married. Perhaps, like some saints, his love for mankind was too all-embracing to concentrate on just one person; perhaps, when the old man went to heaven, he found a serenely brooding goddess waiting for him.

I have returned to the island on the ferry (the *Morning Star* this time) and am now prowling around the antique area about Cat Street and Ladder Street. As much as the goods behind the shop windows, I appreciate the sign writing above them: the onomatopoeic names sounding out like a chiming of gongs and bells – Kwong Tai Hong, Chap Tu Tong, Koon Ku Kok, Yue Po Chai, Wa Cheong. There are interesting captions on

the photographs of 'Old Hong Kong' in a junk shop: 'Black Pussy the prostitute Bathing'; 'Fortun Telling'; and a man stitching at a skirt – 'Broken Dress Repairing'. There is a photograph of some men in a howdah being attacked by an elephant. And that reminds me of Khristian Borganstrum.

Nepal tigers. *Spring 1985.* We should have realised that the only elephant with tusks is the only bull, and that a bull in company with a lot of cows cannot keep his trunk to himself.

Charles and I had made a bee-line for this particular elephant. His magnificent tusks and massive size made him stand out impressively among the herd of grey hulks which lurked and swayed in the shade of the trees by our thatched quarters. We mounted him by climbing a flight of steps onto a platform and from there clambering down into the howdah. This is simply a wooden frame upon a a mattress-sized cushion. Each howdah has a brass plate engraved with the elephant's name. Ours is called Khristian Borganstrum. 'This,' I think, 'is a rum name for an elephant, I'd expect something like Puggaree or Chuntah Singh.'

Our mahout is a small man with huge toenails and a spiked iron bar. He uses the latter to reprimand his steed and the former for steering and accelerating: an energetic scraping with his toenails behind Khris's ears indicating 'left', 'right' or 'faster'.

We have moved off into an ocean of elephant grass, so tall that it reaches halfway up our legs which dangle down from the howdahs. Riding an elephant is rather like being in a boat: it rolls and undulates slightly; there are almost no jerky movements, so one glides through the grass and shrubbery like a barge ploughing through a weed-filled lagoon; only a continuous cacophony of rumbles and blowings emanating from the stern spoils the general impression of silent grace. Like all vegetarians – human or others – the elephant ceaselessly farts. The Indian elephant, unlike the African one, has two large round bumps on top of its head. They are sprinkled with a few sparse hairs. I feel rather

sad looking down on this defenceless bald head; it seems to belong to some poor old man.

We have reached the banks of the river and wait in a queue as there is only one elephant-sized gap in the bushes by the ford. We are going last, as rearguard. As we stand, Khris reaches out with his trunk and gives the cow-elephant in front of him a rude tweak in a naughty place. Our mahout reacts in shocked disapproval, banging Khris on the top of his head with the iron implement and gibbering cries of reproof. Khris is ignoring these reprimands: his roguish tweaks have developed into rather embarrassing fondles. Charles and I sit looking po-faced and scanning the far horizon. The rage of our mahout attains such a frenzy that I fear he might annoy Khris, who could reach up with his trunk, pluck his tormentor off his nape and hove him into the nearest thorn bush. Then we will be left without a driver.

Our quarries are the Royal Bengal tiger and the Great Indian one-horned rhinoceros: the former Mowgli's magnificent Sher Kahn, the latter with folds in the skin which make it look armour-plated; both of them rare, large and bad-tempered. We see plenty of rhinos. The elephants advance through the long grass in a wide rank about fifty yards apart, like a squardon of tanks in battle formation. A lookout stands on the rump of one of the elephants. Occasionally he shouts and points and all the elephants hurry up and group in a semicircle around a resting rhinoceros, who lumbers to its feet and looks embarrassed, like someone caught secretly sunbathing in the corn. It then hurries off and we follow, photographing and shouting excitedly. I feel quite sorry for the uncouthly harassed beasts. We meet a large and tetchy bull rhino in a small lake. To our alarm, Khris is sent into the water to chivvy it out. The rhino cruises slowly off as we advance, but keeps looking angrily over his shoulder. Suddenly he stops and then whirls round in a billow of spray. From head-on the dark bulk and horned prow makes him look like a battle-ship. Charles and I sit as quiet as mice on Khris's back. Even our mahout sits still, goggling. We stare at each other for a bit, then with a contemptuous snort the rhino spins round and lumbers off into the reeds.

The lookout sets up a great caterwauling and pointing. All the elephants halt in their tracks except Khris, who is toenail-manoeuvred to

the lookout. He points down, below my dangling feet, and with a twitch of alarm I see, in the sandy soil, the impression of a huge pad: a tiger's pug mark.

The lookout speaks to us in a breathlessly eager manner: 'There is a gulley over there. Tiger's track goes into it. Khristian Borganstrum is big and brave. Has big tusks. He is elephant best able to defend himself. We always send him to flush out tigers.'

Charles and I do not share his enthusiasm. I think Khris is not too keen either, for now that we have plunged down into the thicket-filled gulley he has began to whoofle uneasily through his trunk. I draw my legs up clear of the undergrowth. The frightful little mahout scrabbles away with his toenails. We quest about with much rustling and snorting. Cries of encouragement and excitement peal out from the mahouts and passengers of the other elephants – it's alright for them, they're all safely far away. My eyes bulge with the intensity of scrutinising the herbage, every bush and tussock seems to have tawny patches and stripy shadows. What's that? A flicker, a running flame as of a bush fire suddenly lit and quenched; urgent yells of the 'GONE AWAY' type ring out from the lookout, disappointed cries are uttered by the onlookers, sighs of relief escape from Charles, me and Khris.

In the late afternoon we trek home. As the sun begins to set it becomes cool. By the time we reach the river, twilight has spread across the sky and the copper and gold gleams of the setting sun reflect on the wide expanse of the calm river. A dark shape with great hanging tail flaps across the waters into the heavy darkness of the jungle on the far bank. It is a peacock. From long, narrow punts men are fishing, their black silhouettes throw nets into the water and then stoop to haul them aboard; egrets are also fishing, standing motionless in the shallower waters. We dismount from our elephants, the mahouts unsaddle the howdahs, then all of us wade into the water. The elephants lie down and we scrub their round flanks and mop and rinse. Khris burbles contentedly through his trunk and squirts up a fountain of water. Our mahout squawks an affectionate reproof. Beneath the water his toenails have a mother-of-pearl gleam in the rising moonlight like two rows of clam shells.

We saw a tiger later.

During the day we had passed a glum little mixed herd of goats and

young buffalo grazing in a desultory manner on the wiry scrub by the banks of the river Reu. 'Live bait,' said our mahout.

'What for?' we asked.

'The goats are for leopards, the buffalo for tigers. They are tied to a tree in the jungle in the evening. Big cats come and kill them. Then you come and watch.'

I gazed at the poor doomed animals with sympathetic awe.

Dinner was in the huge thatched rotunda that acts as general assembly hall, dining-room, restroom and bar. Some of the other tourists were quite frightful: 'That seat, which you have just taken, belongs to me,' said a German in a hectoring Teutonic voice to one of our party, Lavinia, as she sat down.

'Then doubtless you are pleased with the opportunity of giving it up to a lady,' Lavinia replied frostily.

Halfway through the meal a bell rang. 'That means that there has been a kill,' said the manager. 'It's too late in the evening for it to be a leopard, it must be a tiger. Those who want to see it must go now and get into the Land-Rovers.'

Earlier, I had resolved not to go, as I rather disapproved of the whole thing but, realising that the wretched buffalo was dead anyhow, I changed my mind. My conscience is flexible.

We drove between the tall treetrunks of a jungle track with our headlights dimmed for about twenty minutes. Then we disembussed and walked down a small winding path, the only light being a dim torch held by the bearer in front and the flick and gleam of the occasional ray of moonlight slanting through the black columns of the trees which sighed above our heads. I thought of the poor terrified animal which must have been driven along that path a few hours earlier. Finally the bearer extinguished his torch and whispered that we must take off our shoes. We tip-toed the last two or three furlongs and entered a low-roofed underground hut. It had slits in it, like a pillbox. I looked through. There, in a lamp-lit arena below us, a tiger sprawled over the corpse of a buffalo. It looked sated and languorous, like Nero lounging on a couch at the end of an orgy. Occasionally, with slow, sweeping strokes of its tongue, its eyes half closed, it licked blood from its prey's hindquarters. As magnificent as the tiger was, as macabre the scene and as great the

[194]

sacrifice of the bait, I soon was feeling guilty by being rather bored and hankering for my dinner. We finally left, tip-toed, tramped, and drove back to the rotunda; finished our meal, had a bath and went to bed, to be woken by the cheerful crowing of the jungle fowl at the crack of dawn.

It would be hypocritical and sanctimonious to say that my stay here has not been interesting and memorable, but ... the Nature Conservancy Council issued the aims for nature reserves: Conservation (protection), Research, Demonstration & advice, Education, Amenity & Access. So, the bureaucrats have decreed that animals are to be tolerated so that they may entertain the human being. Sometime, perhaps, a less condescending function may be admitted: the privacy of the animals.

 **Tokyo aerodrome, 8 August 1997.** Hong Kong to Japan and back, all in one day; I did not even leave the aerodrome at Tokyo. The first aerial sight was of Honshu, the largest of the archipelago of over 3000 islands which comprise Japan, and the one where Tokyo is sited. It appeared out of the sea as a colossal bay stretching in an almost perfect crescent from horizon to horizon. I then flew over neat farmland, very similar in its crowded busyness and flatness to the somewhat overpopulated countryside of south-east Essex. The most noticeable difference was the colour of the roofs of the agricultural buildings: most had been painted a pale, Cambridge blue. Then, again in perfect, natural symmetry, the cone of Mount Fuji appeared, hovering in the air above a haze of pollution.

My escort has been posted in this country for nearly two years. I asked him if he liked it. He was a thoughtful, analytical fellow, not like a lot of overseas Brits who are conditioned to dislike any strange place and despise any foreigners.

'The Japanese are remarkably like the English,' he said. 'The obvious similarity is that we are both islanders, with an islander's instinctive xenophobia and self-satisfaction. A spin-off is that the sea is a very important element in the national psyche: for example in both states the navy is senior to the army. Both islands are very overcrowded and

although the Japanese and British are great industrial nations the hearts of the civilians are still in the countryside. The two artistic practices of which both countries excel are poetry and gardening. And of course both countries are monarchies with long and esoteric traditions.'

'A big difference between the Japanese and us,' he continued, 'is their sense of humour. We think a man slipping on a banana skin is quite funny, but not as side-splittingly hilarious as do the Japanese. The screams of pain of a traffic accident victim may be drowned out by the laughter of the happy onlookers. On the other hand they can be serious about the most ridiculous things. Out of curiosity I went to the Museum of Parasites. I thought it would be a "Mickey-taking" set up, not a bit. They have 45,000 parasites carefully stored in earthquake-proof shelters, the pride of place in the exhibition galleries is a human tape worm, thirty feet long. The in-house shop sells T-shirts with the slogan "The Wonderful World of Worms".'

'Also they are utterly at variance with our individualism. They have a saying that "the nail which stands apart from the others is the one which the hammer hits first." And they have this thing about schoolgirls. A short while ago there were slot machines where for 700 yen, you could buy a packet of used schoolgirls' knickers.'

We debated the grammatical niceties between 'used schoolgirls' and 'used knickers' and then I felt thirsty and he went off to a slot machine – selling tins of drink. He came back beaming: 'Here, I bet you've never drunk a can of this before.' The name on the tin was 'SWEAT'. It tasted of fizzy lemonade.

I have returned from Japan and am sitting up in bed, late at night, sleepless with time-lag. There is an astonishing Japanese film on the television at the foot of my bed. It is a two-hour long cartoon and is a horrifically compatible mixture of the beautiful and the foul. The story is based on a motor-bicycle gang in the future of a doomed, urban mankind. Inter-gang-cum-tribal warfare takes place as a knife fight: disembowelled intestines writhe in iridescent coils on a pavement where a lithe cat-shadow slithers along the doorways; a kamikaze rider splatters himself against a wall and his bones and flesh explode like the bursting of a chrysanthemum firework; a girl with an enchantingly beautiful face

has her head torn off and her severed neck arteries spout fountains of blood in slow, beautiful curves against the lowering sky of a purple twilight, while with ballet-like grace her headless corpse sinks to the ground as her arms gesticulate and her legs totter in a final dance of death.

Peking, 9 August 1997. Peking – that ugly city of magical and entrancing names: the Garden of Floating Greenery, the Gate of Heavenly Peace, the Pavilion of Eternal Spring, the Hall of Exquisite Jade, the Park of Purple Bamboo, the Temple of White Clouds and the Chapel of Universal Brotherly Love; and those of the tombs, the Dong-lings, such as the Yu-ling, the Jing-ling and the Ding-dong-ling of the Empress Dowager Cixi.

As usual I have been quartered in the Jianguo Hotel, the favourite of all my Queen's Messenger accommodations throughout the world: I always feel a surge of pleasure as I step into the large but cosy entrance hall and see all the eccentric characters sitting sipping tea or swilling beer round the little tables, and the row of smiling faces along the long reception counter. However, stepping outside today is a less welcoming experience: it is only just after nine o'clock but already very hot, and I have planned a three- or four-hour walk, up the main drag to Tien-an-men Square, down to the antique shops of the Liu Li Chang area, then on to the Hot and Prickly, where I shall later have lunch.

First stop: to shop at the Friendship Store in Jianguomen Avenue. Buy Candy the mah-jong set she wants, a book (*100 Tang and Song Ci Poems*) and a toenail clipper. Tell them I will collect the mah-jong set later, don't want to lug it round all morning.

In the open space in front of the store there is the normal terrific bustle of people buying and selling: furtive sellers of pirated cassettes or 'antique' pots and figures; one-stringed fiddles are tweetled at me, flutes are tooted, bicycle bells are tinkled; vendors of huge fans made of peacock feathers strut and display; beggars show their contortions or miseries; furtively I slip a couple of bananas (given to me free in a bowl of fruit by the hotel) to the Tibetan woman with two small,

grubby infants. Further on, touts sit in a row on the low walls, their wares arrayed at their feet – toys made out of slivers of bamboo, cards of buttons, children's shoes, sunglasses or handbags. Four men are sitting on the pavement, playing cards. Amid all the delicate, graceful Chinese, most of us Westeners look great lumps, with our red hairy faces and piggy eyes.

Capitalism has spread along the road. Under the fly-under, where once two Queen's Messengers had to dodge from a line of tanks when taking the diplomatic mail during the Tien-an-men Square massacre, there are now stalls selling magazines, or orange juice, or bicycle bits. I have reached the long line of lawns and flowerbeds. I have often found four-leafed clover in these lawns of rough grass . . . yes! here's one – tweak – put it in my notebook. The air is full of ginger-coloured dragonflies. Many of the cosy little dwellings are being pulled down. In their place new skyscrapers are rearing out of the ground: banks, hotels, office blocks. The one I am walking past at present is entitled the 'Women Activity Centre'. There is not a single woman in sight, just five men lounging against some cars parked in the forecourt. Another masculine touch is that with its white-tiled façade and curved shape it resembles a huge urinal.

Having passed the massive hulk of the Peking Hotel it has become a pleasant perambulation under rustling poplars which shade the pavement to my left; to my right is a high wall painted the dark red of Old China. Couples are sitting on the low benches alongside it; here is a man asleep. There is a smell of sweet potatoes being baked in a converted oil-drum; several vendors are selling iced water from the little carts hitched on the back of bicycles.

Into the 100-acre expanse of Tien-an-men Square. From the archway which marks the entrance into the Forbidden City the huge photograph of Mao Tse Tung gazes blandly over the crowds, over the square to his mausoleum where, presumably, his ghost is busy explaining and making excuses to the other, angry ghosts which live in the square.

As I stand, musing at the picture, I notice three tiny girls beside me, looking up into my face.

'Hello,' one says.

'Hello,' I reply.

I could not have said anything more witty: they run off, screaming with laughter.

Liu Li Chang is a collection of alleyways and lanes which have been renovated in the Qing style. It is pleasant to walk on the flagged paving, between the low buildings whose tiled roofs have the traditional upturned eaves. For a total of fifteen American dollars I have bought three stone rubbings. They are in black wax on thin white paper and show different carriages being driven by divinities and pulled by different steeds: on one, by a pair of winged horses, on another, by a dragon, on the third by ordinary horses being guided by a bird. The stone slabs they have been traced from were originally carved between four and five thousand years ago.

I am now leaving the Tibetan shop, having successfully (30 per cent off) bargained over a block of wood with lines of delicate carvings on each side. From a few of the symbols I assume it is Buddhist, but I cannot guess its use, and I do not know what the different lines of figures carved on each surface represent. Neither does the salesman. It is of a close-grained, slightly yellow wood, perhaps box. It smells strongly of a heavy, exotic smoke. Perhaps it is loot from one of the monasteries, burned down during the Chinese invasion of Tibet in Mao's deliberate attempt to break the Tibetans' hearts and destroy their culture. (Later: I have been told that it is a *torra* mould for the dough of ritual bread.)

I had lunch at the Hot and Prickly with Yun Qing who made me try the 'Princess's Tears', i.e. the fried jellyfish. I thought it would be slimy and runny, but it was rubbery and tasteless. Yun Qing and I are now together in a rickshaw. Yun Qing (pronounced Yoon Shing) is aged twenty-eight, but she looks eighteen. She is a 'modern' girl: her hair is cut short, she wears smart jeans and an expensive jacket; to be unmarried at her age is rare, and disapproved of. She and I are mutual friends of Josh Green, who is a travel agent – and nightclub owner – in Peking, and she is acting as my guide this afternoon, on an afternoon's wander round part of the city. The rickshaw is a heavier edition of the normal bicycle, with a longer wheelbase; the 'engine', a burly Chinese, sits on the bicycle seat

[199]

and we sit side-by-side behind on a comfortably furnished sofa. An overhead awning keeps the sun off our heads. The whole contraption seems flimsy but strong, like a micro flyer. Only the wooden pedals seem crude. The sensation is very like being in a punt, or on an elephant: the smooth gliding, the sudden surge forward, or the swoop to the side. As we sit serene, all around us there is intense activity: the traffic hoots behind and beside us, lorries rumble past, buses cut in, pedestrians zigzag between the vehicles; discernible among the mini-skirts and military uniforms on a pavement there are people having their hair cut, a hawker selling eggs, another mending punctures; distinctive among the fumes is a sudden stink of lavatory, now the scent of cooking.

When I am on a bicycle, the locals – if they notice me at all – generally look friendly, some even smile. Now they stare coldly. They are very racially conscious and I think disapprove of Yun Qing and me sitting together.

We arrive at the entrance of the Bai Hai Park and find Jo-Ann waiting for us, as planned. She is my American counterpart, sent to Peking with some urgent diplomatic message. I invited her to come with us, after she had finished her work in the American Embassy. She is tallish and fair-haired and athletic, her rather angular good looks are feminised by her fussy anxiety about anything unusual, particularly if it looks unhygienic.

I thought that the 'theme' for our walk round the park would be 'names': I have given Yun Qing a list of places I want to visit, to see if they live up to their titles.

We cross the Bridge of Eternal Peace (a bedlam of screeching children and babbling pedestrians), over the waters of the lake, and arrive on Qiong Hua Island. Yun Qing waves an elegant hand over the whole scene, explaining that the Bei Hai Park was in the enclosure called the Imperial City, which surrounded the Forbidden City. There had been a variety of different gardens here for about one thousand years, but the park was landscaped properly into a single area by the Mongul invader Emperor Kublai Khan about 700 years ago. It is all centred around a chain of lakes and ponds, of which the most important was called the Great Pool of Saliva.

Jo-Ann's nostrils flare, she looks with fastidious disgust at the dank water about us.

'We will now go and see the nearest place on George's list: the Palace of Purple Effulgence.'

'What's effulgence?' Jo-Ann hisses at me in a nervous aside.

'Sort of shiny radiance, I think.'

'I guess you may be wrong. It sounds more to me like a kinda fog which might steam off huge pools of saliva.'

The Palace, a small pavilion, is shut, as is the Temple for Cultivating Good Deeds – not a Boy Scout in sight.

The Tower for Reading the Classics is cool and empty and rather dank. Jo-Ann begins to sniff. 'They think it rude to use a handkerchief in public,' I tell her helpfully.

'My Gard, what I am supposed to do?' she mopes.

'Use your fingers or sleeves,' I suggest. She looks at me crossly and takes out a handkerchief into which she trumpets defiantly.

The Pavilion of Shared Coolness is not cool, being an open, long, two-storeyed veranda, almost a corridor. We clamber up the hill behind it to a tall column, on top of which a bronze man stands, holding a brass container over his head.

'That is the Plate for Gathering Dew. One of the Emperors thought that dew mixed with powdered jade could make you immortal.'

'Collecting dew, eh?' says Jo-Ann, 'I can think of worse. Effulgences.'

We leave the park by crossing the Bridge of Perfect Wisdom and enter a smaller garden, not much bigger than a bowling green. Yun Qing calls it something like 'shi-sha eh hok-hai' which she translates as the 'Park where the old peoples meet'.

Everyone is dressed in blue, with Mao-type peaked caps. Most are huddled into groups, all peering inwards and down, they look like tableaux of rugger scrums. They are watching players. All the games are gambling ones. In typically methodical Chinese fashion, the gamblers have grouped into areas: near the small beds bounded by privet are the chess players, poring over the pieces, wooden disks with characters painted upon them, a chattering of advisers being in noisy contrast to the studious and silent deliberations of their onlookers; those playing dominoes seem best to like an area of low walls, upon which they can

sit and arrange their pieces; the card players are assembled in a large area near the bicycle park – each game needs six people and, as in the other activities, there is an intent surrounding of advisers, praisers or insulters, all commenting at the top of their voices. Through the hub-bub of the bedlam one can hear, harsh and staccato, the 'kkkkkk-spwt' as men hawk and spit. Jo-Ann sees little of the scene because of peering down anxiously to see what her feet are stepping on. 'Seems they're trying to keep the Great Pool topped up,' she says moodily.

Under the flared roof of an open pavilion a circle of men stand and watch a trio of musicians tuning up. There is a fiddler. His instrument has one string and a soundbox about the same shape and only slightly larger than the cardboard tube of a lavatory roll. His fingers slide up and down the string as his bow saws and the result is a plaintive but not unpleasant wailing. The other string instrument is a pear-shaped guitar-cum-banjo. It emits a tinny plonking. The last instrument is a handful of wooden slats, clicked together.

I cannot see the point of all the tuning-up, for now that they have finally started there seems to be neither recognisable melodic shape nor harmonious connection between the instruments. The fiddle wails, slow and sad, the banjo-like thing plinks and twangs with a George Formby abandon, the sticks click and pause and clatter and snap at random. Now an old man stands up and begins to yell. Is he criticising the playing? No, by the sentimental expression on his face he is probably singing. He begins to speed up, the clinking and the tweetlings and the twangs begin to harmonise as their speed co-ordinates. I see to my amazement smoke coming from the frenziedly sawing strings of the fiddler's bow. The musicians cease, pausing to pant. Suddenly Jo-Ann realises that she and Yun Qing are the only women around and insists that we leave. We exit the park and enter a maze of hutongs.

Hutongs are alleyways and narrow lanes. Many of them have intriguing names such as Iron Bird, Tea Leaves and Sound the Drum. They range in width from mere passageways, four feet from side to side, to roads just wide enough to allow two vehicles to pass. They are lined with low, one-storey dwellings. These are roofed with rounded tiles. A profusion of chimneys seep out coal-smoke. Sometimes we can look up little passages into tiny yards. They are cluttered with bicycles, lines of

washing, basins, bowls and ewers, the odd potted plant and stacks of coal-dust briquettes.

Yun Qing points to a door. 'We have an expression which could be translated as "marrying into the same door". The door is very important in a hutong. It gives evidence of the family who lives behind it: their income, the usefulness of the husband, the tidiness of the wife. If a person becomes engaged to marry, the family all hurry round to look at the door of the fiancée's house. They see if it is clean and smart: if it has well-painted good-luck signs on the end of the beams, if the hinges and door fittings are of good metal; very important is the threshold, the wooden strip you have to step over when you enter, it is good if it is high, and thick, and has a metal covering to protect the top. If the door is as good or better than the family's, then they are pleased, but if they think that the door of the fiancée's family is poor and beneath them, then they try to stop the wedding.'

Thus, even in the most humble of the dwellings in the back streets of erstwhile Communist Peking, the human instinct for keeping up with the Joneses, or the Patels, or the Changs is irrepressible.

We pass a public lavatory, a couple of doors in a dusty wall. Yun Qing says 'wait a minute, I want to use this.' Jo-Ann says 'I may as well go too – as you must know, George, in our job we learn to use a bathroom whenever we find one.' They disappear through the entrance in the dusty brick wall. Jo-Ann rapidly reappears.

'My Gard,' she says, 'Oh my Gard.'

'Not a nice bathroom?' I ask.

'Just a row of holes in the ground, not even any partitions.'

I unfold my map of Peking: 'We are not far from a couple of hutongs I particularly want to see, because of their names, I wonder if this fellow can help us.'

He is oldish and burly, in a Mao suit. He smiles affably as I approach him.

'Chou pi?' I ask. 'Ku dang?' He does not seem to understnad. I try a variety of pronunciations. Suddenly his expression of bland affability reassembles into one of ferocious indignation. His eyes grow round behind their narrow frames. His teeth jut out nastily. He spits at my feet and strides on.

'What was wrong with him, I wonder?' I say, looking after his departing back. 'Let's try this chap.' He is a youth: denims, gym shoes, rather dirty buck-teeth.

'Chou pi, Ku dang?'

He starts back and goggles at me. 'Sha bee!' he snarls, and walks on.

Jo-Ann looks worried. 'They seem upset, what do "Chou pi" and "Ku dang" mean?'

'Stinking Skin and Pant's Crotch.'

'Oh my Gard! You maniac! No wonder they're angry. They think you're being personal.'

Yun Qing appears from the Ladies. 'What does "Sha-bee" mean?' I ask her.

She looks prim: 'That is not nice. It means "unintelligent female sexual organ". Why?'

'Oh, no reason really, I thought it might be an interesting new name.'

 **Ulaan Baatar, 13–14 August 1997.** We are on the North China Air flight to Ulaan Baatar from Peking. I feel fidgety: a thin line scratched on the beige surface of the Gobi Desert 30,000 feet below me marks the course of the Trans-Manchurian Express, the train I used to take on previous journeys to Outer Mongolia, eighteen times out, eighteen times back – 36,000 miles in all, and not a mile that was boring. Now I am on the dull, newly founded aeroplane flight. Perhaps the slightly cranky aeroplane is typified by the advertisement written on the back of my boarding pass:

Dear passenger,
Wish you have a joyful journey!
When you are in public talking and laughing and drinking and singing . . . living a happy life, suddenly, you feel some part of your body is too itchy to endure.
How embarrassed!
Please dial Huachuan Disinfect and Health 2-in-1 soap, you will gain an unexpected result.

To remind myself of times more elegant but also more adventurous, I re-read a sentence from the book on my lap: a battered old edition of Ian Fleming's *Travels in Tartary*, published in 1934: 'the diplomatic world of Ouida and Oppenheim, that wonderful world where chancelleries are always tottering, and across which Kings' Messengers post madly to and fro, hotly pursued by beautiful women with a penchant for wearing secret treaties next to the skin.'

14 August. We travel in pairs in this part of the world. My fellow Queen's Messenger this time is Anthony B***. We are staying in Greyhound Cottage, the little stone-built bungalow in the Embassy compound which is where the Queen's Messengers are quartered. We have cooked and eaten breakfast and are looking at the scenery all around us, poking above the roofs of housing and tentage: undulating grassy slopes of mountains all dappled with cloud shadows and patches of vivid green in the early morning sunlight. We decide to walk to the top of the highest peak on the other side of the city. It will build up an appetite for lunch and some afternoon shopping.

We have now crossed the whole of Ulaan Baatar: walking along the main road with its stark lines of Russian-built shoeboxes, through the vast empy expanse of Sukhe Bator Square, along the pot-holed chaos of the road verges edged with the huge suburbs of *ger* (yurts) where a third of Ulaan Baatar's population still lives, thence over the bridge across the river Tuul. We have now started to climb the sloping flanks of the mountain. Anthony is a particularly compatible companion as he, too, is a keen gardener, so good that his garden is occasionally open to the public. As we stroll uphill we identify the flowers growing around us. They are mainly of the alpine species: suited to the harsh existence in the steep, gritty slopes of the mountain we are climbing; able to endure winter temperatures of −40°C. There is a particularly pretty little sedum, with the normal fleshy leaves of the 'ice plant' but with orange flowers, a type of monkshood and of gentian, both large and blue, a tall species of the clover family with attractive flower heads like a puce ramrod, a large variety of vetches, saxifrages, stonecrops and a multitude of others. However, we have often seen more interesting and abundant flowers: in early spring when some of the valleys are felted

with edelweiss, or later when the vales are full of tulips and lilies and the boggy places have orchids and the rocks are scrambled over with 'lemon-peel' clematis.

When we have reached the woodland – mostly larch with some birch and poplar – it becomes even more interesting because this is where the two plants I am seeking might be found. One is a rose: low-growing, pink-flowering, open-petalled. It has an unusual tolerance to hard conditions: the heavy shade of the woodland, and the cold. I remember being here on Midsummer's Day a few years ago and it was snowing, and the roses looked lovely with their pink petals cupping the snowflakes. The other plant is one the Botanical Gardens at Kew have asked me to look out for. It is the Mongolian lime ('a small tree of compact rounded habit and dense twiggy growth, with glabrous, reddish shoots. . . . An attractive species with prettily-lobed, ivy-like leaves', as it is described in Hilliers' catalogue). The tree at Kew originates from the mountains west of Peking. It was Przewalski who discovered it in Outer Mongolia (1871), where he also discovered the primitive wild horse named after him. (John Aspinall, who has a herd of Przewalski horses in his zoo, asked me to find out what the Mongolians thought of the releasing of the animal back into the wild. The Mongolian Ministry of Agriculture told me that they thought it a good idea, but reckoned that the horses would stay in the wild for only one season, after that the nomadic herdsmen would round them up for domestication or food.)

I find some interesting patches of wild raspberry, a clump of leaves which look like peony, and a thicket of thin stems which, although fruitless, I think are a type of snow berry, but no roses in hip, nor any sight of a lime tree of any type.

At the top of the mountain there is an *ovoo*: a cairn with a horse's skull on the top. We should run round it clockwise seven times for luck, but after climbing 1500 feet, having started at an altitude of 5000 feet, I prefer a sedate amble. Then we sit and gaze at Ulaan Baatar beneath us, its lines of neat housing and its untidy suburbs of *gers*. There is a panting. A Mongolian appears, jogging. He has a round red face and is wearing minute running shorts which reveal ballooning thighs as pink and glossy and hairless as boiled pork sausages. Like the majority of the

Mongoloid race, whether Red Indians, Eskimos or the Japanese, the Mongolians have very little body hair. We nod and smile and utter the standard greeting: 'Sain baina uu.' He soon trots off down hill and we slither down the scree more slowly.

Lunch: spam sandwich, cheese sandwich, bloater paste sandwich, corned beef and pickle sandwich, potato crisps; tinned mandarin segments: few will deny that we Queen's Messengers have culinary expertise.

Now we are shopping. In the old days there were only very few state-run shops for the locals, and the 'Dollar Shops' for foreigners, who were mainly the staff of the many Communist country embassies. Now there are several little private enterprise booths, mostly selling basics like cigarettes, newspapers and potatoes, but occasionally selling interesting old books. There are also several art shops. The pictures are mostly watercolour landscapes, village scenes or *tanka* (religious scroll paintings). The landscapes are modern and even the bad ones are attractive because the scenery is so beautiful: camels silhouetted against sunsets, a community of *gers* pitched near a pond with mountains in the background, a rolling plain with a far off speckling of antelope and semi-wild ponies. The village scenes are usually older, painted on fabric with a base of a chalk compound, with perspective ignored: all the different events are given equal size and importance – women arguing, a dance, some people running from a snake, someone slaughtering a sheep, a gang of people fulling a blanket of felt, a couple copulating under a wagon, a woman giving birth inside an open-doored *ger*, a string of pack-camel being led from a merchant's, some horsemen lassoing ponies. I do not like the religious scrolls much: they are modern copies of old paintings and endorse my view that Mongolian Buddhism is a religion of fear and punishment rather than serenity and peace. Today I buy a hunting scene with horsemen, wearing their long boots and colourful robes, in pursuit of some wild boar – ten American dollars. There are some attractive airack bowls for sale. They are of silver and big enough to hold about a third of a pint of the alcoholic mare's milk (the milk is alcoholic, not the horse). Dominie told me that I have bought enough, so the only other thing I buy is about twenty postcards.

The art shops also sells cassette recordings of Mongolian music. I like it, much to the puzzlement of my family. It has some rousing tunes which are in tempo with the galloping of horses' hooves. There is also something called mouth-music which to European ears is a bit weird, a cross between the twanging of a Jew's harp and the blaring of a cheap clarinet. But I am looking for a recording of *The Reconciliation Song*.

Some animals desert their young immediately after birth: they are so horrified by the experience and so disgusted by the result that they want nothing more to do with it. (It is remarkable that more human beings don't do so, considering what most babies look like.) When a she-camel deserts her calf, the Mongolians sing a special song to reunite them. A woman from our Embassy saw it happen:

'We were taken to a farmstead of half a dozen *gers*. The abandoned little calf was being held by one of the women, a man held the mother-camel by a rope. She was not the slightest bit interested in her baby, in fact she looked everywhere except at it. And it, poor little thing, kept struggling to get free so it could run to its mother. If it had, it would have been kicked away, as had happened several times. Then two men appeared. They took over from the man and woman and started to sing this very plaintive-sounding song. And as they sang they kept looking at the calf sympathetically. Eventually the mother began to look at her baby and then – I promise you that this is true – enormous tears began to fall from her eyes. And in the end she walked up to her baby and bent down and it seemed as if she was saying "I'm terribly sorry, darling, I didn't mean to be nasty, and I love you – here, have some milk." When we left the calf was sucking from its mother.'

I thought I'd see if there was a recording of this; it could be useful on some of my sheep and Dominie's ponies.

No success finding *The Reconciliation Song*, so back to Greyhound Cottage, to listen to the Russian television and write twenty postcards. Luckily each one needs so many stamps that there is not much room left to write much. The first one to Dominie, then each of the grand-children: Ranulf, Charlotte, George, Hamish, Daisy; then somehow fourteen more.

The Great Wall, 15–16 August 1997. After Anthony and I have delivered the diplomatic bags at the Peking Embassy we will have two spare days in Peking, so I have asked my travel-agent friend Josh Green to think up something unusual for us to do. He has arranged that we are going to see the sunset over the Great Wall of China, spend the night in the dungeons of a newly restored fort, and then get up early to see the sunrise. A mini-bus with driver, dinner and breakfast will be part of the 'package', the total cost will be about thirty pounds each.

The mini-bus has arrived to collect us. Anthony and I pick up our luggage – a minimum of spongebag, book and camera – and hurry out. The mini-bus is like any other mini-bus, a sort of white thing on wheels; the driver is a squat, beetle-browed, rather slab-faced youngish man with an artificial smile; there are two stunning girls. Anthony is the most amiable of people, with a dry wit and a face in repose of a slightly sardonic cast. However his face is completely expressionless as he looks at these women: carved from stone, it seems to be. I remember he is a lay preacher, and rather prim at times. 'I didn't order them,' I say hastily, 'perhaps they're some sort of extra thrown in by Josh.'

During the two-hour drive we learn that the driver is named Chang and the girls are called Wong – the larger, more voluptuous of the two – and Cao, smaller and elfin. Anthony and I, in hushed whispers, cannot make them out: perhaps they are a bit of private enterprise of the driver; perhaps they are merely his girlfriends.

The ramparts of the Great Wall are a thin, jagged line far above us. We can see about two miles of its 3700 miles; this section was built in the Ming period.

Chang smiles, toothily: '700 feet uphill to the wall; 1110 steps. Do you think you can manage it?'

'We'll try,' says Anthony, dryly.

As we follow up the first flight of steps he points worriedly at Wong's left ankle. It has a fine gold chain around it. 'What's that mean?' he asks, even more dryly.

'I don't know. I think it may mean she's a kind of – well, you know what – she'll do it if you want – but perhaps not – if you see what I mean.'

'No I don't. And look at their toenails,' – the charming nails peeping out of the sandals have deep red paint upon them – 'I think that sort of colour is very suggestive.'

'Suggestive of what?' I ask.

'Sort of – well, you know, as if they were sort of available if one wanted it that way.'

'We'll have to wait and see,' I try to say consolingly, 'when we get to the fort.'

We've climbed the first 500 steps. To begin with, Chang and the girls to either side of him scuttled up like lizards up a wall. Anthony and I plodded stolidly after them. Chang kept turning round and cheekily gesturing us upwards with flips of his hand. 'Tired?' he kept shouting, 'we are not even one quarter of the way up yet.' The girls giggled admiringly at his agility and his facility in English.

Anthony and I plodded on.

After a bit Wong began to twitter, a shade petulantly, and Chang took her by her hand.

'His girlfriend, perhaps. And Cao is her friend, asked to come as chaperone,' I said.

'Let's hope so,' replied Anthony. 'Look, they're slowing down.'

Wong let go of Chang's hand, and began to help herself up with the use of the iron pipe which serves as a bannister. Cao followed suit.

Chang stopped and waited for us to catch up: 'You will want to rest now, you are tired.'

'No we're not, and once I start I like to keep on going,' Anthony said.

A twinge of unease darkened Chang's face. 'We move on, then,' he said a bit sourly. Rested by their wait he and the girls hastened upwards. Anthony and I plodded on. It was only about fifty steps later that we came upon them leaning on the rail and staring glassy-eyed into the distance.

'Very good place to stop and look at the view,' lied Chang.

'Have a look, but we'll carry on.'

'So will we,' said Chang crossly. The girls twittered in dismay. 'We might as well wait a bit and let the girls rest,' I suggested, saving Chang's face, which wasn't my intention, and also saving mine – Anthony is two stone lighter than I am, and five years younger.

[210]

I am sweaty and panting now that we have reached the halfway mark, but I sweat and pant at the slighest opportunity, and my muscles are feeling the effect of the 1500 feet I climbed in Mongolia yesterday. So I have persuaded spring-heeled Anthony to rest a bit. Far, far below we can see the three glossy black heads of Chang and the girls. The girls are giggling weakly and clinging to each other. Chang has his head down and is half-hauling himself up on the bannister. He looks up.

'Tired?' I shout. 'Keep it up, you're nearly halfway there.' I am not one to miss an opportunity to kick a cheeky bugger when he's down.

Anthony and I have reached the fort. Like the rest of this part of the Great Wall it is built of large grey bricks. The roofs of the three rectangular outer buildings are pan-tiled and their up-swept eaves have four little statuettes of animals and demons at each corner. These buildings rest on the bulk of the fort, a rectangular block sunk into the body of the Wall. There is access down a steep flight of wooden steps to a central hall, barrel-vaulted and supported by arches. Each arch leads to one of nine rooms, ranging in size from the small cell to the multi-recessed storeroom; all the rooms also have arches and barrel vaulting, to support the doors, the ceilings and the slit windows. Throughout, the whole building is flagged with stone paving. It is very attractive in its spartan simplicity.

I go upstairs and join Anthony, who is leaning against the ramparts that surround the whole fort. He is photographing the view. The fort has been built on the sway-backed col of a mountain ridge. To either side the broad, battlemented road-like top of the Great Wall meanders uphill towards other, smaller forts; past them one can glimpse the Wall writhing over the mountains, sometimes a mere ribbon on the steep face of a valley, more often like the jagged back of a dragon, its crenellated spine silhouetted sharply against the cool blue sky. The land drops below us to either side, almost as sheer cliffs, but angled enough to take a growth of shrubs and trees: oaks, with very large leaves and mossy cups for the acorn, sweet chestnuts, some sort of acacia, wild fruit trees – too far to identify accurately but seemingly pears, apples, plums and cherries. After a great drop of 700 to 800 feet into the shrubby valleys below the land rises again, tier after tier of mountain ridges, hazing into

the far distance, to blue silhouettes paler than the sky. As in traditional Chinese landscape paintings, the feet of the mountains are hidden by mist so that the ridges seem to be hovering in the air; and to add to the unreality little fortlets are often perched on the very pinnacles, and the Wall meanders up to them and away, and all over the place, as if planned by a manic mandarin with a million men to spare.

The central outer building is a combination of a kitchen-cum-dining-hall with the living quarters of Li Shun Bao who is the manager-cook-waiter-chambermaid for the fort. He can get along in English, enough to make us welcome, to tell us dinner will be ready after nightfall, and that he will show us our bedrooms when the driver and his wife and her friend (sighs of relief) arrive (we can see them tottering towards us on the broad surface of the Wall, still a couple of furlongs away).

While we are waiting I wander off to one of the outhouses and peer through the window. There are two beds in it, each is a shelf taking up one whole wall and each has half a dozen pillows and half a dozen sleeping-bags aligned upon it. 'Looks as if we're going to be sleeping with those girls after all,' I say to Anthony, who comes to see what I am looking at. That inscrutable, stone-faced expression again.

Li Shun comes up. 'You are not here, you are downstairs. The others have arrived, come, I will show you.'

He leads us down, he opens a door, he discloses a room which is furnished with a bowl, a chamberpot and a double bed with a pink satin headboard and pink satin eiderdown. Nothing else.

'Do you like to sleep on the left or the right?' I ask Anthony. No answer from Stone Face.

'We would prefer to have a bed each,' I tell Li Shun.

He looks puzzled: 'But that will cost you each another twenty yuan' (about £1.50).

'Money well spent,' says Anthony, heavily.

Our new room is furnished as before but with an extra bed and a larger chamberpot. The walls and ceiling are an extraordinarily complicated assembly of niches, windows and arrow slits, barrel vaulting and arches – eight of them.

We dump our bags on the floor beside our beds and hurry out, for it will be sunset in half an hour and Li Shun tells us that the best view-

point, the next fortlet, is a twenty-minute walk away. It is only about 100 feet higher than where we are, and looks in spitting distance away: 'A bit weedy these fellows, it won't take us more than ten minutes,' I tell Anthony.

We reach it twenty-five minutes later: Anthony is as cool as ever, I am as sweaty and panting as usual. It was not nearly as level or as close as it looked. The Wall is about five paces wide, its surface is sometimes like a gently undulating pavement, but in most places it is stepped, for it climbs up and down mountainsides and undulates upon the crests of ridges, and some of the steps are so steep that one has to use one's hands as well as one's feet, as if using a ladder – steeper even than the precipitous sides of the Mexican pyramids I climbed a couple of years ago. It must have been utter misery to be a Chinese private soldier, burdened with heavy winter clothing, crude armour and weaponry, and being marched up and down by some pig-tailed martinet of an NCO.

The fortlet is on the top of a pinnacle. Much smaller than our fort, which was the headquarters of the local guard commander, it probably held a watching section of ten to twenty men. It has one basic room whose internal pillars support a flat, battlemented roof. We cannot see the sun, it is hidden by the hazy clouds, but the view of glooming valleys and floating mountains as the twilight falls is so magical we don't mind.

Hastily, before it gets dark so that we won't be able to see the steps we will have to negotiate, we leave for the return journey.

It is cosy in the little yard in front of the central outhouse: lamps have been lit, Chang and the girls sit round one table, Li Shun and a couple of friends sit nearby, gossiping with them and playing mah-jong; our table already has two cups of tea steaming on it, and bowls and chopsticks have been arranged for the meal.

While we sip the tea we chat with the others but not very interestingly as no one is fluent in the other's language: the most I can make out is that Li Shun's friends come from the village below and their main village activity is collecting and selling sweet chestnuts and a special kind of pear which is unique to the locality. Far away, in the bottom of a valley towards Inner Mongolia, trees and shrubbery are lit up by

flashes of light. Fireworks, they explain, it is someone's birthday or wedding.

Dinner: the air is warm, the silhouettes of the mountain ranges zigzag across the starlit sky, the girls look pretty in the light of the lanterns and murmur and giggle, the crickets chirr in the valley far below, the smell of cooking wafts from the kitchen. The food is indecipherable: sliced onions and beef and tiny chopped-up potatoes and tomatoes and God knows what, but it is good and hot and steeped in gravy; when the chopsticks can't pick it up the Chinese show us how it can be shovelled straight from the bowls into our mouths and they all laugh but in a companionable way and I'm feeling drowsy.

Anthony spent much of the night lying on his stomach, reading. I awoke and asked if he couldn't sleep. 'Don't worry,' he said, 'but no. Your snoring is quite amazing. Your poor wife must have the patience of Job.' He'd know that sort of thing, being a lay preacher. My subconscious clock woke me again at 4.30. Anthony said: 'Don't bother about the sunrise, it is pouring with rain.' I fell asleep again, lulled by the rustle of rain on the leaves in the valley below.

Wake up two hours later: it has stopped raining and Anthony has disappeared, presumably gone for a walk. Chuck on my clothes – short-sleeved shirt, trousers and shoes – and sally out into the rain-washed morning. Wisps of mist flow up from the valleys and forestry below. The forts in the mountain ridges to the west are being lit by the sunrise to the east. The surface of the Great Wall wriggles away from me into the dawn. The smell of wet leaves wafts up from the valley sides – it reminds me of home. Off I go. I seem to be walking in the sky above a world of utter isolation. I walk through forts: once they were full of worried soldiery, staring towards Mongolia and the avenging hordes; now they are as empty as caves and are cold and dank. A hoopoe flips below amid the sweet chestnuts and oaks. After an hour I turn about and meet Anthony back at the fort; he has been walking in the other direction.

Breakfast is hard-boiled eggs and, to quote Anthony, 'a huge heap of tapeworms, sprinkled with lumps of jellified fat, my God it's frightful.' His chopsticks ply – 'and this odd gravy it's all floating in, it's completely

grey and smells of condemned bedding – pass the bowl, I've got to keep my strength up – yeugh, see how the lumps of fat stick to the tape-worms, can you hear Chang sucking them up, he sounds like an industrial hoover – pass the bowl again, it's better than nothing, I suppose – eugh! And it's tepid. God, this is filthy, all this fat – there's a bit left, pass the bowl please . . . is that all? I'm starving. Let's try another of those eggs, how the hell do you eat an egg with chopsticks?'

Down 1110 steps, into the mini-bus, a two-hour drive back to Peking, into the cosy confines of the Janguio Hotel by ten o'clock this morning. A glass of beer to replenish the liquor lost in all that sweating yesterday: 'Wo-te-peng-you, ta-fu-chien – my friend, he will pay.'

 **Phrase books – – –** Most phrase books are totally useless: by the time one has finished hastily flicking through a plethora of superfluous remarks about the weather or the laundry or the museum opening hours, the taxi driver has driven away, the waiter has gone to another table, the porter has gone on strike or the dentist has gone on holiday. The British do not often need them for, having ruled a third of the world, we have found that the English language, particularly when shouted, is understood by almost everybody. Some veterans, however – Old China Hands, Globe Trotters, the more experienced diplomats, foreign correspondents and traders – admit that there are two phrases which are always useful in a local language: 'My friend will pay' and 'please take off your clothes as quickly as possible.'

The Americans, being continuously torn apart between the priorities of personal comfort and cultural necessity, have another priority: 'Is the place of easement nearer the cathedral or the railway station?'

Of all the phrases ever written, perhaps the best known is the pleasantly archaic complaint: 'My postilion has been struck by lightning.' This was in a phrase book for the travellers of the eighteenth and nineteenth centuries: those on the Grand Tour, or King's Messengers, or

'Culture Vultures' and wife hunters. Such out-of-date books have an immense charm and eccentricity when compared with the mundane phrases of the present world. During my travels I often make a bee-line for the oldest and shabbiest bookshop I can find to see if its shelves still have any obsolete phrase books. They often have, and Africa is a good gleaning ground for such a harvest. I have four African phrase books: the *Kaffir Phrase Book* by 'James Stewart, Missionary', published in 1899; *The Northern Sotho Phrase Book*; *An Elementary Handbook and Language Guide to Learn Setswana*; and *Up-country Swahili*.

I have just opened one at random: 'Boloko bo a fisa,' it says, and adds in explanation: 'The dung is hot.'

I open another book. The first sentence which catches my eye may once have been useful for the average Empire builder but, alas, I have never found any reason for using it: 'That man is a witch-doctor, see the frog in his pocket.' Similarly, I have never had the need to complain to anyone on my farm that: 'Boy, my razor is spoilt, you have used it to shave your head, see, it is still dirty with your black hairs.' Nor even have I suggested, kindly as the intention may have been, that: 'If you want leave to be circumcised I will sign your certificate.'

Some of the comments about other people show a flattering interest, but are a bit personal: 'These little old women are very black.' 'He is obviously suffering from dysentery.' 'That soldier is drunk.'

Life is full of incident: 'A tall man injured a stout woman with an axe.' 'Screwed together, they are put in the borehole.' 'My grandmother is fainting.'

However, there are quieter occasions when one can say to one's love: 'You may scratch me,' or 'You have a nice odour,' and then go for a spin in the country, either by traditional methods 'The oxen were out-spanned,' 'We camped for the night,' 'Next morning we inspanned again' or in a more modern fashion 'He is riding a vehicle making the sound vuu-vuu'.

It is often a worry when returning home, sometimes because of a disaster – 'A hippopotamus has destroyed our hut' – but usually for more mundane reasons: 'The latrine is full of fleas.' 'The cook is drunk.'

Probably the most famous of all phrase books were those issued by

Karl Baedeker of Leipzig. I have one he published in 1888 called *The Traveller's Manual of Conversation in Four Languages* (English, French, German, Italian). For the present-day reader, there is much interest in browsing through it and gleaning evidence on what strange problems beset travellers in nineteenth-century Europe. Doctoring, for example, was not quite the same: 'Have you some fresh leeches? These do not bite.' The modern complications of buying a car were substituted for those of buying a carriage – though perhaps the salesmen, unctuous and glib, were no different from many of those of today:

'Have the goodness, Sir, to walk into my warehouse, where you will see carriages of all kinds: coaches, berlins, vis-a-vis, post-chaises, calashes, phaetons and cabriolets; there are plenty to choose from.'

'There is a carriage that would suit me perhaps?'

'This is a very neat, good travelling chaise, although second hand.'

'The wheels are in a very bad state, the body is too heavy, the shafts are too short, and the pole is too thin, and the shape is quite old fashioned.'

'I beg your pardon sir, you are mistaken: it is a carriage in the latest fashion; it is not six months since it was built, and it has been on only one journey.'

'I think the seats are too high and uncomfortable.'

'It seems so because the stuffing of the cushions is new.'

The character of the voyager rapidly becomes apparent. He is fastidious of his travelling companions: 'Give that little girl a handkerchief.' 'Steward, assist this lady to go on deck, she is very unwell.' He is pernickety: 'Soup weakens the stomach, and therefore I never eat it.' 'Have this chest of drawers wiped out, it is quite dirty.' He is full of minor suspicions and anxieties: 'What are you thinking about?' 'Are there any fleas here?' He is fussy about his appearance: [*my trousers*] 'fit very badly. They are not high enough round the waist: they are tight between the legs, and too wide at the knees.' He is a frightful social climber, as can be seen by this conversation over the supper table:

'Good evening, Gentlemen.'

'Oh! Lord A., are you here! What has brought you into this country?

Answer: 'I have just come from Italy with my wife and the Marquis.'

'Lady A., I have the honour to repay my respects to you.'

'Let us sit down; the supper is getting cold.'

'I shall be very well placed here opposite the Countess.'

Next day he is agog to see the sights, suggesting either: 'Let us go and see the king,' or 'Go and see the princes.'

In spite of being a famous traveller, he does not enjoy his journeys, being continuously beset by fear and foreboding. His detailed and fretful questions, both before and during a trip, display mounting anxiety. This is probably not alleviated by some of the answers:

'Is the road good?' 'Are there many ruts?' 'Is the road safe?' 'Do you ever hear of robbers?' 'I have heard that it is not prudent to travel along some parts of that road at daybreak.'

Answer: 'That's true, where there are woods, forests or ravines.'

'Are the postilions insolent?'

Answer: 'No, never when they are well paid.'

'Is the road over the mountains very steep?' 'Postilion, mind you go slowly when the road is bad and when you make a turn; we do not wish either to be jolted or overturned.' 'Where there are ruts or stones, drive on the pavement.'

There is a pause, when he tentatively enjoys himself: 'To whom does that large country-house belong? It seems very fine.'

Answer: 'It belongs to prince N.'

But then he gets in a panic again: 'Postilion stop: we wish to get down.' 'A spoke of one of the wheels is broken.' 'Some of the harness is undone.' 'A spring is also broken.' 'One of the horse's shoes is come off.' 'It begins to get dark.' 'Do not leave us in the middle of the road during the night.' 'Whip your horses, get on, and take care not to over-turn us.'

Answer: 'You need not be afraid.'

'Keep away from that ditch, it is full of mud.' 'Do not drive so near to that precipice.'

Finally his nerve cracks: 'For my part, I shall get out of the carriage and walk.'

Answer: 'It is unnecessary; here we are, thank God, at the inn, safe and sound.'

He is no better afloat. As he is rowed out to his ship, he complains

uneasily: 'I think the sea is very rough.' 'The vessel is a great way out; and, if a gale of wind come on, our boat might upset before we could reach her.'

He is petulantly surprised when they reach the ship safely: 'Well, here we are at the ship; but not without a great deal of trouble; you were obliged to row hard.'

He boards, and becomes frantic, in spite of soothing replies from the crew. Nausea steals upon him: 'The wind increases.' 'See that great wave which is coming to break against our vessel.' 'I fear we shall have a storm: the sky is very dark towards the west.'

Answer: 'So far the wind is favourable, and the ship sails well.'

'But the sea is very rough; the waves are very high; the rolling of the vessel makes me sick.' 'I have a headache.' 'My head is very bad.' 'The smell of the tar affects me.' 'I am very much inclined to be sick.' 'I am very weak; I must lie in my hammock.'

He perks up after his sleep, and dares to chat a few inanities: 'I am better again, the rest has refreshed me.' 'The wind has fallen. 'What bird is that?'

Answer: 'It is a seagull.'

'I can distinguish the land quite plainly now with my telescope.'

So he lands, and babbles in relief: 'Well, here we are safe and sound; but not without having run some risk: what do you say to it, Captain?' The captain, fed up with his hysterical passenger, snaps: 'On the contrary, we have had a very good voyage.' 'We have done in a day and a half what commonly takes three, four, or even five days.'

I once bought, in an excess of misguided and optimistic zeal, a strange little booklet called *I am Learning Armenian*. From it I learned a little of the daily life of the average Armenian: 'He found a grey frog.' 'Give sweet almonds to this fat she-ass.' 'This is a rusty scale for weighing, carry it away and give it to my grandfather.' 'The hen did not lay an egg this week.'

This humdrum activity is offset by the complexity of some of their names: 'Biedzarr has got a large goat, Roopen and Razmeeg have a lambkin.' 'Mr. Hampartzoom is a tall, white-haired old man.' 'Hrier respects his father and loves his mother.' 'Yezneeg ate the sausage, he

likes very much the meat of the hen.' 'Varooj, give a rose to Vartoog.' 'Frolicsome Kheegar ate a sour apple.'

To make it all the harder, they have their own script: 'The Armenian alphabet was invented by Saint Mesrob in AD 405' is another useful phrase. The writing is pleasant, looking like the arcade of a Roman aqueduct but, to most of us, it is illegible. No wonder 'The pen with which I write is getting rusty.'

I have only once seen a phrase book in use: it was used on me. I saw a middle-aged couple with greying sandy hair, rimless spectacles and pale blue mackintoshes. He was staring despondently at a map of London, she had the phrase book in her hand. I always seem to be the person approached by waifs and strays: perhaps I – deceivingly – look benign. 'Pray, excuse me,' she read, 'I wish to ascertain the whereabouts of Piccadilly Circus.' Taking the book, I rifled through it. Finally I read out: 'Xrntpf zzyrd n't ug winsmetr.' Apparently this meant: 'You are in it.'

She took the book back, scanned the index, turned to the correct page, and read out, gratefully:

'I thank thee kindly, good my fellow.'

'Fare thee well.'

Buenos Aires, 4 September 1997. It has been an irksome day trying to fly from here to Uruguay and back. The aeroplane was delayed for over five hours. At least I was comfortable in the VIP lounge. I chose a corner by a window so that my bags and I would be reasonably inconspicuous but I could also have a good view of the landings and takings-off. My driver, who was also acting as escort, did not mind the wait a bit; he sat on the sofa beside me, sucking his teeth and staring into space. His placidity made me even more fretful. I do not understand people being content when doing nothing: they should be bored, like me.

After several hours together a group of strangers are likely to start coagulating into a community. I had learned in my anthropological days that such an organisation of people is likely to contain stereotypes: the

Leader, the Eminence Grise, the Sycophant, the Joker, the Buffoon, the Scape-goat, the Rebel, the One Voted Least Popular. There were not enough of us to make all of these, just a couple of elegant American women, six men and a large family of Arabs, but the Leader quickly asserted himself. He was a distinguished old Argentinian: the President of a bank in Montevideo. The incompetent airline kept telling us: 'You soon will be boarding, we estimate in one half hour.' The banker, Alfredo, was our only source of accurate information, via his mobile telephone to his secretary; she was in contact with the Montevidean end of the proceedings. The owner of another mobile telephone was the 'One Voted Least Popular'. He was a thirtyish man, sleek and scented. He wore a very expensive but shiny and lightweight suit, and shoes cobbled from the skin of some small, glossy reptile, to match his belt and watchstrap. He also had a voice like a banshee and he used it to scream down *his* mobile telephone.

While he was bellowing down it, to some underling in his office, saying that he was going to miss a meeting (a disaster as dire as God being late at Mount Sinai with the Ten Commandments) I said to the American women: 'I don't know why that bloody man bothers to use a telephone just to speak to Uruguay, he's loud enough without it.'

'Yup,' the tall one in a camel-hair cape replied, 'and I'd guess he's only some itty-bitty contractor.'

'What's he do then, Bett?' asked the one with red suede boots.

'He hasn't said yet, Louise, maybe he's the man who bores the ass-holes in Barbie Dolls.'

'Or bores the ass-holes *off* Barbie Dolls,' replied Louise.

They both tittered.

The aplomb with which some of the more sophisticated American females can utter the most startlingly crude remarks always fills me with admiration.

Bett switched her attention to the Arabs: 'Do you reckon those three women are his wives? I couldn't share my husband with another.'

Louise raised her eyebrows: 'You surprise me, Bett, you've had four husbands, and they've had nine wives between them.'

'I had 'em one at a time. Anyhow he's not my type.'

'I wouldn't mind Alfredo,' Louise mused, 'he's kinda old, but he's tall

and he's got nice manners and good hands and his clothes are well made.'

'Is that your priority in men?' I asked.

'Sex and diamonds,' she replied briefly. 'And what do you look for in a woman, George?'

'Pretty and witty, clever and kind, listens and laughs.'

'And have you met this paragon?'

'I've been married to her for thirty-four years. But after all that time she doesn't seem to listen quite so much any more.'

'Thirty-four years? Thirty-four years! Jeez.' They were stunned into silence for a bit, but not for too long and by the time we had finally reached Montevideo I was quite sad to see the departing backs of my amusing new friends.

I am now back in Buenos Aires. It is late afternoon, not much time before nightfall. I am walking from my hotel to the Plaza de Mayo, one of the central squares of the city which contains some important buildings, including the cathedral. I am not on the Buenos Aireans' wavelength: normally, when walking on a crowded pavement, one's subconscious informs one of any obstacle in front and one automatically steps out of the way, but here I keep on bumping into people. Come to think of it, looking at the erratic driving on the road alongside me, perhaps it is not my fault after all.

The cathedral is basically Palladian (the façade) with a dash of Islam (the rather tatty mosaic-covered dome). The pediment is supported by a fine row of a dozen Corinthian pillars, but the whole edifice is dominated by a huge backcloth of Urban Shoebox: a blank-walled skyscraper. It is an utter disgrace that it was ever given planning permission. Inside, it is Baroque. The altarpiece is a massive convolution and encrustation of gilt and gold and florid carvings. The main body and the side chapels are pleasantly painted in cool colours, pale blues, whites and terracottas, with gold ornamentation.

Dolls are the world's third most popular collectible (after stamps and coins) and I am reminded that dolls probably originated as religious figures because the cathedral is full of them. One doll of the Madonna wears a fantastic dress all aglitter with golden thread embroidery, inlaid

with jewel-like chips of coloured glass. 'Nuestra Señora de la Paz' is a larger doll, with a golden crown; the baby doll she is holding wears his crown rakishly askew. It is strange to see life-sized statues also dressed in real clothes, reminiscent of dummies in shop windows: Santo Cristo del Amor wears a purple dressing-gown with a golden, tasselled dressing-gown cord; a female saint lurks in a corner, wearing a black evening dress, she must feel a bit of a frump amid all the satins and velvets. Most of the smaller dolls are in glass cases, and I wonder why until I see a woman touching the glass pane of one saint and then crossing herself. Unprotected by glass the life-sized figure of Christ on the Cross has a knee blackened with the devout touching of countless, imploring hands.

There is a side chapel with a massive tomb covered with the Argentinian flag. (I think it one of the world's more attractive national banners, with its Cambridge blue and white stripes – neighbouring Brazil has the ugliest of them all.) There is a guard of well-turned-out soldiers with swords and shako, they are changing the post. Much stamping and saluting and five men march off, the impressive solemnity of it all somewhat spoiled by their peculiar, loping Groucho Marx gait. I cannot see whose tomb it is: I suspect it must be José de San Martin who, having done more than any other man in the liberation of Chile, Peru and the Argentine from Spanish rule, died in poverty and exile. One hopes he feels that his expensive tomb is compensation for his bankrupt's death-bed.

It is getting dark. My 'crib sheet', a page of notes assembled by Queen's Messengers to pass on advice and tips, says that we are always welcome at the English Club. It is a short walk away: I'll see if I'm welcome.

It is not unlike my London clubs: esoteric pictures of former members, comfortable chairs, a smell of tobacco and a well-stocked bar. I flitter my Queen's Messenger card about and the next thing I know is that I am sitting at a table with several convivial fellows and several glasses of whisky and soda in front of me.

They seem thoroughly English: they are generally taller than the man in the street outside, and fairer, but I suddenly realise that when they are not talking to me most are speaking to each other in Spanish. They are

mainly third-generation Argentinian: their mothers may have been Argentinian, their wives probably are, their children certainly are; they have names like Carlos Silversides and Eduardo Potterton.

It was difficult for these fellows with their divided loyalties during the Falklands War and we do not even mention it. They have had their Annual General Meeting today and one of the problems has been recruitment: a suggested inducement to membership is to change the name to the 'British Club'. Logical, I suppose, but a pity in a way. Although I have become somewhat discouraged in insisting on my own nationality – any ginger-haired fellow with freckled knees can fill in a form and say he is 'Scottish' and is received with open arms and cries of admiration – but if I put 'English' in any immigration form, there is bound to be some pipsqueak of an official who will purse his lips, scratch it out, and replace it with 'British'. About a third of the world can legitimately call themselves 'British', whether they are from Canada, Camden or Karachi. There are only about forty million of the true English.

After a great deal of drink and convivial conversation the President of the club and his exotic Argentinian wife, Irma, take me to a restaurant and with immense hospitality ply me with more food and drink and finally I weave through the streets back to my hotel. Odd, I don't seem to be bumping into people any more: they step out of the way.

 **Santiago and Isla Negra, 6 September 1997.** I flew to Santiago yesterday and it was cloudy almost all the way from the Argentine. It was only half an hour from our destination that the sky cleared and I saw, with a shock of surprise, the snow-covered massifs of the Andes all around us. Soon the crags and canyons were mitigated by the more gentle undulations of downlands, then flat plains where isolated mountains reared out like barren islands in seas of green. There were great yellow patches on the green – some type of flower.

The snow-caps are above us as my Chilean friend Ricardo drives us off on a hundred-mile trip to the coast. Ricardo is a Professor of

Engineering, specialising in mining. He is large and burly with a pugna-
cious chin; his impressive, hawk-like nose is sandwiched between a
donnish pair of spectacles and a black moustache. We are travelling
west-south-west, through the low farmland of the Plain of Santiago.
There are some little shacks beside the road containing large baking
ovens; whenever any baker has bread for sale he hangs out a white flag.
A red flag is a butcher's sign. I ask if a green flag is for a grocer or a
greasy rag for a garage or a bandage for a doctor's. Ricardo says 'No'.
Some trees have plastic bags tied to their branches. I ask what is being
sold from the adjacent houses. 'Nothing,' Ricardo says, 'they are full of
rubbish for the sanitary removals.'

As it is very early spring there is little to see in the way of flora: the
dominant flower is the one which made the huge patches of yellow seen
from the air. Ricardo stops the car so I can inspect one closely: it is of
the crucifer family, a type of wild mustard. Another wild plant in abundance is a large thistle which looks like a globe artichoke: Ricardo says
it is not eaten, but if I visit here in the summer I think it may be worth
picking some and asking Angélica, Ricardo's wife, to cook some as an
experiment. We pass orchards: the ones full of peach trees are particularly beautiful, a haze of pale pink flowers. The orchards are immaculate, every tree spaced at an exact distance with its neighbours; even
neater are the vineyards, for as well as the spacing they have all been
pruned to the same height, in preparation for the imminent budding.
Ricardo says that there has been a terrific boom in Chilean wines
recently: their root-stock is based on a particularly excellent French one
which was exported in the last century. Disease killed it off in Europe,
so that 'French' wines of the ancient lineage are produced here rather
than in the mother country. I do not see many birds, a large black and
white plover being the most noticeable ones. Ricardo says he often sees
condors further up in the mountains. I see some huasos (gaucho-type
cowboys) rounding up cattle: most of them are Herefords, a few of
them are Zebu. Almost all the livestock looks healthy here; I do not
have the inclination that I have in so many countries to reach for my
worming tackle. The huasos were very smart, with huge boots and hats
with circular, flat brims.

'Do you ride?' I ask Ricardo.

[225]

'Not if I can avoid it. When I was young I helped a friend whose father had a cattle ranch and I was on horseback so much that all the hair of my legs was rubbed off so that I looked like a woman.'

Occasionally we drive over bridges. The rivers are swollen with floodwaters and brown with silt. It has been raining all day so far, a pleasant mizzle. Everyone is wearing rubber boots and mackintoshes, particularly the yellow sou'-wester type. They take rain for granted here, particularly after this season which has been the wettest winter for years. The road is full of puddles, the fields are sodden, the gutters and ditches to either side are full and running, the leaves of the trees gleam and drip.

'It is like your weather,' Ricardo says, 'I always love it when I am in England and the weather man says: "Sunny spells, becoming cloudy." So ridiculous, it sounds, and so English, like "A man is helping police with their enquiries".'

The Isla Negra strikes me as a sort of Chilean Frinton with a dash of the Wild West. There is a wide street, bounded by low buildings – shops and pubs and restaurants, cosy little seaside cottages, many of them shuttered up as they are only used in the summer. One of the houses, larger than most, has been turned into a museum in memory of its inhabitant: Pablo Neruda.

Neruda was born of working-class parents in 1904. Through a combination of hard work and natural ability he became a diplomat (speaking five languages fluently, and finishing his career as Chilean Ambassador in Paris) and an internationally famous poet (Nobel Prize for Literature in 1971). His politics were inclined to the left (he was a Communist Senator for a period) and his inclinations to the right (three private houses and poems in praise of individual liberty). It would be fascinating to hear him in discussion with the poets of Azerbaijan who were persecuted by the Communists. Alas, impossible, unless in heaven or hell: he died in 1973.

Our guide is a friendly but firm American, with a neat blonde pony-tail and crisply ironed trousers. She is obviously so well read on her subject that she has become enamoured of him, and finds some of my comments not only distracting interruptions, but irreverent.

'Pablo Neruda had several houses but this one is the one that he

loved the most, and it was here that he lived with his second and third wives.'

'Three wives, eh?' I remark. 'Well, you know the saying: "One wife is an accident, two a coincidence, three times a habit."'

She waits coolly until my self-induced merriment subsides and then she continues: 'Pablo Neruda was a great collector and this house is full of his favourite playthings and objects of art. Here you will see the collection of bottles assembled by Pablo Neruda, his collection of African and Polynesian sculptures, and of butterflies and bugs; Pablo Neruda loved things because of their shape, he collected shells for example, and although Pablo Neruda could play no music he collected musical instruments. Above all the great interest of Pablo Neruda was the sea. You will see that the interior of this house was disguised like the inside of a ship, with wooden planking on the arched ceilings, and edgings of rope, and the doors are narrow and low. Everywhere you will see items reminiscent of the sea: his collection of compasses, and miniature ships in bottles, and ships' figureheads.'

The figureheads are indeed impressive. I particularly like one of Marie Celeste. It is carved from a dark wood from which – unusually – glass eyes gleam.

'After a good party here in the evenings, when Pablo Neruda and his friends had been talking and drinking and eating and smoking, this figurehead would be seen crying: tears would trickle from the eyes down her cheeks. Some people thought it was a religious emanation: can you guess the real reason?'

'The tobacco smoke,' I suggest.

'Condensation,' she snaps. 'The vapour from the sea and the heat from the fire would cause moisture to condense upon the glass eyes, and then spill over in awesome display.'

'However, although he loved the sea, Pablo Neruda could not swim and disliked going out in boats.'

'What's that little dingy doing on the lawn, then?' I ask.

'You see it has seats in it. Pablo Neruda would sit there in the evenings, with his friends, and drink his cocktails there. Pablo Neruda said it was like being at sea, but not so dangerous or uncomfortable.'

My heart warms to Pablo Neruda: he was obviously a nut case.

[227]

One of the rooms is dominated by a huge fireplace encrusted by a massive mural made from stones and boulders, mostly in lapis lazuli and onyx. I think it grotesque and say so and am rewarded with a look of sad reproach.

'When asked what it represented the artist, a friend of Pablo Neruda, would reply that she made this "in a free-flowing form so that everyone can interpret it into what it means to them".'

'A better answer than "haven't a clue",' I suggest, and am rewarded with an icily raised eyebrow.

'I remember when I was his guest and the fires were lit, it was a very comfortable, welcoming house,' Ricardo says.

Our guide gapes at him: 'You knew Pablo Neruda?' she breathes.

So must a very early Christian have regarded Saint Peter.

We arrive at a little desk. 'Pablo Neruda always wrote in green ink, he said green was the Colour of Hope. And Pablo Neruda would wash his hands both before and after he had written anything.'

My heart hardens a bit. There is a difference between being genuinely bonkers and artificially affected.

We inspect a bedroom. There is a stuffed toy sheep by the bed.

'His wife's?' I ask.

'Pablo Neruda's.'

'Did it have a name?'

'Pablo Neruda called it "Dear".'

Hmmmm.

A cupboard door is opened. It is full of shoes, suits and hats.

'These are his shoes, suits and hats,' she says, awed.

Odd. I remember being shown Napoleon's clothes in Fontainebleau, and Ataturk's in Ankara, with the same devout respect. A cupboard full of clothes means little to me: if anything, it is rather depressing, like going to an abandoned monkey house and being shown a wardrobe full of skins.

The view from the bedroom window is magnificent, typical of this country in its mixture of exotic and the mundane: the Pacific Ocean batters against the crags below us – but its waters are the pallid grey of the North Sea off the Essex coast; a skein of birds fly past – not geese, but pelicans; palms and cacti grow in the gardens to either side – trudg-

ing on the beach are four people with their heads well down against the driving rain.

The last room we visit has been specially designed and installed by a 'Fans of Neruda' organisation to exhibit some of his shell collection. It is one of the rummest places I have been to and with its eccentric bad taste and inappropriate associations reminds me of King Farouk's animal museum. The low-ceilinged rectangular room is a hermaphroditic combination of a small cinema and a chapel. It is dimly lit, mostly through stained-glass windows. At the far end is a wooden statue of a badly vandalised figure of Christ. In the centre there seems to be, at first sight, an altar, flanked by an open pair of angel's wings; on second sight they are divulged as a pair of giant clam shells. Spiking out between them is a narwhale's horn, if this erection looks like anything, it is the genitalia of some space alien. Cabinets of shells are positioned here and there. Nothing can spoil the natural beauty of seashells – though disguising them as a Martian's bollocks is a pretty ingenious effort – but as a distraction from their beauty there is a tank of small, dull fish who swim amid the plastic fronds of some artificial flowers.

Ricardo has driven us back to Santiago and we are now in the assembly hall/gymnasium of his daughter's school. Daniéla is to be confirmed here, with about one hundred other pupils. It is quite spartan, the only religious symbolisms being a crucifix hanging from the ceiling, a makeshift altar on a raised platform, and above it a large portrait of a man with a soulful expression and ginger moustache. I suppose it is Christ, but I've never seen Him with just a moustache, so perhaps it is the headmaster. If it is, he needs a haircut. I can hear the rain thundering on the roof and it is cold enough to see people's breath when they sing. By the altar there is a row of six priests and a Monseigneur, in scarlet. He is a former pupil, very popular. He talks a lot and is evidently quite amusing, to judge from the intermittent laughter. On one occasion I recognise the words 'Princessa Diana' and 'muerté' and 'funerales' and everyone looks sympathetically at me and I look mournfully at my hymn sheet. The service is quite enjoyable: everyone is cheerful and at ease; the singing is good, there are even tunes I recognise and I can follow the words on my sheet; there is a

happy band of flutes and guitars and other twanging and plonking things; there is much kissing and hugging and congratulating.

After two hours of this we all leave the makeshift church and drive to Ricardo and Angélica's house. Ricardo designed it: it is of connecting rectangles, low, and painted white. There is a large veranda. This overlooks the garden, which includes a couple of shrubberies each side of a lawn that slopes down to a round swimming-pool and a small orchard. While Angélica spreads delicious things on little biscuits, as starters for the dinner we are to have in a restaurant, Ricardo has found a bilingual book of Pablo Neruda's first published poems: *Veinte poemas de amor y una canción desesperada/Twenty Love Poems and a Song of Despair.* They seem mainly about women:

> Ah your mysterious voice that love tolls and darkens
> in the resonant and dying evening!
> Thus in deep hours I have seen, over the fields,
> the ears of wheat tolling in the mouth of the wind.

I can forgive him his handwashings and green ink.

We are in the restaurant. I have asked for something typically Chilean so am eating conger eel with shrimps. There is a small cleared area amid the tables where the cabaret is playing. There are five people: two women in chintz dresses with flounces at the hem and sashes, one plumply pretty, the other plumply pleasant; the men are dressed as huasos, the head man being fattish and oldish and twanging a guitar; then there is a tall, youngish one with a squeezebox and the slightly gormless look of Private Pike of Dad's Army; the third man, with huge thigh boots and massive spurs with multi-spoked rowels and a ravaged, handsome, tragic face like a debauched Dirk Bogarde, doesn't seem to do much except stamp and clap.

Daniéla is still at that stage when One's Parents are Embarrassing. Angélica is holding her hands above her head and is clapping them in time with the music, Daniéla scowls at her and mouths the Chilean equivalent of 'For God's sake, Mummy, shut up or I'll die.'

The cabaret, which has been dancing with each other, splits up and

Dirk Bogarde comes up to Daniéla and asks her to dance. She shakes her head and shrinks completely until all you can see is her school blouse, with the top of her head peeping out of the collar. After a bit an eye appears, it sees her mother waving a handkerchief and cavorting with Bogarde: they are miming a cock and a hen in some traditional Chilean dance. There is a muffled groan and the whole head disappears back into the blouse. I find myself lumbering about with a cabaret woman. I must look a complete fool but at least she is the pretty one.

Smells – – – It is a pity that it is not possible to capture smells and store them in some way, as one keeps sights on photographs or sounds on a tape-recorder, because the sense of smell can be the most evocative of all the senses.

If I had such a scent album it would start with my first experience of foreign travel which was the conventional one for an Englishman of my generation: a visit to France. That journey was a sequence of smells: of steam and sooty smuts from the engine of the Golden Arrow as it panted by its platform in Victoria Station; of seaweed and salt in Dover harbour; of nausea on one of the heaving, pitching, rolling, tossing little Channel ferries, forecastle proudly emblazoned with the war efforts at Dunkirk and D-day; and then the first proof I was on alien ground – a nasal wallop – the breath of the porter at Calais, a combination of garlic and Gauloise.

Each type of civilisation has its own characteristic aroma: most communist countries, particularly those of the former USSR, smell of boiled cabbage and damp serge; alternatively capitalism, particularly in its home ground of the USA, has a blend of two completely different scents, the blowsy aroma of popcorn and the acrid stink of pizza.

Religion is an obvious source of smell. Last year I drove Dominie and some friends to Venice, visiting a few churches on the way, and it seemed that even styles had different scents: Gothic has a sharp, flinty and slightly damp aroma that percolates the vast, stone-cascade walls of

the cathedrals of Rheims and Amiens; Romanesque is of the sweet, slightly cloying scent of incense which fills the magnificent arcaded interior of Saint Mary Magdalene's abbey in Vezelay or the magic stillness of Saint Filibert's in Tournos further south in Burgundy; Saint Mark's in Venice has the old Byzantine blend of myrrh and frankincense (or it did when I first went there, now it smells of sweat). Buddhist, Hindu, Muslim, all are identifiable. The only peculiarity I have found are in the *dzongs* (fortified monasteries) of Bhutan: the great doors are opened and you are enveloped in a waft of cold boiled potatoes and stewed yak.

In the sterile cities where people usually visit only for business, such as Qatar, Brasilia or Bonn, there is an all-pervading smell of ink, synthetic carpets and air-conditioning, noticeable as one arrives in the airport terminals. Holiday places have a greater variety. The western Mediterranean, for example, has two distinctive atmospheres: in the French Riviera it is of the slicks of suntan oil that slurp sullenly on the contaminated beaches; on the British-visited Spanish Costa Brava it is of vinegar and lager.

Many cities also have their own characteristic smell: a walk past a stagnant canal can send one back to Venice, Bangkok or Amsterdam, the last of which also has a very personal aroma of cigar smoke – not so Havana, which is pervaded by the slightly sickly fumes of petrol refined from sugarcane. Everyone who returns to Paris recognises with pleasure the warm, rubbery smell of the Métro; Athens, on the other hand, is scented with hair oil. Peking has the unexpected ability to send Englishmen back to their youth, with its old London throat-catcher of coal fires and smog; 1000 miles up the railway line, Ulaan Baatar smells of mutton fat – and once you have been there a week, so do you.

After about two million miles of travelling I consider that the most appalling smells are the sewage lagoons of Calcutta, where you see half-naked tanners, crutch high in the glob, dipping raw skins in and out, and the rubbish tip which bestrews the once lovely slopes on the outskirts of the Sherpa capital of Namche Bazar, an exception to the basic rule that hot places are more noisome than cold ones.

Food is the most obvious source of smells: I remember the surprise

I felt when as a small schoolboy I toured the massive battle-ship HMS *Vanguard* and discovered that it was percolated with the peaceful smell of newly baked bread. Not so soothing are the aromas which waft from the huge modern block which is the food market of Dakar. This is in three layers. In the basement, which is reserved for the locals, the smell is not a smell but a massive stink, blended from a combination of the blood of the animals butchered before one's eyes, of the urine of the beasts excreting in fear, of burning feathers, and of fish. The ground floor is dominated by Europeans, and is less intense; instead of one conglomerated lump of animal, the smells come in pockets, the sultry luxury of mangoes and melons, the cools of apples, mint, lettuce and cucumber. The top floor serves mostly the local hierarchy, the Lebanese, elegant, sharp, subtle: boxes of crystallised fruit, marrons glacé, multi-spiced pot-pourri.

Most evocative of all are the smells which remind me of home: apples in a Peking market; roses in an municipal bed in Islamabad; floor polish in a safari club in Kenya. Chrysanthemums, horses, sheep, wet leaves, a newly mown lawn – strange how even a slight, insubstantial drift of smell can result in an overwhelming nostalgia.

Rome, 23 September 1997. I am staring through the keyhole of one of the most stared-through key-holes in Italy. The metal plate around the aperture has been polished to a silvery shine by countless eyelashes. The view through the keyhole is a perfect scene in miniature: a gravel path leads away from the viewer; it is shaded by a tunnel of evergreens – bay, box and laurel – and through the far end of the tunnel, which acts as a picture frame, the sunlit dome of Saint Peter's glows on the skyline a little under five miles away. The keyhole is set in the gate of the Priory of the Order of the Knights of Malta (Priorato di Malta).

The order is a religious one, the aims of which are 'the glorification of God through the sanctification of its members, service to the Faith and to the Holy See, and welfare work'. It is also an order of knighthood, with the knights following codes of religion and chivalry. The

order is recognised as a sovereign entity, and has diplomatic relations, together with the accompanying ambassadors, with fifty-two other countries; it also has official representatives with international organisations such as UNESCO, the World Health Organisation and the International Institute for Human Rights. Because of this unique position, the diplomatic members of the order have remarkable influence in international circles: they are able to undertake much behind-the-scenes work, for example acting as the liaison and even the negotiator between warring parties. It is rumoured that they did much subtle and skilful introductive work in the civil war in the Lebanon, and remain busy there, the place of their origin, the Near East. Although Britain does not recognise the sovereignty of the order (perhaps because in doing so we would have to admit that our take-over of Malta was a contravention of the Treaty of Amiens, 1802), nevertheless, according to rumour, they were helpful to us in certain contacts with the Argentinians during the Falklands War.

The door opens and I am admitted into the cool shade of the green tunnel. My guide is slightly disappointing. I had hoped for a mysterious figure in the order's black cloak with white Maltese cross, but he is a gnarled little man in a tartan shirt, accompanied by an amiable Alsatian dog.

We pass an open anteroom, the walls of which are covered in coats of arms. The present master, Fra Andrew Bertie, is the first Englishman they have had in that position for 700 years. His escutcheon is quartered with the Cross of Saint John and three battering-rams – rather magnificent weapons with ram's head business ends and handles along the pole. I walk to the far end of a gravelled yard and see the brown waters of the Tiber almost immediately below me and afar off I see the hill surmounted by Saint Peter's.

Here is a neo-classical church with an elegant façade (designed by Piranesi in the eighteenth century), its pediment surmounted by the Maltese cross. I climb the flight of wide, low steps and enter. Armorial banners hang to either side. The side niches each contain memorials: some are impressive – knights in armour; some are simple – clerical. The seating and kneelers are covered with red velvet; there is a gilded

throne near the altar, it is upholstered in a jacquard design of red on red. The altar reminds me of the Austrian Baroque, an ascending arrangement of platforms and shelves, dotted with cherubs and swirls and scrolls. Everything is very impressive but slightly shabby: some of the upholstery is holed, the plaster flaking, the paintwork fading; yet it is not the shabbiness of poverty and neglect, rather the reverse, it shows the wear and tear of frequent use, like the well-worn wig of a venerable judge or the battered crozier of a busy bishop. One feels that the ornamentation and the fittings are there for a purpose, not as mere showpieces.

I wander along the gravelled paths of the Italianesque garden. Most garden beds are edged with neat hedges of miniature box: the scent of it fills the air. There are roses and the occasional striking clump of angel's trumpets (*datura*), with their large, hanging white flowers. Discreet fountains bubble out small jets of water which trickle down to pellucid pools where goldfish drift in serene sloth. There are large terracotta urns, beautifully planted, statues and busts of impressive old men in armour, pretty and aged well-heads. There is a fine line of tulip trees (*liriodendron*), also oranges, palms and oleander; part of the garden is shaded by a huge cedar. In this oasis of peace even the traffic of Rome seems muted. My guide has disappeared; the dog and I wander alone.

The door opens and I am once more in the little Piazza dei Cavalieri di Malta, its whitewashed walls surmounted by urns and obelisks and covered with coats of arms. The square is deserted and seems to doze in the sun; it is silent but for the rustle of palm trees which rear their shaggy heads from the gardens behind the walls. It will be a two-hour wander back to base. Off I go down the cobbled alleyways and side streets.

The whole of Rome is a multitude of arches. Once the Romans had invented their arch they went mad over it: it acts as roofs and basements; it supports viaducts and bridges; it stands alone; it comes in tiers and arcades. And it is surprising how many dead ends there are here: I keep walking up alleyways, vaguely lost, and finding that, at the end, there is a barricade with a little man in a box selling tickets which will

[235]

admit me into a huge brickyard of ruins. All interesting enough, but I am trying to get back for lunch. And it is all up and down: I am reminded that Rome was built on seven hills; and it took longer than a day.

As I tramp along some obscure (to me) side street, I look down and see below an elegant flight of steps leading to an enchanting little assembly of courtyard, roofs and a circular building. I buy a little leaflet which describes the place. It is San Teodoro di Palatino. The original church was built between 583 to 590 but all that remains of this is the apse; the rest of the church was renovated in 1454. The leaflet informs me that the Church was committed to Jesus' Heart Confraternity, the so-called "Big White Sacks".' Why? Were they a group of huge nuns in baggy habits? What did they think when people shouted out: 'Here comes a Big White Sack!'? Did they object? Or were they proud for some esoteric reason?

I descend – seventeen steps. The basic layout is a double flight of stairways leading down to a brick-walled yard: straight-sided length-ways, rounded at the ends; at the far end is the little church. Almost in the middle of the yard there is a stumpy, crudely carved pillar, about waist high. It is a pagan altar. A rectangular depression has been chis-elled into the top – presumably for offerings. Two things strike the eyes when entering the dimly lit interior of the church: firstly the utterly hideous and eye-wrenchingly vile jaundiced yellow of the trashy moquette which is upholstering the semicircular arrangement of the shoddily made pews; secondly the charming Byzantine mosaic whose golden chips glow within the domed apse. Christ sits in the centre on a huge globe; to either side of Him a saint is introducing a martyr. One of the martyrs is rather attractive with a pretty face, long golden hair and wearing a nightshirt. I am embarrassed to find that it is no girl at all, but San Teodoro himself. Apparently he was a Roman soldier mar-tyred in Turkey for some insubordinate behaviour. Two recesses on each side of the church act as shallow side chapels. Each is dominated by a large picture. One is of San Crescentino painted by Guiseppe Ghezzi in 1705. The saint is staring upwards at a cherub and is point-ing to a dead dragon on the ground. I know nothing about him except, now, that he has a liking for sissy footwear, his sandals being bound

halfway up his shins in ribbons of blue satin. The other picture is by Lorenzo Masucci and is of San Ranieri and San Giacinta Mariscotti, of whom I also know nothing, except that one may be a monk and the other a nun and they are staring apprehensively at a disembodied heart hovering above their heads.

I leave the nice little church and tramp on.

I am now in the vast shadow of the 'Typewritter', Victor Emmanuel's monument. Some guide is rabbiting on about this vast erection. His group of tourists are mostly middle-aged and pinkly scrubbed and raw but one of them, standing apart with her head turned to one side in interest, is a nun. She is not your normal nun: a little old hen pottering and pecking busily about, and perhaps clucking to a following brood of chirping children; this young nun has a handsome, serene face and huge green eyes of such slumbering languor that I carry on my way thinking 'What a waste! What a waste!'.

A couple of furlongs more and I have arrived at Trajan's Column. The long epic which spirals up the 131 feet of the pillar is a meticulously detailed cartoon of the emperor's successful campaigning in Dacia (Romania) – showing the beginning, as the Romans prepare for invasion – to the finish, the Dacians being ousted from their country. What I did not know is that the massive block which forms the podium is carved with plunder: helmets, arrows in their quivers, battle axes and spears, armour both scaled and chained; there are S-shaped trumpets with animal heads, presumably lurs; what interests me most are the shields, very similar to the Celtic ones known as the 'Witham' and the 'Battersea' shields which are, to my taste, among the most beautiful examples of metalwork made in England.

As I lean and brood a man and woman with a couple of smallish girls come up and lean on the rail near me. They are English. 'What's that, Dad?' asks one of the girls.

'Cleopatra's column,' says the great wally.

'That's in London, that is, on the Embankment. I've seen it,' says the larger girl.

'That's her needle, this here is her column.'

[237]

'It says here, Dad, on this little notice, that this is Trajan's Column.'

'Same person,' says Dad. I quit. It not my business to tell him he's an ignorant idiot. From experience, I learned long ago that's what daughters are for.

 **Isle de Gorée, 30 September 1997.** I am in Senegal. I have already toured Dakar, the capital, on previous visits so when I was having lunch in the elegant residence of David and Anne Snoxell, our ambassador and his wife, I asked David what he would recommend as a place to visit for such a short while.

'The Island of Gorée,' he said.

Only a twenty-minute ferry journey of under five miles from the city: a schoolboy's dream, littered with the cannons and guns of 500 years of war, yet only 1000 yards long by 330 wide, so tourable within two hours. A small island, yet crammed with history, from the early Neanderthal settlers, through the wars fought between the Portuguese, the Spanish, Dutch, French and British, to times of settling, slave-trading and finally independence. The first European settlers, the Portuguese, used it as a resting and revictualling base for their journeys on the way to the Indies. The Dutch bought it for a few iron nails in 1627 and gave it the name 'Goe-ree', 'Good Harbour', a name it has retained in French form. It became a haven for some of the settlers and traders of the West African coast, being one of the few healthy places there; it became a hell for others, the slaves who were assembled there before being shipped off to the Americas. The British, who had captured and lost it several times, handed it back to the French in 1817 when we were generously returning parts of the pre-Napoleonic French Empire (mostly the sandy, useless bits).

Some of the most interesting remains are the massive fortifications and gun emplacements built by the French against their enemies in the Second World War. 'And not against the Germans, as you may think,' the ambassador said, 'but against the British, culminating in "Operation Menace".'

This naval battle was one of the more unsuccessful of the British naval actions in the Second World War. The actual fighting took place in the three days between 23 and 25 September 1940, but the preliminaries began five months earlier. Arthur Marder, the author of *Operation Menace: The Dakar Expedition* (1976), wrote that the operation:

> exemplifies, in its genesis, planning and execution, all that can go wrong in warfare: an operation fouled up by unforeseen contingencies, the accidents of war, and human error, and against a background of undue political interference, inadequate planning, and half-baked cooperation between allies.'

The intention of it all was based on De Gaulle's theory that once Dakar was taken, then the whole of Vichy-occupied French Africa would swing over to our side. The British intelligence information suggested that this was correct. They were completely wrong: French Africa was thoroughly on the side of the Vichy. This misinformation proved to be the biggest mistake of the whole exercise and was the basic reason for its eventual abandonment.

The invading British armada consisted of a mixed collection of ships, many of them of First World War vintage. There were two battle-ships (the *Barham* and *Resolution*), one air-craft carrier (*Ark Royal*), four cruisers, nine destroyers: 4270 British troops and 2400 Free Frenchmen. The French ships sheltering in the habour of Dakar included the battle-ship *Richelieu*, which was armed with eight fifteen-inch and fifteen six-inch guns, two super destroyers, one destroyer and three submarines. There were also flights of aeroplanes and six coastal batteries, one of these being on the Island of Gorée. The guns there included a turret of two armour-plated 'Vergniaud' cannon.

There were some impressive characters on both sides. The British were commanded by the (later) highly successful Vice-Admiral John Dacres Cunningham. The French commanders included three men who, rather typically, were admired by the British and denigrated by the French. The British assessment of the French commander, Governor-General Pierre François Boisson, was 'Deafened, and lost a leg in the

last war. Is very pro-Vichy. Good character – anti-British,' and of the French C-in-C of French West Africa, General Jean Joseph Guillaum, 'a very honourable and delightful man. Fine military record. Will certainly obey orders from Vichy.' The French said of their own Vice-Admiral Emile Maria Lacroix that he was 'a foul-mouthed, hairy old sea wolf, who looks as though he was hewn with an axe.'

One of the Free French captains, Commander Jacquelin de la Porte des Vaux, was a quick-witted fellow with a sense of humour. As his sloop, the *Dominé*, was sneaking close inshore within the fog, the mist cleared to reveal the *Richelieu* beginning to train her massive guns upon him. Instantly the Commander ordered his bugler to sound the 'garde-à-vous' and as the crew of the *Richelieu* obediently leapt to attention the *Dominé* turned about and got the hell out of it.

From here, beside the bridge of the blunt-ended rust-bucket of a ferry, the island looks like a tadpole, with its long low tail covered with an attractive muddle of red-roofed buildings, the tail and body rear up a hundred feet to become a head covered with a wig of trees and bushes and ending abruptly at sheer basalt cliffs. A view of the chart I can just see on the bench beside the steersman shows that the tail of the tadpole is curved, with the harbour in the hollow of the bend.

We are mooring alongside a crude jetty. There are swarms of children in the little sandy cove adjacent, swimming in the clear waters or just running on the beach, all hopping about as busily as sand fleas.

I disembark and walk into a cosy sandy area bounded by a line of cannon enfiladed on one side, and with areas shaded by trees and para-soled tables and chairs set out on the other. The next 'square' is larger, also shaded by many venerable trees, baobabs and acacias. There is a very attractive Place du Gouvernement to one side. It has lovely old shutters and a balustrated top but is dangerously unstable and has been wired off. In the centre of the square there is another attractive construction. It is octagonal and looks like a pulpit but is actually a ridiculously versatile watertower-with-bandstand. It is all a scene of serenity and peace: once it must have been as busy as the cattleyard in Colchester market, with crowds of abject, heart-sick humans being herded into groups before boarding the slavers.

As I plod further into the village I become surrounded by charming little houses, all in soothingly faded colours, mostly ochres in pinks, yellows and ecrus. There are little squares, floored with sand; the wider streets have central pavements of cobbled basalt, polished by generations of bare feet. There is not much sign of activity except for the children, sometimes a few may be seen playing in one of the squares; if I see anyone moving in the side streets, it will be a child. The main activity of the women is either plaiting each other's hair or watching the laundry dry. The men do even less: they just lounge and stare, willing you to drop dead. From whom are they descended? The lucky slaves, on the island at the very moment that slavery was abolished? Or the warders and prison guards – the Quislings? Or even the slave traders themselves? (The Europeans and Arabs may have been the buyers, but the Africans were responsible for the selling.)

I am now beginning to climb more steeply, between a fine avenue of baobab trees. The barrels of old cannon are used as markers.

I reach the level plateau of the 'highland'. The guns-and-turret of the old Vergniaud cannon dominates the skyline. It is now sixty-two years old. From afar, it resembles some huge rust-red animal, a vast crustacean which has crawled out of the sea and died: its armoured head sprouts two massive antenna which are slumped upon the ground. I pace them out: ten steps from the muzzle to the breech block, then four more to the breech – each gun is over forty feet long. I measure the thickness of the turret armour – about eight inches. All is corrosion and weeds and silence, but it must have been tremendously exciting in there during the battle. Monk, my retired gamekeeper who was a naval gunner during the war, once told me what it was like in a similar turret. There would be eight men. The independent shell with its belt of copper (to bite into the rifling) would be loaded first. Then the two bags of ammunition would follow, having come up from the magazine below by lift or hoist. The blackpowder/cordite/blackpowder sandwich of explosive had been bagged in silk, because silk does not leave smouldering bits which could ignite the next load of ammunition. At the same time as this loading, the sighter and rangefinder would be assessing the success or failure of the last shot and re-aiming. The gun would be fired, the breech opened, and a huge

wet mop would be reamed up the barrel. While all this was going on there would be messages pouring in from headquarters and the enemy was doing his best to blow you to bits. From the firing of one shot to the next took about five minutes.

I walk the few paces off to look at the sea almost immediately below: from here I can see a vast oceanic horizon to one side, and the long stretch of the African coast to the other. Closer by, all about on the plateau top, there are constructions in concrete: other gun emplacements, trenches and ramps leading underground to stores and ammunition magazines, the occasional metal-reinforced building, large tennis-court-sized areas of concrete which sometimes drum hollow beneath my feet; bits of metal are scattered around, chunks and tubes and turrets, all corroded and rusting. Between it all are patches of vegetable gardening, fenced off from the odd wandering goat. I start to go down into one of the underground rooms but then hear voices coming from it; a line of washing and some bedding is in one old circular gun emplacement; eyes peer at me from the few buildings still standing. In the site of a long-gone gun turret I find a 'Peace Pole', each of its four sides inscribed with a prayer in a different language. A group of friends plant these talismans in 'appropriate' places throughout the world, a custom I find eccentric but sweetly optimistic.

I have now arrived at the other end of the island to explore the North Battery (also known as Fort Estrées). This was built in the reign of Napoleon III. It is shaped like a doughnut with a bite taken out of it. The bite is the site of the fortified entrance. Inside there is a little circular yard from which one can enter the thirteen cells which look out to sea. On the ramparted walkway at the top there is just room for ten cannon – the fort is surprisingly small, another of the schoolboy's ideals.

Before the ferry arrives I have time to relax: to have a glass of beer from a beach-side tavern and to write a postcard to Edmée di Pauli to tell her that her Peace Pole is working well here.

I am sitting in the shade of an ancient baobab tree. It gives me an eerie feeling to think that over 200 years ago, maybe under the shade of this very tree, Captain Samuel Courtauld stood, watching the loading of his ship, the *Vela Ana*, slave trader.

 **Newspapers**———My experience with local newspapers has generally been amiable. I was a District Councillor for twenty years, and the *Halstead Gazette* and the *Braintree & Witham Times* ('Brainless & Witless') reported most of my statements with reasonable accuracy. It was the national tabloids that taught me what lying and distortion of truth can be done. After I had talked on Radio 2 about Queen's Messengers, the *Daily Mail* telephoned me saying that they were interested in my mention of collecting plants for Kew Gardens and particularly interested in the possibly unknown 'Siberian Potato' that I had brought back. The reporter asked such questions as 'Do you think that you can be compared to the discoverer of the first potato?', to which I replied: 'That is a nice thought, but no.' This was printed as 'George Courtauld is proud to be following the footsteps of Sir Walter Raleigh' which made me out to be an utter twerp. The paper asked if it could have an example of the tuberous root to photograph. I replied that Kew Gardens had all the plants I'd brought back. Nobody bothered to contact Kew. The article was dominated by a large photograph of a root – from a dandelion, I think – which had absolutely no resemblance to the real thing. Thus, in both word and picture, much of the article was half truth at best, with deliberate lies at worst.

During the last week I have been travelling up the West African coast from Nigeria to Ghana, the Ivory Coast, Sierra Leone, Guinea, the Gambia and Senegal. Much of the time was spent hanging about in waiting rooms. A pleasure in this particular journey is the extraordinary things I read from the newspapers left by previous passengers. Here are a couple of indignant letters:

I wish to complain about the modern habit of unmarried mothers leaving their babies on rubbish tips. This is not only very bad for the infants at an early stage in their life, but sometimes they are found by unscrupulous persons and sold into slavery, or used in sacrifices.
Your disgusted
***
Port Harcourt

I was last week conned by a theatre company operating along Jogoo Road. The company advertised through your daily that they would screen love films *Sea of Love*, *Master of Love*, *Women of Desire* and *Benils Babe Watch*, all to be shown concurrently from mid-day. But to our surprise, we got a rude shock to find that all they were showing was *An Officer and a Gentleman*.

Yours,

***

Nairobi

Interesting news items have included:

POLICE BURY THREE STUDENTS THEY SHOT DEAD

The police had carried the corpses to Port Harcourt cemetery and buried them in a mass grave after their eyeballs had been removed [for sale]. Port Harcourt council officials have said the internment was done without permission of the council. 'Your request for assistance to exhume the bodies for postmortem examination was not accompanied by a coroner's form, nor an order issued by any of the approved authorities, for such exercise,' the council observed.

NUJ (NATIONAL UNION OF JOURNALISTS) CHAIRPERSON ASSAULTED

Mrs Eke-Agbai was beaten up by security guards at Government House. The union has broken into two factions – one comprising workers who do not see anything wrong with the assault and others who insist that the Government apologises for the humiliation it meted out to the union.

MENTAL ART FORUM AVERTS DOOMSDAY

Professor Gabriel Okunzua of the Lagos University Teaching Hospital has said that October 9th is the Doomsday for the globe but his mental Art Forum has developed a protective formula to nullify the cataclysm. Speaking at a gathering of staff and students Professor Okunzua has disclosed that while the space craft Pathfinder was exploring Mars, he and his mental art colleagues were communicating with 'Important Personalities on Mars'.

POLICE DEFEND ROLE IN DEMOLITION

The Lagos State Police Force has defended its role in the demolition of nearly 200 buildings rendering over 10,000 people homeless. They claim they were only obeying orders and object that if the orders were wrongly worded and mistaken it was not their fault.

In a bizarre innovation to warfare, irate youths in Ife-Modakeke sustained the mayhem in their domains with bullets improvised from edible rice grains . . . Once fired into a victim's body, doctors are unable to retrieve them . . . when the rice comes into contact with the warm human blood it swells up and dissolves. . . . Rapid poisoning of the circulatory system leading to death. . . . The price of the rice has escalated.

A snippet from the *Lagos Guardian*'s 'Junior Page' particularly appealed to me:

FACT FILE

Fact 1. The largest mammal is the blue whale. The newborn calves measured between 6 and 8 metres long and weigh up to 3 tons.
Fact 2. The smallest mammal is bumble bee.

Compared with the 'news' reporting, the articles written by many of the regular columnists in Nigerian papers are not only interesting and lucid, but written by brave men who are pushing their luck by attacking the powerful and tyrannical government. Among these are Tunde Oledepo, who wrote of 'the primitive and insane policies and programmes of Government which lead unelected and unaccepted "leaders" to pass collective insults on the citizenry in their futile bid to give reasonable explanations to unreasonable decisions', and Ferni Fani-Kayode:

They forget that the sacrifice of today's truth is a denial of tomorrow's justice. They forget that if there is no Nigeria left they will have nobody to rule and nothing to pillage. What can one say about a

government that places more value on the protection of the state than the rights of human beings. . . . in Nigeria today the truth is not only absent but it has been completely drowned in a cacophony of deceit and an orgy of perversions.

In the *Sunday Tribune*, there was a headline above the photograph of the military ruler:

IN THE NAME OF GOD, BEGIN TO GO.

When I boarded the last aeroplane, on my flight to England, there was only one English newspaper available, a trashy tabloid full of gossip with almost no news but gossip and a pompous editorial by a brainless bigot. There was a particularly spiteful column by a sour woman who has no heart to wear on her sleeve, so wears her gall bladder there instead. The smug but stupid opinions, the malice, the disinterest in anything except sex and sport of the British journalists was a shaming contrast to their Nigerian counterparts, with their great causes, so bravely and intelligently put.

 **Delhi, 14 October 1997.** I had a moment of strong anxiety this morning. I had landed after the all-night flight with three bags: a large diplomatic-mail one; a small one containing emergency supplies for the High Commission doctor; the third, equally small, was the Royal Household bag. Having delivered the first two, I was driven to the imposing President's Residence (formerly the Viceroy's Palace). My escort and I tramped through the tall, pink corridors, guarded by the President's Bodyguard, very smart in their turbans and sashes of red and gold. We finally found the Household Secretaries in a room overlooking the red courtyards and green lawns of the west gardens. I handed over the bag. The nice girl whose job it is to open the bags started sawing away at the seal with a knife and suddenly I knew, with dread certainty, that the Royal letters were cooling in a fridge in the clinic, and all that the Queen and her

entourage would have to read would be the labels on snake-bite serum bottles.

But my fears were unfounded.

In the evening I went to the High Commissioner's Residence for a reception held for the Queen and the Duke of Edinburgh. It was all very pleasant: efficient and picturesque. I arrived in the daylight and wandered round the garden of expansive lawns and good trees and flowerbeds; kites wheeled overhead and green parrots darted about, screeching. Darkness fell to the music played by a band of Royal Marines and swarms of servants handed out quantities of drinks and very good nibbles on salvers: they were tactfully labelled 'Vegetarian' and 'Non-vegetarian'. It did not seem too crowded, although some 1 500 people were there. The Queen and Prince Philip strolled along a wide red carpet which was zigzagged over the lawns and talked to the crowd of guests lined up and goggling at either side. I was winkled out of the crowd by the Defence and Military Adviser to meet Her Majesty. Last time we had met was aboard *Britannia* in the middle of the Pearl River during her China tour. After that I talked to many more people, including some retired, nostalgically reminiscent Gurkha officers, three giggly yet elegant Indian women in saris embroidered in gold; a charming American-born Lady-in-waiting, with whom I discussed how greedy our respective children had been; a peculiar but smiley ambassador's wife who gave me the receipt for a 'salad' made out of tinned mandarins and chopped boiled beetroot (it sounded horrible, I don't know why she told me about it); and an ancient monk with a white goatee beard (we talked for five minutes and I did not hear a single word he said, but he seemed agreeable). A very handsome and elegant woman in her seventies said: 'Ah, you are the Queen's Messenger. I will write a message for her,' and she solemnly wrote out a note on the back of her invitation, folded it neatly and gave it to me, saying: 'You can read it if you like.' (I did, later. It was a note of sympathy and 'complete under-standing' – underlined twice – about the wives of one's sons.) I gave it to one of the Secretaries to pass on. Nice for a Queen's Messenger actu-ally to pass on messages to the Queen.

Finally I scrounged a lift back to my hotel in the bus carrying the Royal Marine band.

15 October 1997. I have been to Delhi a score of times and have 'done' all the right things: the tombs, the Red Fort, the Jama Masijid mosque, Gandhi's house, the Mogul ruins, the Imperial edifices of Lutyens and Baker. Today, instead, I have decided to see more of the local life: the view from the pavement rather than the mini-bus window.

My companion and guide is Nigel ***, someone I met at the reception yesterday. He is an old soldier, a remnant of the Raj: aged seventy-seven yet still bolt upright so that his shock of white hair towers above the dark-haired bustling of the people all about him. His driver, Samuel, is a melancholy little Christian with the most remarkably protuberant lower lip: I have been trying to find a simile that does it justice – a diving-board? a window sill? the tailgate of a waggon?

Having collected me from the Mogul Gate of the British High Commission, Samuel is now driving us across Delhi to a Sikh temple, where we are to meet another sightseer, an American called Chip.

As we traverse the busy chaos of the city, Nigel points out things which he thinks will be unusual to my European eyes: the Pumper-up of Bicycle Tyres – a scrawny man in a dirty *dhoti*; the Mattress Beater; the Ear Cleaner, with his instrument box, the *puggri*, which holds tweezers, picks, scoops and cotton buds, all for the removal – and satisfied scrutiny – of ear wax; the elegant Hod-carrier – a heap of bricks on her head, a green and gold sari draped about her; a man having his hair cut, squatting on a couple of bricks to bring him to the right height; a sacred cow munching marrows off the stall of a thus honoured – nevertheless somewhat despondent – greengrocer; an elephant with an ornately painted trunk; an ox pulling a mower on the lawn of a large roundabout; the Collector of Cow-pats; the Leprous Beggar-woman. There is a terrace of refugee hovels. Each is about eight foot square, cobbled together from an assortment of bricks and blocks, with no windows and roofed with rags and litter; yet each door – of corrugated iron – has a little number painted proudly upon it. We pass an orphanage, the 'Delhi Council for Child Welfare'. Beside the main entrance there is a recess in the wall, in it is a wicker basket. About twice a week, during the night, a baby is placed within. We overtake a small convoy of tiny three-wheeler cabs absolutely crammed with arms and legs, pigtails and ribbons, solemn little faces with round brown eyes, satchels and food

boxes. It is a kindergarten outing. We reckon that each vehicle is holding at least a dozen children, plus a driver.

The Sikh temple, the Gurdwara Bangla Sahib, is white with a golden dome. In front, there is a courtyard; to the side, a large formal pool within an aisled and arched enclosure of white marble. The courtyard is full of impressive men in turbans with huge bushy beards. A lot of them seem angry, and shout and wave banners: they are farmers complaining about something – the weather? Chip is waiting for us by the main entrance. He is a rubicund fellow in shorts: his shiny pink face either creased in smiles or agape in wonder.

Nigel tells us that Sikhism is a sort of 'Protestant Hinduism', which merged what their gurus thought as the best of Hinduism with some of the tenets of Islam and other creeds. Perhaps its basic differences from Hinduism are the belief in one god only and a disapproval of the caste system.

We enter the temple. Men and women are sitting together: unusual for an Eastern religion. We walk round the central altar, canopied and with a gilded dome and heaped with marigolds, whose colour is the holy colour of saffron. We leave through a side door where we each receive a dollop of *kurrah pershas*, a special offering which is cooked in an iron vessel, stirred with a sword and made from a mixture of wheat, sugar and ghee. It tastes a bit like semolina pudding. From the temple we walk to the *langar*, the 'open kitchen': a sort of alms dining-room. On busy occasions it feeds up to 10,000 people; at present it is mid-morning and there are only about thirty people squatting alongside a strip of woven jute which acts as a table. They are sipping hot, sweetened tea. Further off, two lines of women with rolling-pins are shaping chapattis, a hot plate is tended by others who toast the dough disks and pack them ready for the midday meal.

We clamber into Nigel's car – a bit of a cram: I am fat, Chip is fatter and Nigel is six foot three – and Samuel drives us off to the Nigambodh ghat (cremation yard). I do not particularly want to see it, but Nigel says that it will give us a good insight into the 'psyche' of the Indian way of life and death.

The first thing I notice is a huge heap of firewood. We enter the compound. There is a haze of smoke. I have a sickly dread that I will smell

burning flesh. When it wafts into my face I am relieved that all I can smell is woodsmoke and sandlewood. We pass a few pyres. They are burning fiercely. Sinister, dark shapes are in their centre. I try not to look, it would be salacious at the least, and possibly bad mannered at worst. The pyres are below open roofs of metal, on platforms of brick. Each platform has three man-sized, rectangular depressions.

'Six to seven hours,' Nigel replies to my only question.

We stand back to let some mourners walk past. They are carrying a stretcher, the shrouded figure on it looks very flat, except for the high mound of the feet. They are jostling about, looking a bit lost: it all seems rather amateur and makeshift.

Nigel explains: 'They have no undertakers, no priest. Once you are dead you are taken here as soon as possible by your family. No hearses either, sometimes you may be on the back of a lorry, nicely ornamented with garlands and your photograph on the front, sometimes you may be strapped to the back of a tricycle-rickshaw and pedalled here. The average funeral costs the equivalent of twenty pounds.'

A smut blows into my eye. I wonder of whom and from what it is. My eye starts to water. I think with embarrassment that people will suppose that I am grieving.

We walk past more pyres. I feel the heat from one. Someone is warming me.

We mount the steps to the 'dipping tank'. This is where bodies are ceremoniously dunked three times in the holy water of the river before they are put on the pyre. Water is spilling over a channel into the tank. It looks foul. People are cupping it in their hands and drinking it. Perhaps this is to ensure a speedy return to this place – feet first.

A stretcher is carried past and put down beside the tank. The shrouds covering the body are adjusted and I see the top of a poor balding head, then a greeny-grey face with a jutting nose. I look away. On a platform below me some people are piling wood on top of a stretcher. 'Anyone got a match?' asks Chip cheerfully.

We have reached the far outskirts of the city, to the site of the Coronation Durbar where, in 1911, George V was officially proclaimed Emperor of India. At that occasion there were 50,000 troops, thou-

sands of officials, including a hundred mace bearers; there were Maharajas and Rajas and Ranis, generals and admirals and countless spectators. The Emperor and Empress, in their diamond crowns, were enthroned beneath a canopy of velvet surmounted by a gilded dome: all around them was the glitter of jewellery, the gleam of swords and the waving of plumes. All that remains of this magnificent scene is a flight of steps leading up a stone obelisk, alone amid a wide, flat expanse of dusty ground.

There is a small enclosure near the obelisk. It is half-moon shaped, about the size of a bowling green, and railed in. The rusting gates are partly ajar. We squeeze through, into the shrubby, scruffy interior. It is a prison for statues. When independence was declared it was decided that the statues of the British notables would be expelled from the public places throughout India and incarcerated here. Tall plinths of red sandstone are placed in a semicircle before us. Alone, in front, they are dominated by the colossal statue of George V in full regalia, his robe trailing down behind him like the tail of a peacock. It is the statue which once stood in the Rajpath, the great parade, two miles long, which started from the Viceroy's Palace. Apart from the Emperor, there are only about half a dozen potentates positioned on their plinths. The cities of India wanted to keep their statues. So the little squad of imperial nabobs stand still and lonely amid the scrub, their blind eyes staring towards the solitary figure of their Emperor, their King of Kings, their Ozymandias.

We leave. The lonely obelisk is in front. To one side, on the flat dusty ground, a score of ragged children have started to play a meticulously organised game of cricket.

As we drive back to Delhi we pass some water-buffalo wallowing in a pool.

A terrier at a rat-hole, a cock crowing on his dungle surrounded by his wives, a lark trilling in ecstasy above a hay field, two octopi in a passionage sixteen-arm embrace, a pig rootling in a trough newly filled with warm bran and potato peelings, a lamb bounding with youth and *joie de vivre* – examples of Nature in bliss, but none of these can compare in luxuriation and fulfilment with the bliss of a water-buffalo in its wallow. The beast cannot live without water – it originated in marsh-

lands – and it is born with that chin-up stance suitable for an animal which likes to lie almost submerged. It would be interesting to see what sort of aquatic creature it could develop into in the future (probably a stuffed curiosity in a museum among all the other extinct animals). I have been told that they are very stubborn: although stronger than horses, they are reluctant to pull wheeled vehicles. They generally acknowledge only one person as master and will attack anyone else presumptuous enough to try to control them. Their main purpose is to pull ploughs in rice paddies, where they are at home wading in the waters and where their splayed hoofs are suited to the squidgy soil. The milk is almost twice as strong as normal cow's milk, and sours less easily. The curds are a pure white.

We lunch at Maidens Hotel, another remnant of the old Raj. The walls are covered with Empire photographs. In one of them the Prince of Wales (Edward VIII) is reviewing a company of Seaforth Highlanders. In honour of the occasion his flared-out jodhpurs are of the Mackenzie tartan. I suddenly realise what Samuel's lower lip resembles: the undone 'drip-trap' fly of a pair of breeches. Chip is terribly impressed by this garb so I don't tell him that the last time I saw anything similar was at the circus, worn by a chap with a red nose and pointed hat. There is an Indian couple at the next table. He is sleek and dapper. She is plump and has an angelic face. She wears a sari. Between the bottom of her blouse and the top of her skirt there is a spare tyre of naked flesh: it has the shape, colour and delectability of a newly baked doughnut.

Now we are in Old Delhi, wandering through the bazaars of the trading and shopping centre. The walkways are narrow, averaging four paces in width; there are side alleys even narrower, mere slits between walls, litter-filled and stinking. The maze of streets is divided up into sections: the Street of Tractor Spare Parts; the Bazaar of Cooking Implements; the Street of Things to Put in the End of Bottles – corks, plugs, stoppers, caps and bungs; the Alley of Wax Vendors – of blocks of bee's wax, slivers of shellac, cans of petroleum jelly, cakes of palm-tree wax, candles, sealing wax, greases and ointments; the Street of Smell Sellers – gum arabic, rose petals, crystals of menthol, lumps of frankincense, phials of clove oil, sandalwood (either as faggots, spills,

shavings or powdered); in olfactory comparison we pass the Corner of the Rubbish Sorters, untouchable men who pick through unspeakable heaps of yuck whose unbearable stinks make your eyes water. Not much more hygienic are the little alcoves where food is sold, identifiable from their accompanything buzzments of flies: an elephant made of sugar is covered with a creeping of small bees; a customer buys a kilo of crystallised pumpkin, his eyes fixed beadily upon the vendor's primitive scales; here is a Miller, a complete with sacks of flour and a resident mouse, you can have your own wheat ground in a little electric grinder. We meet a friend of Nigel, an Oil Presser, whose ox will walk round and round and round and round in a little cell, pulling at the bar which turns the pressing stone. The ox is an amiable zebu called Moti, which means 'Pearl'. We feed him with chunks of a small marrow that Nigel has specially brought.

'Do they worm their animals,' I ask, enquiring after one of my obsessions.

'Why should they? They don't even worm themselves.'

Everywhere percolates the smells of joss-sticks, of spices, and of the tiled, open-air public pissoirs. People are all ajostle, amid them porters barge and shove, carrying sacks on their heads, or goods in round wicker platters; or they push long, two-wheeled barrows which can hurt if they ram you on the back of your legs; an ox pulls a tumbril past, with one driver to guide and six men on the back to shout 'Make way!'

The walls around us are mostly of flaking plaster, but sometimes when you look up you will see a Mogul window, or a fretted balcony, or you will pass a massive door with ornately carved lintels. All around, embedded in modern masonry, are the remnants of 3000 years of at least eight civilisations.

I stop to write out the contents of some little bowls a vendor has arranged on his counter: 'pepper, clove, cardamon, saffron, mace, nutmeg, chilli, ginger, coriander, cumin, fenugreek, turmeric . . .'. The stall-holder, a small wry-looking man, says: 'Who are you, my friend? Are you the tax inspector?'

'I'm just interested in all the different spices you've got for sale here.'

'So, you observe all our region's culture. Perhaps I should ask you for a fee? Tourists who take photos sometimes contribute due rewards.'

I laugh uneasily, 'You speak English very well.'

'My friend, can you not deduce that I am an educated man.' He glances at Nigel: 'It is not clement, sir, and you are no longer in the bloom of your youth. You should be wearing your woollens.'

We leave the unlikeable, sardonic little man and ascend a steep, narrow, unlit and stinking flight of steps to emerge onto a balcony which runs round a square enclosure. Below us the bazaar bustles; at eye-level there are elegant windows and carved shutters; above, there are domes and pinnacles. It is an old caravanserai. Typical of Delhi, Nigel says, you may suddenly see that the cement walling of an office block has been built on foundations of red sandstone of the time of Shah Jehahn, that the dusty flooring of a yard being used as a children's cricket pitch will suddenly betray the ghost of a formal garden in the evening shadows, that a litter-filled niche in a back alley will have patches of plaster painted with exquisite flowers.

But all is decay, nothing new is imposing or beautiful, the past is ignored and the present will not be worth remembering and all that the future offers is poverty and despair.

Back to the High Commission for mulligatawny soup, an excellent mutton biryani and a couple of pints of Guinness.

Perhaps things aren't too bad after all.

Hints, tips and recipes – – – I once heard a Frenchman say, not completely disparagingly, that the British Empire was run by schoolboys. I think he was correct. During the reign of Victoria, the inhabitants of our islands were swarming out into the world like bees from a hive, sent out by their Queen to explore and report; but whatever the motives of politicians, financiers and industrialists, most people who went out to the colonies did so because it was an *adventure*. Some were callow youths sent away from home because their fathers thought them unfit to run the family business (instead many of them found that they were administrating, single-handed, little-known tracts of land the size of Wales). Some were eager

young missionaries, stifled in clerical collars and thick serge. Others were botanists, or lecturers, or soldiers, or merely lunatics, but whoever they were and whatever the excuse, they were there for the excitement.

Their attitude is well summarised by Sir Francis Galton who wrote a book entitled *The Art of Travel: or Shifts and Contrivances Available in Wild Countries*, first published in 1855. In his introduction he says:

If you have health, a great craving for adventure, at least a moderate fortune, and can set your heart on a definite object, which old travellers do not think impracticable, then – travel by all means. If, in addition to these qualifications, you have scientific taste and knowledge, I believe that no career, in time of peace, can offer to you more advantages than that of a traveller. If you have not independent means, you may still turn travelling to excellent account; for experience shows it often leads to promotion, nay, some men support themselves by travel. They explore pasture lands in Australia, they hunt for ivory in Africa, they collect specimens of natural history for sale, or they wander as artists.

That is his first paragraph. In the second he makes two remarks also characteristic of his carefree abandon: 'Savages rarely murder newcomers,' he says soothingly, with the further encouragement that 'ordinary fevers are seldom fatal.'

Galton's chapter on medicine does little to mitigate the unease his book might induce in the modern reader, even though it starts cheerfully: 'the traveller who is sick, away from help, may console himself with the proverb, that "though there is a great difference between a good physician and a bad one, there is very little between a good one and none at all".' While many of his remedies seem sensible and harmless enough, such as his suggestion for preventing blisters by breaking raw eggs into one's boots, there are others which are considerably more drastic. Gunpowder seems to be an important ingredient in his medicine chest: for snake bites or scorpion stings, 'explode gunpowder in the wound'; for a purge, 'drink a charge of gunpowder in a tumblerful of warm water' (this seems to work on the same principle as the purge made out of fermented figs by our neighbour Mrs Rutland).

Whatever the remedy, Galton writes with cheerful commonsense and ingenuity: I would have found it helpful, in my mountain-rescue days, to know that 'the main arteries follow pretty much the direction of the inner seams of the sleeves and trousers.' His lighthearted optimism seems to know no bounds, even when starving ('all old hides or skins of any kind that are not tanned are fit and good for food; many a hungry person has cooked and eaten his sandals') or about to drown ('a few yards of intenstine blown out . . . makes a capital swimming belt: it may be wound in a figure of 8 round the neck and under the armpits'). If you are likely to become cold while thus swimming about swathed with innards, remember that 'the chilliness consequent on staying long in water is retarded by rubbing all over the body, before entering it, about twice as much oil or bear's-grease as a person uses for his hair.'

In those days, before the invention of the motor-car, the traveller depended greatly upon beasts of burden. Sir Francis is particularly interesting on this subject, whether discussing something abstract, such as their sociability ('men attach themselves to horses and asses, and to a lesser degree to mules and oxen, but they rarely make friends of camels') or being more practicable (to stop donkeys braying, 'lash a heavy stone to the beast's tail. It appears that when an ass wants to bray he elevates his tail, and, if his tail be weighed down, he has not the heart to bray').

His advice on how to treat the locals is likely to be considered a straightforward, tactless example of nineteenth-century attitudes, long before the notion of 'political correctness' existed: 'MANAGEMENT OF SAVAGES: A frank, joking but determined manner, joined with an air of showing more confidence in the good faith of the natives than you really feel, is the best.'

I had often suspected that 'trading beads with the natives' was a fanciful item of legend, but no, *The Art of Travel* has much to say on the subject, suggesting that a large quantity of beads be taken ('40 or 50 lbs weight goes but a little way') and that the most suitable are 'dull white, dark blue, and vermilion red, all of a small size'. However, he also advises that travellers take such items as needles or tobacco because, for example, 'the chief at Lake Ngami told Mr Andersson that his beads

would be of little use, for the women about the place already "grunted like pigs" under the burdens of those that they wore, and which they had received from previous travellers.'

He deals with many other problems, but whether they are peaceful, such as how to tame cormorants for fishing, or more urgent, such as how to defend a stockade, an impression pervades the book that the whole world is an adventure and it is glorious to be alive.

I too, as a traveller, have been collecting helpful hints throughout my travels. Here are a few of them.

Pest repellant: garlic gin
This is the most effective of all repellants, and the most versatile, keeping away mosquitoes, horseflies, lions, polar bears – even the beggars of Calcutta and the whores of Lagos:
  Ingredients: cloves of garlic, lumps of sugar, gin.
This is made in the same way as the more conventional sloe gin, namely: fill a bottle 50/50 with the garlic and sugar lumps. Top up with gin. Cork. Keep topping up every day until there is no more absorption. Strain away the garlic (which can be used with roast venison). Drink a large quantity of the garlic gin before going to bed or whenever you wish to be pest-free.

To destroy cockroaches
Cockroaches have existed for millions of years and their metabolism quickly adapts to insect killers. This method relies on their natural greed (it is used in the back-streets of New York):
  Scatter yeast on the floor of the kitchen or infested place. After it has been gobbled up put out saucers of water . . . Wait for the bangs.

To relieve aching feet on a forced march or other long walk

Rub aconite (aconitum anglicum – also known as monkshood and wolfsbane) on the soles of the feet.

This was used by Essex witches: the powerful effect of the extremely poisonous aconite numbs the feet so that you cannot feel yourself walking, and it seems as if you are flying.

To divert charging animals, particularly bulls

Turn you back to the animal, open your legs and, bending down, look at the animal from between your parted knees.

I do not know why this works – or even if it works: I have not tried it. An umbrella opened and shut in the animal's face will also often frighten it off (apparently).

To float

Take off your trousers, tie a knot at the bottom of each leg, put a leg under each armpit, so that the rest of the leg is hanging down behind, open up the waist end of the trouser towards the water and jump in. The trouser-legs will fill with enough air to act as water-wings for about thirty yards.

To catch fish

Eat asparagus, then pee into water. Fish are attracted by the urine. Chuck in a hand grenade.

Packing

Always travel as light as possible. I now go round the world with a bag small enough to go in the overhead locker of a small aeroplane. The most necessary and versatile of all equipment is a toothbrush. Apart from the spongebag all one needs is a change of socks, pants and shirt. Most things can be washed and dried overnight. Sleep nude; the only time pyjamas are useful are as underclothes in freezing conditions. (A pair of pyjama trousers under one's ordinary trousers are infinitely more warming than the layers of women's tights and long-johns some people wear.)

A good book is the only other necessity. I learned that as a yarn and fibre salesman in Yorkshire, sometimes having to stand in a queue for up to four hours (occasionally in the snow) before reaching the buyer's little kiosk.

Admittedly, if one has a hobby, it is sensible to take the equipment. Several of my fellow Queen's Messengers play golf and have attempted ingenious methods to travel light. One had a golf club with a ratchet which changed it from a putter to a driver to brassie to a niblick to whatever those things are called; another had a shaft with detachable heads, but in an x-ray machine they looked like pistols.

Ottawa, 22 October 1997. I went to bed last night in the autumn and woke up this morning in the winter: a couple of inches of snow lay on my windowsills. There had been no wind during the night so that the snow had settled and stayed: the buttons on top of the row of flagpoles outside my window each wore a little white dunce's cap; there was a small park outside my windows and each branch and twig had a ridge of snow transforming the trees into crystal candalabra amid whose stems the leaves flamed in gold and amber and scarlet. Later, as we drove through the woodlands outside the city, the sight of the coloured leaves amid the snow was one of the most beautiful sights of nature I have ever seen.

[259]

Before the drive I had had a most pleasant breakfast, eating behind the conservatory windows of the dining-room, so that I was snug and warm and greedy with my fried eggs and bacon and coffee. On the other side of the plate glass, office-going pedestrians shuffled through the snow or stood in a bus queue, all hunched and fluffed up like a row of brooding hens, their breaths floating veil-like into the still air.

Ottawa is a place to admire, and then to leave. It is built on the cliffs which overlook the river Ottawa. The public buildings look more Scottish than English, being built from the local heavy stone in the Aviemore–Gothic style. The public gardens, particularly during tulip time, are beautiful. The food, perhaps because of the French influence, and because of the abundance of adjacent fresh and saltwater fish, can be extremely good. There is an encouraging lack of litter and graffiti, the people are gentle and well-mannered and likeable. However, once you have toured the few museums and galleries, there is not that much to do unless you like winter sports.

After breakfast I walked outside into the clean crispness and wandered below the arboretum which has been planted alongside the Rideau Canal. People skate along this in winter but now it is still full of water. I then pottered around the cliffs which overlook the river, admiring the trees and the snow and chatting to the squirrels, some black, the others of the darkest chocolate brown, then I was driven to the aerodrome though the autumn-winter colours and hopped onto an aeroplane and flew off to . . .

New York, 23 October 1997.

Dear Mr. George Courtauld:
In answer to your letter I would like to suggest a 'tailor made' tour that would focus primarily but not exclusively on gargoyles. We will see hundreds of gargoyles of various types, along the way I will talk about New York City's architecture and history and point out many landmark buildings.
Yours Truly
Alfred Pommer.

I am slightly disappointed in Mr Pommer. His name, together with his advertisement in the New York guide (which described his 'Private Walking Tours Given At Your Convenience') suggested someone rather old and dotty. But he is – for New York – rather conventional: a middle-aged ex-hippie, with flowing grey locks and dressed entirely in black, including black woollen gloves and a small black rucksack.

I had written in answer to his advertisement saying that I had been to New York about fifty times and had seen all that visitors were expected to see, so could he show me something unusual? He has suggested this gargoyle tour but in fact it has turned out to be a general amble around mid-town, interesting and quirky. I have seen or learned that brownstone houses are so named because they are faced with a thin slab of stone which turns brown after slicing; the buildings usually have a flight of steps leading up to the first floor and a half-basement below it (most were built between 1860 and 1930). Many of these houses (and even ones of later dates) enclose squares of gardens similar to the green squares of London, but not so accessible. There are many extraordinarily grandiose interiors in the Art Deco Style, including those of several banks and hotels such as the Waldorf Astoria, whose main lobby has a magnificent two-ton, nine-foot high English-made clock. There is a shop called Le Chien which is entirely devoted to dogs and cats: among the rhinestone-banded dog bowls, the hair and tail ribbons, the cookery books for dog's dinners, I found a shelf of scent bottles – CHRISTOPHE, 'a fragrance for the elegant male dog', and MARTINE, 'eau de parfum for the fashionable female dog'. In the St Regis Hotel on 55th Street there is a mural behind the 1930s bar which depicts 'King Cole passing wind', his Italianesque courtiers looking askance at him. I see a car-salesroom designed by the architect Frank Lloyd Wright (he was so small that he made all his building interiors to his size, so that the average man keeps on banging his head on door lintels and chandeliers). One shop, at 714 Fifth Avenue, has windows of engraved glass designed by Lalique. And the gargoyles – all over the place.

Before today, New York has been a ground-level place to me; ironic perhaps, as it is famous for its skyscrapers. But once you have looked up at the massed concrete canyons towering miles above your head, you are inclined to stay at eye-level, and it is one of the best cities in the

world for that: the extraordinary collection of people of all types and races, the magnificence and variety of the goods in the windows. But Mr Pommer made me look up again, to the scowling faces halfway up the blank wall of a brick skyscraper, to the frieze and row of grinning faces above the first floor of an apartment store, to the medieval-Brooklyn faces peering under the eaves of a church, dwarfed by an Art Deco office block which in its turn has an utterly unexpected face below a copper-towered roof.

One of the nice things about Mr Pommer is his excitement. He sometimes talks with such animation about a gargoyle that he causes passers-by to stop and stare, and I find I am in the middle of a small bunch of total strangers, all peering up at a face which they have never noticed before. He carries an enormous loose-leafed folder in his rucksack, and occasionally unpacks it to illustrate his explanations with photographs of the buildings when new, or show what the owners looked like, or their family trees. We've been at this for three hours now; another hour to go and I am utterly freezing as an arctic wind howls up the concrete canyons, but I do not have the heart to stem Mr Pommer's enthusiasm, which is more peculiar and interesting than many of these ruddy gargoyles (to be honest, I never want to see another gargoyle again, ever).

North Essex, 31 October 1997. *Colchester.* The Mongolians who are waiting for me must feel thoroughly at home: early-morning frost glistens on the pavement they are standing on; their living quarters, the Essex University students' block which looms behind them, resembles one of the spartan barrack-buildings of Ulaan Baatar. They pile into the Land-Rover and I drive them off. Battsengel, being the one I know, is sitting in the front passenger seat beside me. It was August when I last saw her, in our Mongolian Embassy, where she was an interpreter. She had told me that she and her husband and daughter would be living in Colchester for a year. Erdenebayer, her husband, was a senior police inspector in Ulaan Baatar. A couple of years ago, when in his late thirties, he learned

English, then he won a scholarship to study human rights: 'Humans did not have rights under the Communists, just the State, so I am having to learn a completely different new way of life and thinking.' He has served five years in Siberia as a policeman, then a couple of years in Hungary, and spent another year in a university in the USA but, as Battsengel says: 'This is the very first time we will be seeing the countryside life of any of the countries we were staying in. We have always lived in big towns and did not know any of the country people.' Their daughter, Bolor, is fourteen. She is already taller than her parents, and by the time she is eighteen will be graceful and beautiful. At present, she is gawky and blinks shyly behind round-lensed, state-issued spectacles.

As we drive out of Colchester into the countryside Battsengel keeps up a running commentary: 'Look at all the different coloured leaves in the gardens! – there are still apples on some of the trees, and they are very big – *everywhere* is farmed – the country is cut up in small pieces by all the hedges – the Old Queen's Head, the Cooper's Arms, the Shoulder of Mutton – there are many public houses in this village – we must go to a public house before we leave England, it is very typical – what are those big trees everywhere with round shapes? – [they are oaks] – how beautiful, and you see the farmed land is all around them – look at all the flowers in the gardens, but you cannot eat flowers – *white* geese! – many of these little pet-dogs do not look very useful – the grass is still very green. Is it not yet winter?'

The lane which leads from Millbrook to Colne Engaine is thickly hedged by a mixture of tall scrub. A sudden gust of wind sends the autumn leaves pouring forth: 'Like yellow and red snowflakes, all falling from the sky and flying around us!' exclaims Battsengel, entranced.

We drive through the village and pass World's End Farmhouse: 'That is where my eldest son George lives, with his wife Fiona and their children, George – the Eighth – and Hamish. Their house is about 500 years old.'

'Oh dear.'

We pass Bullocks Valley. 'What are those men planting?'

'Trees, another 3000 of them. Half of them will be those oaks you like, the other half will be other hardwoods like lime, ash, gean and

hornbeam. We already planted 14,000 trees this February. Then it didn't rain for eleven weeks and I lost over a third of them.'

I show them some of the livestock. They quite admire Dominie's Welsh mountain ponies ('very pretty') but I reckon that they think them a bit spindly. They get into ecstasies over the stocky furryness of Albert, the old Shetland pony, and photograph each other patting him. Two of the horses at livery are in Park Field. The Mongolians fall about in helpless merriment to see horses wearing overcoats, but when they stand next to the 16.2-hand mare they become awed: 'So huge, so very huge.' I say that the sight of their cows wearing bras to keep their udders warm is just as funny as our horses wearing coats. The Mongolians are particularly knowledgeable on sheep, so we go to Goldingtons Meadow to inspect the ewes. The Mongolians marvel at their size. I remember a Mongolian from Leeds University telling me that of all the things he missed most, it was boiled mutton. 'We are having one of my sheep for lunch,' I tell them.

They are pleased it is to be mutton rather than lamb. 'You can only get lamb in this country, it is strange. In Mongolia we think it not kind to kill a little lamb who has not lived very long, also they are small and uneconomic, and they do not taste as good.'

When you approach a stranger's *ger* in Mongolia you shout 'Hold on to your dogs!'. I should have warned the Mongolians about the five dogs which swarmed out of my house after I had opened the door. Dominie had made everything look welcoming with the fire roaring in the front hall. Candy and her husband Alex had taken an early day off from work and had already arrived, also Matthew, a young friend at Essex University who I thought the Mongolians might be pleased to meet.

We finished off a whole saddle of mutton which they pronounced 'as good as Mongolian sheep', also a large apple tart on which they congratulated Dominie. She smiled blandly: I did not mention a large empty box I had seen in the scullery labelled 'Sainsbury's'.

After lunch I took them on a tour of some of the countryside and we ended up at Greenstead Green, where my brother Sam was muffling the church bells for a funeral tomorrow. We went up the spire into the bell loft and Sam explained the purpose of muffling the bell clappers,

which was to make them sound more impressive and solemn, and he showed them how he did it (some bellmen use special little leather bags, with laces round the top, Sam uses horses' knee-pads). He let them ring the bells, which they found surprisingly hard and heavy work. Probably the first Mongolians ever to ring an English church bell.

I am driving back home, having dropped the Mongolians back at their Colchester digs.

'Why do you want to go all over the world, when you have such a lovely home and family, and there are so many things to do on your farm?' Battsengel had asked.

I often wonder why. Sometimes I think the purpose of travelling is to help in the appreciation of home. But nobody must stay only on the inside of their garden fence. If I had done that I would not have clambered over the ruins of Jerash in the twilight, or given a sermon in a cathedral (with a knuckleduster in my pocket, just in case), or scaled up to a mountaintop castle in a country I'd never even heard of, or slept in a dungeon on the Great Wall of China, or have eaten a jellyfish and drunk half a pint of Sweat, or have knocked on the door of the Lord of the Green Mountain, or have found an aunt's Peace Pole in a gun turret off the coast of Senegal, or have seen a whip made of fish's whiskers and a table made from an ear or have heard the lammergeyers calling high above the mountains of the Karakorum – and so much else besides.

It is getting dark. I must hurry home: the fires will need more logs put in them, the smell of mutton casserole will be coming from the kitchen, and Dominie will be waiting for me.